TIGER CATE

A NOVEL

B.E. JACKSON

This book is a work of fiction. Other than a few major cities and a certain delicious burger franchise, all names, places, characters, and incidents in this book are the products of the author's imagination. Any resemblance to actual events, persons, or places is purely coincidental.

For reprint rights and permissions, please contact:
B.E. Jackson
P.O. Box 256
Skull Valley, AZ 86338

bejacksonauthor@gmail.com

ISBN
979-8-9882980-1-4 (Paperback)
979-8-9882980-2-1 (Ebook)

Cover by: 100Covers.com
Interior Formatting by: 100Covers.com

Dedicated to anyone who has ever burned with ambition, been told no, and did it anyway.

This story is for you.

PART I – Homecoming

"Life is just choices. You follow the voices
And hope they're your friends."—B. Christensen

Chapter 1

August 2, 2019 Los Angeles

Cate Finley dangled like a fly on a spider's thread, high above Wilshire Boulevard on an early August morning. Moments earlier, she'd felt the floor give way beneath her feet and heard a splintering crash below her, wincing as the straps of her climbing harness grabbed her ribcage.

Sweat cooled on her temples and adrenaline shot through her torso and out her arms as she tried to listen to the voice in her head.

Release the paintbrush, Cate. Now grab the rope overhead and pull yourself up slowly.

Only after she was clutching the scaffolding frame that anchored her harness did Cate peer down at the platform where she'd stood painting moments ago. It lay in pieces on the concrete, a hundred feet below. She shuddered and hoped, at this early hour, that no one had been on the sidewalk.

The slick steel scaffolding she clung to shifted slightly.

No, stop, this isn't happening!

Her lungs compressed as a scream sought an escape route. Eyes closed and jaws clamped, she told herself to breathe deeply through her nose as she listened to the strangely calm voice in her head.

Don't panic. Someone will come. Just ... hang on.

A siren blared in the distance. Was help on the way already?

Her sweaty fingers lost their grip, and she dropped back down, her stomach lurching as the harness grabbed her ribcage again. The momentum swung her into the side of the building she'd been painting, close enough to touch. But unlike the climbing walls she occasionally worked out on, there were no handholds, nothing to cling to. She was stranded next to its smooth, painted surface.

A twenty-year-old memory came to her—the scowling face of her father, "Doc" Finley, who had forbidden his teenage daughter to climb the enormous granite monument known as La Cabeza Rock, which loomed near their ranch in Arizona. The thrill of doing so on the sly was short-lived. When the mountain rescue team finally got Cate off the ledge where she'd gotten stranded, Doc had crushed her in a hug and wept.

"Wherever you go, Catie, you take our hearts with you. Please remember that," he'd murmured in her hair. Then he grounded her for a month.

She often thought of that father and daughter moment shared at the Rock. How easy it was to dice into small pieces the hearts of those who loved you. Doc and her mother, Fiona, had been just days from boarding the private plane that would end their lives.

A breeze came up, sending her into a slow spin, like a reluctant circus aerialist. With each rotation, the unpainted spot on the mural came into view amid swirls of vibrant color—yellow, red, blue, and green. There was the blank spot she'd been reaching to paint with her artist signature "Catify" just before the platform collapsed.

Conner Ping, the L.A. Arts Council rep, had called her into his office and told her there were problems with the scaffolding.

"The Council said, do *not* do any more painting until we've had building maintenance check it out," his raspy voice had warned.

"Aw, Conner, you know they take weekends off." That meant

not getting paid until midweek. They'd bonded over their mutual love of musical theatre and she liked to make full use of that. She'd dropped to her knees like an orphan in *Oliver*, pleading in exaggerated Cockney, "Please, suh, oy need moh porridge to eat and coal for the fuh-nace. Oy promises to be good."

Cate's theatrics never failed to amuse him. When he started to giggle, she knew she'd gotten her way. Now she'd catch heat for going rogue.

Now a fire truck pulled up below her and a handful of men scrambled, preparing to launch the ladder. A small group of spectators had gathered. Cate thought of the one person who would love—would even pay—to see her smash onto a sidewalk: Joseph Russo. Wait, was that him in the crowd? No, no, he was on the East Coast nurturing his political career. Still, a sliver of fear had found her gut.

Stay in the now, purred the voice in her head. *Stay focused and survive.*

Her paycheck, sent to a secure online account under the name Catify, would have been enough to live on if the work was more regular. This was only her third mural in the last ten months— and probably her last for the Council.

Up came the ladder, edging closer to her as the hydraulics whined on the fire truck.

"Hold still, miss. Gonna be all over soon," barked a cheerful voice from just below her. She took a long shaky breath and held still to be rescued, once again.

When they deposited her on the sidewalk, Conner Ping was the first to greet her. With a tragic smile, he told her the Council board was suspending the mural projects for the foreseeable future due to, um, *insurance concerns.*

"You are *such* a talent, and it's been *such* fun having you on the team, Catify ... such fun." He held out an embossed envelope. "Here, I've written this letter of recommendation for you, and your check's in the mail, er, email," he sang. He gave her an elfin smile, then turned to amble back down the street like a leprechaun wheeling away his pot of gold which, in a way, he was.

At the McArthur Park station, Cate hopped the Metro Red Line bus that would take her over the hill to San Fernando Valley. In the past eighteen months, she'd gradually made peace with LA's sprawling public transit. It was hideously slow, but it beat the hassle of finding parking anywhere in the downtown area. Sure, there were rideshares for hire, but she'd grown leery of stepping into a stranger's car.

In a perfect world, Cate would be selling her artwork for epic wages and living in a high-end loft. She would not be sleeping in a 1978 camper truck parked on various streets within sight of the Ventura Freeway. Getting the camper, which she'd named "Max," had marked a new direction for her, after years of sharing roach-infested apartments with fellow artists in lower Manhattan. Once she'd arrived in L.A., though, Max had made a better bedroom and art studio than transport. The truck's engine would need major repairs soon, something well beyond her current income.

Cate's stomach growled, and she envisioned the breakfast her friend Levi would be making back in the camper—scrambled eggs with chorizo and a side of buttered toast. She turned on her phone and it chirped, startling her so much that she nearly dropped it.

Expecting to see Levi's number on the screen, she saw instead two texts from an unknown number. She clicked on the first.

Cate, have you heard from Margaret? She's missing.

She stared at the phone for a beat. Margaret? The only person she could think of was her older sister Margaret, whom she hadn't seen in nearly twenty years. What did the text mean by *missing*? A single butterfly fluttered in her sternum. She clicked on the second message.

M. missing a week and they're stealing the ranch. Pls call me.

An image of the last time she'd seen Margaret flashed on her mental screen. Her sister, leaning over a sick horse under the stable lights, as Cate made her stealthy way to the ranch Jeep with a packed suitcase and a plan for her life that did not include staying in rural Arizona.

She and her older sister hadn't spoken much since that summer when teenage Cate had brashly raided the ranch office safe and hopped a bus to New York, chasing her dream of becoming an artist. Now someone in the dusty little town where she grew up appeared to be texting Cate's prepaid phone. That was a mystery in itself. Besides Levi, only two people had gotten the new number after she'd changed it eighteen months ago. On a hunch, she texted one of them—a lawyer named Tyson, who kept her informed about Joseph Russo's activities.

Getting strange phone texts. Joseph messing with me?

The "low battery" flashed on the phone screen and Cate pocketed it as the bus pulled up to her stop. She hopped onto the sidewalk, now feeling tiny spiders running loose between her ribs. A hulk of a man was jogging toward her, panting and waving his arms. Levi.

"Hey, they're towing your truck!" He looked stressed and spent.

"What? How could—is street cleaning today?"

Levi nodded. "The guy showed me the statute. Said I could

move it," he panted as he caught his breath, "but it won't turn over."

Now they were jogging side by side, and Cate could see the tow truck's blinking lights ahead. Max was hooked up—shackled like a prisoner—and ready to be hauled off.

"Crap!" She sped to a run.

"Cate, you just need to show him some paperwork!" she heard Levi shout.

The tow truck driver, sporting a Judas Priest t-shirt and a buzz-cut fade, was climbing into the cab when Cate reached him.

"No, please don't do this." Her voice sounded thin and whiny to her own ears.

"Miss, I'm just following orders. Take it up with the LAPD." Was there a hint of sadism in that smug smile?

"But I—I have all my stuff in there."

Her hiker's backpack and its contents—a hoodie, change of underwear, toiletries, and about forty dollars in cash—were crammed below the tiny dinette. More importantly, the camper held her art supplies and the dozen portraits she'd painted over the past six months.

Judas Priest looked her over, studying the climbing harness hanging over her shoulder.

"Okay, but before I can let you in there, I need to see either a current driver's license, a current registration, or an insurance card. Got 'em?" He waited a moment, then sneered. "Didn't think so. Plate tags are way expired."

He flipped a business card out the window, shifted the diesel into gear, and pulled away from the curb.

"So, how do I get any of those without a physical address?"

But he'd already rolled up his window and cranked up the headbanger music.

Her throat tightening, she tracked the teal-and-white truck with its vintage white camper shell until it disappeared around the corner. Over the past few hours, she'd lost her job, learned her sister was missing and just watched everything she owned get towed away. An errant tear splashed on her hand as she picked up the card and read the address. The Northwest Valley Impound was at least a six-mile hike in her tattered running shoes.

Chapter 2

For the first time in their friendship, Levi looked upset with her when she told him what she was planning. As they sat on a park bench, he leaned forward to rub his face and scrape back his tangled hair. Cate hoped this wasn't the start of one of his chronic migraines. Then he spoke, eyes fixed on the ground.

"Look, you can't just sneak in there and steal your truck back, Cate."

She prickled at the words. Imagine anyone telling her what she could or couldn't do at this point in her life. Then she threw a glance at his worried profile. Hadn't he been a military cop or something? If anyone had a right to shoehorn some common sense into her right now, it was probably this guy.

A year ago, Cate had pulled up to one of her usual overnight spots in the San Fernando Valley and noticed a mountain of a man snoozing on a nearby park bench. She'd watched from the safety of the cab as the derelict had slowly tilted to one side and caught himself just before spilling onto the ground. She couldn't resist cracking her window and calling out, "Great way to bust your head open."

Startled at first, he'd looked around until he saw her. Then she'd gotten back a smile so amiable and genuine, she'd felt herself melt a bit.

"Oh, been there, done that," came his rich baritone reply. Then he yawned, stretched, and checked his watch like he'd been waiting for the bus. So, not drunk after all, just very sleepy. And he wasn't kidding about hurting his head. A vivid purplish scar ran along his left temple, disappearing under a shaggy mop of black hair.

Built like a linebacker and medically furloughed from the U.S. Army after an IED explosion in Afghanistan, Levi Saaga became Cate's first friend in California. She'd guessed he was in his mid-twenties, almost a decade younger than her. The mystery was why he was sleeping on park benches since he must have been drawing some kind of military pension. One morning, over a shared breakfast of burritos, he'd admitted he was working night shifts in the IT department at a local hospital and saving up to bring his mama over from American Samoa. For a second time her heart melted, and she'd made him an offer.

He could sleep in her camper from early morning, when he got off his shift, until late afternoon when Cate returned to paint on her canvases and sleep. With the amount of crime among the homeless in the area, it made sense to team up with a male twice her weight and almost a foot taller. He was polite, a good conversationalist, and he loved his mama—what more did she need to know? Even better, he somehow managed to make delicious meals in the camper's tiny kitchen. Of course, with his hours, it was mostly breakfasts, but who could be choosy?

Now Levi's mocha eyes were on her and his usual good humor was missing.

"Cate, that's an LAPD impound. If you try to break in, they'll jail you."

"Don't have a choice," she said softly. "No current insurance or registration. All that takes money and a physical address."

An expired New York driver's license was the only searchable information on her in any database, and she'd worked to keep it that way—to stay one step ahead of Joseph and his people—since arriving in California.

The texts were haunting her like ghost children. Out came the phone, but now it wouldn't even turn on. Her charger was in the camper.

Trying to keep her voice light, she asked, "Hey, IT, got a charger?"

"Not with me. Plenty at work if you—"

"I need my pack, I need my pack," she mumbled, half to herself.

Levi seemed poised to say something, even as he stifled a yawn.

"You look done in," she told him. "Please go find someplace to sleep before your shift tonight." Flicking the impound card with her fingers, she got up and started toward Van Nuys Boulevard.

"No, wait, dammit! Ah!"

She glanced back to see him massaging his head. A migraine had indeed begun, an effect of his head injury. On a normal day, she'd splurge on fuel and drive him over to the VA in West Los Angeles to get his migraine injection. In this harsh landscape of haves and have-nots, they had come to care for and about each other in such ways.

Cate sighed deeply, feeling the toll the day had already taken on her. Impulsively, she walked to where her friend sat, lifted his shaggy hair, and leaned down to softly kiss the scarred forehead. Suddenly his arms were wrapping around her, gently pulling her closer. His body felt strong and warm.

Startled at first, she relaxed into his embrace and lifted her arms to cradle his head. The first time they'd touched like this, really. It felt so natural ... so soothing ... okay, and also something more. Were they about to cross out of the friend zone?

I don't know how to do this and not have it be a disaster, she thought, gingerly stroking Levi's tousled hair.

For a moment, neither moved. Then a ticking clock in Cate's mind started up, and she pulled away. *Texts. Margaret. Ranch. Joseph?*

"Come on," she said, pulling on his arm. "I'll walk with you over to the hospital. They should have that shot you need, and probably even a spare cot in the staff room."

He withdrew his arm and gave her a wide, valiant smile, a hint of humor back in his eyes.

"Nah, I can make it to the VA, Cate. No worries. You should—you should do whatever you have planned to spring Max. Just, you know, be careful."

She flashed him an I've-got-this smile, but it was all for show. In reality, she didn't have anything. Hunching her climbing harness over her shoulder, she took a few steps and turned.

"I'll text you when I get my stuff and know something about Max, okay?"

"Don't text. Call," he said, massaging his forehead again.

"Okay." She managed a smile for his sake. Phone calls were hard for her. Then she turned and headed up the street.

#

Three hours later, Cate was staring at the Northwest Valley Impound with its imposing hurricane fencing topped with razor wire.

She spotted her truck right away, parked against the far wall. Jingling the keys in her shorts pocket, she saw the surveillance camera setup and abandoned her plan to sneak on the lot after closing. Instead, she walked straight into the office prepared to say whatever she needed to get her belongings.

Once she had her backpack and her finished artwork, she'd

surrender the rest of it, Max included. Much as she loved that truck, updating the paperwork—let alone affording the repairs—was out of the question right now.

The solitary man behind the desk was the same tow truck driver from earlier. Death metal screamed from his phone, forcing Cate to raise her voice.

"Hi. I need to get into my truck, please." She mustered her most winning smile, but her face felt as fragile as a china plate. The guy looked up, seemed to recognize her, and then went back to his scribbling.

Cate heard the growling hiss of a big cat fill her ears as she felt heat spread from her chest, through her shoulders and neck, and into her face.

I will rip his throat out, came the voice in her head. She shook it off and lowered her gaze. Time for a different tack.

Suddenly her eyes and nose were leaking, and a loud sob escaped her open mouth. Startled, the guy shot her another look as she struggled to catch her breath.

"Look, you can see that ... um, that I'm homeless," she gasped, the tears flowing freely now. "Please don't make me ... beg ... just let me get my stuff!" It felt humiliating to use them, but tears might work at this point, so she let them flow. Resting her forehead on the counter she let out one more sob.

Had she overdone it, scared him maybe, and was he now dialing the cops? Her head still down, she saw the man's track shoes out of the corner of her eye as he got up and walked over to the counter. A clipboard with a sign-in sheet slid toward her. She looked up at his deadpan face as he spoke.

"You got exactly ten minutes. Put the truck keys on this desk— in ten. And here," he pushed a tissue box toward her, avoiding her gaze. "Mop up that mess." Then he sauntered back to his paperwork.

Cate wiped the counter dry and made a dash for the door. Thirty seconds later, she was inside the camper, surveying her belongings. She changed into jeans, grabbed a handful of running shorts and a few t-shirts from the closet, and tossed them into the backpack. Then she carefully lifted each of her twelve finished eight-by-ten-inch canvas panels and placed them inside an oversized black portfolio. Scanning the space once more for any of Levi's belongings, Cate saw none and exited.

Ten seconds later, she was back and grabbing a plastic Goodwill bag from below the sink. She yanked a black knit sheath off a hanger in the closet, jammed it in the sack, and added strappy sandals and a zippered makeup bag. Because you never knew when you might need to clean up your act.

Chapter 3

Seated next to a wall outlet in a mid-valley coffee house, Cate sipped from the steaming cup in front of her and waited for her phone to come back to life. Eventually, the screen glowed white and then chirped as it flashed the menu. There were the two texts, but no new ones and no phone calls. She reread the messages and set the phone down on the table.

It could be a trick, but someone would have to know her history to pull that off, and she hadn't told anyone in L.A. the truth about where she was from. It might even be her sister Margaret playing a weird mind game on her.

Cate had communicated with Margaret exactly three times in the last two decades. Five months into living in New York, sixteen-year-old Cate had been deep in crisis, facing a potentially life-changing decision. She reached out for help, instinctively calling the number where her mother Fiona had always answered. Instead, she got Margaret's flat voice telling her the only possible choice she'd support, financially or otherwise. It hadn't been the one Cate wanted to hear and she'd hung up.

The second time, almost a decade later, Cate had called from a hospital bed, gravely injured and desperate to make amends and return home. Nothing ... crickets ... It was true, there was bad blood between them. Cate had stolen money, run away to New York, and had hung up on her sister the last time they'd spoken. But what kind of family just doesn't respond to a stricken member?

The third and last call had been eighteen months ago, when Max broke down in Omaha, on the trip out to Los Angeles. Standing in the blazing sun outside a noisy automotive shop, Cate had left a voicemail pleading with her older sister to send money to her online CashPay account so she could fix the truck. She hadn't expected a response and indeed Margaret hadn't returned her call. But a thousand dollars had miraculously turned up in the account later that day.

So, were these Margaret's texts now? If so, why this pretense? Cate picked up the phone and called the texter's number. The recorded female voice that answered wasn't her sister's.

"Hi, this is Brownie. Sorry, I'm not able to answer ..." Cate ended the call. The name, the voice—none of it was familiar, and it alarmed her this person had her cell number.

With a sigh, she went in search of a bus stop. She needed to sell the paintings and then she'd decide what to do.

An hour later, Cate was standing on Ventura Boulevard in front of the high-end pawn shop that fancied itself an art gallery. There was quite a crowd for eight-thirty on a Saturday night. Dexter, an artist friend from her early days in New York, looked surprised to see her peeking in the window at what appeared to be a private party. He raised his hand in an elegant gesture to come around to the alley. A moment later, he opened the back door and ushered her into the office.

"Hello, darling, what's up?" he asked with concern, after deciding against an embrace. Cate felt him appraising her grubby attire and taking in the current state of her hair—six inches of dark chestnut roots followed by a foot of scraggly, pink-tinged platinum, pulled into a high messy ponytail.

"Love the extreme *ombré*, but what happened to last spring's fuchsia?"

Normally she'd banter with him about her hairstyle choices, but she needed to get to the point.

"Max got towed and I … I need some cash. Remember those portraits the gallery bought? I've been working on some more." She lifted one carefully out of the portfolio and laid it on the table.

Dex gazed at the richly detailed study of an elderly homeless man with a beautiful smile holding a half-eaten sandwich, who had sat for Cate in exchange for some food and good conversation. As with the other portraits, she'd captured his face in her trademark hyperrealism, the super-saturated skin tones popping out of a graffiti-splashed background.

Dexter carefully pulled out and examined each canvas before finally looking up and smiling.

"Cate's babies … I would know them anywhere. It's the moisture in their eyes." Now she was daubing at her own eyes because, well, the day. He pulled her in for a hug and patted her back.

"The not-so-good news is, small isn't selling along the coast right now. It's gargantuan wall-high work—more like those building murals you paint—that's really taking off. These are more, well, bathroom art." He wrinkled his nose, smiling ruefully.

"And worth nothing?"

He sighed, eyeing the canvases again and calculating.

"I can front you, uh, two-fifty against future sales. Will that help?"

She mentally added up her mural paycheck and the advance, plus the fifty in cash shoved in her backpack. She shook her head, feeling tears well again.

"I need to bail out and fix Max, then drive home to Arizona." Seeing Dex's eyes widen, she went on quickly. "My sister is … is in some trouble there and," she took a breath, "this might be a good time for me to get out of town for a while."

Dex nodded, looking more alarmed. They'd met her first year in New York, and he was well aware of the threat that had chased her out of that city. In fact, Dex had been the one who'd encouraged her to come out west.

Walking to his desk, he removed a metal box and began counting some bills into his hand. Then he turned to her with a new thought.

"Hey, maybe you could take the bus? Shouldn't be too long a trip, and it's got to be cheaper than buying gas for that thirsty truck." He handed her the money. "Geez, I had no idea you came from Arizona."

Cate smirked. "Long ago in a galaxy far, far away ..."

"Bet it's hotter than hell right now."

More like heaven, she thought, as childhood memories of the monsoon season began to float through her mind. The summer mornings with luminous gray clouds that built to thunderstorms by afternoon. Air shimmering like gossamer while cicadas sang their eerie love songs from the trees and cattle grazed in jade-hued fields ... heaven.

She felt Dexter's stare and tried to shake off this strange wave of nostalgia.

"We, um ... we live up north in the high country. Cold enough to snow in the winter, and summers aren't nearly as hot as Phoenix."

Cate folded over the cash and shoved it into a back pocket. Before today, she hadn't thought of her childhood home in years. But saying "we" just now had been effortless, like riding a bike again after two decades. *We—I live somewhere. I belong somewhere.* That felt good, like a missing puzzle piece finally sliding into place.

Just then, her phone chirped a text and she checked it nervously. It was Tyson, the lawyer friend who kept her up on his uncle, Joseph Russo.

He knows we talk and he's pissed. I can't help you with this anymore. So sorry. Be safe.

A familiar clock had started ticking in her brain. *He knows ... be safe.* It really was time to run.

Chapter 4

Dex dropped her off outside the downtown L.A. bus terminal at just past one a.m. At the counter, Cate bought a one-way ticket to Copperton, Arizona via Phoenix, and then dragged herself over to a line of seats. Was she really starting a new day without the benefit of a night's sleep?

Two hours into her wait, sprawled across three seats in the nearly empty bus terminal, Cate awoke to someone groping her. A man with obscenely large biceps waved the small roll of cash he'd just lifted from her jeans pocket.

"You can earn this back if you're nice—" was all he could whisper before getting a face full of aerosol deodorant from the travel-size can she'd been clutching when she dozed off. No doubt the guy had mistaken her for a teenage runaway in her jeans, t-shirt, and scraggly two-toned hair. She lunged for her money roll as he wiped at his eyes, but he jumped back just in time and sprinted out of the terminal. She looked around for the terminal guards, but they were apparently all on a coffee break. Grimly, she pulled her pack into her lap and sat upright, as she waited for her bus to arrive. *You've been scrounging for money your whole adult life,* she thought bitterly. *Shouldn't you be used to the feeling by now?*

Another hour later, Cate had boarded and was tucked into one of the transport's generous seats. As the bus rumbled forward, city lights blurred outside her window while old memories began to visit.

In truth, Cate had never thought much about money until her parents' private plane crashed while returning from their anniversary trip to Baja. Doc and Fiona Finley's deaths had put thirty-year-old Margaret in sole charge of ranch management, family finances … and her younger sister Cate's immediate future. And Margaret had managed all of it like she managed the thousand-pound horses she rode—with an iron fist.

At the time, Cate had been a carefree fifteen-year-old, a budding young artist finishing her sophomore year at Copperton High and winning art awards at the county and state fairs. Carefree right up to the moment she'd stood in the late afternoon sun and watched a sheriff's SUV roll up the driveway. It had been Sheriff Mack Griffin himself—not one of his deputies—who had stepped out and looked up at the sisters standing on the patio. She'd felt a kick in her stomach like nothing she had ever experienced. Before any words were spoken, her body had told her the news would be terrible.

Mack had looked near tears himself, as he spoke to the sisters. He and Doc had been as close as brothers.

"Girls, I'm sorry to tell you your parents' plane went down—" was all he got out before Cate had begun wailing and grabbing onto Margaret, who stayed still and silent.

Rosa, their cook, had tearfully urged Cate to eat some dinner that night, but she had no room for it. She had cried for four hours straight, lying on the sofa in the high-ceilinged great room. Alone.

At some point, Cate had wandered outside in search of her sister. A single light shone at the stables and she headed for it, the full moon illuminating her path. In the farthest paddock stood Margaret with her arms around her favorite mare, her body heaving. Of course, Margaret had preferred to grieve in the presence of her cherished horses. "Her place of worship," their mother had called it.

The sisters never did share their grief about their parents' death. Cate would have loved to confide in her older sister, but by then she'd grown fearful of Margaret's increasingly dark, alcohol-fueled moods. The funeral came and went, with Rosa and her husband Diego preparing the ranch house for the memorial service and cleaning up afterward. Dozens of neighbors and family friends hugged and fawned over Cate at the funeral, but Margaret was not among them.

Halfway through that summer, Margaret had announced one evening that Cate would be going off to a boarding school outside Flagstaff for her junior year. Shocked and heartsick after their parents' death, Cate lacked the energy to resist. Besides, living under her domineering sister's rule had already crushed her social life. How much worse could boarding school be?

That year away from the ranch where she'd been born and raised, felt to Cate like she was doing hard time. But it had also been the true start of her real education. Loneliness gave birth to a feeling of independence, bringing out the fighter in her. In her mid-semester evaluation, the school counselor wrote that Cate didn't "mesh" with the other girls in her class and appeared to have "anger issues."

Without a doubt, she felt angry, hostile, sad, and guarded. Her coddled classmates, whose doting parents showed up every Friday to whisk them away for fun weekends, considered Cate a whiny, boring bitch. At least that's what she'd once overheard from a bathroom stall.

By Thanksgiving, Cate had stopped trying to get a ride home on weekends. Instead, she began to look forward to the dorms clearing out for Saturday and Sunday. She ate stale oatmeal cookies in the cafeteria, where she sat at whichever empty table she liked and sketched or painted from morning until dark. When she wasn't doing art, she was plotting her great escape to New York.

Then it was late May, the prison sentence at school had ended, and Cate arrived back at the ranch with a plan to get out of her sister's hair for good. Attending a New York art school after graduation was a goal that she and her mother had set years earlier. Over the past year, Cate had begun to wonder, *what if I could just make it happen sooner?* Late at night, holed up in her bedroom at the ranch, she went to work on an action plan.

A decade later, while cleaning out an old satchel of sketchbooks, she came across her neatly printed list.

What I Will Need to Get to New York City
1. $$$ for travel and housing
2. Job. Look in Mom's address book for her NYC friend's (Brent? Brenden?) restaurant (Foxy something?)
3. ID proving I'm 18, for job apps. (Create on Mom's laptop.)
4. Transportation to the bus station in Flagstaff.
5. Good enough excuse to leave here without setting off the Margaret alarm.

The last item had fallen into her lap: a summer internship teaching art to kids at a special needs camp in the White Mountains.

Predictably, her sister had rejected the idea.

"Nope. If you do anything this summer it'll be summer school to improve your GPA so you can get into that accounting program at the community college. None of that art crap Fiona indulged you in." Margaret had an annoying habit of using their parents' first names. "That way, you'll have some skills we can really use around here," she'd growled, swigging from her beer as if to punctuate.

Curled up on the buck-stitched leather couch in the great room, opposite Margaret's overstuffed chair, Cate had laughed at first, thinking she was being teased.

"Accounting? You're kidding, right? You've seen my math grades, right? ... Right?"

Margaret had remained silent and stony-faced. Cate felt herself losing control.

"Margaret, the only thing I want to *do*—the only thing I'm any good at—*is* art. Mom knew this. And this internship will help me get a scholarship—get me low-cost tuition to a quality art school in New York."

Margaret had looked at her for a moment with narrowed eyes. At thirty-one, she was already beginning to carry extra weight around her middle, no doubt from all the beer she'd thrown down since their parents' funeral.

"Scrap the New York idea, Caitlyn. You're not cut out for that life. You'll stay."

"The hell I will. Since when are you the boss of me?" Now Cate was standing, looming over her sister's chair. "You're not Mom, so don't try to act like it. I'm doing what I damn well want to, and what I want is *not* to go back to that fucking boarding school."

She had never sworn like that before, and Cate braced for Margaret to lash back at her. Instead, a smirk spread over her sister's face, as if she'd just thought of the punch line to a joke. Then she'd let out a low belch, stood up slowly, and left the room.

That was the last straw. In mid-June, three months shy of her sixteenth birthday, Cate had finalized her exit plans. She kept a packed suitcase of clothes hidden in her closet while she waited for the right moment.

Then came the night Margaret had to care for a sick horse at the stables. The horse was a high-priced broodmare with a serious post-foaling infection. There would be the usual all-night vigil attended by Margaret and the ranch hand Diego until the vet arrived.

As part of her plan, Cate had gotten her learner's permit and practiced driving the ranch Jeep back and forth to town with Diego's supervision. Her plan was to drive to Copperton and take the last shuttle to the bus terminal in Flagstaff. There, she'd use her newly minted ID to buy her bus ticket to New York City. Hopefully, the Jeep wouldn't be missed before Cate was seated on the eastbound bus leaving at six a.m.

The biggest hurdle had been getting hold of some cash. Over Memorial Day weekend, with Margaret at a horse show in California, Cate had scoured Doc's office looking for the safe combination. Finally, she'd discovered it scrawled on a sticky note and stuck to the underside of his desk drawer.

When she opened the safe, the banded cash stacks seemed greatly reduced from what she'd seen in there before Doc's death. Even so, there had been enough to fund her escape. She hadn't taken that much, less than a year's tuition at the snooty boarding school.

Once in Flagstaff, she paid for a bus ticket to New York City and then stashed the rest of the cash in a flat pack she wore under her clothes. Hopefully it was enough to cover a few weeks in a student hostel while she secured a job and scanned the roommate ads. At a dinner stop in Amarillo, Cate had mailed the Jeep keys home with a short note. *Dear Margaret — Sorry about the money. Not sorry about leaving.*

That had been nineteen years ago. Now Cate was coming home to ... search for Margaret who'd gone missing? It felt surreal. And more than a little ironic.

Over the years, Cate had often wondered why no one had

come looking for *her*. When no officers stepped forward to handcuff and haul her away as she got off the bus in the city of her dreams, she'd felt weak with relief. Even after getting hired by her mother's friend Brenden to wait tables at his Foxy Hound bistro, she'd kept one eye on the television in the bar. With each trip through, carrying a tray of food, Cate had expected to see her photo and news of her disappearance. But there was none, she finally realized, because Margaret hadn't bothered to file a missing person's report on her. Never. Margaret had simply written her off. Who does that to their sister?

The spiders were climbing up her ribcage again. Would Cate now be filing a missing person's report on her sister?

Chapter 5

Gradually, the transfer bus climbed out of the Sonoran Desert on the interstate that connected Phoenix to Flagstaff. Saguaro cactus, agave, and paloverde gave way to rolling hills filled with scrub oak, pinion, and mesquite—the high desert flora of Cate's childhood memories. This year's monsoon storms had already cloaked the pastures in lush ryegrass. Herds of red and black cattle dotted the hills. As familiar landmarks began to appear, the pangs she felt in her stomach weren't just from hunger.

She found herself staring at the phone in her hands. Not at the mystery texts, but at the number she'd promised to call. She didn't know what to tell Levi. There hadn't been time to fill him in on the messages, let alone to finally reveal something about her history. She knew so much about him—from the names of his siblings and the volcanos that surrounded his island village to his academically gifted mother, who'd raised five children while pursuing a master's degree in health administration. She felt the momentary security of those arms wrapping around her again and dialed.

"Hey," the rich baritone voice poured over her like a healing balm.

"Hey. Where are you?" she asked. He was in a crowd somewhere, probably at the hospital cafeteria.

"Getting something to eat. Where are you?"

She gazed out at the vast splendor of the Arizona high country and wished she could tell him. Despite their bond, something made her hesitate.

"The, um, boondocks."

He chuckled. "The what?"

"I couldn't spring Max, so I'm ... on a bus. Headed home."

"Really? For good?" He sounded less happy now.

"I ..." It was hard to answer at this point. "I don't know, but I doubt it. Home is a cattle ranch. Not really my," she took a deep breath, "not my jam, you know?"

"Okay." She heard him talking to someone on his end. "Hey Cate, I'm holding up the line here. But thanks for—I just wanted to, to hear your voice. Call me when you get where you're going, okay? I care ... a lot ... about you. Be safe, Cate."

"Yep, that's the plan," she said, ending the call and staring back at a woman across the aisle who'd been leaning in to listen. Cate turned to the window and felt tears on her cheeks. Where *was* all this emotion coming from?

An hour into the trip north, the bus turned onto a state highway and soon rumbled down the main streets of one small town after another. First came Bryant and then, fifteen minutes later, Keener's Valley popped into view. Twenty years had not changed the two towns much. A once-popular café now sat derelict, and a 1960s-era laundromat had morphed into a feed store with a mountain of furry hay bales stacked in the parking lot. There was still plenty of open space surrounding the towns. She imagined the lack of local jobs had kept their populations low.

Someone on the bus opened a potato chip bag noisily, reminding Cate she was hungry and had zero money to do anything about it. That also meant no money for transport once they arrived in Copperton. Ironically, the bus was about to take them through

Cabeza Valley and past her family's ranch before it climbed the final twenty miles through alpine mountains to Copperton.

At the terminal in Phoenix, she'd asked the transfer bus driver if he could let her off in Cabeza Valley. Busy helping people stow their suitcases, the man hadn't even looked at her. Instead, he'd barked that this was the *express* run, and the only stops he was authorized to make were in Copperton and Copper Valley. He'd looked overworked and sleep deprived.

Now chatter on the bus quieted as the distinctive rock formation for which Cabeza Valley had been named came into view.

"That's Cabeza Rock," a woman in front of Cate told her companion. "Cabeza means 'head' in Spanish."

From this distance, her childhood haunt really did look like a giant human skull erupting from the earth. A seven-hundred-foot-tall white granite monolith that had been shaped and smoothed through centuries of pummeling by the elements, it was a perennial challenge for rock climbers. To be sure, Cabeza Rock Monument made national news whenever an unlucky soul fell to their death off its slick facade.

The turnoff to Finley Ranch was coming up soon. As the passengers continued to gawk at the monument, Cate got an idea. Nervously rolling a small vial of artist's turpentine in her hands, she tried to gauge how long it would take for the smell to reach the driver and for him to pull over and investigate. She loosened the cap on the vial, then paused to debate once more the wisdom of pulling such a stunt. *I mean, you're not fifteen anymore*, came the voice in her head.

Just then, the bus hit a pothole and lurched sharply. Her hand collided with the seat back and lost its grip on the vial, which dropped to the floor uncapped and rolled forward under the seats.

She snuck a look around. Had anyone been watching?

All eyes were still on the big granite boulder, voices commenting on how much it looked like a man's bald head. People pointed out that you could almost see the eyebrows, and that the smaller granite rocks jutting perpendicularly from the base of the monument looked like a pair of hunched shoulders. They were really using their imaginations now.

The bottle had barely made a sound rolling on the rubberized floor and was now lodged between a woman's two shopping bags, three rows down and across the aisle. The chemical smell, however, was beginning to waft everywhere. There was nervous murmuring, and a few people covered their noses. Cate knew turpentine came from tree sap and even had medicinal uses. But most people still considered it toxic, and she counted on them having a negative response to the fumes.

Someone was asking the bus driver about the awful smell, and he responded instantly by pulling the bus over. Cate had a hand over her nose, too, but also had her backpack ready for a speedy exit. Once the bus was stopped in a turnout, the driver pushed the door release to let in some air. A couple of people immediately scrambled out of the bus, gasping dramatically.

"Hold on!" said the driver. "I'm not authorized to have you disembark anywhere but at the Copperton terminal—" but his voice was lost in the stampede of passengers rushing out the open door. Cate let several people get off the bus ahead of her and then casually stepped off, her hand still cupping her nose and mouth. With the milling crowd buffering her, she ducked around the back of the bus unseen.

She'd inhaled far worse fumes in artist studios over the years. They'd all survive. Soon the bus would load back up, minus one passenger, and continue on to Copperton. She crossed the empty highway under the baking August sun and started walking. In the distance lay a vast green pasture and the tree-lined lane that led to Finley Ranch. Somewhere beyond that road lay the clues to the mystery that was drawing her home.

Chapter 6

Cate stood gazing at the sign directing visitors down the mile-long road to Finley Ranch. The familiar *F-over-R* brand made her smile, even as her throat tightened a little. A memory came of seeing Doc touching up the paint on that sign as her rural school bus rolled up to let her out. He often drove his ATV out to meet the bus and shuttle her down the dirt road that she'd be walking today. On the way home, he'd stop to check on a newborn calf or an irrigation pipe while she picked wildflowers for the dining room table.

Cate had banished such memories to the far reaches of her mind after her parents' death and during her time at boarding school. Margaret had done this to her—first pushing her away and then sending her away. Eventually, the ranch stopped feeling like home.

Twenty years hadn't shrunk the cottonwood trees any. Their massive branches arched elegantly over the road, creating a tunnel of green this time of year. On a different day, Cate might have captured shots of the enormous gnarled trunks for future canvas ideas. But who knew what situation lay ahead of her? Better to stay focused and keep moving.

A moment later, she was startled to find a panting dog walking beside her. The Rottweiler didn't look friendly enough to pet but seemed content to travel with her, so they walked together in silence with Cate throwing him sidelong glances. Occasionally he would peel off and chase something into the weeds, bringing back a stick once and a lizard another time.

She and the dog soon arrived at the bridge over Cabeza Creek. Consisting of two flatbed railroad cars that her grandfather Mike Finley had installed some sixty years earlier, the bridge allowed traffic to cross the creek year-round. A healthy runoff flowed today, the golden-brown water making a gentle roar as it swirled against cottonwood seedlings along the banks.

Lining the northern and eastern edges of her family's hundred-acre cattle pasture was a small neighborhood of six homes. Twenty years ago, two of them had housed Finley Ranch employees, and two had been rentals owned by Sheriff Griffin. The one nearest the bridge had belonged to the family of her childhood friend and high school sweetheart Drew Mason. The sixth one ... she couldn't quite remember. She saw it now, across the pasture—a quaint little gingerbread house nestled in dense foliage.

The dog went digging in the bushes again. This time, he returned with something soft and dirty hanging from his mouth. A dead gopher? No, more like a piece of cloth. A filthy white sock. He brought it right up to her and dropped it. Without thinking, Cate reached for it. As she did, the dog let out a low growl and hovered his head just next to her hand. Having handled a Rottie or two at her dad's vet business, she knew they were dead serious about their toys, but liked to play the old "Do you feel lucky, punk?" game.

"Oh, we're playing *that* game, are we?"

He wagged his nub of a tail but kept up the growl. She withdrew her hand slowly, mindful of her father's well-worn advice.

Always look a horse in the eye before climbing in the saddle, but never return an aggressive dog's stare.

Keeping her gaze averted, she carefully stepped around the dog and his trophy. The threat gone, he casually retrieved his sock again and trotted up to the entrance of the nearest house—the Masons. As the dog approached, two little boys ran across the yard and called to him.

"Samson come here! Where have you been, you bad boy?" Samson trotted past them and disappeared with his sock into a massive wooden doghouse painted the same salmon pink as the main house.

"Pink now, huh?" Cate chuckled, remembering when the two-story farmhouse had been apple green, a quarter-century ago. Drew's aging hippie parents, Carrie and Norris Mason, had built much of the house themselves and had corralled the neighborhood kids into helping with the painting. Even though nearly twenty years had passed, Cate instinctively scanned the yard for Drew's vintage Camaro, finding instead an old quad and a dirty white minivan.

Spring break of her year at boarding school, Cate had hitched a ride home and "surprised" Margaret with a painting of one of her champion show horses. In return, Margaret astonished Cate by handing over the keys to her Ram truck so she and Drew could drive up to Copperton.

"It's safer than your boyfriend's chop shop relic. Don't speed," Margaret had said stiffly as Cate hugged her and snatched the keys. Cate had thought it might be the start of better times for the two sisters. The talk about Cate's future as an accountant, a scant two months later, would destroy that notion.

The trouble had begun much later that night when she and Drew were on their way home from a party in Copperton. Drew had started to take the back way to Cabeza Valley, a seventeen-mile dirt road that ran up and over the Bradshaw Mountains before plunging down the other side in a series of switchbacks. Just as they'd crested the mountain, Cate made Drew stop and let her drive. He'd been drinking heavily at the party, and Cate—newly licensed and well-practiced—felt she was the safer bet to get them home.

Then, out the rear window, they'd both seen a pair of head-lights rapidly catching up to them.

"Gun it!" Drew had barked, a panicky sharpness to his voice she'd not heard before.

"I'm not gonna gun it with a curve coming," Cate had fired back. They'd been arguing all night after she'd witnessed him sell-ing meth to some strangers at the party.

As they rounded the bend, a closed gate across the road brought the truck to a screeching stop. Drew hopped out and was opening the gate when the other vehicle caught up to them. Three large guys exploded from the truck and ran up to Drew.

Cate had stayed put, her temples throbbing. Watching the four in the headlights, she'd felt scared and vulnerable. It looked like a conversation, at least, and not a pending fistfight. Then Drew was casually walking back to her.

"You take Margaret's truck back, okay? I got this," he'd mur-mured through the open driver's window. He was trying to keep his voice calm, but he looked pale and shaken. She had never seen him so scared. Her anger at his earlier stupidity now turned to protec-tive fear. Why was he telling her to drive off?

"No, Drew. No! I'm not leaving you here, fool."

That was when it came out of nowhere—Drew's hand hitting her face. Somewhere between a slap and a punch. She had gasped and grabbed her face, the darkness all around her sparkling. Then his furious words had ripped through the night.

"You think I want Margaret gunning for me 'cause I got her shiny Ram all busted up?" He spat out the words. "It's business, 'kay? Be sure to tell her that, too. Now, get the hell outta here, Cate!"

Since his high school graduation, the previous year, Drew's "business" had been meth— cooking it and selling it. Cate had returned home from boarding school to see a vintage Camaro with an expensive paint job in the Mason yard and Drew looking about fifteen pounds skinnier. Margaret had begun shooting him savage looks whenever she saw them together, which was why Cate had been so surprised by her offer of the truck that night.

The slap had been a turning point for them. Cate had stepped on the gas and driven home alone, although she'd barely slept that night. When she'd called the Mason house the next morning, Carrie Mason had said she heard his Camaro start up in the middle of the night, waking everyone in the house. Then he'd driven away.

"I have no clue where he is now, Catie." Carrie's voice sounded tired and annoyed. "Since he turned eighteen, he hasn't really stayed here much."

There were so many things to be furious with Drew about— his recklessness about his new "business," his not driving with her back to safety that night. But mostly the slap. No one had ever hit her—ever. Had he been alive, her father would have ripped Drew a new one. Still, she wanted to give him a chance to apologize. She even left him a message on his "business" phone, but he never returned the call. Turned out, they had broken up without her even knowing it.

Until she left for New York, she never passed Drew's house without searching for his Camaro in the yard. Over the years, whenever she found herself thinking about him she imagined the worst. Something terrible had happened to him, she just knew it. But no one in his family showed much concern that he'd moved on so abruptly.

Now, as she strode past the pink house, a solidly built woman opened the screen door and called for the two kids to come in. Cate could see it was a boy and a girl with short hair. The woman—thirtyish, with strawberry blonde hair caught up in a topknot and wearing a too-small tank top over fringed cutoffs—was vaguely familiar. On impulse, Cate called out through the line of desert willows from where she stood on the road.

"Desi? ... Desi Mason?"

Drew's sister Desiree had been a grade behind Cate at Copperton High, but in no way had they been friends. Cate had dominated too much of Drew's time and attention for his sister's taste. Although three years apart, everyone had jokingly called the Mason siblings "the twins" back then. They'd shared the same red-blonde hair, freckles, and golden eyes—not unlike the two children currently playing in the yard.

"Desi, it's Cate ... Cate Finley." She felt a sudden need for someone from her old life to recognize her.

Desi shaded her eyes and looked out at the road just as Cate parted the willow branches and sidled up to the fence. She watched Desi's expression change from confusion to delight.

"Oh, my God, Cate? What—how long has it been?"

"Well, I left halfway through 2000. It's ... it's my first trip back.

Desi had walked up to the low picket fence, still staring at Cate. Suddenly, the woman reached across and pulled her into a hug. Surprised, Cate returned the hug briefly, then stepped back to take in her old neighbor. A waif back in high school, Desi now sported ample hips and breasts under her snug top and cut-offs. Brightly colored floral tattoos spanned from bicep to wrist on each arm. Cate nodded at the sleeves with approval.

"Nice artwork."

"Wow, you look great, you skinny thing! You're not one of those spin class fanatics, are you?"

Cate inwardly guffawed at the idea of affording a gym membership.

"No I, um, run." *And climb buildings*, she thought.

"Well don't look at me," Desi tugged her tank down over her full midriff. "I've got a three-month-old asleep in the house. Still carrying baby weight." Cate laughed, grateful for the woman's easy camaraderie. Desi tilted her head as she studied Cate. "I love the pink hair. Still doing the art thing?"

"Yep. Still, uh, baking?" She had a flash of preadolescent Desi winning pastry awards at the county fair.

"Are you kidding? We're in deep. Remember the bakery across from the old Courthouse? We co-own it with another couple. Plus, my husband preaches down here at the church on Sundays. Busy!" Desi gave her a cryptic look before she spoke again.

"Are you staying a while? You ... you have got to meet Rae-lene, our 'foster,'" she said, holding up finger quotes. "I need to stop using that word. She's not been doing too well all week, but when she's feeling better, for sure. Cate, you are not going to be-lieve whose kid—"

But Cate's inner voice was speaking to her again.

"Hey, Desi, I came home because—I mean, I got a message about Margaret. Have you seen her? I mean, lately?" Cate felt her-self blushing. It sounded too dramatic to describe her sister as missing.

"Margaret, your sis? No, not really." She frowned as she tried to recall. "Saw her and Leelee Ruiz out riding horses a couple weeks back. Why? What's going on?"

A baby's wail came from inside the house.

"Shoot, somebody woke up. You're staying at the ranch house, right? Let's catch up later."

She turned and retreated up the front steps, leaving Cate baffled. If Margaret's disappearance wasn't a hot topic on the neighborhood grapevine, maybe this was all a false alarm.

At the door, Desi turned back to Cate.

"Hey, now that you're back, there's a meeting at the Community Center that Bronnie Taylor's trying to organize. They'll be talking about the dreaded Cabeza Rock Estates development. What I hear, Finley Ranch is involved." A louder wail came from the house. "Oops, I'm wanted. Bye."

Bronnie Taylor ... Cate pulled out her phone and stared at the texts again. When she'd called the number, the voice on the message had said, "This is Brownie." Or had it said Bronnie?

Chapter 7

Rae

Peering out the second story window of her bedroom, Rae saw her new foster mom—who wanted to be called Aunt Desi—talking with a skinny lady with a silvery pink ponytail. They'd said Margaret's name loud enough to draw her to the window, but now they were talking about something else.

Margaret ... Rae shook her head violently, trying to erase the pictures that were haunting her from last week. They made her feel bad—like she was the one who'd done something to Margaret, instead of just seeing her lying in the field like she did.

"Not my circus, not my monkeys." That was what the cab driver had said when he'd dropped her mama and her, along with her older brother Davy, off at that freeway bridge five years ago. Before the police had put her in foster care. Before all the foster families had tired of her ways and she'd ended up here. Before last week, when she met a lady named Margaret who owned all the beautiful horses across the field.

One day, not long after she'd come to live there, Rae had gotten up the nerve to walk over to the Finley Ranch stables and ask the lady about letting her work there.

"What are you, about ten?"

"Thirteen, ma'am. I'm just ... short is all."

"You have a name?"

"It's Rae. *R-a-e*, not like the boy's."

The lady had nodded, pulled out a shiny black case—a smartphone—and typed something into it. Then she'd put it back in her vest pocket. The denim vest had black and gray horses running across the chest and around the back, each outlined in tiny sparkling rhinestones. *Bedazzled*, Rae had thought.

"I'm Margaret. Margaret Finley."

"Miss Margaret—" Rae had started to say, but the woman's laugh cut her off.

"I'm running a boarding stable, not a boarding school. Margaret's fine."

Then they'd both laughed a little. Margaret's phone had made a chiming sound in her vest. She'd pulled it out to look and her smile cramped into a scowl.

She'd glanced up at Rae and said, "You can start scooping poop tomorrow morning at six, okay?" before slipping the phone back in her vest and stomping off towards the huge house that sat on the hill.

Remembering the woman's scowl had made Rae not want to be late the next morning. Ducking through a fence into the large pasture that separated Desi's house from the stables, she'd trotted across in the early light and tried not to step in any cow patties. She passed the cow herd as the sun edged above the horizon, the light growing stronger until it shone on the thing that had looked like a sleeping cow.

At twenty feet away, Rae stopped. Her hands and feet prickled like she'd touched something electric but she couldn't look away. Not a cow. A person—a woman. Lying on her side, faced away. Large, round hips dressed in denim. Barefoot, with arms stretched over her head like she was diving into a pool. Short-cut graying hair. A dark T-shirt under a denim vest. Rays of early light were hitting the black and gray bedazzled horses that raced across it … Rae knew where she had seen that vest.

That's when she shut her eyes and whispered, "Not my circus, not my monkeys, not my circus, not my monkeys …" Then she'd turned, then she'd run, all the way back to the foster home.

Later that day Rae thought maybe she'd dreamt it all. So, she went back to the pasture. There was no body lying there, only the cows, so she guessed it had been a dream. Then she saw something shiny in the grass. A phone. She knew whose it was, had seen the lady with all the pretty horses—Margaret—take it out and tap on it.

Lying on her bed just now, she reached under the mattress and pulled out the phone. It was dead. She didn't have a charger and couldn't ask for one. They would make her say why she needed it, then ask where she'd found the phone. And why was she out in that field? Why, why, why?

Rae had been asked the "why" questions before, at other foster homes. "Why don't you talk to us?" "Why do you hide shit from us?" "Why can't you act normal?" Why, why, why? The looks they gave her. It made her not want to tell anyone anything, ever again.

Chapter 8

Cate

Just past the pink house on the cottonwood lane, Cate stared at the two empty lots where old Sheriff Griffin's rentals had been. The displaced dirt looked fresh. The sheriff would be in his eighties and retired by now, maybe even passed. Perhaps there were new owners planning to build their dream homes. The two lots combined made up a good chunk of land, five acres at least. Enough for someone coming from Copperton who wanted to keep horses and chickens.

As Cate stood musing, a vintage gray truck nearly passed her before lurching to a stop. Out of the cab came a slightly built man with the Mayan features of his forefathers. Smiling, he spread his arms wide and, Cate, laughing, dropped her pack and moved in for the second hug of the day. Diego Ruiz had worked for Finley Ranch since before Cate was born.

"*Hola, Señorita* Cate. *Bienvenido a casa!*"

"*Hola, Señior Diego,*" Cate murmured, stepping back to look at him.

He had to be nearing fifty, but looked older, the southwestern sun having etched deep lines into his cheeks and brow. Seeing how he had aged made Cate grieve for how long she'd stayed away and she hugged him again fiercely. When they separated, Diego wiped away tears and surveyed her backpack and portfolio where they sat on the ground.

"But why are you walking?" Laughing and shaking his head,

he picked up her pack and set it in the truck bed. "*Venga,* we will go and surprise *mi familia*—Rosa *y los niños,* Liliana *y* Diego *Júnior.* We call them Leelee and D.J."

"You still live in the little house down by the stable?"

"Oh, *sí.* Leelee is the horsewoman, but D.J. is not happy here. Wants us to move to Phoenix." Diego's face darkened momentarily, and he shot a glance toward the main house. Then he turned cheerful again as he updated her on the ranch's activities for the past two decades.

The Ruizes' modest bungalow stood on its own half-acre next to the ranch entrance. Rosa greeted them at the door, as excited to see Cate as her husband had been. Younger than Diego by a decade, she'd been a pregnant twenty-something when Cate had last hugged her.

After saying Cate looked thin, Rosa fluttered to the kitchen and returned with a snack of *queso* and *tortillas.* Cate tried not to show how starving she was as she devoured the plate of food. Periodically, she offered some to the other two, who smiled and shook their heads.

The front door opened just as Rosa was taking her empty plate, and a grim-faced young man strode in with a fistful of mail. Bitterness hung on him like frost-bitten fruit. Diego turned to welcome his scowling son with a warm smile.

"*Recuerdas a*—you remember Miss Cate, *sí?*"

D.J. tossed the mail on a side table, then swiveled to stare at Cate with open hostility.

"Another Finley, just what we need," he said with a sardonic smile, before turning back to his father.

"Tell Leelee that old mare is down with colic again. I'm done doing her work." He shot Cate another dark look and left with a door slam.

What was that all about? Cate wondered, feeling the hair on her arms prickle.

Just then, a willowy girl in her late teens entered from the back hallway. Dressed in skinny jeans, boots, and a black tank top, with a ball cap in her hand, she radiated good humor as intensely as her brother had broadcast his misery. The wide-set cheekbones under jade eyes and her full lips made Cate want to grab her sketchpad.

The girl was headed for the door but detoured when she saw Cate and walked over to shake hands. When Cate stood, the girl loomed over her by a good four inches.

"Hi, I'm Leelee. So nice to meet you," she said. Her smile was amiable enough, but tension creased her jaw. No doubt she'd felt her parents' embarrassment at D.J.'s rudeness.

"Hi, I'm Cate. Your brother was a toddler and I think you were just a baby bump the last time I was here."

Leelee giggled momentarily, then she was all business again, opening the front door while she and Diego spoke in rapid Spanish. Cate caught the word *bella* and had a flash of memory. She took a step toward the two.

"Wait, you aren't talking about a horse named Bella, are you? Before I left, there was a mare with that name that I ... used to ride."

"*Sí, es Bella,*" Diego answered, nodding.

Leelee turned to Cate. "A little bay mare with a big star on her forehead?"

Cate nodded. "She'd have to be in her late twenties by now."

An image flashed of the mare's burnished red coat gleaming in the sun and the enormous patch of white on her forehead as she rubbed her face against Cate's hands.

"Yeah, she's our chronic colic case these days," Leelee was saying. "Hey, you want to help me with her?"

\#

The Finley Ranch stables sat on a three-tiered slope and looked like it had gotten a recent paint job—claret with stone trim—making the place look more like a New England farm than a southwestern ranch. The highest level of the stable was divided into three large paddocks. The middle level contained a twenty-four-stall horse barn and veterinary offices and a large arena with plenty of parking took up most of the lowest level. Beyond that was a fifteen-acre irrigated horse pasture.

A half-dozen horses were out in the pasture, and one of them was rolling and flailing its legs in the farthest corner. Bella.

Cate's jaw tightened with a remembered sense of urgency. She'd heard her father tell numerous horse owners over the years that colic was a life-or-death issue in horses and needed prompt treatment. Leelee handed her a halter and lead rope, then entered the barn office and returned with a syringe of fluid, a packaged needle, and a towel laid over her arm. They headed out to the pasture at a fast pace.

"So, did you learn horse vetting from Margaret?" asked Cate.

"Yes, she and *Papá* were excellent teachers." Then she dropped her light tone and turned to Cate with an anxious look. "Look, I'm trying not to get too worried, but Margaret should be home by now. I ... I just don't know what would keep her away for this long."

A twinge of panic started up in Cate's chest. She took some deep breaths and stared back at the girl. Was this evidence her sister was indeed missing?

"Exactly how long has she been gone, Leelee? Is anybody

looking for her? I ... only heard about this yesterday." Was it just twenty-four hours ago she'd first read the texts?

But they had arrived at where the horse was violently thrashing on the ground. It was indeed the Bella she remembered, drenched in sweat and with deep creases along her belly—a sign of extreme stomach cramping. The horse alternated between rolling on her back from side to side and struggling to get up.

While Bella was still down, Leelee quickly haltered her, handing the lead rope to Cate. The girl deftly probed a vein in the horse's neck, slipped in the needle and attached the syringe. Then she delivered the sedative as though she'd done it every day of her life. Within minutes, Bella had begun to relax and lick her lips. Leelee coaxed her to stand and put an ear against her flank to listen for gut sounds.

"Now, we do the belly lifts to get her insides moving again." She stepped to the other side and reached under the mare's midsection, handing Cate one end of the towel.

"Hold it flat and firm against her stomach, starting just behind the front legs. I'll count to ten while we lift up ..."

The mare grunted softly and lowered her head as they worked. She stood patiently, as if knowing the two were trying to help her. While they lifted, Leelee counted in a low, calm voice. Slowly, they moved the towel pressure along the bottom of her belly toward her tail. Periodically the mare raised her tail and Cate heard soft whooshes of air. Leelee smiled and then giggled a little.

"That's a good sign. Things gotta move along. Right, Bella? Now you walk her for a while, and we'll see if she'll pass some manure. Otherwise, we call the vet." She patted the phone in her back pocket.

Cate led Bella up the hill then along the fence to the far side of the pasture. When they got there, the old mare drifted over to where there were several manure piles and immediately dropped her own on top of them.

"Good girl," Cate crooned to her, then lifted her hand in a thumbs-up signal back to Leelee, watching from the stables.

The mare's coat was drying now and becoming the color she remembered, a rich blood-red bay. The last time Cate had seen her, Bella had been in her prime—her coat gleaming like a ruby in the sunlight. Now her black mane and tail were dull and brittle with age.

Suddenly melancholy, Cate scrubbed the dried sweat on the mare's neck with her fingertips and smoothed the black mane down, impulsively burying her face in it. She took a deep breath of the pungent horse scent. A memory came—climbing on the fence to throw her leg over Bella and race her bareback down the sun-dappled cottonwood lane. Riding bareback had once been Cate's refuge from the world. She had forgotten it, forgotten this horse, forgotten where home was.

Chapter 9

A woman of Amazonian proportions opened the front door of the main ranch house and peered down at Cate with a hint of amusement. Jet black hair captured in a tight chignon, impressively drawn black eyeliner rimming ice blue eyes, makeup base a little too dark for her skin tone, and deep crimson matte lipstick. A black blazer partially concealed a frilly magenta blouse that emphasized her substantial breasts. Below that, skin-tight English riding breeches wended their way down long, if plumpish legs and disappeared into knee-high black riding boots. It struck Cate as way too formal for Cabeza Valley. More like suburban realtor meets Olympic equestrian.

"Can I help you?" The woman asked in a contralto voice that sounded comfortable with wielding power. Her smile was dazzling, jaw jutted forward, both upper and lower teeth exposed.

Cate stood in silence for a moment, so startled she thought she might forget her own name.

"I'm Cate ... Cate Finley. Margaret's sister. Who are *you*?"

The woman's expression barely changed save for a slightly raised eyebrow and a muscle flexing in her jaw. Cate felt her own jaw beginning to tense in response.

"Hello, Cate ... Cate Finley ... Margaret's sister," came the flat reply. Had the woman just mocked her? "I'm your cousin, Estelle Parker—Margaret's ranch manager. What brings you back to the homestead? New York—isn't that where you were last bound?"

Cate felt warmth creeping up her neck and wasn't sure why. Clearly this woman knew of her, but she couldn't remember ever hearing of a cousin named Estelle. Should she ask more about that?

Without being unfriendly, the woman was managing to make her feel like she'd come to the door selling something. As Cate struggled for words that wouldn't make her sound loony, Estelle discreetly checked her watch.

"Look, I'm here because—I got a text that Margaret is, well, has gone missing." Cate scanned the woman's face for signs of understanding but found none—just a blank stare in return. Mortified, Cate gestured at the open door. "Do you, uh, live here at the ranch?"

Estelle had been gazing at her intently, eyes narrowed and with a slightly puzzled frown as if Cate were speaking with a thick accent. Suddenly she threw her head back and laughed. An open-throated, high-spirited laugh that made Cate chuckle along uneasily. *Oh, my gosh, yes. Hilarious.*

The woman was leaning over now, still laughing, holding her stomach and shaking her head. Cate pressed on.

"So ... what, not missing, then?"

Estelle caught herself in mid-guffaw and reached forward to pat Cate's shoulder comfortingly. "You poor thing! Who ... who told you that? That's ..." She was trying to control herself now. "That's rich ... so," she took a breath, "so very funny, ha-ha ... ," and another fit of laughter.

Cate felt irritation watching the woman struggle to gain control of her giggles. It was starting to seem, well, excessive.

"Then, Margaret is here at the ranch?" she asked, leaning forward to peer at Estelle's downturned face.

If she was here, Cate realized she would have to explain this sudden return to the ranch. But Margaret would have to explain why

Leelee Ruiz and this other person—Brownie or Bronnie—were worried about her. Either way, it would be an uncomfortable reunion.

Estelle was recovering, straightening to her lofty height and her tone changing to gentle sarcasm. "So, has the town started to form a search party? Bronnie Taylor and her cronies? What a scare you must have had, poor dear. Come in, come in." She gestured grandly for Cate to cross the threshold. And as she did, family memories flooded back.

Here was the worn Persian carpet in the foyer, where her mother had taught countless rescued puppies *not* to make deposits. Along the hallway hung empty wrought iron wall holders that had once carried different candles depending on the season. Green and blue in the spring and summer, orange and yellow in the fall, and red and green at Christmas.

As they stepped into the great room, Cate recalled the eight-foot-tall pine trees her father would drag in for the Finley women to decorate before hosting the community holiday party. So would begin the annual making and stringing of colored popcorn, the wrapping of twinkling light strands, and the placing at the top, not a star or angel but a tiny hand-carved cowgirl on her horse. Because Margaret had insisted, and they couldn't say no to Margaret. Not after her favorite horse—a golden palomino like the one in the tree ornament—had the misfortune to break his leg one Christmas morning.

The right wall of the great room was still devoted to Margaret's winnings in the horse show ring. Twin glass-fronted trophy cases held several dozen trophies of all shapes and sizes. A sea of blue ribbons, a few red, and even fewer yellows hung on strands at the back of each case.

Flanking each side of the displays were photos of the dozen horses Margaret had taken from yearling futurity to senior championship by the time Cate left. There didn't seem to be many recent photos in the collection.

Estelle had turned her back and was furiously tapping at her phone. Cate crossed the room to stand next to Estelle and gaze out the floor-to-ceiling window that offered a panorama of the horse stables, pasturelands, and the Cabeza Rock Monument looming in the south. Sensing her presence, the Amazon clicked off her phone and turned to Cate with her hostess smile in place.

"Well! ... I, uh, just texted your sister that you were here. She is *de*-lighted. Yes, ma'am, just *tickled*. She's actually been in Albuquerque all week at a horse sale of some kind. Getting," she glanced at her phone screen, "some new prospects—always so exciting for her."

"Oh, really? Leelee seemed to think—"

"Oh, little Leelee's doing some thinking, is she?" There was a sharp edge to the dismissive smile. "Well, no worries. Margaret will be hauling back," she flicked her phone back on to check, "tomorrow night. Right. Monday at the latest."

"Hauling horses?" Cate turned her gaze down to the stable yard where a six-horse living quarters trailer sat hooked up to a dually hauler with the Finley Ranch brand emblazoned on the cab door. Why hadn't her sister taken that nice rig on her horse-buying trip? Maybe she had another rig ... maybe.

She looked to see whether Estelle had followed her gaze, but the woman was oblivious, stabbing out more texts and pausing to read. Unsure what to do next, Cate scanned the room for familiar artifacts of her own childhood achievements. Nowhere in sight were her art awards or even any photos of her. Had every scrap of her existence been purged from the house?

"So, can I get you something to drink?" Estelle asked, snapping her phone case shut. "I usually have a glass of wine in the afternoons. Or we have beer from the local microbrewery."

A more sociable person might have said yes to alcohol—a lot of it— at this point, but all Cate craved was some alone time with her memories.

"Um, could I just get some water?

"Fizzy or flat?"

"Not carbonated if that's—"

"Flat it is. Coming right up."

A few minutes later, they were sipping their drinks, seated opposite each other in the leather loveseats that flanked the enormous sofa in front of the picture window.

"Well, then, I'm so curious where you've been all this time, Cate. With a *c* or a *k*? I want to get it right."

Cate peered back at her and thought, *Why don't you know this if you've been texting with my sister?*

"Um, it's Cate with a *c*, and Caitlyn with an *i* and a *y*," she said with a tight smile. This whole conversation was setting off bull crap alerts in her brain. But maybe it was best to go along with the charade until either her sister came home or this Bronnie person turned up. "And, as you said at the door, I left to go, um, study in New York."

"Wow, Cate in New York Ci-*tay* ... That must have been a shock. Was it a shock, Cate?"

The name repetition was getting annoying. She wondered if the woman had already been drinking when she knocked on the door.

"Um, there was an adjustment period. I learned ... some things."

"About survival, I bet." The woman took a giant slug of wine and broke into her charming smile again. In a softer voice, she asked, "Did you learn to survive there, Cate?"

Cate chuckled despite herself. *Oh ... hell ... yeah.*

"I held my own. But enough about me. What's your story, Estelle?"

"My story?"

"Uh huh, where did you come from? You're whose cousin? Or niece? Because I don't think I ever heard about you from either of my parents."

Their eye lock was brief but intense. Estelle looked away first. She dropped her gaze to her wine glass as if in grief over such a tragedy.

"No. Understandable. I'm your dad's second cousin. Our families were estranged a generation back."

"I see." Although not at all convinced, Cate did know a little something about estrangement. "And your family's name is Parker?"

"What? Oh, no. That's my married name. Rest in peace, Rudy. Poor dear."

"And where are you from, Estelle?"

"Nevada, most recently." Estelle gave an abbreviated version of The Smile and launched into her cheerful hostess voice.

"Listen, Cate, I've got to make a call. You're staying here tonight, right? Rosa will cook us up something for dinner if I ask her *por favor.*"

"That's very kind of you *and* Rosa." Regardless of how hungry she felt, Cate didn't think she could keep up what was feeling like a cat-and-mouse game with Estelle for a whole evening. "I'm pretty beat from travel and all. I think I'd just like to turn in early tonight."

For the first time, Estelle looked genuinely sympathetic and a little relieved. Maybe Cate had just come at an inconvenient time.

"Oh, absolutely, Cate. Pick any of the spare bedrooms upstairs. That one at the east end was yours, I believe. I'll have Rosa leave a sandwich for you on the kitchen counter."

Then, like a queen rising from her throne, Estelle stood and strolled out of the room.

How easily this woman directed her around her own family's house, authoritative in her role as hostess. Estelle had ... charisma—that's what they called it, right? Charisma, and all that height. In her flat-heeled riding boots, she was at least six feet. Was that what made her so intimidating?

Oh, shut up. You worry too much, said a nagging voice in Cate's head.

"Maybe I do, but that woman's got a strange vibe." Suddenly drained, she rose and crossed the room to the stairs. On the upstairs landing, she pulled out her phone to try Bronnie's number again. She needed to talk to the woman who had lured her back here. It went to voicemail immediately, and this time she left a message.

"Hi ... um, this is ... this is Cate Finley. You ... texted me—yesterday? Okay, anyway ... I'm—"

But the recording had cut off, probably due to all her pauses. Suddenly she was too tired to pursue anything but a nap. When she opened the door to her old room, nothing registered except the softness of the bed as her body plopped down on it.

Later that night, refreshed from a few hours of sleep and one of Rosa's delicious chicken salad sandwiches, Cate luxuriated in the privacy of a full-sized private bathroom. After a long soak in the tub, during which she laundered her underwear and t-shirt, she studied her naked body in the mirror.

Her tanned arms and legs evidenced the hours spent climbing the sides of buildings in t-shirts and running shorts. She still had a runner's body, with decent muscle tone and barely any fat. But her thin, weary face showed the stress of a nomadic life. Too many sleepless nights and restless days spent looking over her shoulder. And now she was home at last, but did it feel like home? It did not. In fact, there were no signs that she'd ever lived there.

Yawning, she slipped on a clean t-shirt and shorts and headed for the bed. On the way, she opened the window facing the eastern pasture and the valley beyond that. Crickets chirped in the nearby brush. Faint snuffling sounds of horses came from the stables. A distant coyote yipped, and a baying dog responded. Under it all, the frogs' song droned at the flowing creek. All were a welcome respite from the harsh traffic noises she'd grown used to in the city. Climbing into bed, Cate soon drifted off to this concert of nature.

Chapter 10

She startled awake from a dream with a sickening sense of violation. A hotel room bed, on a different morning, long ago and across the country. Her naked body aching, injured and woozy under a blanket of fragrant yellow roses. The memory brought her to her feet, poised for flight. Then she saw where she was. A different bedroom in a different world. *Relax. You're safe. Breathe.*

Her old room, but not hers. Margaret had completely changed it. Beige. On. Beige. Gone were the orange and magenta swirled walls that her mother had agreed to let her paint after Cate had worked so hard to get A's on her freshman midterm report card. Gone were the paintings and drawings that had covered the vibrant walls, along with her 4-H awards for textiles, hand-painted fabrics that had won her first place at the County Fair three years in a row. Most likely, Margaret had fed them to a bonfire when she found out Cate had run off to New York with stolen funds. This was how her sister took revenge? Erase all memory of her from the place?

Feeling as grim as the walls, Cate pulled on jeans and a clean t-shirt, tied her running shoes, and went downstairs in search of caffeine.

The house was silent and empty, but the coffee machine had a half-full pot of what turned out to be excellent brew. Next to it, a carton of flavored creamer wallowed in a small ice-filled tray, and a plate of blueberry scones beckoned to her. Heaven.

Standing and sipping at the picture window in the great

room, Cate saw some kind of event taking shape down at the stables.

A line of trucks and horse trailers that stretched out past the ranch entrance rolled slowly into the oversized parking lot next to the riding arena. A man, probably Diego, was waving each rig into the spot next to the previous one, making a parallel line of parked vehicles. People were unloading and saddling horses. Far in the distance, a few riders drove a small herd of black calves toward the arena. Clearly, the ranch was hosting a cow horse event, probably roping or team penning.

Although not the true "horsey one" in the family, Cate was enough of a ranch kid to have done her share of team penning. She had often made up the third member of Team Finley, alongside Doc and Margaret. As she recalled, a team of three riders each had to separate their assigned calf from the herd and guide it into a pen on the other side of the arena. Scoring was based on how fast each team could pen all three calves without losing one back to the herd.

Coffee mug in hand, Cate wandered down the stone-lined path to the stable area to get a closer look. Directly in front of her, a familiar figure sat on a stout white horse, poised to ride into the arena. Dressed in a white Stetson hat, a cherry red western shirt, and matching jeans, Estelle Parker sat looking tense and uncomfortable in the saddle.

I'll bet you wish it came with a seatbelt or handrails, Cate thought.

The arena gate was opened, and Estelle jabbed her horse in the ribs with her spurs. The animal dutifully trotted into the arena while she stood in the stirrups to avoid the bounce.

Behind her followed young D.J. Ruiz on a tall chestnut gelding and his sister Leelee on a prancing cream-colored horse with blue eyes and an abundant mane and tail. Cate drew up to the fence to watch the three riders. Estelle was barking orders at a scowling D.J. while his sister's shoulders slumped miserably. The siblings could probably have ridden circles around this woman, but she seemed to have some sort of control over them.

"Is that really you, Cate Finley?"

A rider had sidled his horse up to where she was hanging on the fence. When she turned to face him, he took off his cowboy hat and broke into a wide cherubic grin.

"Oh, my God. Jimmy?"

Jimmy Lee Baker had been assigned to the same chemistry lab table as Cate during sophomore year at Copperton High. They had instantly become partners in crime. Their bond solidified after a shared lab experiment had resulted in a small explosion and a 911 call to the Copperton Fire Department. There'd been no injuries but it had made the local news.

"Hey, torched anything lately?"

He hopped off his horse, and she climbed down for an awkward hug, mainly due to a height issue. Jimmy had reached his full stature in middle school—a whopping five-feet-one. While he'd been a superb athlete in individual sports like running, swimming, and diving, his height had made him a lightning rod for all the jocks at Copperton.

At Cate's suggestion, Jimmy had joined the drama club just in time to be cast as Puck in Midsummer Night's Dream.

An entire semester of raucous laughter amongst the "drama geeks" had steered him away from sports and into the theater. He'd even found his soulmate, an equally tiny thespian named Marisa.

"What brings you back to town?" he asked, looking her over approvingly.

"Actually, some family business. I guess it was time." She

smiled back at him sheepishly. Really, it was too early to start talking about the mystery texts. She'd wait and see if her sister came home tonight as Estelle had promised.

"Family business with Margaret? I mean, your parents … back then. So sad." He paused for a moment of respect. "But, in a way, you're saved from having to watch them go downhill slowly. My dad took early retirement due to 'old-timers' disease. Ugh, pretty miserable."

"So, did you end up joining your dad's law firm?"

"Yep, but only on the condition we steer the practice toward estate planning."

A voice on the PA system cut in with a request for Team Baker.

"Oh, hey, that's my team. Cate, so good to see you again." He reached in his pocket and handed her a business card. "Call when you're in town. We'll do lunch at the Palace."

Then he stepped onto the first rail of the fence, propelled expertly onto his horse's back, and trotted off toward the arena gate.

The announcer broke the news that Team Finley had been disqualified after letting a calf escape back to the herd. Cate saw Estelle's horse open his mouth and set back on his haunches as she yanked savagely on his bridle. Then the woman slid clumsily out of the saddle and threw the reins at Leelee. As she leaned in to hiss something at the Ruiz siblings, her eye strayed toward the house on the hill.

A large black SUV was parked next to the house, and a line of suited men stood peering down at the crowd. Estelle waved animatedly and was headed toward them when she noticed Cate and made a detour.

"Good to see you're up, Caitlyn. Did you want to join in the fun? Liliana can saddle you an appropriate horse, I'm sure." Then she noticed Cate's empty coffee cup and held out her hand with the air of a schoolteacher shaming an offender. Cate smiled back, lazily handing her the cup.

"Not quite dressed for riding this morning, Estelle. All good. Happy to be a spectator."

"Wow, you are *so* not Margaret," Estelle said, dusting off her jeans and chuckling. "Well, I'm off to conduct some meetings this afternoon, but I wanted to invite you to a little dinner party for my, uh, visitors." She gestured up the hill, speaking at a fast clip. "We'll have drinks starting at six, then a presentation you will find very interesting. Then some delicious catered barbecue. Hopefully, your sister will arrive in time for it, but at least you'll join us, yes?"

"Um, sure. Thanks, Estelle," Cate replied, feeling the muscles contract in her stomach.

The prospect of this woman and some strangers witnessing her reunion with Margaret was unsettling. Her gut was telling her something was way off in that house and to keep her distance. But her mind wanted to know just what kind of presentation the woman was planning, and for whom.

Wanting to get Leelee's take on the situation at the house and connect some random dots, she looked around for the girl. Finally, she spied her hanging a hay bag in front of Bella's stall. Cate walked up to her old mare and scratched her ears gently.

"How's our patient today?"

"Well, she's eating and drinking, so all good, I guess," the girl replied tonelessly. She looked deflated, and Cate longed to ask what Estelle had said to her.

"Nice effort out there in the arena this morning. Couldn't have been easy."

Leelee looked at her with genuine curiosity.

"How well do you know—?" she began.

"Estelle? I was going to ask you that," Cate replied. Leelee nodded and looked slightly relieved.

Well, this wasn't good news. Cate hadn't realized how much she'd been counting on the Ruizes to reassure her about Estelle. Her heart started to race as she stroked Bella's neck.

"Honestly, I've never heard of a cousin named Estelle before yesterday. Dad didn't have many relatives, and my mother had no family here and no contact with her family back in Ireland. Wish I could talk to my folks or Margaret about her. What did Estelle say to you and D.J. before your ride? I can't help asking; you looked so miserable out there."

"She … she likes winning, but … she's just a terrible rider. I feel so bad for Pete, the horse she rode. His mouth was bleeding. She's heard what I think about it. Said she'd get me fired if I continued my sass. You better ask D.J. what she said to him, though. We don't speak for each other anymore."

At the breakfast burrito concession, Rosa said D.J. had taken the hay truck into town. Just then, there was static over the PA, followed by an announcer calling out, "Cate Finley to the arena, please. Cate Finley, arena gate."

Startled, Cate turned and saw Jimmy waving from just outside the arena entrance. She walked down to see what he had in mind. In answer, he held out the reins of the brown and white spotted horse standing placidly next to him.

"Hoping you can help. Our third rider ducked out before the second go-round, and we've got a shot at some prize money." His smile was mischievous.

"Do I look dressed for horse sports?" she asked, matching his smile.

"Nobody much cares what you're wearing, Cate Finley. They care if you still have cow sense."

"I haven't stepped in the saddle in nearly two decades," she said, laughing because this was going to happen. "Jimmy. I'm begging you. Please don't make me do this."

"You're in good shape—haven't let yourself go, at least. Hop up. Cochise will do all the work."

"Hope I don't regret it," Cate said, adjusting the stirrups. She gave the gelding a pat on the neck and hauled herself onto his back.

As it turned out, riding a horse *was* a lot like riding a bike— once you'd ridden enough, you would always know how to do it. It helped that Cochise's trot was smooth as silk, and he proved easy to turn. Once in the arena, Jimmy introduced her to the other rider, Paco, and explained their strategy. When the buzzer sounded, they would each take a turn separating their assigned calf from the herd and then driving it toward the pen at the end of the arena. Jimmy volunteered to take the first calf, counting on Paco's and Cate's calves following their buddy into the enclosure without resistance, and thus shaving time off their score.

It worked like a charm until Cate got distracted by Estelle, standing on the hill flanked by her entourage. Out of the corner of her eye, Cate saw her calf double back and head for the main herd again. Without a cue from her, her horse spun on his haunches and raced to cut off the calf's escape, managing to chase it back into the pen at the last possible moment. The crowd whistled and whooped their approval. Once she'd regained her breath, Cate reached down and rubbed the spotted horse's neck as he blew out.

"Good boy, Cochise," she crooned.

Suddenly she was fourteen again and riding Bella out of the arena behind Doc and Margaret after a superb round of penning.

They'd snagged the trophy, and Doc had let the sisters split the cash prize. Winning these events had always created a fleeting camaraderie between the Finley girls. Margaret had beamed at her and given a rare thumbs-up that day. Recalling it now, an ache found Cate's chest, and her eyes stung.

Now the PA was announcing the morning's winners. In the end, Team Baker took the second-place jackpot of $210, which Jimmy and Paco gave to Cate for being such a good sport. While she was relieved to have some unexpected cash, she quickly rebated them fifty dollars each. A girl had some pride.

Wanting to delay going up to the house until she'd talked to D.J., Cate grabbed a grooming bucket from the tack room and headed for Bella's pen. On the way, she passed the Finley Ranch horse rig that she'd seen from up at the house and veered off to take a closer look.

The trailer was a monster, with six stalls and what looked like a dozen feet of living quarters, hooked up securely to a Freightliner hauler. Cate guessed she was looking at well over a hundred thousand dollars of horse transportation. She imagined Margaret climbing into the cab and feeling like the queen of the world. What would make her sister leave it behind on a horse-buying trip?

The door of the living quarters wasn't locked, and a shocking mess lay inside. Clothing and food containers were strewn on the floor. A pile of empty Jack Daniels bottles and numerous beer cans occupied one corner. A human rat's nest. Who was living in the trailer and trashing it? She refused to believe it was her sister, who had once torn into Cate for dropping a gum wrapper at the stables. She would need to ask Estelle about this along with some other troubling details. But first, a visit to Bella's stall.

But the mare wasn't in the barn. Cate saw her out in the stable yard, where a man in a filthy cowboy hat was about to load her into a stock trailer. A magnetic sign on the trailer read, "Copperton Livestock Auction." Panicked, Cate looked around for Leelee and saw her carrying a saddle to the tack room.

"Leelee, what's going on with Bella? She's not going to auction, is she?"

Leelee shot her a furtive look, then stared down at the saddle in her arms. "Well, Estelle just told me she has to go. Too many colics."

"Estelle? Since when does Estelle make decisions on the horse operation? I thought she managed the office or something."

"Cate, I don't—" Leelee pleaded softly.

"If Doc was alive, he would *never* send Bella—a beloved ranch horse that he'd bred and raised—to an auction. Because you know why? At her age, they go straight to slaughter." Cate felt her voice shaking as the emotion began to build. "I can't believe Margaret would *ever* allow this." Not the animal-loving sister she remembered.

"Well, I think she must have told Estelle to do it, Cate. That's ... that's what I think," the girl said defensively.

"Tell you what, you keep Bella off that trailer, and I will deal with Estelle, okay?"

Leelee nodded and headed over to talk to the driver.

Cate could hear the drone of voices coming from the dining room as she walked through the front door of the ranch house. In the foyer, she stopped before a painting of her parents and gazed into her father's gentle eyes.

"You wouldn't do this to Bella, not after all the years she's given the ranch."

She went into the kitchen for a glass of water and tried to

eavesdrop on the meeting. Estelle stepped through the door, a peevish finger to her lips.

For a moment, Cate took in the towering woman, freshly changed into a cow print shirt over her fire engine red jeans that she'd tucked into black and white cowhide boots. A woman of her age and size, dressed like that, might have been laughable had Cate not been so furious.

"Estelle, Leelee seems to think Margaret told you to send Bella to the livestock auction. True?"

Estelle looked at her blankly for a moment.

"What? Oh, uh, sure. She said to sell all the excess horses."

"Really? Bella? To the slaughter auction? Because back in my day, we avoided doing that to our beloved animals." Cate could feel her face heating up.

"Don't shoot the messenger. Talk to your sis. I'll give you her cell."

There was that smirk again.

The last thing Cate wanted to do was have another ugly phone conversation with Margaret. And, gauging how she felt right now, it would be ugly. Someone was jerking her around.

Cate stared back at the woman, speaking slowly and deliberately.

"I have canceled the haul to the auction yard until my sister gets home. You look like you've got plenty of other things on your plate, am I right?" Cate asked, throwing a look in the direction of the dining room. "Who are those men?"

"Oh, you'll meet them tonight," Estelle said with a look that made Cate's spine shiver a little. "Don't forget, happy hour starts at six."

The woman headed for the door only to turn back to Cate,

her face now looking wounded.

"And listen, I'm truly sorry if my stepping in to do some operations management disturbed you. Margaret has said countless times she wished you had stayed and become her partner in the ranch."

Stung, Cate watched Estelle disappear into the dining room. The woman had gotten one part of the story right, at least. Cate had ruined her sister's grand plan when she ran away to New York.

Chapter 11

When six o'clock rolled around, Cate put on the black sheath and sandals, along with the department store makeup, and studied herself in the bathroom mirror. Not bad. If she was to be the Finley clan representative at dinner, she was determined not to feel like a poor relation.

Quietly taking the back stairs down to the kitchen, Cate glimpsed a panel truck with "Copperton Charlie's Texas-Style BBQ" parked outside. The tailgate stood open, revealing a portable slide-out grill. A mouth-watering aroma of barbecue wafted into the kitchen.

Rosa stood assembling ingredients for an enormous tostada on a silver platter when Cate leaned in for a side hug. She resisted the urge to remain there all night, embracing this woman. The summer after her parents died, Rosa Ruiz's nurturing had been the only thing standing between Cate and starvation.

"*Que bonita, mamacíta,*" Cate murmured. Rosa beamed and hugged her back briefly, then shot a worried look over her shoulder in the direction of Estelle's voice in the great room.

"*Ten cuidado, mi preciosa.* Be careful!" Then she quickly resumed the salad preparation.

Cate nodded, feeling somewhat like she was entering a lion's den. She picked up a wine glass, filled it with tap water, and entered the great room.

Their names were Hugo, Dirk, Randy, and Gabe, and they

were already on their second round of cocktails when she strode into the room.

Conversation stopped, which was flattering. Cate was glad she'd taken some extra time with her hair, brushing it into a loose topknot with tendrils carefully pulled out and wound into spirals. A chic version of her girl-living-out-of-a-backpack look.

Hugo turned out to be the eldest nephew of Sheriff Mack Griffin, who had indeed died a few years back and left him the two rental properties next to the ranch.

"With all original plumbing and laden with termites, they were twin white elephants, I'm afraid," Hugo said in a slight British accent. She looked at him curiously, and he laughed. Aristocratic and well-tailored, with the air of a friendly, well-built stockbroker, Hugo was the polar opposite of his folksy uncle.

"My great-grandparents were originally from England. My father Colby—Mack's younger brother——spent his senior high year with relatives in London and basically never returned to the States. So, I represent a whole branch of the Griffin family composed of repatriated Brits."

"Wow, someone who strayed farther than I did," Cate quipped.

"Yes, I've heard. New York, right? And this is your first trip back since high school?"

Yes, yes, that was becoming *the* question to ask her.

Estelle came by just then with a towel-wrapped champagne bottle.

"Fill you up, Cate?"

Cate started to protest, but the liquid was already pouring into her empty glass. In general, champagne held no appeal for her—bad memories of Manhattan hotels.

Dirk and Randy appeared to be twins or at least related,

but maybe it was just the shared male pattern baldness and lack of fashion sense. Flashing realtor cards along with their dentist-enhanced teeth, they seemed in awe of Estelle's charisma. *Estelle's minions*, Cate thought.

The fourth man, introduced as Gabe and standing apart from the others, was by far the most interesting. Between answering and asking questions from the others, Cate kept her eye on him as he inventoried the fixtures and furnishings in the great room. Antique dealer? Either that or he was painfully shy. Or a well-dressed burglar. He had a face that clenched like a fist, even when in repose. Dressed impeccably, he seemed reluctant to touch anything for fear of ruining his inky black suit with dust and animal hair.

He caught her looking his way, and a smile spread across his features. It made him look like a ravenous thug. Charming ... friendly ... but no less a thug. She hated feeling so paranoid, especially now that she was back in her family home. This was the lasting damage from having spent so many years in a harsh city like New York. You picked up on dangerous energy.

She noticed the waning fire in the oversized brick fireplace and seized a wrought iron poker to stoke it. The logs instantly fell apart, being the wax and sawdust kind for sale at supermarkets. Cate closed her eyes and imagined her father, a master builder of real wood fires, rolling over in his grave.

A sudden nostalgia for Doc's corny jokes and easy company came over her. God, she missed him, more so now she was back in the home they'd all shared. There was something undefinable and ominous in this room right now, making her feel nervous and edgy. She had an impulse to keep the poker handy.

Gabe moved to stand next to her, his back to the fire.

"What an exquisite property you have here." His voice was

smooth and practiced. "Must have been hard to leave all those years ago." Clearly, an invitation to draw her out.

She'd changed her mind about him. A lawyer or corporate operative of some kind. The kind that might have a nondisclosure agreement from a powerful man tucked in his coat jacket. She knew that was crazy. There was no way Joseph had followed her back to this dusty little Arizona town. Even so, she turned and gave the man a cold stare, hoping to discourage more conversation. He nodded, slightly amused, and they both turned to view Estelle's floor show.

"Why don't we start the presentation, shall we?" Estelle had recorked the champagne after refilling Cate's glass and now set it under a side table by the bookshelf. "I'm most interested in what you gentlemen have come up with since our last meeting."

Estelle ushered everyone over to a line of folding chairs that faced the picture window. She switched on some spotlights, then closed the ceiling-high drapes with a flourish. The room instantly transformed into a cabaret, with Estelle as the main act. Pulling down a screen that hung on an easel, she stepped to the side as Dirk—or Randy—started a PowerPoint presentation.

The first slide showed a wide span of houses that looked like they backed right up to Cabeza Rock National Monument. It took a few moments to register that some of the structures in the vast sea of homes would have to be located on Finley Ranch property. Specifically, the bottom half of the hundred-acre irrigated cattle pasture that had been her father's pride and joy.

Halfway through emptying her wine glass, Cate set it down and rose to her feet, peering at the screen. "Wait, what? Is this a housing development? How is that even possible? I thought the land around the rock was part of the national monument."

Hugo fielded her comment as smoothly as he'd done

everything else.

"Ah, the monument encompasses only ten acres each to the north and south, and a scant five acres each direction east and west. So, that's an optical illusion that the homes are right at the base of the rock. Though, there will also be an easement road between the community and the monument."

The next slide showed Finley Ranch with a caption reading "Cabeza Rock Estates Recreation Area and Clubhouse." There sat a modernized version of the ranch house on the hill. Below it, happy crowds of people hit golf balls, swung tennis rackets, and strolled the turf-covered grounds where the stables now stood.

The second text message Bronnie had sent was beginning to make sense—*"Someone is stealing the ranch."* Was this it?—the "Cabeza Rock Estates"? Hadn't Desi Mason mentioned a meeting coming up that Cate should attend?

She felt briefly woozy and grabbed the arm of her chair for stability. Something was happening to her—a floating, unsteady feeling that made what she saw on the screen seem like part of a dream. She pulled her focus together and faced Estelle, who was looking back at her with intense interest.

"What's going on here, Estelle? Where is Margaret? Did she ... did she okay this ... this development plan or whatever the hell we're looking at?"

"But of course," Estelle replied as if soothing a fretting child.

"Well, I want to hear that from *her*."

"She'll be coming later, dear," the woman crooned. "Why don't we all have a bite to eat? We'll continue when everyone has a full stomach."

Cate didn't want to eat with them, but her blood sugar seemed to be crashing. It was probably the damn champagne. This would all be cleared up when Margaret arrived. It was too bizarre to believe otherwise.

When dinner was served in the formal dining room, minutes later, Cate dove into her plate of food—barbequed chicken, frijoles, and salad. Estelle handed off each person's plate personally, emerging from the kitchen like an Italian mama feeding her brood of hungry youngsters. Cate half expected her to go around tucking napkins under chins and saying, "*Mangia, mangia.*"

As soon as she was done eating, Cate knew she was in trouble. The room floated like it was filled with water whenever she turned her head to look at something. It was difficult to focus her eyes. She blamed that second glass of champagne Estelle had poured. Not a good idea in this crowd. Must keep alert and sober ... must.

She excused herself from the dinner table, picking up her plate as if to help with the clearing. It was dusk outside, and the kitchen was empty of Rosa. Cate set the plate down with a slight clatter on the counter before heading for the back stairs to the second floor. She heard a lively conversation continuing in the other room and was startled when Estelle's voice called from the kitchen.

"Caitlyn? Are you all right?" The tone in her voice could have passed for genuine concern.

"Yep, just going up to the room for a moment. Keep the party going," Cate called down the stairs with what she hoped was a fun-loving lilt in her voice.

By the time she reached the top of the stairs, she was crawling, dragging herself along the hall toward the door of her room. This wasn't just alcohol in her system, no, no, no. Something had gone wrong with her muscles. They felt like unset gelatin. Something—in the food? Yes, it had been in the food—and maybe in the champagne. Why had she been so trusting? It had hit her hard and was getting worse each minute, soaking into her system. In the bathroom, she turned on the tap and stood gulping water, knowing what she would need to do next.

Minutes later, she crawled out of the bathroom with an empty stomach. Still not steady enough to stand, though. She felt profoundly tired suddenly.

She inched toward her backpack, intent on the bottle of dark gray capsules she kept ... buried deep ... for the occasional iffy street truck meal.

Her fingers found the round cylinder as a whine began in her head, and patterns appeared in her vision. Back to the bathroom for water. But first, she hauled herself over to the door and pushed the button on the doorknob, her heart racing while her body grew even weaker. She had begun to sweat. It dripped down her face and soaked her dress.

In the bathroom, she downed charcoal capsules with handfuls of water as her mind chewed on bits of thoughts. *Estelle had done this, but why? Am I that much of a threat? How? And how had she gotten to my food? Oh, right.* Cate remembered taking the fully loaded plate. Peculiar, since weren't most barbecue dinners buffet-style?

Cate eased down onto the floor and closed her eyes.

She was drifting on a raft in the Sea of Cortez. Summertime with its oven-hot temperatures ... Fiona, Doc, and Margaret on the beach in the distance. With the float gently cradling her ... so peaceful ... But someone kept calling her name, kept up a pounding racket.

"Cate? Cate! What's going on in there? Are you okay?" It was Estelle, talking through the door. There was a pause as someone farther away—a man's voice—said something.

Then Estelle's voice again, saying, "She wasn't feeling all that well. She's been under a lot of financial stress, you know. Both the sisters …" Then a mumbled reply, followed by "… runs in the family." Then more mumbled words. "Okay, I'll tell her. Okay, I will do that if … if it comes to it. Safe journeys, you two."

"I am not opening that door, no matter what," Cate said quietly, more to herself than Estelle. She rolled onto her back and felt the room pinwheel around her. Her arms and legs felt so heavy now, she couldn't have crawled over to work the lock even if she wanted. What had they drugged her with, and why? She was so sleepy, and yet her heart was racing.

"Cate, I need you to open the door right now!" A different tone to Estelle's voice than a moment ago. Strident and menacing. She was speaking sharply to someone behind her now. "Well, I can't very well do that if she's locked herself in, can I? Here, give me those and go get the house keys from the kitchen. We need to do this within the hour."

Adrenaline surging, Cate had gotten on her hands and knees and was searching for a chair. There was a sturdy one at the desk—metal-framed. She crawled to it, carefully pulled herself up, and then used it as a walker, pushing it in front of her. When she got to the door, she tipped the chair forward, fitting the back under the knob. Something she'd seen in a movie.

Bracing against the door, she kicked the chair legs into the hardwood floor to make it hold fast. Next, she half-crawled to grab her phone from the nightstand, tapping 911 just as her knees buckled and she slid down to the floor again. A voice came over the phone.

"911, what is your emergency?"

"Finley Ranch, Cabeza Valley." On her knees but bent forward, she had to stop to catch her breath. "Come quickly ... the bedroom, second ... floor. I ... I've been poisoned."

Sparkling windowpanes floated before her eyes. A roaring in her ears. Then a sinking sensation ... way, way down. Silence.

Chapter 12

August 5, Copperton Medical Center

There was a moment when she'd awoken to a wailing siren and a bouncy ride that soon smoothed down. Two men leaning over her, a needle poking her arm, an oxygen mask covering her lower face.

Then nothing until she opened her eyes to the white-on-white of a hospital room. Tears of gratitude over still being alive seeped from Cate's eyes. A single golden splinter of sunshine beamed through the shaded window and onto the foot of her bed. Someone was at her bedside, leaning over the tubes in her right arm.

"You saved me," she whispered hoarsely to the woman adjusting her IV. The woman looked up with a start and then smiled at her. It was a tender, patient smile. Calm, slate-colored eyes and a gentle face fringed with silver curls. The kind of face you wanted to wake up to in a hospital. Something familiar about her smile.

"From what the EMTs said, you saved yourself," the woman replied with a chuckle.

She smoothed down her nursing scrubs and sat in a chair beside the bed. Cate tried to focus as she felt her hand lifted and held. The woman leaned her face in. Cate blinked her eyes to get a clearer view. That familiar feeling about her again.

"Do ... I know you?"

"Possibly. I'm Bronwyn Taylor. I sent you those texts about Margaret ... and the ranch."

After a moment, Cate croaked, "Brownie?"

The woman chuckled and squeezed her hand.

"Well, close. My nickname is Bronnie."

"You?" Cate croaked, feeling tired and weak, but safe now. Safe.

"I'm a friend of ... of your mother ... of Fiona."

An image came to her of someone hugging her tightly at her parents' funeral. Comforting arms and a sad, gentle face. This woman's face.

After a slight glance over each shoulder, Bronnie leaned in confidentially. "I'm so glad you came home, Cate. We really need your help."

The furtive movement and comment felt absurd, like something Princess Leia had done in a *Star Wars* movie. Cate started to chuckle, which quickly turned into coughing spasms. Suddenly, Bronnie was all nurse again, helping her sit up and offering a small basin to spit in.

"Look, we'll have plenty of time to talk after you've recovered. I'm ... so sorry you had to go through all that." Her expression had become grim as she tucked in the sheets and set a cup of water on the table next to the bed.

Cate fought through fatigue to get a question out.

"Bronnie, how did you ... find me?"

"Cabeza Valley grapevine at work. Rosa told Desi, who phoned me here at the hospital. I'm a neonatal nurse."

"No, I mean ... before, when you texted me. How did you get that number?"

The woman drew back and sat down, her mouth in a tight smile.

"Well, that's going to be part of a longer story. Not for today. Just know that I have good intentions, unlike the person who did this to you."

Cate stared at the older woman. She had to mean Margaret's ranch manager, Estelle Parker. Now it was all coming back—the dinner party, the guests, the barbecue. She felt a sudden wave of nausea.

"I feel like crap. Did they pump my stomach?"

"Yes, you got the whole drug protocol, including charcoal and some atropine for your heart. You know it was ketamine, right? Apparently enough to knock out a horse." Cate took a deep breath. Yes, now she recalled where she'd felt this way before—back in the days when Drew had convinced her to boost some "Special K" from her dad's veterinary supplies. She'd dabbled in recreational doses a couple of times but hadn't liked it.

"Somebody put it in my food, Bronnie. At dinner. One minute we were talking at the table, then—"

She pictured the fist-faced Gabe laughing harshly at something and a chair screeching. Had he moved his chair back from the table and followed her? Had he and Estelle planned to do something to her?

A memory of Estelle calling out her name as she crawled up the stairs, of the woman standing outside the bedroom yelling. What happened next? A blank. The blood pressure machine next to her started a high-pitched, pulsing whine. She tried to move her feet to get out of the bed, but though her pulse was racing, there was no energy left in her.

"Let's not talk about it right now," said Bronnie. "You need to recover fully. I'm going to ask your nurse for more medication to help clear this from your system. I'll keep checking in on you today. You need to drink plenty of this," she handed Cate the cup of water, "and rest, okay?"

"I need to find out—"

"Yes, you probably do, but not quite yet. Just rest."

Bronnie headed for the closed door and turned back.

"You're going to get a visit from the psych doctor on duty. Part of the protocol. Estelle told the EMTs you seemed depressed and had stolen drugs from the stable supplies. They—we have to follow up on self-harm cases."

"What? No. No shrinks—police. I need to ... file a ..." Cate felt cold sweat breaking out on her body. The monitor started its alarm again, and Bronnie opened the door to the hall and called out, "Can I get a floor nurse in here, please?" Then she was gone.

Within a minute another nurse came in, followed by a woman of about Cate's age. She wore a white lab coat over street clothes and her name tag read "Dr. Lana Sontag." Her straight auburn hair was chopped off at chin length and her oversized, black-framed glasses threatened to slide down her nose, negating any gravitas she may have sought. Cate flashed on a Lana she'd known back in school.

"Hi, so I'm Dr. Sontag? I wanted to talk to you about your, um, mishap?" Her voice was soft and she seemed to have retained that juvenile habit of making statements into questions.

Cate sat up with newfound energy. The water and IV drugs were starting to work their magic.

"My *mishap*? You mean how I was drugged by people staying at my family's ranch? Are they in jail? Because, if not, I want to press charges."

She did not like talking to shrinks and the prospect of speaking one now had coaxed her alter ego out of hiding, what Levi had nicknamed "Tiger Cate."

The doctor glanced at her clipboard, then tried again. "Your cousin—Estelle, right?—contacted the hospital and said your sister Margaret had been trying to enact a guardianship over you for some years now?"

Cate felt a sharp laugh escape her lips. *What utter rot.* "A guardianship, really? My sister Margaret whom I have barely spoken to in twenty years? That's rich. How the hell was she going to pull that one off?"

Appearing not to have heard her, the woman extended the clipboard.

"Anyway, I just have some intake papers for you to look over—"

"Is anyone going to follow up on the fact that I was poisoned at my family's ranch last night? Police? Hand me that phone and I'll call them myself." *Don't push me,* growled the tiger. *I will push back so much harder.*

Beginning to sense the futility of her mission, Dr. Sontag gave it one last try. "If you could just sign this? Then we could get a bed ready over at the psychiatric hospital facility." She recoiled from the look on Cate's face. "Really, it's ... it's just a few blocks away? Then, once you've been stabilized, in a week or so ...?"

"Nope." The tiger and the doctor faced off for a silent moment.

"I mean, this is ... this is voluntary, Cate—um, Miss Finley— but it could be very beneficial for you right now."

Cate had underestimated Lana Sontag's tenacity. She was dug in.

"No. You need my signature, right? Let me see that." Cate took the clipboard and began checking boxes. "No, I won't sign a release of medical information. Yes, I'm declining further treatment. Signing ... there. Are we done here?"

Groggy a few minutes ago while talking to Bronnie, Cate was fully conscious now. Still feeling weak, but fully aware. She'd been about to say that she knew quite well what a stay in a psych ward was, but that was the kind of information they might be seeking right now. They still might get it from New York somehow, but not with her help.

Somewhere inside her, the tiger had begun to pace. She felt a little like she was gaining superpowers.

"I'll take my clothes now, Lana," Cate announced, pushing herself up from the bed by her elbows and bending her knees. Getting up was going to be problematic, to put it mildly. Needles and tubes still connected her to what was probably just hydrating fluids at this point. Tiger Cate or not, she would need this woman's assistance.

"And let's stop pretending we don't know each other from the junior high track team, okay?"

Lana blushed and consulted her chart again.

"Look," Cate went on, "your best option right now is to call someone to unhook me before I do damage to my vein and sue the hospital for malpractice."

The last twelve hours had been more surreal than any canvas she could have painted—ever. And the arrival of a shrink with commitment papers? It was like stepping into one of those dystopian novels she enjoyed reading.

To Lana's credit, she was now standing her ground. Maybe it was the last straw in what had been a hellish week for her, but her face hardened as a new argument seemed to percolate.

"Cate, you—you can't be released until the attending doctor checks you out and signs off. Because you were a 911 call, there's protocol and certain rules—"

Cate cut her off. "Fine, send in the doctor, Doctor." She was over it now. Where was her savior and new best friend, Nurse Bronnie? She needed to get out of the hospital and back down to Cabeza Valley to look for her sister. She was not going to go quietly into a psych hospital. Not ever again.

But it wasn't the attending doctor or Bronnie when the door opened a few minutes later. It was the law.

Chapter 13

A nurse led a uniformed man into the room and Cate's first thought was, *They've sent the oldest Sheriff's deputy in the department, maybe in the world.* He didn't *look* so much as *move* like an old man—slightly stooped and with a hitch in his stride.

"Hello, I'm Deputy Gomez, here to take a statement from you regarding the 9-1-1 call last night. Are you"—he nodded at her disheveled state—"up to talking?"

Cate hauled herself up against the pillows, primly smoothing the covers over her legs.

"I'm fine. Where should I start?"

He took out some reading glasses from his breast pocket and put them on self-consciously.

"Well, I have some questions here." He checked a list on his small clipboard. "Where did you get the drugs that you took?"

Aware she was talking to an officer, Cate bit back her anger and spoke carefully and civilly.

"Well, Deputy Gomez, I didn't *take* any drugs. I ate *food*. And had some champagne." He looked up from writing. "One full flute and a couple of sips from the second glass. What's that, about six ounces, maybe?"

He went back to writing while the artist in her instinctively took in his features. The arched black eyebrows and aquiline nose, the hard lines along the jaw, and ironic tilt to his mouth. It was a handsome, lived-in face of someone familiar with pain, who hadn't yet lost his sense of humor. In a different setting, she might have talked him into holding still for a pencil sketch.

Noticing her intense stare, he made his next query.

"What is your permanent address?"

Another difficult question. "Hmm, that's hard to say. Can you just put that I'm in between residences and staying with friends in Los Angeles?"

"Their address?"

"And I don't know that from memory. Have to … check my phone. It's in my backpack. Did that make the trip to the hospital?" Or was it now in Estelle's clutches at the house?

The deputy scanned the room before replying, "I'll ask the nurse. Let's keep going. What was your business at the Finley Ranch?"

"Besides the fact that I'm, you know, a Finley? I got a text that my sister Margaret was missing. Did you guys get a missing person's report on her … maybe from a Bronnie Taylor?"

For the first time, Gomez looked truly interested.

"The Bronnie Taylor that works here as a nurse?"

"Yeah …?"

Cate waited for him to say that Bronnie was a clueless hack who constantly nagged their office with UFO sightings, but Gomez simply returned to his notes.

"Sorry, go on, please."

"Well, when I arrived here a couple of days ago, I was greeted by a 'cousin' named Estelle Parker. Tall gal. Told me Margaret was on a trip and was returning Sunday night—last night, correct? Maybe you could ask Estelle whether my sister actually came home?"

"Hm, I will check on it when I get back to the office." He wrote a note and then looked up at her. A moment went by.

"You think someone drugged you at a dinner party at Finley Ranch? Who was there? Can you give me their names?"

"I just caught their first names. Um, Randy and Dirk. They were, uh, realtors. Gave me their cards. Then there was Hugh—Hugo … spoke with a British accent. Didn't catch a last name but he was—is—a nephew of old Sheriff Griffin. There was a slideshow of Finley Ranch being developed into … uh, Cabeza Rock Estates." She paused to take a breath. Well, that part had come back pretty easily.

In fact, over the past hour, much of the evening had come back to Cate. Right up to that crawl up the back stairs to her room. Gomez pulled a sheet of notes from the clipboard.

"Yeah, here is Estelle Parker's account of the evening. She had a business meeting with her associates, and then they left. The two of you had a quiet dinner. Champagne was poured, she wasn't sure how much because she went to bed at some point and left you still drinking—"

"Wait, that's not—" Cate tried to interject, her heart pounding in her ears. She felt Gomez studying her and let him go on.

"Um," he searched for his place, "the next thing she knew, some hours later, a lit-up ambulance was in the driveway. She said that you had seemed depressed, had talked about poor choices you'd made in your life, financial problems, and a bad breakup. She said she had no idea you were—in her words—'so fragile' or she wouldn't have left you alone."

For a moment, Cate just stared at him. *I am Alice through the looking glass,* she thought, *and the Red Queen wants my head.* Again, she felt trapped in the room, tethered to beeping machines. She had the urge to yank herself free of the tubes and run away.

"Okay, okay—that?" she gestured to the deputy's report with her free arm. "That's all a load of bullshit!" Cate rolled her head to loosen the tension that was quickly seizing up her neck. "Go ask those realtors. ... Ask Rosa Ruiz—she cooked for us. There was ... a barbecue caterer there from town, Copperton ... Carlos? Charlie? There were *six* of us at the table, for God's sake."

Looking flustered, the deputy tried to calm her as a nurse entered, summoned by the beeping alarms on the monitors.

"Well, that's quite a different story. How do I talk with Rosa ... Ruiz, is it?"

"The Ruizes live on the property. Right before you get to the ranch entrance. Go left toward the stables and you'll see a little red clapboard house—same trim as the stable. You can't miss it. Diego has worked for my family forever. I know Rosa will back me up."

"Okay. You said there were four men—who was the fourth?"

"Gabe somebody. Not from around here. Sounded like he might be from New York." That was a hunch on her part. "Maybe a lawyer?" Another hunch.

After Gomez left and Cate was alone again, she leaned back on the bed trying to figure out her next step. Because wasn't that what heroines in adventure stories did? Alice and the rest of them? In truth, what she wanted was a bus ticket back to LA. What she wanted was for her sister to materialize and fix this mess because, from all appearances, it was Margaret's mess, not hers. Why had these people, or rather Estelle, felt the need to drug her? Why did Estelle lie to the cops about the dinner party? What might have happened if Cate hadn't managed to barricade the door last night? And where was her sister? Where *was* Margaret?

Chapter 14

La Cabeza National Monument, "Cabeza Rock" to the locals, cast an ominous shadow across the valley in the late afternoon sun as Bronnie's vintage silver Volvo made its way down the mountain from Copperton.

Since leaving the hospital, Cate had been working on a list of questions, and now Bronnie was in the hot seat.

"So, how did you get my phone number?"

Bronnie threw her a quick glance, then resumed her focus on the sharp mountain curves.

"Margie gave it to me for safekeeping. Said you'd called from somewhere in the Midwest a couple of years back, asking for money to fix your vehicle. She hadn't been up to returning your phone call but then felt guilty and turned to me for help in wiring you the money—to that Catify email account. She ... she felt bad she didn't talk to you back then, but she was going through a ... complicated time here at the ranch."

Cate had more to ask, but "Okay," was all her throbbing head could muster. The nine hundred dollars had been both a shock and a lifesaver. It had gotten her back on the road after her truck's engine crapped out in Nebraska.

Why had no one come looking for her? Unlike more recently, Cate had been highly traceable during her first year in New York. Margaret could have found her via their mother's friend, Brenden, who owned the bistro where she'd found work. Their mother had mentioned Brenden and his bistro numerous times at the dinner table. Her sister could have reached out to him if only to make sure Cate was still alive.

"I should have called her when the payment came through, but then I hit a wall trying to get gigs when I got to LA. I guess ... I put off talking to her until things got better."

An uncomfortable silence followed until Cate resumed her list of questions.

"How did Margaret and Estelle become partners?" Because it was clear that was what they were. Cate just didn't know how far the partnership went.

The woman next to Cate was visibly struggling now.

"They, uh, knew each other as girls." Another pause as Bronnie suddenly braked for a small herd of deer that sprinted nimbly across the road. "When Estelle arrived at the ranch five years ago, something shifted in Margie's mindset. Estelle seemed to undermine her mentally and physically, to the point she stopped socializing and even quit riding for a while. It was weird. Margie's always been strong, rarely backing down from anyone, even ... even Doc when he was alive. I don't know ... the accident could have taken a greater toll than we thought."

"Wait, what accident? You don't mean our parents' plane crash—?"

"No, about ten years back when she got tossed off a colt. Concussion, fractured ribs ... some disc trauma. Compressed nerves in her lower spine. She was on an oxy regime for a while. I ... I wrote her a script myself. It was all we knew to do at the time."

Cate winced at the reference to oxycontin. Once upon a time, she'd been more than acquainted with the drug herself.

"Her back pain—it was substantial. She had to stop competing and that made her miserable. She gained weight—about thirty extra pounds. Then she went in a new direction, boarding horses and taking on some students. That's when she brought on Liliana Ruiz to help her. Leelee was fourteen but already had all that height. Having someone young to mentor was just what Margaret needed. Perked her up a bit."

They had passed the road to Finley Ranch and were now traveling down the dirt road that ran parallel to the highway. Bronnie turned at a whimsical-looking sign reading, "Loose Cow Lane," and Cate saw it was taking them to the far side of the hundred-acre cattle pasture. To their right, a herd of Angus clumped together in the dense grove of trees that marked the center of the acreage. The Volvo finally pulled into a tangled yard in which sat a charming gingerbread cottage right out of a fairy tale.

"Wow! This was the mystery house I couldn't remember when I walked in from the highway the other day. How long have you lived here?"

"About a decade. Margie helped me get into it when the housing market had taken a dip. Reasonably priced, as there's only about an acre of land. But it works for me and the kitties."

As if on cue, five felines in various colors ran up to them as they emerged from the car. Bronnie looked sheepish.

"Okay, don't say it. Little old lady, gingerbread cottage, cats, the tangled yard. I know you're wondering if the oven's hot and where I stash my broom."

Cate laughed in spite of her pounding headache, feeling residual tension melting away.

"Well, maybe if the cats were all black," she teased. She picked up a calico kitten that had been rubbing against her leg. "Strays?"

"They come and go, thanks to the coyotes. This batch was

from a pregnant stray who dumped them on my porch and then said *adios*. That's right, we're poor widdle orrr-phans," she squeaked in a high-pitched voice, wiggling the paw of the ginger kitten she held.

Cate smiled and looked far across the field toward Drew and Desi Mason's pink house, the empty Griffin lots, and Diego and Rosa's cottage by the Finley stables. Way in the distance and halfway up the mountain rise sat the majestic Finley ranch house. From this distance, it was easier to appreciate the unique blending of Santa Fe and mid-1960s architecture, with its high-ceilinged great room and exterior of adobe stucco and exposed logs. Bronnie unlocked and opened the double doors in the patio and turned to gaze across the pasture as well.

"I was glad to be close by to help Margie through her dark times after the accident. Neighbors are … pretty important when you live in the country."

Cate felt a brief twinge of, what—guilt? In a different life, she would have been the one filling that role. And how strange that her sister's emotional trouble ten years ago had coincided with her own trauma in New York.

"Neighbors are pretty important in the city, too," Cate agreed.

Cate had learned the importance of friendly neighbors in the East Village. Hers had been a fellowship of struggling artists who had each other's backs, sharing their lodging and even their food. Having the right neighbors could take the place of family.

"And, speaking of neighbors, I need to get my backpack from the ranch house."

"Not tonight," Bronnie's voice was soothing as she retrieved a small pack from a pantry shelf. "Here's an extra toothbrush. Let's get a good night's sleep, and then see what's what in the light of day."

Cate smiled at her hostess. "What's what," indeed. The woman was adorable, but Cate had already hatched a plan to visit the ranch that night under the cover of darkness. She just needed a little food and a quick nap to fix her lingering hangover.

Bronnie cooked a dinner of sautéed chicken and steamed vegetables with clarified butter. After eating, they settled on the couch and swapped fond memories of Doc and Fiona.

"Fiona would have loved seeing the strong woman you've become, Cate," Bronnie murmured, putting a mug of chamomile tea on the end table next to the couch.

Cate's eyes welled up as her mother's Irish lilt came back to her, speaking soothing words in her ear. She felt the opposite of strong ... overwhelmed. She closed her eyes, just to rest for a bit, and didn't open them again until morning.

Chapter 15

"What time is it?" She felt like she'd been asleep for two days, probably the effect of the drugs departing her body.

Bronnie was leaning over a pan of fragrant food cooking on the stove and turned to give her a sunny smile.

"Almost six o'clock. I have a shift that starts at seven, so I'm off to the hospital in a few minutes."

Cate was on her feet and headed for the door, running shoes in hand. Bronnie beat her there.

"Cate, there is nothing in that backpack that isn't available in this house in some form or other." Bronnie took a breath and continued more calmly. "Please wait until I can go with you. Estelle's not... she's—"

"She's a nut job. Is that what you wanted to say?"

Bronnie smiled sadly as she plated their food.

"Yes, but sort of—worse."

What's worse than a nutter? Cate wondered.

"Estelle is very ... wily, so don't underestimate her. And Margaret may have put her in charge. Legally, I mean."

Cate fought the urge to snap a retort, then circled back and flounced onto the couch, feeling oddly petulant. Bronnie went back to her skillet, adding, "Look, it's your call, but if you *do* end up going, just be careful."

They ate outside on the elevated porch, taking in the spectacular view of the pastures, the cottonwood lane, and the four houses lining it, including Desi's pink two-story. The homemade brown bread and softly scrambled eggs were rapidly disappearing off Cate's plate.

"You say Margaret put Estelle in charge," Cate said between bites. "What does that mean?"

"Hm, well, your sister was too proud to admit it outright, but she was terrified of the ranch business failing, so it's clear she brought in Cousin Estelle to manage the finances. She's used to, uh, managing real estate."

Cate had been trying to do the math on all the improvements she'd seen. The original ranch buildings still stood, but that paint job on the stables and the road surface improvements, not to mention the deluxe horse hauling rig at the stable, had most likely cost Margaret a small fortune. Had she mortgaged the ranch?

"Where did the two of them meet? I asked Estelle at our first meeting, but she was vague about it. Man, I want to talk to Margaret so badly right now!" Cate plinked her fork down on the empty plate.

"Cate, can I make an observation? You eat like you haven't had a meal in a month. What exactly is your situation in California?"

"Me?" She glanced down at the empty plate. "On the high side of homelessness. I mean, I'm not sleeping under freeways or anything, but I've … I've had some rough patches."

"Well, I must say, as a medical professional, you look healthy enough, given that kind of lifestyle. Just, you know, hungry."

Cate leaned back, folded her arms, and fixed Bronnie with a knowing smile.

"Very nice try getting me off topic. When was the last time you saw my sister? Did she mention a trip?"

"I passed her on the lane, as I was coming home, and she was driving out. That was almost two weeks ago. She didn't slow down or stop, just waved like she'd be right back."

"What was she driving?"

"That monster truck she pulls with. When she didn't show up at our usual Friday lunch date, Estelle said she had left with her clients on Thursday. But it isn't like Margaret to leave town without letting me know."

Cate nodded.

"Since I got here, Estelle's been telling me Margaret is headed back from Albuquerque, that she's been out buying more horses for the ranch. How does that jibe with her worrying over finances?"

"Well, Margie doesn't buy horses for herself anymore. Just for clients."

"Okay, that makes more sense. So, a client took her along just to check out horses? Maybe that's why the hauling rig is currently parked at the stable. By the way, I looked inside, and it gives new meaning to the term 'trailer trash.' Looks like it hasn't been in use for a while and a human pack rat has moved in."

Bronnie picked up both plates and stood up. Cate wanted to keep the conversation going, now that she was getting answers.

"According to Estelle, Margaret's been headed home for a couple of days now," Cate rattled on, following her host into the tiny kitchen. "I left a message on her phone yesterday, and it's weird she wouldn't be curious enough to even return the call."

Bronnie stopped midway to the sink and turned to Cate, her face suddenly anxious, her voice quavering.

"I think we can assume that Margaret isn't returning from New Mexico. In fact, let's assume nothing Estelle has told you in the last few days is true. Nothing." Tears were welling in the woman's eyes, and Cate realized they'd been there all along.

Cate stood and awkwardly took the plates from the woman.

"Go to work. I've got this, Bronnie. I want you to know I'm … I'm up to this. Really. We'll get a missing person's report filed and an investigation launched."

A few moments later, as she stroked the kitten in her arms and watched Bronnie pull her Volvo out of the parking space, Cate wondered why Bronnie hadn't filed a report herself, given her long history with the family and her own suspicions.

PART II – Consequences

"How do you know I'm mad?' said Alice.
"You must be," said the Cat,
"or you wouldn't have come here. "
—L. Carroll, *Adventures of Alice in Wonderland*

Chapter 16

August 6, Cabeza Valley
Rae

Everybody was gone from the house, but Desi had said she would be back real soon. She said it with a worried look that told Rae they were going to call the foster agency if somebody didn't shape up real fast.

Rae had been through it before. She had dark places in her that made people nervous.

In the past, she'd been okay with changing foster houses. It had happened so often that she was over it. But this time was different. This time she loved living here, on this lane, with a dog to pet and all the pretty horses to look at. Desi had said that she wasn't foster, she was family and she wanted to believe that.

Standing in the backyard of Desi's house and playing fetch with big Samson, she saw a man walking across the pasture.

He came from the ranch direction and headed straight toward the clump of trees—the "copse" was what Desi's husband Jake called it, but she hadn't known what he'd meant. The only cops she knew wore uniforms and pulled you back from freeway rails so you couldn't see your dead mama and brother.

A memory flickered before she could stop it.

She is standing on the oven-hot bridge over the freeway. Mama and Davy sitting on the wall, calling to her. They're drunk on tequila and smoking something Mama bought on the street in Phoenix. Before that cab driver picked them up and dumped them off on a stretch of nowhere. The wind blows like a roaring furnace as Rae peers up at their laughing faces. They are dead, dark angels, eyes blank and shiny, urging her up on their cloud.

Mama yanks hard on her wrist and shouts, "C'mere!" But Rae pulls back, breaking her hold. Mama wobbles, her arms flapping. She screams and grabs at Davy. They both fall backward over the wall, feet disappearing last.

"Mama!" Rae reaches forward to grab them. Too late. Did she do this? Did she make them fall?

Then come the noises—a car screeching, then another, and then more cars. She doesn't want to look but she does. Mama and Davy, lying on the hot freeway, dark wetness spreading out. After a while, the arms of strangers wrap around her. They pull her back.

Crouching on the patio, Rae rubbed her face to smear out the pictures. She focused hard on the figure in the pasture as it moved past the house. She could see it was the guy who worked at Margaret's ranch—D.J.—looking so mad, just like her daddy had looked after her brother Jamie got shot dead by the hunter. Her daddy had been mad enough to do something and now he was in prison.

The guy was at the spot where Margaret had lain and he was walking around in circles, kicking at things in the grass like he was looking for something. She thought about the phone upstairs, stuffed between her mattresses.

Someone else was coming, walking the field from the other side—the lady she'd seen standing on the road and talking to Desi a few days ago. Rae had named her "Pinto Lady" because her hair started out brown and then changed to a silvery pink. She wore it loose today, flowing down her back like melted peppermint ice cream.

Pinto Lady walked fast, headed toward the stables. The man ducked behind one of the trees and watched her go by with the look of a dog that wants to bite something. Then he turned and looked back at where Rae had ducked down behind the patio fence. He lifted a finger to his lips, like saying "Hush up," and then he drew it across his neck.

Chapter 17

August 6, Cabeza Valley
Cate

The contents of Cate's backpack were calling to her. Her phone, wallet, and everything else she owned were in her old bedroom at the main house, all within the grasp of the Amazon.

Bypassing the stable, she followed the road up to the parking lot next to the house, which was empty of cars. After climbing the flagstone steps to the front patio, she tried each door, making her way around the rambling Santa Fe structure, but Estelle had locked everything up tight. She stood for a while, studying the fragile-looking trellis she'd climbed as a child, then turned and followed the footpath back down the hill to the stables. Rosa would have a key, and she still needed to get her take on the disaster of a dinner party.

From her view coming down the hill, she could already see that both Diego's truck and Rosa's ancient Corolla were missing from their parking spaces next to the stables. Where was everyone on a Tuesday morning? In the distance, someone chased a white horse around a circular pen. It had to be Leelee. She veered off in that direction.

The girl's back was to her as she worked the horse against the far side of the pen. Cate recognized the technique of getting a horse to change directions using an upraised hand holding a lariat. Back and forth Leelee sent the horse, turning him against the fence and then asking for a few paces at a canter, then raising the opposite arm and sending him back the other way.

A memory flashed of being ten and helping to train the young mare named Bella. Doc would stand behind her as they faced the running horse, showing her just when to raise her arm and turn Bella's massive body.

"She needs to see you out of the right eye to know when to turn to the left," Doc had said, guiding her arm up and making the coiled rope swing at just the right time. "Eventually, she will see the pattern, find the rhythm, and that will give her confidence."

Remembering now, Cate ached to feel her father's gentle but firm touch on her arm again, guiding it to lift the lariat at just the right time.

Cate recognized the vanilla-colored horse as the one Leelee had ridden at the team penning. Now lathered and anxious, he was an apparent newcomer to round pen work. Once he'd managed a dozen turns, Leelee gave him a break from the pressure of the lariat. Instantly, he stopped and faced her, his sides heaving from stressful exertion. Leelee stepped back and crouched slightly—almost like performing a dance step—signaling him to come to her. He lowered his head and licked his lips as he stepped up to her. She noticed Cate standing at the rail and waved.

"Pretty exotic-looking horse, Leelee."

"*Mesteño*—Spanish mustang," she said with some pride. "And look at the fancy eyes. Not too many blue-eyed cremellos in the wild. We call him *Destino*."

Destiny, Cate mentally translated, *or destination*. The horse was stocky, but with the smooth lines, thick neck, and flowing mane of the horses that Spanish explorers had brought to the Americas some four hundred years ago.

"Back in my day, Margaret would have scoffed at getting anything but a registered Quarter Horse."

"Yes, still true. Estelle bought him for me to train."

As she said it, Leelee looked down, uncomfortably. So, this had been a secret and it explained a lot about her relationship with Estelle—or, rather, the woman's hold over the girl.

"Officially, I'm training him for Estelle to ride, but honestly, this horse will never be good for a beginner. He's got too much *brio*, too lively. And he's definitely *not* a fan of spurs or whips. He pitched my brother off twice before D.J. took the hint and kicked off his spurs." She grinned at Destino affectionately. "I want to make him a show horse and compete in Western Dressage. Margaret would've loved that idea."

Cate's chest flickered at this use of past tense.

"Leelee, look at me." The girl turned to face Cate. "Is Margaret on a horse-buying trip or not?" Leelee shot back an anguished look. "I mean, to your knowledge?"

"What did Estelle tell you? Because to be honest, I haven't really"—she picked up the horse's halter and lead rope from the ground and shook it out—"uh, been talking directly to Margaret lately. Estelle just comes down and, you know, gives me my weekly instructions for the horses. *Mamá* said Margaret was having dizzy spells or something. She came off a horse pretty hard a couple of months ago."

Off another horse just months ago? That was news. Leelee had been putting on a brave front, but she clearly shared Bronnie's anxiety and uncertainty over Margaret. Cate imagined what the stakes were for the Ruiz family, especially if her sister didn't come back from wherever she was. This ranch was their whole life, and suddenly it was under the control of someone as ruthless as Estelle

Parker. Cate needed to get into that house and maybe search the office for clues.

Since her recent return home as an adult, a thought had been nagging her. She wanted to take a look at her parents' will, something she'd never laid eyes on. Maybe she could also find a copy of the ranch deed, especially after the other night's presentation. These were things her lawyer friend Jimmy Lee could look into once she got copies. Plus, she wanted to check if the combo to the safe in Doc's office still worked after all these years. Finally, there was a missing person's report to file and a way overdue call to Levi.

"Leelee, do you have a key to the house? My backpack and phone are still in there."

Again, the girl looked uncomfortable. "Estelle changed the locks last week and, um, we haven't gotten new keys yet."

"Really. Changed them last week, huh?" Cate tried to make her voice sound casual, but her internal alarm was clanging. Maybe climbing a trellis would be as easy as riding a horse again.

Chapter 18

After the struggle of the actual climb, getting inside the second floor was a snap. Most of the five doors off the second-story veranda were glass sliders. At the far end, the one leading to Margaret's old bedroom had been closed, but not latched. Oops.

Growing up, Cate hadn't been allowed to spend much time in Margaret's room. The age gap between them meant that by the time Cate could hold an intelligent conversation, Margaret was already an adult. A very private one. Occasionally, they might play a board game together in the living room, but Cate couldn't remember a time she'd been invited into Margaret's room for a sisterly chat.

The room's walls held more trophies and horse-themed posters. Margaret the star equestrian grinned back at her starting at age twelve or thirteen and into adulthood. Gazing at the walls now, it occurred to Cate that there were no photos of Margaret in grade school or as a toddler, let alone a baby.

Family lore was that Doc had inherited the ranch when his older brother died and had moved his family to Cabeza Valley from New Mexico a couple of years before Cate's birth. There had to be photos of the Finley family's life in Albuquerque, but she couldn't remember ever having seen them.

Cate was surprised to see a computer in her tech-hating sister's room. She sat in front of the PC and flipped it on. The monitor lit up, and a password prompt screen appeared. Without thinking, she typed in eight letters, which the screen accepted. Amazing that

Margaret still used the "4Finley4" passcode from when all of them had shared a computer, two decades ago.

The desktop came up, loaded with a clutter of files. Mostly horse show and breeding information—photos, pedigrees, sales documents—all unsorted individual files. After a quick survey, she decided no ranch financials lived there. More likely they would be downstairs in their father's old office.

She was about to power down the computer when a folder caught her eye ..."Starr." That name with its double "r" rang a bell. A vague memory came, from nearly three decades earlier. Six-year-old Cate had found a thick envelope lying on the back stairs, addressed to a Starr somebody in Las Vegas.

As she'd stood holding the letter, Fiona had come down the stairs.

"Mama, did you drop this?" Cate had held the packet up and watched her mother's smile fade when she read the writing.

Later that evening, Doc and Margaret had a heated argument in Doc's study. Soon after, her sister had left the house in a fury—slamming the front door. Yes, it had been a rare moment of raw emotion in the family, one that had left everyone tiptoeing around Margaret for days. That's why it had lodged so well in Cate's memory.

The first file opened to a newspaper article dated 2002 with the headline, "Las Vegas Authorities Question Ex-Stripper Re Wealthy Husband's Death." Well, well, there she was—a younger and slimmer Estelle, posing seductively under stage lights, in a newspaper photo. The piece that accompanied it made Cate eager to read everything else in the file labeled "Starr."

LAS VEGAS, NV—Authorities are looking into the poisoning death of wealthy financier Rudolph Parker, 89, who was

discovered in his penthouse apartment in the Tangiers Hotel and Casino. It is the third mysterious death on the Vegas strip in six months, and officials are investigating possible links to tainted alcohol supplied to the hotel by Pritcher & Sons Distributing. Parker's estranged wife of ten years, exotic dancer Starr Parker, was questioned and released.

Nearly an hour after she'd climbed the trellis, Cate finally descended the stairs and stepped into Doc Finley's office off the front foyer. Surely any financial statements or tax returns would live there. She fought to ignore the inner voice that was urging her to go back upstairs, grab the backpack, and climb back down the trellis for a clean escape.

Exiting through any of the entry doors downstairs might trigger a silent alarm, the kind that alerts your phone. It was easy to imagine Estelle having installed such a device. Cate's conversations with Bronnie had left her curious and itching to dig into the ranch records. Sleuthing like this wasn't her strong suit, but who else was going to do it?

The same oak furniture, Persian rugs—even the light fixtures—that had been in the office when she left, now welcomed her like old friends. She moved to the large leather desk chair and idly spun it on its swivel.

It was here Doc had conducted serious discussions, about house rules, about her grades, and about Drew, including a cringy sex talk. Cate imagined Fiona had deferred to her husband's expertise as a medical professional and her own Catholic modesty. Besides, Doc just had a way of making everything sound sensible and clear-cut. Regardless of the topic, he'd always ended his conversations with Cate the same way: He loved her, he wanted the best for her, and she was making him and her mother so proud with her artwork.

Cate tried opening the top drawer of the closest file cabinet. Locked. Batting zero. She recalled that a single key had simultaneously locked or unlocked all the drawers in her father's file cabinet. After searching for a minute, she found a massive ring of keys in the bottom desk drawer.

The fifth key she tried unlocked the cabinet, but just as she pulled it open, she saw a shadow move past the office window and heard the front door unlocking. Estelle. What to do now—hide? Try to sneak out the front door?

Cate was headed for the office door when it flew open. Dressed in stiletto-heeled boots, skinny black jeans, and a fringed black bolero vest, Estelle stood in the doorway pointing a semi-automatic pistol straight at her. Both women screamed, and Cate instinctively jumped to one side. Estelle's face went from startled to fearful to enraged and, finally, to a forced smile in rapid succession. In any other setting, the whole scene might have been comical.

Estelle lowered and deftly re-holstered her weapon.

"Good lord, I nearly shot you as an intruder! I never close that office door. Never."

"Duly noted," said Cate, recovering her breath.

"How did you get in? Upstairs? A ladder?" She went over to look out the window. "Ah, the trellis. You are quite the monkey, aren't you?"

It really didn't merit a response. Remembering Bronnie's warning, Cate opted not to start her inquiry with, "What the hell, why'd you drug me, Estelle?" The woman was way too clever for straightforward questions. Instead, she mustered all her cheerfulness.

"Oh, hi, Estelle. I was hoping to find Margaret here when I

got home from the hospital. You do remember my sister Margaret? You've been promising she was on her way home for two days now."

Estelle took a stab at a good-natured shrug.

"She's a grown woman with her own itinerary, Caitlyn. Something must have come up. I'm not worried. She's with her client, Dory Banks. Dory's been looking for a new—"

"Horse, yes, so I gather." Cate grabbed a pad of paper and picked up a pen from the desk. "Give me Dory's number, because Margaret isn't answering her own phone."

"Why ever would I know—"

"Because—correct me if I heard it wrong—you manage the ranch, which means you manage client information. Yes? Which also means you should know every damn thing about Margaret's business. But tell me, did I get that wrong like I got wrong how many people were at your dinner party the other night—the one you said didn't happen?"

Like the Cheshire cat, Estelle turned on The Smile. The shift in her demeanor was both chilling and fascinating. When she next spoke, it was again with the poise and haughtiness of a lady of the manor.

"Cate, you do seem to be working yourself into a state. Why don't you go upstairs and relax? I know I could use a glass of wine. You?"

Cate just stared at Estelle as a grim truth unfolded. This woman was laying another trap for her.

"You're a piece of work, aren't you? I did some reading up on you just now in Margaret's room." She paused. "Starr."

Estelle had been about to walk out of the room but snapped her head to look at Cate. The look woke the tiger inside Cate.

"Starr Parker, exotic dancer," she went on. "Catchy. You

danced in Vegas 'til a rich old sugar daddy caught your eye, and you tossed your net over him. You married him and, what, made him completely dependent on you? Did you think no one would blink when he passed away in his sleep? Funny, the cops did, at least for a minute. Then along came a bunch of similar deaths. What a lucky break for you—the hotel facing lawsuits for stocking tainted alcohol and all. How very convenient."

Estelle drew in a deep breath and lifted her shoulders in another shrug. It was the wounded look of a well-practiced martyr, and for some reason, it stoked Cate's fury.

"Then you—what, spent all his money? Lost it feeding your gambling habit? Yes, it was educational to read all about you on Margaret's hard drive. What I didn't see was how, in any way, you are related to the Finley family. Still searching, though."

A full minute ticked by as they stared at each other. Suddenly Estelle was running. Not at Cate but away, toward the stairs. She seemed to catch one of her high heels in the area rug and then dove face-first into the tiled stairway.

Cate gaped at the woman's still form. *What ... just happened here?* Then Estelle pushed herself up from the tile and turned back to face Cate triumphantly. Blood was gushing out of a cut above her eyebrow, a bruise was rising on her cheekbone, and a thin trickle of red was just emerging from her nose.

As Cate stood speechless, Estelle pulled out her cell phone and dialed. She pressed the speaker button. The room filled with the sound of ringing and then a voice answered.

"911, what's your emergency?"

An enormous sob came out of the woman on the floor.

"I've ... I've been attacked by ... by an intruder. Please hurry, she's trying to leave."

Cate realized her jaw had dropped open. She shut it firmly and swallowed. Her voice was shaky but calm when she spoke.

"That's what you'd like me to do, isn't it, Estelle? Run away so you can sic the cops on me?" Instead, Cate pulled up a chair and sat down to wait for the authorities.

Chapter 19

When the sheriff's SUV crept up the driveway a scant half-hour later, Deputy Gomez was not one of the responders. Cate nervously watched through the office window as two young officers clad in khaki and sporting neckties cautiously approached the front door and knocked, their weapons drawn but down at their sides.

After holding Cate at gunpoint for about twenty minutes, Estelle had given in to the constant dripping of blood from her nose onto her ruined blouse and gone into the kitchen for a towel and some ice. So, it was Cate who walked over to the front door and let the officers in.

"Are you the—?" the first officer began.

"D'at was me, officer," Estelle answered as she walked from the kitchen clutching the bloody towel over her nose. "You ... you d'eed to arrest her! For assault and battery. With this!"

In her other hand was a wrought iron fireplace poker smeared with bright red blood, which she gingerly offered them. The poker looked vaguely familiar, and Cate recalled having used something like it to stir the fire at the dinner party. Estelle sneered at Cate as she passed by and handed the poker to the nearest officer.

"That does it! I'm pressing charges. I'm not suffering any more abuse by this crazy family!" The impact of her speech was marred by a comical inability to pronounce "n" and "m" words due to the volume of blood still leaking from her face. She tried to blow her nose into the towel and winced in pain.

"And you are ...?" the first officer asked Estelle as the other moved to stand behind Cate.

"Estelle Parker, Fidley Rach badager." She handed the man her business card and her driver's license. "This person has bid saying she's a relative since she arrived here—with a backpack and on foot—what, a week ago? Less? Feels like more."

The officer turned to Cate, who once again realized she had no current driver's license or any form of ID—certainly nothing listing Finley Ranch as her address. The only current photo ID she carried was for the LA Arts Council, which simply listed her as "Catify." Still, she gave a shot at presenting her case.

"Look—all this? ... is crazy. That woman ran toward those stairs, tripped, and fell. I ... I never touched her, sir." The officer still had his hand out for her license. "My ID is, um, upstairs with my belongings. But I've ... recently moved back to this area from New York and haven't yet changed my—"

"Liar!" Estelle shouted, holding the ice up to her head and pointing at Cate. "She's a homeless vagrant from Los Angeles." She leaned her battered face toward Cate and muttered confidentially, "You're not the only one who knows how to do an online search ... Catify!"

The officer behind Cate spoke into his radio.

"Roger that. It appears to be a ... a domestic dispute. A case of she said,"—he looked over at Estelle and then back at Cate pointedly—"she said. Nope, the claimant has an ID and appears to be at her work address. Nine-oh-one to her face. Recommending an ER trip. The suspect is apparently a transient." More muffled sounds. "Ten-forty. Bringing that one for a full print check."

Cold dread crept up Cate's backbone.

"Well, let me guess who 'that one' is," she murmured dryly.

"Can I at least get my backpack from the upstairs bedroom?"

"I'll get it, miss," the officer behind her said as he headed for the stairs. Minutes went by. Then he trotted back down the stairs like an eager pony, her backpack held gingerly by his latex-gloved hands. He was talking into his radio again.

"We've got a suspect in custody for a two-fifteen. Looks like possible meth or cocaine." He lifted a zip-lock bag out of the pack and held it up for the other deputy to see.

Cate saw the glee on Estelle's ruined face and silently groaned, *Well played, Starr Parker. Very well played.*

As they firmly guided her into the back seat of the SUV, she mumbled, "I can't wait for you guys to drug test me." Then she realized the ketamine she'd consumed at the dinner party was probably still in her system.

#

An hour to the north lay the community of Silver Springs, known affectionately by Cate's Copperton High crowd as "Sliver," due to its sparse population, and home of the county's detention center, as well as its courthouse.

Once there, her conversion from private citizen to inmate took a brisk forty-five minutes, including the paperwork, urine sample, body cavity search, and clothing swap. An hour later, clad in prison orange, Cate sat before a video monitor in a shallow alcove off her assigned cell block. She peered at the image of her old friend Jimmy Baker, sitting in his comfortable law offices in Copperton, as he slowly shook his head and read from the papers in front of him.

"Breaking and entering, we can toss that one out. I talked to the deputies who found no evidence of a break-in *and* you were an invitee of the claimant. Then, assault … with a poker."

Now Cate fully remembered grabbing the poker at the dinner party and debating whether to hold onto it for the night, no doubt all the while being observed by Estelle.

"I didn't touch her, Jimmy. She fell—on *purpose*—and smashed her face on the stairs. I mean, you've seen her. She's, what, six inches taller and has about fifty pounds on me? Somehow, she had this preplanned—at least planting the drugs in my pack and calling the cops on me." She rubbed her face in her hands. "I was warned. Bronnie said to stay away from her. I'm an idiot."

"Look, it's clearly out of my field of practice, but I think you could get the first two charges dropped. The drugs, though—different story."

"Oh, my God, I totally fit everyone's profile of a meth addict, don't I? Skinny, transient female with scraggly bleached hair. I'm practically a poster child."

The way Jimmy was now scrutinizing her put Cate on edge. For the second time that week, she shook off the sensation of being in a dystopic fantasy novel.

"Hey, they did a drug panel when I got here. Can you check on it? Also, can't they, um, fingerprint the baggie? There is no way my prints are on it, and the backpack's been out of my possession for the last forty-eight hours."

"Don't think that one matters."

"Just check, please." They were silent for a moment. "Also, *someone* needs to get a missing person's report done on my sister. I mean, it's going on two weeks. Maybe I shouldn't be the one to do it, all things considered. Can you reach Bronnie Taylor? She's a neonatal nurse at Copperton Medical. Bronwyn Taylor. Lives down in Cabeza Valley, close to the ranch. She brought me home to stay with her after I got released from the hospital so clearly *she* doesn't think I'm a criminal."

Jimmy was nodding and making notes. "I can't believe all this has happened to you within three days of returning to Arizona, Cate. It's just so crazy."

"No kidding—" A two-minute warning flashed on the monitor and Jimmy stacked papers, preparing to end the conversation.

"So, when's my court date? I need … I need to get out of here."

"Your initial appearance happens tomorrow, about midday. In person. We're shooting to get an OR—release on your own recognizance. So please don't say or do anything from this point on that might hurt your case."

Cate drew in a long breath and slumped.

"Wow … Estelle has me right where she wants me. Locked up and out of her way. Meanwhile, no one is actually looking for my sister, and who knows what that woman is doing right now to cover her tracks? Did I mention she is scheming to sell the ranch property to developers? She made no secret of it Sunday night, right before she drugged me. I've heard of people stealing property by transferring the deed into their name when no one was paying attention. Could this have happened already with the ranch? I was looking for the deed in the office files when Estelle walked in on me."

Jimmy brightened and sat a little straighter.

"Now *that* is in my wheelhouse—estates, real and otherwise. I can check with county records—oops, you're flickering. Hey, Cate?"

The screen went blank. Twenty minutes had gone by fast. Cate got up from the video kiosk and shuffled in her soft slippers back toward her cell block. She passed by shivering women, grumbling women, and sad, silent women. In a way, being incarcerated wasn't much different from walking among the homeless on the streets of Los Angeles. A little less cheerful, but at least they fed and clothed you.

#

Late afternoon brought a phone call. Thinking it was Jimmy, Cate instead heard an unfamiliar female on the other end.

"Hi, Cate, my name is Sarah Hamlin, and I'm a reporter for the Copperton Daily News. I, um, I got referred to you by a family friend, Bronwyn Taylor?"

"Yeah?" *Great, now what?* Cate had felt nauseous and exhausted since lunch and couldn't imagine why Bronnie would put the media onto her at this point.

"The thing is, I'm doing a series of articles on out-of-state developers acquiring public and private land amid, well, some concerns from local citizens. So, I understand your sister is out of town, and we were wondering if we could interview you as the Finley family representative about, you know, how the acquisition of your ranch is going."

Cate stared at the phone, beyond irritated. Did this reporter know she was calling county lockup?

"Look, I don't know anything about—" She stopped as a light bulb went off. Bronnie had put the woman in touch with Cate for a reason. "So ... you haven't yet talked to my sister Margaret?" Cate asked, trying to keep her tone neutral.

"No, she hasn't returned any of my calls."

"Well, that might be because she's been missing for over a week."

Cate spoke evenly and slowly into the phone. Then she waited for a response from the other end. When none came, she hurried on, conscious this was her chance to get the word out.

"Margaret was supposed to be coming back from New Mexico, but the only one who claims to have heard from her is *also* the woman who's living in our family home and has been lying to me since I got here."

"Lying? About what?

"Well, that Margaret would be returning home the night before last, for one thing. Also, about my sister making a deal to sell my family's ranch to developers, which was certainly news to me and everyone else I've talked with. I only know about it because I happened to be at a dinner where this woman, Estelle Parker, and a group of developers discussed their plans—right in front of me."

"You say it was a group of developers? Can you tell me who they were?"

"Well, one of them was the former Sheriff Mack Griffin's nephew. A guy named Hugo ... Griffin? There were two realtors from Copperton who gave me business cards that I, um, can't get to right now." She thought about the fourth man but wouldn't know how to identify him at this point. "I wish I could tell you more about the evening, but someone drugged my dinner and I ended up in the ER."

Silence on the other end. Cate realized her story was a plate of crazy with a side of paranoia. She took a deep breath and decided to start over.

"Look, Bronnie contacted me in California about my sister Margaret being missing for over a week. I came back here to see if I could help look for her."

Still no response from the caller. Cate felt perspiration collecting on her neck and forehead. Was this really a local reporter she was talking to? Or ... had New York found her again?

"Hello?"

"Oh, I'm still here. I was just writing notes. I know a Griffin nephew named Hugo. He seems to be connected with several development deals in the county. You say the others were realtors? Was one named Randy Simmons?"

"Well, yes—definitely a Randy, and a Dirk or Dick?" "Yes, the two I'm thinking of are cousins."

Cate breathed a sigh of relief. "Matching comb-overs and the same receding chin? Sorry, I'm an artist. It's in my nature to study people." Like the guy who'd completed the quartet and had tried to chat her up by the fireplace. On a future canvas, she would paint him as a man morphing into a pit bull. Estelle's pit bull.

#

In the evening, still edgy from the conversation with the reporter, Cate had another video chat with Jimmy. He held up a newspaper photo of Estelle's battered face with the headline, "Local Realtor Attacked by Vagrant." He wasn't pleased when he heard Cate had also spoken to a reporter.

"No talking to anyone—especially not to the media—until we've sprung you from there. The other side is definitely pressing charges, and she also filed a restraining order to keep you a hundred yards from her."

"What? She can't keep me from my family's ranch."

"Cate, if she's residing there as the ranch manager and your sister has given her power of attorney, she most surely can."

Power of attorney ... Cate was silent for a moment, feeling a riptide pulling her under the ocean.

"So, what did you find out at County Records?"

"Something quite unexpected, Cate. It explains a lot of

what's been going on this week. It would help if we could talk to your sister, but, lacking that, you will be playing a very big role."

"What? Tell me." Her heart fluttered, as waves of nausea washed over her. "I need to hear something positive."

"I don't want to talk about it under these conditions. We can discuss it after we see the judge." He flashed his mischievous smile. "By the way, I have a surprise character witness for you."

"Who, Desi? Rosa?" But Jimmy was gathering his papers into a folder, aware their allotted time was ending.

"Cate, this character witness is going to, um, give a prepared statement." She guessed what he was implying without saying directly—that some stuff had been massaged or even made up. Who was this person?

A twitchy inmate with cropped red hair and a vicious-looking tattoo circling her neck had strolled over to stand in front of Cate, strongly hinting she should vacate the booth.

"Jimmy. I—" She eyed the inmate who was practically vibrating with impatience. "I need to give up my spot. I'll see you—" but the screen had already gone blank.

Cate climbed out of the booth and, as she stepped past, the woman poked her shoulder.

"Heyyy, I know you! You were Drew Mason's little jailbait girlfriend. Finley, right?"

Stunned for a second, Cate recovered and gave back a non-committal smile and shrug.

"Man, that takes me back. Your sis Margaret paid my boyfriend a lotta cash to mess Drew up good," she cackled. "Hell, yeah, we went to Vegas on your family's dime that night, girl."

Cate stared at the redhead. Was she talking about the night Drew disappeared? She managed what she hoped was a polite nod and casually strolled away. An open cellblock in county jail was no place to take issue with someone, at least that was what her cautious self was telling the growling tiger. At a safe distance, she looked back at the woman. A few years older than Cate, with a deeply creased face and some broken teeth. Probably a current or past meth tweaker, judging from the amount of involuntary movement going on. Had this woman's boyfriend done something terrible—maybe even murdered Drew? That long ago, how would anybody ever know for certain?

Cate walked back to the central pod where inmates were reading, playing cards, and watching television, feeling a cloud of depression beginning to settle on her. Normally, she would dive into her painting or sketching to combat these dark feelings. But the odds of getting a blank sheet of paper and a sharpened pencil were less than zero.

Chapter 20

August 7, Silver Springs Courthouse

Like a well-behaved cart pony, Cate padded along in her jail-issued slippers next to the plump female detention officer. There was just no way to feel credible or innocent while wearing orange prison scrubs, not even if they fit perfectly, which these did not. She'd washed her face and then neatened her hair with a borrowed comb, all the while praying the owner didn't have head lice.

Suddenly, a tall door in the corridor opened, and they entered a sparsely populated courtroom. She'd been in only one other courtroom, about a decade ago, during her days of opioid addiction. That situation had been so traumatic she'd blocked out the memory until just now. She recalled rows of seats like in a church, a judge on a high, throne-like chair behind an enormous desk. The attorney for the other side had hammered her with questions she couldn't answer without sounding guilty. In the end, when she realized they would be taking away the one thing in this life she gave a rip about, the tiger had emerged and she'd lost control. Now, as she walked with the officer straight down to where Jimmy sat, Cate felt her hands begin to tremble. Would the tiger get her in deeper trouble today?

Almost as soon as Cate sat down, the judge appeared and everyone rose, so she struggled to her feet again. Her nervous energy was building—butterflies turning into stealth bombers in her stomach—and now she was shaking all over. She didn't see Estelle anywhere in the courtroom, which was surprising considering how much the woman had wanted to show off her damaged face to the press.

Still standing, Jimmy presented their case very succinctly to the court. Then he handed typed pages to the bailiff, who presented them to the judge. The judge glanced over them and then looked down at Cate, who had again seated herself only to stand back up under his stern gaze.

"Caitlyn Finley, you were arrested for breaking and entering, assault, and suspicion of felony drug possession." He silently read the next paragraph, then put down the paper.

"Well, today must be your lucky day. There is no physical evidence of a break-in, and you appear to have been staying as a guest of the plaintiff, so that charge is dropped. Furthermore, laboratory analysis of the powder found in your possession was ...," he consulted the next page, frowning and pursing his lips, "inconclusive. So ... a court date will be set to address the assault charge only. You don't seem to have a permanent address, in this area or elsewhere—uh, yes, Counsel?"

Jimmy had been waving his hand as if hailing a cab, his small stature making it difficult for the judge to see him.

"Your honor, at the time of the arrest, Cate Finley was visiting her family's ranch and didn't have a current ID with her. But she has been residing in Los Angeles with her fiancé."

Cate snapped her head to stare at him, but then remembered his warning and quickly looked down at the floor as Jimmy continued. "He's here today to testify regarding her character and residential status."

The judge nodded, and a bailiff led a man from the back of the courtroom to stand before the judge. Cate blinked and then blinked again to clear her eyesight.

"What the—?" she murmured before catching Jimmy's warning look.

It was Levi, hair cut short, and dressed in full dark blue army officer's attire, including a beret set at an angle that covered his scarred temple. An impressive array of medals glittered on his chest. Catching herself gawking, she closed her mouth and swallowed a few times.

Levi took a military stance in front of the judge, which emphasized his linebacker physique.

"Your honor, my name is Levi Saaga," he said in the deep, rich voice she'd grown used to hearing daily. "Originally from American Samoa, serving in the United States Army, S2 division, currently on medical leave due to injuries suffered while on active duty. My home address is 2209 Brookline Avenue in Baldwin Hills, California."

Cate's jaw kept wanting to drop, so she clenched her teeth. Either he was perjuring himself big time, or he wasn't a homeless vet after all. Why had he been pretending to be one for over a year?

"Your honor, I've been closely associated with Cate Finley and have never witnessed any behavior that would lead me to believe she was violent or a drug user of any sort. In fact, I've never even seen her consume an alcoholic drink. She and I have resided together for this last year. While I'm confident that she is innocent of the charges against her, I'm even more confident she is not a danger to society. I respectfully request her release from jail on her own recognizance."

Cate felt herself blushing at the man's glowing defense of her. It was what she needed to hear right now—and almost made up for his deceitfulness.

The judge, stout and fiftyish, with tired eyes and a sardonic expression, sat blinking at Levi for a few moments before consulting the papers in front of him.

"Thank you, Sergeant ... Saaga? You may be seated and thank you also for your service."

Levi looked relieved to have his speech over. After a slight pause, he walked to the empty chair on Cate's left and sat. She could smell his herbal-scented cologne and yearned to flash him a smile but didn't dare.

The judge was saying something about the conditions of release. He lifted a new sheet of paper from his pile and glanced at it.

"It appears Mrs. Parker has filed an order of restraint against you, Ms. Finley. That means that you will need to find alternate housing in the area until the trial. You will not be allowed less than one hundred yards from Mrs. Parker at any time. That includes the Finley Ranch where she currently resides and is employed. Is all that clear to you?"

Cate had an impulse to shout in protest, but croaked out a meek "Yes, your honor" instead. Doing anything else would have played right into Estelle's hands. The judge signed her release papers, banged his gavel, and she became a free woman again.

A half-hour later, dressed in clothes sent by Bronnie, Cate walked outside the gates of the detention area and saw something that made her smile for the first time in days—Levi, back in jeans and a black T-shirt, leaning against her teal and white Ford truck with its vintage white camper.

She sighed deeply and murmured, "Ma-ax," but she was smiling at Levi.

Chapter 21

Cate watched the summer tourists pass by the front window of The Palace restaurant in downtown Copperton and tried to appease her inner tiger with bites of nicely cooked filet mignon. She could barely look at Jimmy, Bronnie, and Levi without wanting to burst into tears or a rant—or both. But she remembered the last time she'd lost her temper in a restaurant. Recovery had taken months. *You're smarter now, girl. Stay smart.*

"... And that's why I'm against you going to Cabeza Valley. If Estelle sees you, she will try to taunt you into breaching the restraining order, I just know it," Jimmy insisted.

"Well, at least you agree that she's liable to do that, psycho that she is," Cate replied, stabbing a ranch fry with her fork.

"Oh, sure, but still, a smart psychopath can prevail in court. Trust me."

"So, taking her back to LA is out of the question?" Levi asked Jimmy while keeping an eye on Cate.

"I can't leave. That's just what she wants—no Finley family members in this area to fight her when she steals the ranch."

To change the subject, she asked the question that had nagged her since she saw him standing in front of the judge.

"Levi, how did you find me so fast?"

He and Jimmy exchanged looks and Levi chuckled.

"Cate, I'm in information technology. Did you really think your phone was untraceable just because it's prepaid? You would have needed to pull out the SIM card to lose me."

Cate felt her face redden. "Good to know," she mumbled.

"Once I got to Copperton, it was just a fluke I saw that news-paper headline at the motel." *The one naming me as a vagrant,* she thought. "It mentioned this guy," a nod at Jimmy, "was your lawyer, so I looked up his offices."

Satisfied for the moment, she didn't pursue the next questions, which were, *So, you're not homeless? What the hell, Levi?* and, *do you even have a mother in Samoa, or was that a crock, too?* All in good time. For now, she owed him the debt of humble gratitude.

"So anyway," Cate continued, "I can't and won't leave the area. Not as long as Margaret's still missing and Estelle's active-ly marketing the ranch. I need to file that police report first thing tomorrow morning."

She was chattering now, but it was hard to stay calm when she thought about her last forty-eight hours. Jimmy was nodding his head, hands up as if to tone down the conversation.

"Yes, believe me, you need to stay in this county for more than one reason. Especially with Estelle having access to the ranch business accounts." Cate shot him an alarmed look. "I can tell you more, but let's do it tomorrow at my office with those documents in front of me."

Bronnie stood up and put down some cash to cover her meal, which Jimmy pushed back at her gently.

"You two are more than welcome to stay at my place. I doubt Estelle will venture over to that corner of the ranch, but if she does, we'll hide you in the root cellar." She laughed but then realized no one was joining her.

"I just don't want you to be tempted to go to the ranch house again," Jimmy warned Cate. "You do not want to violate this protective order, certainly not while you have a court case pending."

In the end, Cate and Levi followed Bronnie back to her place, parking the camper truck in the shrubbery behind the house where it couldn't be seen from Finley Ranch. Looking spent, Levi said he was retiring to the camper, which left the two women alone.

Realizing a part of her did indeed want to sneak over and spy on Estelle through a window, Cate tried to keep Bronnie talking for as long as she could. It proved easier than she'd expected. The older woman had something on her mind.

"There's something I've wanted to tell you, Cate, and I haven't—don't really know how. I keep thinking Jimmy's going to discover it and tell you."

Cate took her arm, alarmed at how grave she sounded.

"What? Something about Margaret?"

Bronnie started to speak, then hesitated.

"I'm not the one to—I promised your sister, no matter what, but it may be time. Do you remember the old cabin on the ranch that runs upcountry behind Cabeza Rock? You used to be able to get there by jeep, but lately, the rains have all but washed out the road. The last part's only accessible by foot or on horseback. Maybe a brave soul could get there on a quad."

As Bronnie spoke, Cate recalled the switchback road through pinion pines that got steeper until it leveled off onto a high-country valley. There sat the wooden cabin that her father had taken his new bride, shortly after the wedding. The two had spent a rather low-tech honeymoon camping there. Growing up, Cate had often tagged along when Doc and Margaret rode horses up to check the high valley's fences and have a picnic on the front porch of the cabin.

"Your sister has a soft spot for that cabin, some critical memories tied to it. I was actually worried that we might find her there, so the other morning I hiked halfway up the trail ..." Cate looked at her sharply. "But there were no recent tracks of any kind."

"Bronnie, what are you trying to say? If it's something that would help with the search for Margaret, you need to tell me."

"More like the search for Cate and Margaret. Family stuff. Some missing pieces. But can we continue with this tomorrow? I'm tapped."

And with that, she went into her room and quietly closed the door, leaving Cate puzzled but barely able to keep her own eyes open.

Chapter 22

Gunshots woke Cate in the early dawn. Panicked, she groped around for her jeans and pulled them on, thinking of Levi out in the camper. She met him at the door as he was entering the house.

"They came from the pasture," he said, pointing toward Finley Ranch. She nodded and knelt to tie her running shoes. Then she grabbed a small pen light from the windowsill as she headed for the door to the porch.

"Cate," she heard Levi say behind her.

The bright August moon was just above the horizon, throwing an eerie glow across the dark pasture. In the distance, she thought she could see a figure striding away from her, toward the ranch stables. A dark mound lay in the middle of the acreage and her heart had begun to pound. Was it a human? A cow? She was about to climb the fence to go see when Levi caught her arm.

"Cate—wait a minute! What are you doing? The restraining order—"

She turned to him, fixated on who or what was out there.

"Something or someone just got shot in that field. I … I need to find out." It could be a mistake—Estelle drawing her into a trap—but she couldn't help herself.

She scaled the barbed wire fence in one move, hopping down on the other side. Levi went to follow her over, but then stopped, looking down at his bare feet.

"Wait here. I'll be right back," she said, adding under her breath, "I think."

The gate to the horse pasture stood open and all the horses were in with the small herd of heifers. Startled by the shots, they had formed a roiling clump. Cate could see Destino's ghostly form as he tried to guide the herd away from the solitary shape that lay in the grass.

She moved closer and saw it wasn't a cow or a human. It was Bella, her old horse. The mare lay on her side, groaning. Her sides heaved as she struggled to breathe.

"Bella," Cate said, feeling a sob rise from her throat. The horse made an attempt to raise her head. "Hi, girl. Easy, easy, baby."

Cate knelt over her with the penlight and saw where two bullets had penetrated her neck and a third, probably at point-blank, had entered her forehead at an odd angle. Blood gushed onto the ground from the holes in her neck.

"Oh, God, no … no!"

Whoever had done this couldn't even be bothered with a clean and merciful shot. No, the opposite of that. A clumsy, torturous execution.

A ghostly stack of papers lay under the mare's head. On impulse, she pulled it out and, in the penlight, saw it was the *Copperton Daily News*. The front page had what looked like a photo of Cate standing next to Max outside the courthouse. The headline read, "Woman Fears for Missing Sister's Safety, Questions Finley Ranch Manager's Motives."

Cate hadn't realized she'd been crying—bawling noisily—until she felt a hand on her shoulder. Startled, she turned to see a young girl. She looked like Desi's daughter, Shania, but the hair was longer, the features more feminine. The girl's face glistened with tears.

"She ... she was a beautiful horse," the girl said, looking at Bella sadly. "Was her leg broke? I heard they shoot them when ... when their legs break."

"I don't know," Cate said, swiping at her eyes. "I ... I found her like this. She was my horse ... once."

"She was ... your sister? Margaret?

"Yeah," Cate answered, wiping her face on her t-shirt.

The girl took Cate's hand and put something in it. Cate glanced down and saw that she held a black case containing what looked like a phone. She shone the light and saw three gold letters embossed on the case—*MJF*.

"What? Wait, where did you get this?" But the girl had turned and sprinted toward Desi's house. Was she Desi's foster kid?

She heard the rumble of an engine as some large farm machine rolled onto the field from the direction of the stable, no doubt headed to pick up Bella. Probably not Estelle driving, but Cate didn't think she should stay to find out. The mare was still now and breathing very shallowly. There was nothing she could do here but get arrested for violating the restraining order. She leaned down to give a furtive last kiss on the mare's smooth, still-warm cheek.

Her eyes burned and she felt spent ... defeated. Had Estelle really done this? Of course, she had. The newspaper headline. Message sent and received.

She slipped the phone into her pocket, grabbed the paper, and sprinted back to Bronnie's house. The approaching tractor droned behind her.

Levi was still standing at the pasture fence. He said nothing, just took her in his arms. No resistance on her part. His embrace felt massive and comforting, like being lowered into a warm bath. It was just past five a.m. and already it had been a brute of a day.

#

Back inside the house, Bronnie made coffee and eggs while Cate sat back on the couch with her eyes closed, shaking her head.

"I shouldn't have made such a stink about Bella on Sunday. She killed her to get back at me," Cate muttered. "What kind of monster does that?" But she knew the answer to that one.

Levi read the front-page article on Margaret's disappearance out loud:

"... reporter contacted Margaret Finley's sister, Cate, who spoke of her fear that her sister has met with foul play. She said the Finley Ranch manager, Estelle Parker, who is also a local realtor specializing in development deals, maintained Margaret was out of town on a horse-buying trip.

'She was supposed to return on Sunday, but she didn't. I've been asking around and no one has seen her in nearly two weeks,' said Cate Finley on Tuesday in an exclusive interview.

Planning regarding the Cabeza Rock Estates is continuing in the ranch owner's absence, and a presentation to the Cabeza Valley Town Council is scheduled for next week. Cate Finley stated her deep concern that they are proceeding with their plans for Finley Ranch without her sister being present.

'This doesn't sound like an idea Margaret would support. I'd just like to talk with her about their proposed plan to demolish a ranch that has been in our father's family for over a hundred years,' Finley explained by phone on Wednesday."

Phone. Cate felt her back pocket and pulled out the one that the girl in the field had given her. No response when she clicked the "on" button.

"Does anyone have a phone charger that might work for this?"

From across the room, Bronnie gasped.

"Where did you find that?"

"The girl gave it to me. The foster at Desi's? She asked me if Margaret was my sister, then handed me the phone."

"How ... how did she ...? Okay, that does it. I'm calling the sheriff's office to come out here and get this report done. That phone is Margaret's." Anxiety creased Bronnie's face, and Cate felt her own insides knotting.

"We should charge it just to be sure," she replied with a glance at Levi, who had magically produced a case of neatly stored chargers and adaptors. The first cable he tried fit the phone, and it pinged as he plugged it in.

Bronnie picked up the discarded phone case, looked at it, then threw it on the table again.

"Cate, it's hers. You saw the initials, right? We have to go talk with that child. But I want to get this report started first."

"Ask if they can send Officer Gomez. I spoke with him at the hospital. He seemed sympathetic."

Bronnie smiled faintly. "Miguel Gomez questioned you? Oh, that's almost ..." She shook her head. "We're ... old friends. Sorry, Copperton is still a small town."

"Maybe I should go over to Desi's before the sheriff gets here. The girl might feel less intimidated with just one stranger asking her questions." Cate now recalled having seen her a few times, scampering like a wild creature around corners and behind trees to avoid being seen.

Levi had been poised to go with her but sat back down and frowned at the charging phone in his hand. She crossed the room, squeezed alongside him in the easy chair, and whispered in his ear.

"Have I told you lately how grateful I am?"

"Hey, friends like us? We don't let friends stay in jail," he murmured, a smirk forming on his lips.

"Though we still have to talk about your sins of omission," she whispered.

He wrapped his free arm around her and pulled her closer. She breathed in his scent—herbal and coconut, along with something musky and male. There it was again, that thing stirring deep inside her, like an itch. She rested her head on the side of his neck for a long moment. Could she trust a guy like him? Could he trust her? What would a future together look like? So much of hers would depend on the immediate days ahead. Wriggling out of the chair, she went out on the porch to see if any lights were on at Desi Mason's house.

Chapter 23

Later that morning, Desi opened her door with an impish smile on her face. She was clearly delighted that Cate had asked to come and meet Rae.

"So, you've guessed who she is, right? Whose kid she is?" Desi's over-the-top eagerness was nerve-wracking, given Cate's early morning trauma.

"Your foster child? Uh, not really."

Desi squeezed her eyes shut and gave her head a little perplexed shake.

"Why does she keep telling people that? She's not a foster, Cate, she's family. That's Drew's daughter."

Cate gave her a hard look. This was not the time to be pranking her. She kept staring as Desi nodded and went on.

"Yep, my great disappearing act of a brother. Actually, he re-surfaced a while back. Contacted us from Tennessee, probably a dozen years ago now."

Cate held up her hand, to stop the flow of information while she looked for a place to sit. The porch steps seemed the closest. The other woman looked like she was waiting for her to say something, but Cate couldn't comment. An entire human being—her childhood friend and first love, Drew Mason—was resurrecting from her mental list of the dead.

"He seemed to be doing great—had a good job at a distillery in Lynchburg for a decade at least. Then, all of a sudden, we get word he's in jail—I mean state penitentiary jail—and not for dealing drugs, either. No—attempted murder. Went after some hunter who accidentally shot his youngest son Jamie, oh, about eight years back." She shook her head. "So sad."

Cate wondered if there was a physical limit to the amount of shocking news someone could handle in a day. Desi pulled a chair up next to her.

"Hey, something else you may not know—your sister's the one who made him leave the state back then. Those guys you kept insisting tried to run you off the road driving back from Copperton all those years ago?"

Cate faced her. "Margaret paid them to do it." She was recalling the red-headed inmate's comment to her in lockup.

Desi nodded and went on. "He said they roughed him up good—broke his nose and a rib or two. Told him to get out of town if he wanted to keep living."

Why would Margaret do something like that—go to those lengths just to pull her apart from Drew? Out of some sense of protection? More like rage and jealousy. And what had Cate ever done to deserve any of it?

She debated coming back another time to talk to Rae, but this new information didn't really change anything. The past was in the past. Still, her brain was buzzing from the news.

Drew Mason, her childhood playmate, and first love, was not dead after all. She took a deep breath and then followed Desi up the stairs to talk with Drew's daughter.

Chapter 24

Rae

When the doorbell rang, she knew she'd brought trouble on herself. But she'd felt so sorry for the shot-up horse in the field this morning. Rae had just wanted to give Pinto Lady something to make it hurt less like they'd tried to do for her after her mom and Davy had fallen off the bridge.

Desi had called Rae to come downstairs, but it was going to take more than that to get her to answer. Then she heard footsteps on the stairs and a real quiet knock on her bedroom door. When she opened it she saw Desi and Pinto Lady. They stood there with the smiles people wore who are going to ask hard questions, questions that might make you cry.

"Rae, this is Cate, an old friend of your daddy's. *And* she's Margaret's sister. You know, the lady you're going to start working for, whenever she gets back in town."

That won't be happening, Rae thought. The lady named Cate took a step toward her.

"Hi, Rae. We, um, talked a little in the pasture this morning. You … you gave me something—a gift—and I came to ask you about it."

Rae turned and walked back into the room to look out the window at the pasture where cows and horses now grazed. The pasture where Margaret Finley had lain.

She felt Cate walking up to stand next to her, looking out

the window.

"Rae, you aren't in any trouble, okay?" She was trying to make her voice sound soft.

"I'm just … I'm curious about how you got the phone. Maybe you found it or"—Rae moved to sit on the bed, facing away—"maybe Margaret gave it to you?"

After a long silence, Rae turned to look at the lady. She studied her crazy hair—side-parted and hooked behind her ears today. The shiny dark brown roots turned to dull pink just above her shoulders, then spilled halfway down her back like melted peppermint ice cream. She saw hope and sadness under the smile Cate wore and wished she didn't know what she knew. She wanted someone or something to wipe away everything in her head, all the bad thoughts and memories. Like cleaning grit from a windshield. She wanted to see a sparkling, new world out of her eyes again.

"She didn't give it to me. I found it." Her voice felt raspy, her throat dry.

"You found it?"

"Yes, ma'am."

"Where did you find it, Rae? It's … it's important that you tell us, because … Margaret is missing." Cate's voice had started to shake a little, but she kept it lifted like she was still hopeful. "She's not in New Mexico where … where everyone thought she was. We need to find her, Rae."

Rae looked down. She liked the sound of the lady's voice and wished they could talk more without Rae having to tell.

Now the lady—Cate—was crying again, like she did in the field but more quietly, and it must have shamed her because she turned to go.

"I found her in the field," said Rae, "in the middle. By the bunched-up trees."

Cate turned back to look at her, eyes wide like a spooked cat. What had she said? It had come out all wrong.

"You ... you found the phone in the field?"

"Yes, ma'am."

Cate's voice was softer, not crying now. "Because you said *'her'* just now."

"I ... I did?"

"Yes, you did. You said, 'I found her'."

Rae felt the cage door opening inside her. A wild animal crouched, ready to pounce. Something was rising in her, making her feel like ripping up her room, like punching at things. At herself, at her mama and brothers, at her daddy, at poor Margaret. She didn't want to do this anymore—be the secret keeper, the only one left.

"I saw her—I did! I saw Margaret! She ... she was lying, in the grass, in the trees." Her breath was hard to catch. Small gasps between words. "Her face was—down. But the sparkly vest—so bloody—ruined. Somebody ruined it, somebody—"

Then gasps and sobs—she couldn't stop them. Holding her head, feeling the wail rise up out of her like an injured animal, she sank to the floor. Someone close by her was sobbing. Then arms were lifting her up, wrapping around her, holding her. It was Pinto Lady holding her close now and crying with her.

Chapter 25

Cate

Later that day, Cate slouched on the front porch steps at Desi's with Samson the Rottweiler and watched as a sheriff's SUV pulled into the yard. Deputy Miguel Gomez emerged from the driver's side and a fresh-faced young deputy slammed the passenger door. Cate recognized him as one of the responding officers from the night she was arrested. Perfect. The two deputies conferred briefly by the car while the dispatch radio barked static in the background. It was only early afternoon, but Cate felt emotionally drained and not up to more police interaction.

Too much had happened in too few days. She felt fragile and crabby—afraid she would do or say something rash. Then, just as Gomez approached, a switch flipped in her head, and she became a more capable version of herself. Cate 2.0. She'd be damned if these men would see her fall apart.

"Officer Gomez," she held out her hand. "Thanks for coming down."

"No problem, Cate. This is Detective Royce of Criminal Investigations."

To his credit, Royce didn't refer to their previous contact, but his expression made it clear she wasn't above suspicion. Not at all.

"I hear you have reason to believe your sister, uh, has passed. Is that correct?"

"Yes, I talked to the girl who lives here with her aunt and uncle. She says she saw my sister lying, um, unconscious in the pasture about twelve days ago, maybe?"

Royce shot a glance at the house. "We're going to need to speak with the girl—Rae is her name? She'll need a relative or guardian present."

"That's me. I'm her aunt," said Desi, who'd been listening inside the screened door. "But can we wait for her therapist? Dr. Bauman has been treating her, and I'm worried she might be overwhelmed by the police, you know, questioning her. She's being treated for previous PTSD."

"Maybe we can start by asking you a few questions about the day she says she saw Ms. Finley ... er, Margaret. Is there a reason no one reported this sooner?"

The two deputies walked inside with Desi, and Cate was again alone with the dog. She heard the rattle of a distressed motor and saw Levi riding up in Bronnie's ancient ATV. Cate sidled over to greet him as he parked alongside the SUV.

"You didn't bring it, did you?" Cate asked in a low voice.

"Well, no, not after you phoned me, but are you sure that's wise? It's evidence, Cate."

"Right now, it's the only link with my sister that's still in my possession. Do you think you can get into it?"

"It would be optimal if we could get her passcode. Otherwise, I gotta crash the lock screen and hope she didn't opt for sophisticated encryption."

Cate squinted her eyes at him and tilted her head. "Who are you again?" Levi laughed and studied his fingers. "Seriously, my sister's not very techie, from what I saw of her computer the other day. I'm surprised she even *had* a smartphone."

Gomez came out the front door and walked up to them.

"The girl isn't really talking to us right now. Maybe when the doctor gets here, they can give her something. She's, uh, quite upset."

Cate gazed back at the house and felt a pang for Drew's young daughter.

"Yeah, she was pretty emotional when she told us about it this morning. Can't we—can't you just start searching the pasture? She said she saw Margaret in the grove of trees out there."

"We need something of hers that has her scent. A toothbrush or article of clothing. We just happen to have a search dog in the car today. Doesn't always happen that way."

Now Cate realized why Samson had parked himself by the rear hatch of the SUV. He was crouched down, his nub of a tail wagging, and fixated on something through the smoked windows.

Looking at the hulking dog now, she remembered their first meeting on the road. He had retrieved some cloth from the bushes. She'd thought it was a gopher carcass but then realized it was a dirty sock. He had carried it the whole way home and into his doghouse. A sock.

Rae had said she thought Margaret was barefoot or at least shoeless. Cate had a sudden urge to go find that sock.

As Gomez unlocked the back of the SUV, the Rottweiler's excitement grew. Gomez spoke to him commandingly and the dog immediately sat. Remembering how possessive Samson had been, Cate used this distraction to edge over to the doghouse and peer into its depths as Levi eyed her with curiosity.

The Rottie had a stash of toys. She tentatively reached her hand in and rifled through stuffed animals, garden tools, tennis balls, and half-chewed rawhide pieces.

Behind her, she heard Samson barking at the police dog. Far in the corner of the doghouse, Cate spied a piece of light cloth and grasped it.

Suddenly, Samson was at her side. As she pulled out the sock, he grabbed it and ran off a short distance, turning to look at her triumphantly. She debated letting it go. What were the chances it was Margaret's sock?

Cate walked over to where Gomez was connecting a leash to a ragged, hunched German shepherd with protruding hips and ribs. The dog looked up at her with a benign expression on his grizzled face.

"Wow, is that dog going to be okay?"

Gomez shot her a glance and then laughed. "Considering he's about ninety-three in human years, he's getting around pretty well."

The vet's kid in her spoke up. "So, about fifteen, then. And you're still working him at that age?"

"Actually, we're both supposed to be retired, but you just can't keep a good cop home."

Cate gingerly petted the animal's bony back with new respect. "This is your own dog?"

"After ten years on the job together in NYC, you don't break up the team. This is Jorge," he said, pronouncing it *hor-hay*. "Please don't call him 'George.' He gets insulted."

Levi approached and put his hand out to Jorge, who sniffed it politely before turning his eyes back on Gomez.

"I think we might have found one of Margaret's socks. The bad news is, it's in his teeth." Cate pointed at Samson, who shook the sock and gave them the "You feel lucky, punk?" stare.

Gomez dropped Jorge's leash, and the dog instantly sank

in a crouch. Then the deputy walked over to Samson and stood in front of him holding up one index finger.

"Drop it!" he commanded.

The dog immediately sat and opened his mouth. The sock fell to the ground and Samson hovered over it protectively, just like he'd done on the road with Cate.

"Leave it!" Gomez said, again with a sharp, commanding tone. Samson sat back up, mesmerized by the deputy's upright index finger. With his other hand, Gomez reached down and grabbed the sock before the dog could focus back on it. With a practiced movement, he flipped the dog a treat that had been hiding in his upright hand. Samson opened his massive jaws and caught the treat in midair, then walked off toward his doghouse.

After a moment, Cate said, "Okay, that was pretty amazing."

Levi nodded and chuckled. "So, you're a canine officer."

"Not here, but I do help out in the county with search and rescue as needed. I spent a dozen years in K9 in New York. But this? This was dog whispering one-oh-one." He pulled on latex gloves, and the other two watched as he picked up the sock and examined it.

"Doesn't appear that the dog did much chewing on it, so that's a plus. We'll need to get an analysis back at the lab. We still need to get something of Margaret's for comparison."

The phone was looming in Cate's mind, but she couldn't bring herself to hand it over yet. Not until Levi could crack the passcode.

"Um, check with Leelee at the stables. I bet Margaret kept a sweatshirt or barn jacket down there. If my memory serves, my sister carried used tissues in her barn coat pockets for her allergies. I'd go over and get it myself, but ..." she said over her shoulder as she climbed into the ATV, "I'm banned from entering my family's ranch."

She'd done her part. The sheriff needed to move forward with an investigation into Estelle Parker and her cohorts. Levi climbed into the driver's side of the vehicle. Cate leaned in and whispered, "I'm hungry. Let's see what Bronnie's got in her cupboards and surprise her with dinner when she gets home."

Back at the cottage, they made spaghetti carbonara, using the linguini pasta and canned sauce Bronnie had on hand and adding fresh tomatoes and peppers from her garden. As they sat on the porch of the gingerbread house, Cate chuckled and shook her head. Levi gave her a quizzical smile.

"Share," he insisted.

"Oh, it's stupid. I can't help feeling a little like we're Hansel and Gretel in the gingerbread house."

"Um, weren't they siblings?"

"Yeah, I guess so. See? Stupid."

Levi reached his hand over and ran a finger softly over her forearm.

"What are we really, Cate?"

Seeing his face suddenly made her want to cry. Not whimper, but howl. For the second time in a week, she felt breakable, like a cracked porcelain cup. *Am I too far gone, too broken to fix?* She picked up their empty plates and started toward the kitchen. Stopping at the door, she looked back at him and smiled despite her sadness.

"We are two amazingly lucky people, two fragments of a billion-piece puzzle that miraculously fit together."

A more hopeful smile spread on his face. He picked up the rest of the dinner items on the table and followed her inside.

In the kitchen, their arms free of clutter, they stepped into the embrace that had been on her mind for a long time. A minute passed without any sound but the ticking wall clock and two people breathing each other in. He turned his head to whisper in her ear.

"Do you feel that?"

"Shh," she said, lulled by the humming in her own body.

"But you do feel that, right? It's … it's not just me … ."

"I feel it. What do you want to do about it?"

"Well, there's the obvious, but …"

"Uh-huh?"

"I don't want you to regret it—you know, to think it was a mistake."

She pushed away from him, smiling, and looked into his earnest brown eyes with their fringe of black lashes. Then she turned her head to an imaginary audience.

"I'd like the record to show a man just said that."

He laughed and pulled her close again and gently kissed her neck, then murmured in her ear.

"No, I want you to know how serious I am. And believe me, we Samoans are very serious about this stuff. Ask my *faatina*."

"Your …?"

"Mother."

"The mythological mother you spun tales about all those months we shared the camper?"

"Okay, I knew this was coming," he said, a sheepish smile on his face. "Look, she's real and she is planning to come for a visit—to see all four of her children. So, you can ask her—"

"What? No, I absolutely will not ask your fiercely protective mother about us getting together. Not after the stories you've told me—"

The sound of a car pulling up to the house cut the conversation short. They turned toward the door, expecting Bronnie.

There was a polite knock and Gomez walked in, holding Cate's backpack. Cate lunged for the pack, then noticed the pained look on the deputy's face and stepped back. He'd come for the phone.

"The little girl—Rae—said she gave you a phone she found out there."

Levi went over to where it was charging.

Cate coolly returned the deputy's look. "First, thank you so much for bringing this back. Second, she gave me a dead phone she found in the pasture. We were charging it up to see if it was Margaret's."

"Look—technically, that's obstruction."

Cate stared at him hard, then decided to ignore his insinuation that she had criminal intent. Remembering her own phone had been almost dead, she fished it out of the pack and plugged it into an empty charger on the kitchen counter.

"Speaking of technical, Levi here knows how to crack passcodes on smartphones. Do your CSI folks?"

As if on cue, the phone Levi was tapping into pinged. He looked up from the screen and gave a thumbs-up.

"It worked? You got through the lock screen?" Cate asked. He nodded and she looked over at Gomez as she said, "Brilliant." Cate and Gomez walked over to look at Margaret's unlocked phone.

Suddenly Cate's phone chirped an incoming text. She walked back and checked the screen. Someone was sending her a video file. Without thinking, she clicked on it.

Up came an extreme close-up of Margaret's face, murky in the dim light of the phone screen. She appeared to be outside at night, walking while she spoke to the camera.

"Hi, it's me, Margaret. I ... really hope you get this. Something's ... something's happening here at the ranch. Bad. You better come … home. She's planning something—wants my truck keys—I told her"—*unintelligible sound*—"I'm trying to get to Bronnie's house now but … I don't know if—"

Dead silence. Cate hit play and they all watched the video again. Levi checked something on Margaret's phone.

"That must have been pending in her outbox. Says it went out right now."

"But not when it was made?" Gomez asked, suddenly coming to life.

Levi clicked a new screen and scrolled down.

"Video created July twenty-sixth."

Then, with an apologetic glance at Cate, he handed Gomez the phone. The deputy took an ancient handkerchief from his pocket and gingerly folded the phone in it.

"Want me to look for a baggie? I think Bronnie's got some," Levi offered.

Gomez shook his head, regarding the younger man with grudging respect.

"No, that's fine. We'll need a set of your prints as a rule-out. Hopefully, the little girl didn't clean it, especially the screen, before handing it over. They'll cross-reference any DNA with the sock." He looked strangely energized as he prepared to leave.

"I'll be back tomorrow after we pull a DNA sample from the sock and get a search warrant for the rest of the ranch."

But Cate was only half-listening. She was looking at her phone screen where a new message had come in from Tyson, the lawyer in California and Joseph Russo's wayward nephew.

Just got word they've sent someone to AZ to look for you. Watch your back.

Chapter 26

Bronnie didn't come home until ten. By then, Levi had gone to the camper to sleep. Cate had been tempted to just climb into bed next to him, but she felt too anxious to sleep. She needed to separate herself from this house until she knew who was coming to AZ per Tyson's warning. She thought about just calling him back, but he probably didn't know. He'd risked enough for her already.

Cate needed to talk with Bronnie about some possible escape plans. Staying put wasn't an option right now. She was loading her backpack when she felt the older woman's scrutiny.

"Look, I can't explain this, but I … I hope you can trust me. I need to get away from here for a while. There's someone on the East Coast who's been looking for me and—"

"An ex?"

Cate stopped and looked at Bronnie, realizing she owed her more explanation than she had time to give.

"It's …"

"Complicated. I got it. But how can you leave? You've got to stay in the area until your court date."

"Yes, that's been made very clear to me."

She was trying to be patient with Bronnie and the others. None of them—not even Levi—knew the events that had created this fear in her, this urge to run.

"Let me try to understand this. You need to hide because you think he's followed you here?"

"Oh, he wouldn't need to do that. He has staff—people on his payroll. I might not know who, but—" An image of Gabe's predatory smile at the dinner party came to mind and she shut up. She secured her sleeping bag on her backpack, then stood it up and gave it a shake to settle the contents.

"I know people judge me for the way I've been living, but it's kept me alive the last two years. That's what happens when you get involved with the wrong … family."

Bronnie blinked several times but didn't say more. It was a lot to swallow, Cate knew. But since the cross-country escape, she'd never told anyone her story, not even Levi. The first rule of Flight Club: Shut your yap.

"So, you need a better hiding place. What about the cabin?"

"That's what I was thinking. Just wondering if the well still works. All I need is a water source."

"What about food? Here, take this." Bronnie tossed her a loaf of wheat bread from the counter. "And this to go with it." She handed her a nearly full jar of peanut butter. Cate smiled at her, opened her pack, and jammed them in.

"You're a lifesaver, Bronnie." She pulled out her solar battery flashlight and switched it on. Nothing.

"Crap."

"What? No, you can't take that trail tonight. Are you kidding? When's the last time you went up there—twenty years ago? It's gotten dangerous from erosion. There are animals out there, for Pete's sake. Wait for dawn—*please!*"

"I need to leave before the big guy in the camper wakes up. He'll want to involve himself, and that would be—I'd rather have him mad at me because I left than—"

"Really? Isn't he ex-military? He might be a real asset in

something like this."

But Cate was done talking. She had already sacrificed too much for her one mistake.

"When he wakes up, tell him I called an Uber and headed up to Copperton for the day, okay?"

"What's an Uber?" she heard Bronnie asking as she closed the front door.

It was warm and clear, a typical summer night in Cabeza Valley. The rains had been on a break this week, and a full moon glowed overhead—plenty of light to keep her on the right path. She just needed to pay attention to where the jeep trail veered off to the cabin. Bronnie was right about one thing: it had been decades since she'd traveled that path. But she was fit and, more importantly, motivated.

A twinge of guilt pinched her gut. She'd forgotten to fill Bronnie in about the day's events, but Levi could probably tell her over breakfast. Levi caused another twinge. She wanted to trust him, but hadn't he lied to her about being homeless when they first met? Trust, especially trusting a man, was hard for her anyway. That was the damage done over the last two decades. If she asked for his help, then she'd have to tell him what happened to her in New York. She wasn't ready to face that yet.

About a mile past Bronnie's cottage, Cate came to a locked gate. This was new. Doc had never locked a single gate on the property. A thousand acres of deeded land and he'd never needed to bar anyone from coming in.

She hoisted her pack up and over the fence and climbed over. Instinctively, she *felt* the trailhead to her right. Although there was no written sign, a large granite boulder—almost a miniature version of Cabeza Rock—still marked the beginning of the trail leading to the high pasture where the cabin sat. Cate took a deep breath and started the climb.

An hour later, the trail finally crested and leveled off dramatically. Before her, in the moonlight, stretched a vast high-country valley dotted with the dark shapes of pinion pines. Cate turned and looked back down at the ranch buildings and the moonlit hundred-acre pasture far below. Porch lights twinkled from the handful of residences along its perimeter. She guessed she'd climbed a thousand feet above the valley floor. When the sun rose tomorrow, she would be looking straight across at the bald crown of Cabeza Rock. But now it was time to find the cabin and see if it was still livable.

The jeep trail had ended abruptly at a cleared turnaround amid dense catclaw, chaparral, and manzanita. As she navigated her way through the brush and across the flat expanse, she felt mentally prepared for any creature she might encounter. All except rattlesnakes. Most people didn't think cold-blooded reptiles ventured out after dark, but most rattlers did their best hunting on warm summer nights like this one. She walked forward, listening intently for the sharp hissing that sounded so much like a lawn sprinkler going off.

At what she guessed was mid-valley, Cate scanned the perimeter for the cabin. Her heart sank as she failed to see it anywhere. Had Margaret torn down the cabin in an attempt to wipe out the past and reinvent herself? Then she sighed deeply and let common sense catch up with her. Margaret wouldn't destroy the little wooden house that had been a refuge for her and a symbol of their parents' love. It would be standing even if it was in ruins.

She set down her pack, shaded her eyes from the moonlight, and scanned the perimeter. Far off in one corner, at the start of a rocky incline, she saw the faint outline of a structure. Eureka. She picked up her pack and trudged wearily toward it.

Just as Cate reached the cabin, she heard the distinctive staccato hissing she'd been listening for the entire hike. Despite being mentally prepared, she gave a shriek. The snake lay coiled on the bottom porch step—pale, coiled hose with an angry upright nozzle.

"Well, there you are," she cooed in a shaky voice. "And thanks for the welcome."

Cate muted the screaming banshee in her brain long enough to lift the stick she'd been using to sweep the ground in front of her on the hike. In one move, she hooked the snake under its middle and flung it far into the bushes, just as her father had taught her a quarter century earlier. Her body gave an involuntary shudder as she raced up the stairs and came to stand on the porch.

The idea of entering the dark cabin without a flashlight had lost its appeal. Better at daybreak, when she could check all the corners for more creatures. At one end of the wood-plank porch was a hammock strung between two posts. She carefully balanced her pack on the porch railing, slapped the dust off the hammock, and gingerly climbed on. It creaked a little but held her.

Well, she was here. Morning would come ... the sooner the better.

Chapter 27

August 9, Finley Cabin

In the early dawn, Cate awoke shivering. Her ears picked up the metallic squeak of the rusty windmill, along with soft grunting noises. A javelina herd casually paraded past the cabin, mothers nagging their adolescent young along to the trough brimming with well water. She watched them drink, deciding they were still the ugliest creatures on earth. Really. Just a bunch of skinny, hairy pigs with undershot jaws that featured menacing canine teeth. But somehow their presence brought her comfort this morning.

"However, if I had a bow and arrow, one of you guys might be breakfast," she muttered.

Memories of crossbow hunting with her father flooded in. Sitting on a low hill, their bows across their laps, and gently teasing each other. He'd been so proud to share his bow-hunting skills with her. "It gives the creature better odds," he'd say with a chuckle.

She stood and slung her pack over a shoulder, before carefully swinging open the door to the cabin. Sparse. But it wasn't like she was expecting a refrigerator and microwave. The furniture consisted of two chairs, a table, and an army cot. A built-in bench seat under the front window probably held cookware and tools. Rodent droppings lay scattered everywhere on the floor, which explained the nighttime visit from the rattlesnake.

The one splurge her parents had made was the cast-iron wood stove nestled in a corner. A fire would be cozy this morning.

But chimney smoke might alert someone she was staying up here. She was fervently hoping Estelle didn't know about the cabin, but she likely did if she'd been at the ranch for five years.

Cate opened the screenless windows and got to work sweeping the floor with a primitive broom she found behind the stove. Then she laid out her solar flashlight on the porch railing that faced east, along with a solar charging station for the extra burner phone she'd secreted away in her backpack. Only one other person had that number—Bronnie. She would give it to Levi, eventually. She just needed time to get a handle on her nerves, to calm down. Outside communication could wait a few days.

Covering the filthy table with her rain slicker, she set down her pack and pulled out breakfast—the loaf of wheat bread and jar of peanut butter, plus a small can of double espresso Bronnie had thrown in at the last minute. With her penknife, she spread a generous dollop of the peanut butter on a spongy slice, folded it in half, and gobbled it down—sort of. The dry combination proved hard to swallow, and she quickly chased it with the remaining ounce of water in her thermos. Through the window, she spotted the manual water pump at the trough. Time to see if it still worked.

The dryness of the peanut butter sandwich had brought back another time she'd lived on such food. That first day of waitressing in the East Village, nearly two decades ago. She'd stood on the sidewalk across the street from the Foxy Hound bistro, with cars and people rushing by, nervously trying to wash down her last bite of sandwich with sips from a water bottle.

Her mother had frequently mentioned Brenden Connelly, an old friend from Ireland, who owned a bistro in the Soho district. The day after she stepped off the bus at Grand Central Station, Cate had walked into the Foxy Hound bistro and asked to speak with the owner. A burly man in his fifties, with graying red hair and sky-blue eyes, had emerged from the office. She'd shown him photos of her mother and her, slipped out of the family album before Cate left home In a quavering voice, she'd told him about her parents' plane crash. Brenden had wept a bit, confiding that Fiona had been his first love. Then he'd wiped his eyes and, with hardly a glance at Cate's fake ID, had offered her a waitressing job starting that week. She had solemnly walked out of the restaurant and fist-pumped when she hit the sidewalk. *She shoots, she scores!*

The pulsing energy of the city had been intoxicating. *This is where I begin*, she remembered thinking as she stood on the busy street again. *I can be anyone I want to be in this city.*

Back on the cabin steps, a petite squirrel was playing a game of hide and seek with her. She threw her last crust of bread in its direction and headed over to fill her thermos at the hand pump. The crank was stiff but still drew up the water. She smelled a handful of it. Non-chlorinated, that was for sure.

Decades ago, Doc had told his daughters that the granite-studded mountain rising up behind the cabin was an excellent filter for the snow and rainwater that seeped into the underground aquifer. So, chances were ... slim to none that giardia lived in there? Well, she would be the test subject for sure. She leaned over to fill her thermos and another memory came: filling the water pitchers for the tables at the Foxy Hound.

Cate hadn't told her new boss Brenden that she had no waitressing experience. But learning was half the fun, right? Nor had Cate told him or anyone else she was sixteen. Not when she had masterfully forged an Arizona driver's license saying she was eighteen. Besides, she was used to hard work. Since grade school, she'd helped thoroughly clean the ranch house, buck hay at the stables, and clean the cages for her dad's veterinary business.

Her coworkers at the bistro soon learned Cate was the go-to person for icky messes. She discovered that such skills were a commodity to be traded and bartered. "Sure, I'll handle all the trash cans and clean out the coffee machines," she offered one coworker, "if you'll take my shift on Mondays so I can go to my drawing class." And so forth.

A month after starting her job, she noticed the young man sitting in the corner of the near-empty bistro one day. She'd been instantly attracted to his looks—swarthy, well-tailored, and aloof. The opposite of any boy she'd known in Arizona. Nothing about him then had seemed sinister or dangerous, not compared to finding a diamondback rattler on a dimly lit porch step.

But the most dangerous thing about a man like Joseph was the kind of people who surrounded him—his "handlers." And they were employed by his family for just one thing: damage control.

In the Finley cabin, Cate gazed out the eastern window at the sun-soaked dome of Cabeza Rock and ached to start drawing. She pulled out a small sketchpad and a tin of charcoal sticks from her pack. While her mind wandered, her fingers worked automatically to create the outline, adding contour and shading with repetitive strokes of her charcoal. Then her phone chirped loudly out on the railing and she nearly tossed her charcoal. Recovering, she walked out and checked the screen. Bronnie, of course.

All okay up there? Worried.

She picked up the phone and tapped the screen.

Snakes and rodents. Nothing I can't handle.

Levi left 2 look 4 U in Copperton. I M a bad liar and he knows it.

Cate set the phone back on the rail and wiggled her shoulders to relieve some tension. She didn't really know what to do about Levi. He was a fixer—a solver—and appeared to be really good at it. There just seemed to be no fixing the thing that had followed her back to Cabeza Valley.

Chapter 28

By mid-afternoon, Cate had distracted herself by creating her first masterpiece—a surrealist pencil drawing of Cabeza Rock. Sporting a monocle and a top hat worn at a rakish angle, the mountain evoked *New Yorker* magazine's vintage dapper mascot. To capture the rock's size and detail, she'd used four sheets from her little sketchpad and then tried to anchor the finished drawing together with some ancient duct tape she'd found hanging on a nail just outside the front door. But the tape wouldn't stick to the rough-hewn wall. She needed some nails. Several candidates were visible in the floor planks, but how to pry them loose?

The bench seat under the main window seemed an obvious place to store tools. She lifted the lid and instantly dropped it again. An animal had made a nest of shredded cloth and paper—perhaps the same one that burrowed deeper when she'd lifted the lid just now. She grabbed her snake stick and flipped up the lid while standing back. The shredded paper rustled violently, and a squirrel hopped out, scrambling for the open door.

"All right, anyone else? Let's do this!"

A smaller squirrel peered up at her before diving back into the nest. Her eye caught a familiar object in the corner of the bench cavity. A red metal file case with a handle on top. It looked like the case that had been a fixture under her mother's desk throughout Cate's childhood. She reached in with the stick, hooked the handle, and lifted it out with some effort. Sure enough, a faded label on the lid read "Important Papers" in her mother's meticulous script. What was it doing up here at the cabin?

The box was locked. Not a particularly strong or complicated lock. She thought of all the times she'd watched Fiona working at her desk with the red box in easy reach. The information she'd gone searching for in the office might very well be in there. Had her sister brought it up here for safekeeping?

The tiger was whispering to her: *Cate if you are indeed the last Finley, shouldn't you see what's in there?* Then she took the thing outside, found a rock, and smashed the lock.

An assortment of file folders greeted her—each labeled with her mother's schoolgirl-neat writing—Marriage Certificate, Passports, Car Titles, Property Titles, Births & Adoptions—*wait, what?* Cate flipped to that section and pulled out the first paper. It read "State of New Mexico, Report of Adoption" and was dated August 20, 1982. Cate saw Daniel "Doc" Finley and Fiona Willis Finley listed as adoptive parents of a thirteen-year-old female named Margaret Jean Brown, born in Albuquerque, New Mexico.

Cate stopped reading and pushed back from the table, nearly tipping the chair over. Her sister had been adopted at age thirteen? She pictured Margaret's bedroom with its lack of any grade school or baby photos. Suddenly all the peculiarities of her sister made sense—the use of their parents' first names instead of Mom and Dad, the distressing arms-length distance she maintained with Cate, and the stark contrast between Margaret's lack of interest in family photos and her intense love for the ranch animals.

Cate's eyes fell on a newer page in the file, scrawled by someone with a less tidy hand than her mother's. She took a swig from her water thermos as she scanned the sentences.

Cate,

If you're reading this, you've probably met Bronnie Taylor and know my secret. Don't blame Doc and Fiona. I begged them not to tell you. Just seemed easier.

Looking back I didn't treat you right and I'm sorry. Sorry I didn't return your calls. I'm no good for anyone. If you're home, then things are probably bad. There is someone I let stay at the ranch who you shouldn't trust. You might have already met her. I put Fiona's box up here for safekeeping. Read everything in it.

I'm sorry.

M

Reading past her sister's familiar curtness, Cate felt her sadness and despair and tried to envision a young teenage Margaret coming to live with Doc and Fiona. A girl who had been given a second chance at a happy life—like Rae coming to live with Desi.

Now that she thought about it, Margaret hadn't hit any of the adult milestones. There had been no boyfriends or fiancé, let alone a husband or children. Her closest bond seemed to be with their parents and Bronnie Taylor.

So, this was the secret Bronnie had been sworn to keep? And who the hell was Estelle, that she could wield such control over Margaret? A friend from her pre-adoption days? Cate suddenly realized she should show this letter to Jimmy. It looked like her sister was saying she didn't want Estelle in charge of the ranch. But if so, why hadn't she named her in the letter?

She skimmed through the papers again. According to the date of adoption, Margaret had enjoyed less than two years of her adoptive parents' attention before Cate was born. She imagined Margaret's despair at suddenly having to compete with a newborn. The fact went a long way to explaining her sister's coldness, even if it didn't take away the sting.

Filled with apprehension, Cate reached for the other pages in the file. The first one she touched was a State of Arizona birth certificate. She saw her name listed as the infant, then scanned down the page and saw Fiona and Doc listed as her parents. Comforted, she slipped the paper back into the file box and flipped the lid closed.

She was torn between heading back down the mountain right now to meet with Jimmy and spending another night in the cabin. The papers were in her possession now and would soon enough be in her lawyer's, although she doubted the handwritten note from Margaret would be enough to get the restraining order dropped.

She had a pounding headache, probably a combination of tension and eyestrain. Maybe another night up here would soothe her nerves and give her the strength to wage what was beginning to look like a legal battle with Estelle.

In the meantime, the cabin needed a thorough cleaning, and she needed a break from thinking. She spent the next few hours chasing dust off surfaces and clearing out the squirrel nest in the bench seat, using a dustpan made of folded art paper.

By the time she looked outside, it was nearly sundown and she was hungry again. Was that a motor getting closer? It sounded like Bronnie's old quad with its raspy muffler. She dreaded the prospect of seeing anyone right now, but at least Bronnie might bring food. If not, peanut butter sandwiches would get her through the next day or so. She swiped at the dried tears on her face and wished she had a mirror. Reading the contents of the file box had left her alternately energized and depressed. She didn't feel ready to talk about it with anyone yet.

The quad driver brought another jolt. Deputy Sheriff Miguel Gomez, having exchanged his khakis for jeans and a faded black t-shirt, hopped off and grinned at her before untying a tote bag from the cargo rack.

"Well, look who I found," he said in greeting.

Cate inclined her head. "Don't tell me—on your day off you decided to do a little four-wheeling. Kudos on getting it up that trail, but how'd you get through the locked gate?"

He lifted a bulky set of keys that she'd noticed hanging in Bronnie's kitchen. Then he shifted the bag in his arms expectantly. It was obvious he wanted an invitation to come inside. Cate was just worried why.

"You can report to the Yavapai County Court that I did not, in fact, jump bail or whatever."

"Noted, although I'm here on another matter. Can I come in?" He climbed the steps carefully, juggling the large tote as he grabbed a handrail for support. His limp was more pronounced as he stepped through the open door and awkwardly set the bag on the table.

"Bronnie sent you food, plus some clothing she bought in town, I think. Underwear, jeans—"

"Okay, stop talking about underwear," Cate cut him off, her voice suddenly shaky.

She pulled the two chairs up to the table and sat in one of them. For some reason, the tears she'd fought all afternoon were rolling down her face again. It was just—he was being so nice. It made her think of Sheriff Mack delivering the bad news about her parents.

"You ... you came to tell me ... something." Her voice was getting squeaky, and she was horrified. She brought her hand up to hold her mouth in place and smother a sob.

Staring at her intently, Gomez took a seat.

"I did. I certainly did, Cate." He paused uncertainly, then pressed on. "The girl was not lying or imagining she saw something. The dog found Margaret's scent in the pasture. He chased it all the way to the caretaker's cottage by the stables—the Ruiz family's house?" She nodded. "We found, um, significant evidence your sister had spent time in the house's cellar, probably after death. We did not find Margaret."

"Wait, the Ruizes? They're ... no, now wait! They're like family. No—"

"The older Ruizes weren't at home, but we did bring the daughter, Liliana, in for some questions. The girl is devastated and also had a solid alibi for the Friday night in question."

"We're still trying to locate the Ruiz son. We don't have a, um, body. So, technically, we can't really detain anyone yet. I just wanted to tell you that, um, there is evidence your sister is deceased, Cate."

"Okay," Cate murmured softly as she slumped in her chair. What she'd begun to suspect earlier in the week had just been confirmed. Hearing this now, made her feel empty and robbed of what she'd never had—her sister's truth, and her love. She felt beyond conflicted.

Gomez looked poised to ask a question.

"Not my real sister," was all she could say.

Gomez leaned toward her. "Pardon?"

"Just ... we weren't blood sisters." She pulled the adoption paper from under the box and passed it over to him. Then she stepped out onto the porch and watched the eastern sky turn from blue to rose.

When Cate came back into the cabin, Gomez had unwrapped two chicken salad sandwiches and handed her one. They ate in silence as the last bit of daylight faded. Suddenly exhausted, Cate didn't feel capable of more conversation. Without another word to Gomez, she climbed onto the army cot in the corner of the cabin, dragged her sleeping bag over her, and fell asleep.

Chapter 29

In the chilly early morning Cate roused, pulled on her hoodie, and stepped out onto the front porch. Gomez lay on the hammock, burrowed in a sleeping bag he'd apparently thought to bring with him.

She washed her face at the pump, then disappeared behind the rock outcropping. When she returned to the cabin, Gomez was awake and rummaging through the tote. He pulled out a bag of banana muffins and two cans of the espresso that Cate loved so much.

"Morning. I was going to leave last night, but I didn't have the heart to wake you with that noisy quad motor."

Still not quite up to conversation, Cate grimaced and mumbled, "Well, aren't you the humanitarian."

"Brr, a little nippy this morning. I was just about to crank up that magnificent stove over there."

In response, she sat down, elbows on the table, and stared straight at him. "Why did you really stay over, Gomez?"

Gomez handed her a muffin he'd carefully swaddled in a white paper napkin, an act that seemed so fatherly it momentarily distracted her.

"Uh, well, okay… " Suddenly he looked less confident than he had the previous evening. "You lived in New York before Los Angeles, right?"

"For over a decade and a half. That's not a secret." She watched his weathered face struggle with finding the precise words. "Oh, just get on with it." Irritation was rising in her like a thick soup on boil.

"Bronnie told me a little about why you came up here to the cabin. You have someone stalking you, someone from New York?" He looked at her for a reaction. "Thing is, I think I know why. A decade back, I was working out of Precinct Nine, Lower Manhattan."

Cate had dropped her muffin on the table and was on her feet. The man was both wily and patient, she'd give him that.

"Wait, I just—I mean, the news barely covered it," he continued. "I don't even remember reading your name. Just a whisper through the precinct that a Russo family member had nearly killed some woman, put her in a coma."

He paused for her to comment but she didn't feel like speaking or moving.

"Then I remembered you from that one photo they ran, what, a year later? You were wedged between two officers coming out of a courtroom?"

She just stared at him, feeling flushed, breathless, and fascinated all at once. At what point in the last week had he recognized her?

Gomez gave up on her response and leaned back to focus on his last bit of muffin.

"I get why you don't trust anyone, Cate. That family ... Look, would you relax a little? If I'd come to do you harm or something, don't you think I'd have done it by now?"

His smile was amiable, his manner relaxed. Like her father trying to treat a skittish horse. She slowly sat back down. He pushed her half-eaten muffin toward her. "You look like the photo but, well, different. That's why I wasn't sure at first."

"I was still swollen from surgery after the 'accident.' His family paid to fix my face."

"Yeah, least they could do, right? A mystery how he could

run for office, like he's doing now, instead of spending time behind bars. People's memories are worthless. Nobody remembers further than fifteen, twenty minutes ago."

"You did," Cate said. She picked up her muffin and took a small bite, still wary.

"You were fighting him over custody, right?"

"My—our son ... Will." Out the window, the sun lit up patches of the field. "I haven't seen him in over four years, since I crashed his thirteenth birthday party on ... on Long Island." Images of endless green velvet lawns, Will in the distance playing soccer, the party decorations flapping in the wind.

Gomez was nodding as he munched. "See, that's New York. People with money take you to court to get control of what they want. And if that doesn't work, well, they fix it with a fist."

Wow, almost poetic, Deputy Gomez. She gave him a grudging smile and he grinned back. No doubt he had been a good-looking man in his earlier decades. A Mediterranean ruggedness.

"Look, Deputy G—"

"Hey, it's my day off, so ... Miguel." He flashed the wolf grin again.

"All right, Miguel. You seem likable enough. A good listener. Assets in your profession, no doubt."

"Thanks." His eyes narrowed, waiting for more.

"Just the kind of person they would send to ... talk to me."

"Who, the Russos?"

She laughed, gazing out toward Cabeza Rock.

"Of course not. You're not wearing Armani. No, I mean the candidate he's running against. Janssen? They're the ones reaching out lately. They want to use my story against the Russo machine so he never gets a shot at governor."

Gomez nodded and sat back.

"When they first got in touch in LA, they said it would come out whether or not I told the story. I said I wasn't an idiot and that the attack was still just hearsay until I went public. I've seen what the media—regular and social—do to women who tell their stories, especially during a campaign. Excuse me if I don't jump at the chance to be exploited and then gutted." Final answer. She threw the last of the banana muffin in her mouth.

He wasn't with Janssen's team. Too much of a lone ranger. Too soft-hearted to be anything but a *simpatico*. Bronnie's *simpatico*, it appeared. Gomez, Levi, Jimmy, all the good guys showing up in her life these days. Where had they been a decade ago?

Cate took a deep breath. "Who am I kidding? It's worse than just getting trashed on social media. Russo's camp gave me a message right before I left New York: Cate, you're expendable. Speak out on anything and you're dead."

She tried to keep her voice from shaking. This conversation was bringing it to the surface again, and she did not want to cry in front of this man, no matter how nice he appeared.

"If I speak out, maybe a month or two will go by. But they'll find me. I'll be another tragic story on one of those true crime shows. I'll disappear just like Margaret did. Only this time it will be without any trace."

Chapter 30

By late morning, Gomez was preparing to leave and go get his dog, Jorge, whom he'd left in the care of Desi and her family. He pulled out a folded paper from his overnight bag. It was Margaret's note to Cate.

"Thanks for letting me take this along. It might be supporting evidence if and when your sister's case goes to trial. Jimmy can drop by the station and get a copy for his purposes."

He leaned in confidentially from where he was seated on the quad. "Cate, please take care of yourself. You got a lot of people concerned about you."

She shot him a doubtful look. Levi, Jimmy, and Bronnie for sure, but it was hard to believe anyone else gave a rip about her in this town. Noting her reaction, he took on a more business-like tone.

"We're following up on that dinner party—the guests' names you gave me at the hospital. And thanks for the sketch of the one guy, Gabe. You're skilled. It's nearly as good as a photo. I'm tempted to use facial recognition software and see if he's known in any databases."

"Well, look through the New York State Bar roster first. Something about him screams lawyer, the headline-chasing kind."

Miguel nodded and started the quad.

"Hey, Miguel?" He shut off the noisy engine. "You know Estelle's trying to pull something here with this restraining order. She ... smashed her own face and did all that damage to herself. How crazy do you have to be—?"

The man had enough class to look sheepish as he cut her off. "I'm so sorry, Cate, but I can't comment on that one. It's Detective Royce's case. Just … keep in touch with Jimmy Baker about the order of protection. He'll have updates for you." He started the quad and put it in gear. "Sorry," he repeated before roaring off across the meadow.

Well, full marks to Gomez for keeping ethical boundaries, she thought. He'd probably catch hell from the sheriff's office if they knew he'd spent the night up here. Unprofessional association or whatever. She watched the quad reach the trailhead and disappear over the ridge.

Gomez had told her to take care of herself. But how could she really take care with so many loose ends to gather up? Who was Gabe? Why had Diego Junior been so pissed off at their first meeting? And had he really been the one who'd done something to her sister? Or had he assisted someone else?

She thought of Bella dying in the field as a tractor rolled toward her. Then she imagined Margaret being dragged through the same field, stashed in a cellar, and most likely loaded into a car to be driven off—to somewhere. A flash of D.J. Ruiz's dark expression and angry words on the day she'd arrived in Cabeza Valley. That had been a week after Rae saw Margaret's body in the pasture. It was painful for her to think the Ruiz family might be mixed up in this in any way.

With Gomez gone, Cate went back to the bench seat and opened the lid. Something else had been hiding in there. Another gift from Margaret.

She pulled out the molded black plastic box and set it on the table. Familiar gold initials reflected in the window light—*MJF*. Unlatching and lifting the lid, she peered down at the Walther

PK380 semiautomatic with two extra magazines. Oh, it was loaded all right; she'd checked yesterday. Maybe tonight she'd build that fire in the stove.

#

By mid-afternoon, slate-gray monsoon clouds had gathered on the horizon. Cate could see a brooding clump of them migrating toward her from across the valley. Silvery sheets of rain hung from the clouds, promising a dense downpour when they arrived. Her flashlight was charged, and she'd carried several armloads of firewood from the stack behind the cabin. Although intense, the monsoon storms of her childhood had always passed through quickly. As long as you weren't in a flood plain or standing by a solitary tree in a flat pasture, there was little threat from a downpour or lightning strike. In the meantime, she relished the opportunity to read a few more of the Finley family documents.

Out came the red file box, just as a flash of light outside preceded a deafening thunder crack. Droplets began to hit the tin roof, soon rising to a cacophony of noise. The view out the windows was obscured by cascades of falling water. "Rain on steroids" was how her father described the summer monsoons.

When the full deluge hit the cabin, she glanced up to see how the roof was faring. Still watertight. The rain let up after about ten minutes, only to return with the same intensity a few minutes later. Such was the pattern over the next two hours.

Cate surveyed her full jug of water, the remaining food from Bronnie, and the bulk of firewood next to the stove and knew all her creature needs were being met. All except companionship. She peered down at the sketch she'd drawn on her pad to calm her nerves during the loudest part of the storm. It was a study of a tousle-haired young man sitting on a park bench and leaning forward. His hands cradled his face, where a soft smile had captured his broad features. Amused eyes stared back at the viewer. She wondered what Levi had found to do in a cow town like Copperton and if he would ever forgive her for ghosting him.

Digging through the file box again, a thick folder marked "Estate Planning" drew Cate's interest. She selected a faded manila envelope addressed to Doc and Fiona Finley. Her mother had neatly lettered across its front, "File Copy—Updated Will 5/10/2000." Bingo, the will she'd gone searching for in the office. Cate lifted out the thick sheaf of papers that had last been handled by her parents the very month they'd died. Just what had they updated?

Cate's name turned up all over the document, which was astonishing. Only fifteen when her parents died, she couldn't recall even attending a reading of the will or Margaret sharing any details on the estate with her. She had assumed she stood to inherit it when her sister passed, just as Doc had done when his older brother died.

Words jumped out at her from the page listing the distribution of assets to heirs.

"To our daughter, Caitlyn Willis Finley, we bequeath one-half of the entirety of our estate, to be held in trust until she reaches her twenty-first birthday."

Cate poured over the list of assets, which included the ranch, its livestock, and vehicles, valued at nearly four million dollars; an investment portfolio totaling seven hundred fifty thousand; and a half-million-dollar life insurance policy. The phrase "to be held in trust" kept haunting her. In trust by whom? Margaret?

Her head was starting to ache with nagging questions. Why hadn't Margaret ever told her about her inheritance? Why hadn't Cate ever asked about it? Had Margaret's coldness and hostility toward her really killed all her curiosity back then? True, the two of them hadn't shared many conversations after their parents' deaths, save the ones about Cate's education and career direction, which Cate had heatedly rejected. If she hadn't pushed back so much on Margaret's plans for her, what would her life have been like today?

Cate stopped reading and closed her eyes. There was too much to process here, between her conflicted feelings toward Margaret and eyestrain from reading. She picked up the phone and dialed Jimmy's number. He had said this was his wheelhouse.

A familiar feeling was coming over her. Once again, she'd trusted the wrong person, and it had cost her.

Chapter 31

September 6, 2000, New York City

Cate awoke on a bed of roses. Pale yellow blooms with blushing edges. A vague memory came, someone giving them to her, of holding them in a bouquet, of leaning forward to smell their elegant fragrance. Now they were scattered across the bed with abandon, their petals bruised and wilted, even as the scent lingered.

Moving her legs, she realized with a start that she was completely naked under the sheets. There was a sharp pain between her legs and warm liquid seeping down there. When she lifted the covers, the welts and smears of blood brought her to a sitting position, wildly scanning her surroundings. *Oh, my God, where am I? What happened?*

Her head throbbed as she strained to remember the night before. The last thing she could recall was sharing the back seat of a black town car with Joseph Russo. The clink of champagne glasses. A toast to their second date and to her "eighteenth" birthday. Then nothing until she awoke just now. What had he done to her? As she twisted around to search the room, she felt the pain inside her—raw and bruised ... violated. Her head pounded. The wine. Her stomach lurched. The pasta. Now she remembered there had been a candlelit dinner.

Where was she—a locked room in someone's house? The sudden thought sent her out of bed. The door opened onto a lit hallway and she heard the faint hydraulics of an elevator. An apartment? A hotel?

Back at the bedside, a folded card stood upright, bearing a hotel name and location on the Upper West Side. She was still in New York, at least. A wave of relief gave way to nausea and she headed for the bathroom. Drinking water straight from the faucet, she ignored its off taste as her parched mouth hungrily grabbed for more. Without thinking, she turned on the shower and let it run to hot.

Last night, Joseph had taken her out on a date, supposedly to celebrate her eighteenth birthday. It was her birthday, all right, her seventeenth. And this wasn't how a date should end. She knew what her mother would have called it.

When Cate had arrived in the city, three months earlier, she'd been cautioned about people who would smile at you, convince you to come closer, then steal things out of your pocket or grab your purse. Joseph's smile had been endless on their second date. More than he had ever done as a customer at the bistro.

When they'd first started spending time together, it was just fun walks around the village after her shift ended, swapping stories and laughing easily. Once she'd called him Joe, only to be corrected sternly. Joe Russo was an uncle whom he despised. He would only answer to Joseph. Cate liked the name because it made her think of the Bible story of Joseph and his many-colored coat.

He said he was planning to go into real estate, make a ton of money, and "own this town." She'd teased that maybe then he could afford to buy one of her paintings. They'd both laughed, then hugged, which had led to their first kiss.

When he'd asked her out on a date, she'd accepted easily, thinking this was the kind of boy her parents would have wanted for her. He was well-dressed, clean-shaven, and polite. His family had lived in New York for a long time, albeit in a suburb called Long Island. He was the opposite of her boyfriend Drew back in Arizona—in appearance, in education, in goals for his life. He *had* goals for his life.

When he'd picked her up for her first date, he'd been stunningly dressed, like out of a menswear magazine. Not for the first time, she'd wondered at his age. While he talked about the college courses he was taking and his round-cheeked face looked youthful, he spoke with the maturity of someone a decade older.

As he helped her into the black town car, she caught him eyeing her casual gray knit tunic over plaid leggings and scuffed Dr. Martens boots with a slight frown on his face. But the rest of the night, he never gave her clothes another glance.

From the outside, the restaurant had looked too small to do much business, but once inside it was spacious and exquisite—an ornate cavern. She imagined Alice following the White Rabbit down its hole and winding up in such a place.

Everything on that first date with Joseph had been so magical and romantic that when he'd asked her out again—this time to celebrate what she'd whispered to him would actually be her eighteenth birthday—she'd happily agreed.

"I want to do it up right for your eighteenth, Cate. Welcome you to adulthood."

On September 6th at 9:15, Joseph was waiting in the town car outside the bistro again. This time, Cate wore a short, sleeveless dress of mauve velvet over sheer black tights and her boots. She'd felt the outfit stayed true to her artistic side but was fancy enough for another posh dining experience.

He had an open bottle of champagne and two long slender glasses. It was like something out of *Cinderella*. They'd sipped and talked and laughed while the car made its way uptown and then through Central Park. The driver had let them off outside a midtown restaurant connected to an elegant-looking hotel.

Inside the lobby, Joseph had led her into a private alcove, where they'd ordered linguini with red clam sauce and more champagne.

"This place ... so much history. Do you like history? In the early twentieth century, around World War One, some famous writers and intellectuals met here and formed a round table of Manhattan *literati*."

Cate nodded and emptied her champagne glass, imagining famous people seated at the table next to them. She wished she could look up the meaning of "literati," as it sounded so beautiful. He was trying so hard to show her *his* New York—different from the one she saw every day in the East Village. He'd been so polite, so respectable, so attentive to her. Apart from her parents, no one had ever shown her that kind of attention.

Now in this strange hotel room where she'd awoken alone, she stepped into a hot shower, desperate to rinse off the entire night. Something on her upper chest stung and she glanced down to see a red circle above her left breast. She dragged herself out and to the mirror, gasping. Someone had bitten her hard enough to draw blood. A perfect set of upper and lower teeth marks. A whimper escaped her throat. She'd been drugged, hurt, raped. She should ... she should call the police, right? She should report this. Her whole pelvic area throbbed.

Then she thought about what would be involved in talking to the police—the kind of questions she would be asked. Did she know her attacker? Yes. Was she sexually active? No. But she and Drew had gotten pretty close, right before she'd gone off to boarding school. And anyway, these were questions she didn't think she could bear to be asked.

Mostly, though, she worried they would discover her fake ID. What would Brenden say when he found out? He'd have to fire her when he found out the truth. What would she do then? Call her sister? Cate winced, imagining how that conversation might go.

Now the tears were coming. She couldn't report it. She ... she didn't know—wouldn't be able to say what happened. Did she really want to risk losing what had taken so much to achieve?

I want out of here, she thought as she stumbled back to the bedroom. Someone had folded her clothing on the chair, her Doc Martens placed neatly beneath. Joseph? Had he stared down at her while he carefully folded her things? How long had he played with her like a rag doll while she lay there, completely knocked out and helpless?

She dressed and summoned the courage to walk out into the hotel corridor in her date clothes. Right before the lights had gone out in the town car, she'd felt his arm around her shoulders, drawing her in. Then she'd awakened this morning, feeling like a used and wadded-up tissue. Pressing the elevator button, Cate looked down the hall to see where the wailing child was and realized the sound was in her own head.

On a night when she should have been celebrating with people who cherished her, Cate learned for the first time that people could be both charming and treacherous. Later, she would hear it called psychopathy or an antisocial personality, fancy terms that warn you not to trust what you are seeing and hearing. You had to develop a feel for it, like the sense that told you if a horse was going to buck you off, or when a dog had bite in him, or if a schoolmate was going to trash you behind your back.

Every morning, she would examine the bite wound over her left breast. It was finally healing, but she feared it would leave a scar. Mostly she feared she would see it every time she looked in the mirror, even if others didn't. So, when it was sufficiently healed, she stopped at the tattoo shop that sat opposite the Foxy Hound. She emerged two hours later with the small owl perched on a dream-catcher, inked above her heart. She prayed that the combined symbols would give her future wisdom and protection against snakes and other predators.

For a while, Cate feared she would encounter Joseph in the bistro again, that he'd pretend like nothing had happened. But he never did come back. *Good riddance,* she'd thought. She'd rather devote her lonely nights to her artwork than feel that vulnerable with anyone ever again.

Then she found out she was pregnant.

Chapter 32

August 11, 2019, Finley Cabin

She is on a rollercoaster, climbing high above a fair. Crowds of people swarm below her. As the cart crests the highest hill and begins to speed up, she sees the dark-haired little boy standing apart, his arms stretched out to her. A man stands behind him, his hands over the boy's eyes.

"Mama, I love you. Where are you?" the boy shouts.

She reaches for him but her car rushes past and then heads down and quickly around the tracks until it slows to climb again. She is looking everywhere for the boy. She can't see him, but she hears his voice.

"Mama, I can't see you! Where are you?" He gropes toward her blindly, but the man pulls him away and the crowd swallows them up. She tries to get out of the car, but it has taken her up so high, up into the clouds. Finally, she climbs on top of the car, her arms spread like wings. "Wait!" she calls out to the boy. "Wait..." A red-tailed hawk sailing high above her swoops down to brush its wing against her face.

Cate came to with a start. In the morning light, she stared straight into Levi's eyes. He had been stroking her face and now sat back in a crouch next to the cot. He reached up to the table for the drawing of the man on the bench.

"So, you *were* thinking of me."

Cate swallowed, feeling tears welling. Then she dove forward and grabbed him in a fierce hug. His arms wrapped around her gently and they stayed that way for a moment. Finally, she pushed him back and held his face.

"What you must think of me, of all this."

"What, that you have family problems?" His smile had sadness as he pulled her in. "You should see what's happening with mine right now." He gave her a kiss on the top of her head, gently laid her back on the cot, and stood up. "I came to say goodbye for now. Have to get back to LA. My sister's in the hospital, and her fourteen-year-old is running things at the house—er, at my house," he added a little sheepishly.

Once again, a reminder he'd kept his own secrets from her. She was still adjusting to his actually having a home.

"What? What happened?" Cate pulled a hoodie over her tank top. The rains had cooled the cabin considerably overnight.

"A bad marriage happened. Talia's going to be okay. Couple broken ribs and a leg fracture from when he pushed her down the front steps." He scowled as he spoke about it. "But our fierce mama is arriving, and if I time it right, I can pick her up at LAX. She's a *matai* in our *'āiga,* which makes no sense to you, but trust me, it's a big deal back in Samoa. She'll set things straight."

"You'll take Max?"

He shook his head and gave a quiet chuckle.

"I got a rental up in Copperton. You know I love that truck, but Max has seen better days."

"Max and me both," she said. Tears spilled as she recalled the dream she'd been having just before he woke her.

"All right, enough. You can't say that about someone I love. Come on, show me the tiger. Where is she? Grr!" He held his curled fingers up like claws.

Cate gave him a reluctant smile and lifted her fingers weakly. "Gr."

"And also, do you have a permit or even any training for *this*?" He pulled the Walther out of his pocket, which she'd laid on the floor next to the cot the night before. "Because the safety was off."

"Yes, sir, I have training." She'd grown up with gun safety training from her father, but after Joseph's attack, Cate had secretly gotten in some practice at a firing range in New Jersey. In the end, Cate had decided against buying a weapon due to the dreaded background check. Still, it gave her some satisfaction to picture Joseph's face each time she shot at the gun range.

Seeing Levi now ready to leave, Cate made a quick decision.

"Wait, can you give me about five minutes?" She ran back into the cabin, packed up the Walther, safety now on, stuffed it and a file of assorted documents she'd pulled from the red box into her backpack. Then she put the box back in the bench seat, straightened her sleeping bag on the cot, and closed the door to the little cabin.

"I need that long-overdue talk with Jimmy at his law offices."

As they descended the mountain, the freshly washed green valley sparkled below them like the Emerald City of Oz. They walked through the shadow of Cabeza Rock and Cate spoke of her hilarious first attempts to climb it as a teenager, aided by the equally inept Drew.

"We had no idea what real rock-climbing equipment looked like. Drew swiped his mother's clothesline, and I snuck some riding helmets out of the tack room. At first, we couldn't get higher than ten feet. Luckily, the ground was soft for the dozen times we fell back down. Then, one day, we got halfway up but couldn't figure out the descent. Cue the mountain rescue team."

"Ironically, that snooty boarding school where Margaret sent me turned me into the climber I am today. They imported actual Himalayan Sherpas to teach us," she said as they continued walking.

Levi looked at her, eyes wide, and shook his head.

"In Samoa, our mountains breathe fire, so surviving a fall from one is not even an option. I think you'd love hiking the Tafua Rim, though." For the first time, she was seeing the nostalgia he felt for his island home. She bumped his shoulder with hers, playfully.

"Hey, I would love the chance to climb your fiery mountain," she murmured with a wink. He raised his eyebrows and guffawed in surprise.

Until now, she'd forgotten the details of that ill-fated first climb up Cabeza Rock back when she was fifteen. At the peak of their ascent, she and Drew had shared a joint he'd brought along. When the rescue crew recovered them from that ledge Cate had been higher than a kite. That had been the real reason her father grounded her right before her parents' trip to Baja.

The year they died marked the end of Cate's childhood and the beginning of a harsh reality. All of it—her parents' death, her banishment to boarding school, Drew's sudden disappearance, and the long bus ride to New York—had created a desperate loneliness in her. No wonder she'd been drawn to a charming guy like Joseph Russo.

Chapter 33

August 11, Bronnie's Cottage

For once, Cate was relieved that Bronnie was working at the hospital. Theirs would be an awkward conversation where Cate asked whether Bronnie knew about Margaret's adoption—family friend that she was—and about Cate inheriting half the ranch back when she turned twenty-one.

After leaving a message for Jimmy to call her, Cate took a much-needed shower while Levi fixed some eggs with freshly baked sweet coconut bread in the kitchen of the gingerbread house. The food was simple but immensely satisfying. Sitting across from him at Bronnie's kitchen table brought back their months of sharing breakfasts in the camper truck. How different Levi seemed now. More animated and somehow more accessible. They had both been hiding parts of themselves.

"*Fa'a papa*?" she asked, trying out her pronunciation of the sweet bread, and he nodded. "How do I get you to cook like this all the time?"

"You got to marry me, woman," he teased.

She snorted. "So, living in sin for a few years would be out of the question?"

He grimaced. "Remember, I'm a *matai*'s son. The standards are higher."

"The day I meet your fierce *matai* mother, I'll need to bring Tiger Cate for sure."

Levi guffawed and Cate summoned the nerve to ask a question that had been on her mind all week.

"Um, Levi? Just how old are you?"

He gave her a wide grin.

"I turned thirty in May. Would have invited you to the birthday barbecue but, at the time, I thought it'd be a serious breach of our, um, mutual privacy agreement."

Cate had liked that, how he'd respected her privacy. It had completely disarmed her and fostered a rare feeling of intimacy with this man, who was now turning out to be an enigma. The question that had been on her mind the last few days suddenly bubbled to the surface.

"Levi, you weren't homeless when we met, so why did you pretend to be?"

Now it was his turn to look uncomfortable.

"I really was having a bad headache that day. Just sat on the bench to, you know, rest. Next thing I knew this cute girl was teasing me from the cab of her truck. She kind of assumed I was homeless and I kind of wanted her to keep talking to me."

"So, a ploy to pick up girls?" She grabbed their plates and took them to the sink, trying to suppress a laugh as she recalled their first conversation. But she also understood. The only reason she'd spoken to him that day was because he seemed slightly worse off than her.

With a deep sigh, Levi followed her over to the sink, gently took hold of her shoulders, and turned her to face him.

"Listen to me, Cate. I know I haven't been completely straight with you about my situation. But that doesn't mean I'm not worried about leaving you here, given all that's happened—" He seemed to search for the right words. "G'ah, I wish I could just bubble-wrap you!"

Still scowling, he leaned down and kissed her. Their first real one. Nice. She pulled him down for another one. He leaned back and stared hard into her eyes.

"Promise to do nothing stupid 'til I get back, okay?"

Feeling equal parts slighted and amused, Cate grimaced back at him.

"What? Oh sure, I get ya. And I promise, I won't. I'll lock all the doors and lie low in the gingerbread house with Mr. Walther stuffed between the sofa cushions." His alarmed look prompted her to add, "Safety on."

She reached to touch his face. "Levi, thank you for everything you've done."

He leaned in for one more kiss and headed for the door. It took a moment for her to recover. Oh, boy, she was in it now.

#

In the afternoon, Cate left another message on Jimmy's voicemail— "Hey there, Where are you? I need your expertise as an estate lawyer."

Then, feeling antsy and useless, she spent several hours doing what she called "therapeutic cleaning." With a half-dozen cats now in residence, Bronnie's cottage needed the attention and Cate wanted to surprise the woman before she returned from the hospital.

Surfaces were dusted, floors swept and then mopped, cat boxes were emptied and replaced, the fridge received a thorough wipe-down, and the shower got a good scrubbing. For a while, the heavy labor kept dark thoughts in check. Finding the papers at the cabin had filled her with new anxiety and burning questions she needed to have answered.

By the time Cate looked at the clock, it was already six. Where was Bronnie? Her nursing shift had ended at three and she was home usually by four-thirty or five, even with a stop at the store.

Cate lay back in the recliner, with a microfleece throw and two sleeping kittens in her lap, wondering what to do next. The next time she came to, the clock said ten-thirty and her lap was empty. The couch was just a few steps away, and the microfleece came with her.

Chapter 34

In the cool of the morning, she got up to shut the kitchen windows and still didn't see Bronnie's car in the drive. Had she worked a double shift? She'd texted Bronnie last night, but her phone showed no answer. This time she called, and it went straight to voicemail.

"Hi, there. Didn't know if you'd heard that I came back down. Gomez told me what ... what they'd discovered about Margaret and I'm ... dealing with that reality. Bronnie, I need to talk to you about a few things I found—" She paused to find the right words, and the recording shut off. With a sigh, she turned to go make coffee.

Cate heard the rumble of a car engine pulling up to the cottage and hurried to the window, only to see a sheriff's SUV instead of Bronnie's Volvo. Gomez was riding shotgun this time, and his expression looked grim.

Dreading more bad news, she sipped coffee and watched the two officers walk around the outside of the cottage as if searching for something. When she finally opened the front door and leaned out, the relief on Gomez's face was unmistakable.

"Hello, I'm home from the hills," she said stiffly. It felt awkward to see him after their time at the cabin.

"Hello, Cate," he answered in his deputy voice. "We were hoping to find Bronnie Taylor at home."

"She ... she hasn't been here since I got back yesterday morning." A finger of fear strummed her ribcage. "Why?"

Gomez's partner, whose name tag read "Deputy Tom Friendly," took out his notepad and looked at it.

"Um, we've had a report of what appears to be a silver Volvo at the bottom of a ravine, about halfway up Cold Springs Road."

"Wha-at?" was all she could say. Instantly she was back in Bronnie's old Volvo the day they'd driven it down from Copperton. She imagined it catapulting off the steep road and tumbling down the mountain, with Bronnie still at the wheel.

"That's why I was kind of hoping to find her car parked down here," Gomez said gently.

Cate was remembering Estelle's snarky comment to her on the day they'd first met—*"So, has the town started to form a search party? Bronnie Taylor and her cronies?"* Had Bronnie's hospitality to Cate given Estelle a reason to harm her?

"Is there a rescue team at the site? If she's down there, she … could need help—"

"Cate, it's a long way down, about two hundred feet or more. They're dropping a man by helicopter. But—"

"I need to get up there—" She headed to the living room for her shoes and the truck keys. Gomez followed, his voice low and measured.

"No you don't, Cate," Gomez said so sharply that Cate turned to look at him. "It's tight parking and some emergency response vehicles are already headed to the scene." He gestured to the sofa. "Let's just sit for a minute. I want to ask you some questions about Bronnie's state of mind this past week."

Cate perched on the edge of the sofa, feeling too antsy to relax.

"State of mind? You mean, did she drive over a cliff on purpose?"

"We don't even know if that's her car," Deputy Friendly

chimed in.

"Gee, I wonder how many silver Volvos there are in Cabeza Valley, population four hundred and fifty?" She caught Gomez's warning look and took a breath. "What's making you ask about her state of mind?"

"We first tried to contact her at the hospital, but she'd left work early saying she was sick. Then we find out she didn't come home."

Cate let that sink in. "She ... was fine when we texted the night before last." Then she realized how stupid that sounded. She couldn't possibly know her mental state through an electronic message, or if it was even Bronnie she'd been messaging with. She pulled out her phone to look at the exchange.

Bronnie: **how's it going up there?**

Cate: **swell, nd a shower.**

Bronnie: **i bet. lightning come close?**

Cate: **no, nice show tho**

Bronnie: **food?**

Cate: **ate most of it. got any protein bars?**

Bronnie: **ill bring some up by quad in am. need to talk w you**

That had been late morning, the day before yesterday. Later that night, Cate had fallen asleep for eight delicious hours and awakened to Levi caressing her face. Levi! He would have been the last to see Bronnie. She texted him.

know ur busy but nd to talk urgent

Then she realized she was texting from her new phone number and added,

xoxo cate.

Gomez and Friendly had been inspecting the rest of the cottage and were gazing through the office door when Cate caught up with them.

"Unfortunately, I spent some time cleaning house when I got back yesterday. I didn't get as far as the office, but you can see from just its state that the whole cottage needed it," Cate confessed.

The officers exchanged a look. They walked in, carefully side-stepping the debris on the floor.

"My opinion, office looks tossed," murmured Friendly. "Was anyone else staying here besides you?"

"My friend Levi came over from LA to help spring me from jail." That got his attention, but a head shake from Gomez told him not to pursue. "I just sent him a text to call me."

As if on cue, her phone rang. She stepped out to the kitchen to answer. At first, there was only traffic noise and a siren. She took the phone off speaker.

"Levi?"

"Hey, Cate. Sorry, I'm outside the hospital. What's—"

Cate rushed on, not sure she could trust herself not to break down.

"They think they've spotted Bronnie's car at the bottom of a ravine off Cold Creek Road."

"What—where?" More traffic noises and a siren. It was like trying to hold a conversation at a busy intersection.

She raised her voice and enunciated each word. "Her car might have run off the road up to Copperton."

"Is she okay?" The noise quieted as he moved indoors somewhere.

"No one knows, still trying to get to the car. Levi, how did she seem when you last talked to her?"

"Well, she wasn't at home when I came out of the camper

yesterday morning. I don't think she came home from work the previous night. At least, I didn't see her, but then I wasn't looking too hard. I just got up and headed to the cabin on the trail she'd told me about a few days ago."

"Okay, another question: What was the state of the house the last time you saw it, say the night before last?"

"Fine. Lots of cats on the couch but everything in its cozy place, I guess."

"So, it didn't look like someone had ransacked it?"

He hesitated. "Not … not that I could tell. You okay, Cate? Should I come back?"

Yes, Levi! Come back and hold me again. Make all this go away.

"No, your family needs you right now. Thanks for asking, though. I … I love that you offered."

On his end, she heard an ambulance start up. He raised his voice to compete with it.

"What? I couldn't—did you just say you loved me?"

She fought the urge to laugh—inappropriate, somehow.

"Yes, you stinker. I do—that thing," she murmured back, acutely aware that the deputies were eavesdropping.

"Someday I'll get you to say … 'that thing.' Listen, call me if you get news on Bronnie. I gotta bring the car back to Chaparral Rentals in Copperton, anyway."

Relief. "Okay, good. I mean, I'll see you soon, then. Bye." Putting away her phone she thought, *I'm falling for you, Levi—there. Easy for the mind, hard for the mouth.* She turned to the waiting men.

"Sounds like she's been gone for a couple of days. Did you hear anything from the crash site?"

"No, but we're headed back up there," Friendly said, heading for the door.

"Don't suppose you would let me tag along." She tried not to sound needy, but a dark cloud was descending again, making her desperate for distraction.

"Until we know what we've got, it would be better if you stayed," Gomez told her gently. "I know Bronnie would like someone watching her place and her animals while she's ... away."

Cate nodded, tears welling in her eyes. "Sure, that's—that's okay."

She watched through the window as the SUV carefully backed out of the densely shrouded yard, feeling that familiar sense of loss and loneliness that had haunted her since her teens. In the past, the only way she'd been able to ward off depression was to create something out of the turmoil she was feeling. But first, with her new sense of self protection, she did a quick check that all the windows were shut and locked, along with the front, patio, and kitchen doors.

Cate checked that the gun was between the cushions, safety on, then pulled out her artist case and a three-by-four-foot canvas that had been leaning against the wall.

She sat cross-legged in front of its blankness, staring. Soon, cerulean blue swirled on the canvas. She played with shaping the color and pushing the edges out until it became a deep, murky cave. Next came thick slashes of red and violet, followed by thin green edging. It felt comforting to work the intensity of the hues onto the canvas. She abandoned herself to the abstract color blocks, using a thin knife to scrape off paint and form words.

I ache 4 u Margaret

I ache 4 u Bronnie

I ache 4 u Will
I ache 4 u Bella
I ache 4 u all

B.E. JACKSON

I ache 4 u Will
I ache 4 u Bella
I ache 4 u all

PART III – History

"History is who we are and why we are the way we are."
—David McCullough

Chapter 35

January 2, 2007 New York City

Cate pulled up the collar of her son's coat to protect his neck from the arctic blast as they waited for the light to change. People had told her this winter was a heat wave compared to previous decades, but it hadn't felt that way when Cate led Will out of the one-bedroom they shared with another single mom and her kids on the lower east side of Manhattan.

"First day of school, Will," she chirped excitedly, ignoring the tiny scowl on his face.

While he got on well with adults, her son seemed shy around other children. He'd told her at breakfast he wasn't looking forward to his first day in a room full of them. Cate blamed the homeschooling, which had been their only choice when they'd lived at the artist commune in Woodstock.

So much had changed, on a national and a personal level, since the day she'd taken that home pregnancy test. When she first found out, her boss, Brenden, had been unbelievably kind, letting her continue to waitress into her sixth month. By that time, Cate had joined her friend Dexter's artist collective as an intern and was helping construct edgy window and in-store displays for stores in upper Manhattan. As her due date approached, however, Dexter and his partner Perry had insisted she get out of the city.

"Give yourself and the kid a chance at some decent air," Dex had chided good-naturedly in early March of 2001, as he handed her a bus ticket to their friends' communal farm in upstate New York.

Leaving the East Village behind had felt devastating, but the life growing inside her had demanded she look at "the bigger picture." At least that was what the priest had said on the day she'd gone to Our Lady of Victory Church seeking forgiveness for the sin of being young and stupid. That had followed the brutal phone call to Margaret, where her sister had told her she could come home but not with a "bun in the oven."

Much to her relief, the artists' commune had supported her pregnancy from the moment she arrived, supplying a midwife and helping her seamlessly blend mothering into her other responsibilities on the farm. "Creativity is always a blessing," was their loving motto. Indeed, Will's arrival in May had been joyous, followed by a blissful summer spent working in the communal greenhouses and improving her oil painting skills.

On September 11th, Cate had spent three early morning hours in the greenhouse before striding into the cafeteria for breakfast, toting Will in his baby carrier. No one was sitting at the tables. Instead, twenty people surrounded the vintage television the collective used to keep up on the news. Peeking over a shoulder, Cate had caught the very moment the second tower fell at the World Trade Center. Throughout that day, she and the other members had run the gamut from numb shock to wailing grief. Something had broken in the world. Something it would take years to heal, if it ever could.

Now, nearly six years later, the entire collective had moved back to the city for work. Offered a position on their project staff, Cate had a chance to earn real money, not just barter for meals and a bed.

To do that, she would need to put Will in traditional school.

She knew entering him halfway through the school year would be socially stressful, and she hoped this first day would go well.

It took just minutes to walk from their apartment on Orchard Street to the grammar school on Essex. Growing up on a ranch out west, Cate had endured flying spit wads, food fights, and general mayhem as her school bus made the daily hour-long trip to the town of Copperton. The sons and daughters of Cabeza Valley were a hard group to win over. However, it did help that their families relied on her dad's veterinary skills to treat their beloved pets and livestock. She wished she could send Will off with the same insurance policy on his first day.

As they neared the school, Cate noticed a shiny black Lincoln Town Car parked along the curb, its uniformed driver just opening the backseat door. She thought of the last time she'd ridden in such a car, of what had lain in wait for her that night. Her grip tightened on her son's hand as they walked past the vehicle. She turned her head to glance down at Will, and nearly collided with a well-dressed man emerging from the town car.

"Oh, I'm sorry," she said instinctively, then gave him a second look. Clad in an elegant black wool coat and an Ascot cap, the man stared back at her as he helped a stylishly dressed young woman climb out and stabilize on her towering Louis Vuitton heels. Cate and he locked eyes for an instant before he broke out in a smile. It was a wide and charming smile, a familiar smile. Joseph Russo.

"Is that ... Cate? Why, hello." His gaze dropped to her thrift store clothing, probably similar to what he'd seen wearing while waiting tables at the Foxy Hound. Then he glanced down at Will and his smile froze for an instant. His eyes narrowed, and he flashed his high-wattage smile at her again. "And who is this little man?"

Cate's thoughts were racing. *Are you kidding, Joseph? Did*

you think I was on any kind of birth control when you slipped me the drugs and raped me in that hotel?

For six years, Cate had fantasized about meeting like this and saying those words, but for some reason she could only stand and stare at him.

Will was smiling back at the well-dressed stranger and spoke up, just as Cate had coached him to do when meeting adults for the first time.

"Hello, my name's Willis Daniel Finley." Then he held out his small hand to shake. Joseph laughed and removed a glove before shaking the boy's hand.

"Well, aren't you the charmer?" he said with a chuckle. "Yes ... charming." He raised his gaze to Cate again and she realized she was holding her breath. *Breathe and blink, girl,* said the voice in her head.

"I ... I didn't know you lived ... here in Manhattan, I mean," she stammered.

"Oh, we moved into a townhouse in Soho while Dina finishes her fashion degree at Parsons. Right, babe?" He and his wife exchanged tight smiles. Nordic and patrician, Dina clearly suspected she was meeting one of her husband's past hookups. She turned and helped her daughter—a diminutive ice princess also wearing a scowl—climb out of the car.

As Cate gazed at the woman slipping her arm into Joseph's, a surprising emotion came over her—pity. Okay, and a little envy, but only for the design school part. She had long ago discarded her own dream of pursuing an art degree. Dina was more than welcome to Joseph Russo, although, from the look of their daughter—Will's age or maybe a year older—Dina had already been in the picture when Joseph took Cate on that fateful date.

A bell chimed in the school building, rescuing Cate from the situation. She grabbed her son's hand.

"Come on, Will, it's time for school to start," she murmured with feigned excitement as she pulled him forward. The boy glanced back at the trio of Russos before falling into step beside his mother.

Later, Cate would reflect on the chain of escalating disasters that chance meeting on the street had unleashed. It began with an envelope from Joseph, left for her at the school office. The card inside was an invitation to his daughter Portia's seventh birthday party. It was to be at the Long Island home of Mrs. Leona Russo, presumably Will's paternal grandmother.

She'd peered down at the embossed invitation and thought how artfully, how flawlessly some people lived their lives. In the six-plus years since that fateful night, Cate had learned the terms, "girl on the side" and "baby mama." She was one step below that—a one-night hookup that he, a married man, had drugged and then raped.

She ran her fingers over the expensive print job. Plenty of children grew up just fine without knowing all of their lineage, and her son would be one of them. She'd ripped the invitation in two and thrown it away.

#

A week later, Cate had started a new assignment uptown with her artist cohorts. What she liked most about designing store windows uptown were the hours. Three nights a week, from ten p.m. until five or six in the morning, she took the subway to Midtown Manhattan while her roommate, Heather, stayed with their sleeping children.

When Cate combined the pay from that job with the tips and wages from waitressing part-time at the Foxy Hound, she could pay nearly all her bills. She told herself she was working as an artist in New York City, even if she didn't have the fine arts degree that she'd come to the city to pursue. It was the best possible plan, and it was working.

Then came the night Will went into convulsions on the apartment floor.

It had been a particularly tough week for Cate. Brenden had sold the bistro and the new owner had reduced the staff, announcing she'd need to take on more hours. Will had been cranky for days, running a fever off and on. That night, she had finally managed to get him to bed with a dose of liquid acetaminophen.

At eleven-thirty p.m., Cate was in the window of a posh purse store on Fifth Avenue, applying a base coat of white to a showcase wall when her phone rang, and she grabbed it reflexively out of her jeans pocket.

"It's Will. He's rolling and shaking on the floor and I think … I think he's having a seizure," her roommate Heather whispered breathlessly. Cate could hear the barely contained panic in the young woman's voice.

"I'm coming now. Call 911—please!" She'd clicked off her phone and headed toward the store entrance, her mind already racing ahead to the subway station. Her friend Dexter was working on the crew that night and followed her to the door.

"Cate?"

"It's Will. He's very sick—having seizures.

His face looked stricken.

"Go! Call me when you know something." She nodded and hurried out.

On the subway, she read a text from Heather saying they'd taken Will to New York Presbyterian. Cate rode the transit all the way to City Hall and then ran down the traffic-lined streets to the hospital. She burst into the emergency waiting room and within minutes was in the examining room staring down at her child's reddened cheeks. The attending doctor, a strikingly beautiful East Indian woman, came into the room to speak with Cate.

"Hello, I'm Dr. Patel. We think that this was caused by his high fever and upper respiratory infection. But I'd like to keep him overnight and run blood work, just to be sure. You say this is his first seizure?"

Cate nodded, beginning to tear up. "Ever. He's been the healthiest kid. ... I should have—" What? Should have known better? Foretold the future? Never left the apartment?

"Don't beat yourself up. Your roommate did the right thing by calling 911." Yes, thank God for Heather. Cate texted her, profusely thanking her and giving an update on Will.

She slept in a chair by Will's bed, waking hourly to peer at his face. In the morning when she opened her eyes, he was awake and smiling over at her. The relief felt dizzyingly delicious. The hospital released him midday and she splurged on a cab to get him home. Then she took the rest of the week off to nurse his respiratory infection.

A month later, reality set in when the medical bills began arriving. Cate applied for Medicaid, something she'd let lapse, and it covered some of the expense. The remaining bills totaled just over three thousand dollars, which she didn't have. The bistro had let her go for taking too much time off, and now she was anxious about leaving Will overnight to do the window display work.

Her only other possibility was her estranged sister. The two hadn't spoken since the night Cate hung up on Margaret angrily demanding she get an abortion. That door was permanently sealed, as far as she was concerned. She didn't have many other options, which is why Cate responded to the second invitation that came from Joseph Russo.

Chapter 36

June 14, 2007 Long Island, New York

"What a pleasure to meet you, Will," said the child's paternal grandmother, extending her porcelain hand with its manicured nails, tastefully done in rose pink. Whether or not Joseph's wife knew, it was clear that Leona Russo had been clued in about Will's parentage. Although a DNA test was still pending, anyone seeing them standing side-by-side at the party could see Will was a miniature version of Joseph.

Cate had gotten the unspoken message that she was to fade into the woodwork, which she did, grateful for the substantial Russo check that had gotten the debt collectors off her back. Raising a child in New York was expensive, and considering what he'd done to her, Joseph stepping up to his financial responsibility had been a great relief.

Cate turned to gaze out at the sea of people gathered to celebrate a seven-year-old's birthday. So much money spent on a single day. It was more like what other people spent on an upscale wedding. Well, not her problem. Time to sample the various food trays offered by a small army of uniformed staff. She threw a glance back at her son, as he held his grandmother's hand and walked with her down to the garden. She had wistfully daydreamed about Will meeting her own mother, Fiona. But she had accepted her rapist's financial help, hadn't she? Enduring scenes like this was the price she would pay.

Later that day, Mrs. Russo stopped Cate in the hallway.

"Could I have a moment with you, Cate?"

Leona Russo was a study in white and gray. Platinum hair coiffed just below the ear, pale gray eyes with heavy lids on which were drawn slender lines of charcoal gray. Elegant long neck on a spare body built for couture fashion. *A really northern Italian,* Cate thought. North to the point of Scandinavia, not unlike her daughter-in-law, Dina.

"How is Will's health? I understand we had quite a scare a few months back. Any more seizures?"

Cate tensed at the woman's use of "we" but caught herself before she said something rude. After all, it was these people's money that had paid her bills when they'd started stacking up a few weeks after Will's hospital stay. Within a day of her contacting him, Joseph had sent payment to the hospital.

"He's fine," Cate told the Russo matriarch. "Thanks for ... for asking. He's very healthy. So blessed, really." Then she smiled while her teeth bit into the softness of her cheek.

"Well, he's an extraordinary boy, Cate. Very special. We need to take ... good care of him. And I wonder..." The woman's voice trailed off, and she looked uncertain for the first time all afternoon. Cate found herself leaning in, curious to hear the woman's question.

"I would love it if, sometime soon, you could let him come stay with me for the whole weekend. You're invited too, of course. It's just"—she waved her pampered hand casually at the gathered masses—"so hard to get to know anyone at these large freak shows."

Surprised, Cate laughed outright at the woman's comment. How refreshing to hear her own thought expressed by the last person she would have imagined saying it.

"Well, of course, Mrs. Rus—"

"Please, it's Leona." She flashed an exquisite, feminine version of her son's smile. "Let's just be Leona … and Cate."

Cate returned her smile, nearly forgetting that this beaming woman had raised a rapist.

Chapter 37

May 3, 2009 New York City

Cate sat in the booth of the midtown restaurant glaring at the digital time on her phone and poised to leave the moment it blinked one-fifteen. Screw Joseph Russo's bloated ego. Her window for indulging tardiness was fifteen minutes, no exceptions.

For sure, exceptions had been made. Allowances and concessions in the last two years, mostly involving Cate counting to ten and agreeing to Joseph's requests. First the DNA test. Okay, reasonable. Then he'd asked her to switch Will to another school, one more prestigious and convenient for the limo to park next to on the weekends they went to visit his grandmother. It hadn't been long before the message came that Cate could stay home on these visitation weekends. Joseph had made each request so politely and reasonably, citing Leona's needs and desires, not his own.

At fourteen after the hour, Joseph slid into the booth across from her and flashed his wolf grin. How had she ever found that leer appealing?

"Hi, Cate, thanks for meeting me." He picked up a menu and gave it a token glance, then plopped it down again. "How's the job treating you these days?"

"Jobs," she corrected. "They're great, Joseph." Cate used the measured tone she always reserved for him. He didn't care about her new waitressing job or her ongoing window design work. Someone like him, whose "work" was massaging the egos and assets of the well-heeled clients in his uncle's financial management firm, didn't care what actual working people did to earn their pennies on the dollar.

It was now common knowledge amongst the Russo family and associates that Joseph had a certified out-of-wedlock son with a baby mama attached. As much as this humiliated her, she couldn't quite wean herself off the ample child support checks that had begun two years ago and now faithfully arrived each month. And all she had to do was keep letting her son visit the Russo mansion on Long Island twice a month. Aware that Will would never get to meet and know *her* parents, Cate had a hard time denying him a relationship with his living grandmother, Leona.

Still, that didn't mean Cate had to listen to everything the man sitting across from her had to say. Time to set some boundaries.

"Joseph, you said you wanted to discuss something. I've got about forty-five minutes of my lunch hour left," she prompted evenly. She'd actually taken the afternoon off, but he didn't need to know that.

"Okay, then ... let's ... let's get down to it." He put a hand up to the waiter, signaling he'd like to place an order. "I have a business proposal. An interesting venture, if you'll indulge me." She waited for him to go on, but instead he jumped topics. "Will and his Nana have really taken to each other, have you noticed? She often rides into the city when Uri picks him up for their weekends, and that is saying a lot. My mother does not love Manhattan," he said with a chuckle.

Cate's fingernails made a small ticking sound as they tapped the table in impatience. *The way you chatter on about your family,* she thought, as *if I was part of your inner circle.* She could feel her annoyance swelling to irritation. *Get to the point, Joseph.*

"Our family and their funny little ways, honestly. For instance, there is this ... this clause in my uncle Joe's estate that says no male relation shall inherit any of his millions who hasn't produced a male heir by age thirty." He gave her a conspiratorial look of exasperation. "I mean, crazy, right? Here I have three beautiful daughters, but I'm about to turn thirty and will be cut out of my uncle Joe's will because Dina can't seem to get her zygotes or X chromosomes straight, or whatever."

She felt a smile creep onto her lips and thought, *well, aren't you in a mess. I'm sure it's all your wife's fault. Is there trouble in paradise?* She took a sip of water and blatantly checked the time on her phone.

"So, what I'm proposing—it won't really change much," he said with a reassuring tone. "I would ... I would just need to record Will as my child—"

"What?" She couldn't have heard that right.

"You know, legally adopt him through the courts and—"

"Uh, no." It came out of her mouth reflexively, even as she only half comprehended what he was saying.

"You would still be his mom—"

"I *am* his mom. And no."

Suddenly she got it. She saw how the last two years had been leading up to this conversation. Joseph had "invested" in her child, and now came the payoff ... a multi-million-dollar payoff from the sound of it. He was trying to buy Will. She grabbed her purse and slid out of the booth.

"Now, Cate, listen to me. You would be a much richer mom, who could go to art school and not have roommates and, well, enjoy life a bit. You'd be set up. I'd make sure of that—Cate!" But she was already at the exit.

Out on the sidewalk, she was headed for the subway when Joseph caught her arm.

"You've got a lot of nerve acting like that in a public place," he said icily. "My family's been nothing but kind to you and the kid."

She wrenched her arm loose and faced him.

"*I've* got nerve? Let me get this straight, Joseph. You want to buy my child. You want to take him and set him on that shelf of playthings you call a family and teach him to treat women like you treated me? In case you've forgotten, you drugged and raped me. Why? Why would you do that, Joseph? And were you ever sorry about that? Because I didn't hear an apology."

He stood there, his eyes darting around as she went on.

"I've seen your wife and daughters at those events. I can't imagine what you do to make them cower like that in their own home, but well done! So, my answer is no. I'm not handing over to you a human being I carried in my body and lovingly nurtured, just so you can make bank on your uncle's fortune. Go get a real job."

She turned and started walking down the street, taking deep breaths to calm herself. The tears were coming, and she wouldn't let him see that. She and Will would leave New York, travel out west to the ranch in Arizona. Cate would get hold of Margaret and grovel, beg her forgiveness, tell her she'd enroll in business classes like she should have done nearly a decade ago. She would not take any more of this family's filthy money.

She felt Joseph grab her arm again, and this time he dragged her into a small alley just past the restaurant. His face had gone a deep crimson, and he bit into his words like a savage dog.

"I should have known you'd be too stupid to see what a good deal I'm handing you. Listen, you little redneck whore, I'm—" Without realizing it, Cate had brought her hand up and it made a smacking sound on the side of his face.

His jaw dropped as if in shock. Then he snapped his mouth shut and she saw what was coming —a raging canine cut loose from his chain—just before his fist came straight for her face. It made a crunching sound, shooting stabs of pain into her sinuses and launching twinkling star patterns before her eyes. The next one knocked her to the ground, stunned. Liberated teeth clinked loosely in a well of blood, which began seeping into her throat and nose. She coughed and spat weakly, trying not to choke.

Someone else was yelling and pulling at Joseph, whose weight she could feel. Still, the blows came. One knocked her jaw loose. A hard fist found her right cheekbone, a cracking sound, and her head rotated left sharply. Humming rose up in her ears and the sound of voices under water. And still the thudding blows came, until she blinked out like a burnt lightbulb.

Chapter 38

One week later

And then the light bulb blinked on again. Under a veil of gauze, in a bed, in a room, machines beeping. Intense throbbing, through the haze, a face coming close in soft focus, eyes that smiled at her. Then back to a dreamless sleep.

The third or fourth time, she stayed awake longer. A cup with a straw came near, some liquid to drink. Throat so sore, but too thirsty to refuse. The face came near again, a nurse saying her name … Sarah. Halo of sandy hair and freckles, with sad blue eyes.

Cate's eyes stayed open longer now, but her vision blurred after a moment. In a while, men came into the room and wheeled her down a hall, through a door, and into a place where light shone out of a wall. A window.

She was alone again and wanting to sleep before the throbbing returned. Sarah came in, chatty now, supplying answers to questions she couldn't yet ask.

What happened? "Apparently you were in a car accident."

Where am I? "You're at Tisch Hospital."

How long? "You were three days in an induced coma due to a brain bleed. So much trauma to your head, my goodness. You woke up four days ago, but kind of in and out." She leaned in and smiled reassuringly. "S'normal."

Cate squeezed Sarah's hand to thank her and then gestured with her fingers for something to write on. She had no memory of what had happened to her, but she did know she had a child, a son. Willis Daniel Finley. Will. She scribbled weakly as Sarah held the pad for her.

date

"It's May tenth." Cate heard fast and loud beeping on the monitors next to her.

will

Sarah frowned, confused. Then she turned and fiddled with the machines. Cate scribbled again.

son birth day where he is

Sarah gave her sad smile again. "I ... I don't know anything about that."

find out

Sarah looked at her for a moment, then nodded and left the room. She was gone a long time. Then the door opened, and a man walked in. He did not look like hospital staff, but he did look vaguely familiar as he came close to her bed. Middle-aged and stocky. Bushy blond eyebrows. Ocean-colored eyes. Deep creases in his cheeks.

"Hullo, Ket, you do not know me so well, I tink." Thick Slavic accent. "I am Uri, Missus Russo driver. I drive boy to see her, twice month, yes? Sometime drive Mister Joseph." He stopped talking and snuffled his nose. Was he crying?

"You ver so lovely. Then the ... accident. Now look et—" He took out a handkerchief and blew his nose.

Her mind was slowly clicking along.

Driver ... accident—has something happened to Joseph? I was in a car with him? Where were we going?

"I must go beck Ukraine now. He get med I try to stop—to pull him off *blub-bub—*" the words were turning into underwater sounds again, "*blub bub* … no way to trit woman. I have dotters."

Cate felt like she was going under an ocean wave. She grasped at his hand and held on weakly and tried to make sound, to speak her son's name through her wired jaws. Uri leaned closer, trying to hear.

"Hm? Ah, Vill. He stay at Grandmama's. Safe, good, no problem." He patted her hand. "I … I em sorry, Ket."

Was he apologizing for getting them in a car wreck? "No way to trit woman." Why had he said that? She let go of his hand and felt him slip out of the room. Too much effort for her throbbing brain. Sleep now.

#

The next time she woke, curiosity guided her hands over her injuries. The damage started at her neck, in a brace, or was that for her jaw? Jaw wired shut. Stitches in lips, broken nubs where her front teeth were. No food coming her way for now. Then her fingers crept upwards to something that felt like a house roof over her nose. Gauze wrapped around her skull, probably an inch thick, with holes for her eyes. Head shaved?

How had she gotten so injured? Slammed face first into the privacy window of a town car she didn't remember getting into? And if that were true, why wasn't Uri—the driver—injured? Was Joseph also in this hospital?

The next day, orderlies came into the room, unlocked her bed and rolled it out into the hall. Nurse Sarah waved to her as she was loaded into a small chamber amid hydraulic sounds of an elevator. She drifted off and awoke in a different hospital room with new bandaging on her jaw and face.

A different nurse came in, followed by a small man in a doctor's coat. He looked like a handsome elf. Dark hair with gray at the temples, and finely chiseled features offset the fact that he barely came up to the nurse's chin.

"Well, hello. It's great to see your eyes open. I'm Dr. Stuart Littleton, and I'm the one responsible for your fancy grillwork and the nose tent, ahem."

Cate thought of a book that she and Will had read together, *Stuart Little*. Will … her son. She ached to see him. A choking sob came up from her throat, alarming the munchkin doctor and his nurse.

"Oh, not to worry, Cate. You're on the mend. Now, we'll let you rest a day and then remove the bandages to see how it's going, shall we?" Then an edge to his voice. "So hard to believe a car accident did all that damage."

#

Later in the week, Cate was elevated in her bed dozing when she awakened to the familiar scent of Chanel No. 5 and saw a silver-haired woman seated uncomfortably in the visitor's chair. Cate had raised her hand in greeting and tried to smile, but the muscles of her face weren't prepared to cooperate yet.

"Hello, Cate, my dear," Leona Russo said in her familiar clipped cordiality.

"Oo-eh's Oo-ill?" Cate asked through her caged teeth, hoping her meaning was clear. She tried to look around the room, but the neck brace prevented it.

"Will? He's … home. I mean he's back at the house in Glen Cove." She leaned toward the bed as if to tell a secret. "Cate, I hear you've been asking for him to visit, but we think seeing you in this condition would be, well, unnecessarily traumatic for him. You probably can see my point. It's all … a bit much for such a young one."

She rattled on for another ten minutes, doing her part to hold a one-sided conversation. But Cate had stopped listening. Instead, eyes closed, she was remembering how her infant son would giggle with delight when her breath ruffled his feathery soft hair. Would none of the medications they gave her soothe this deep ache in her heart?

#

Weeks of slow recovery followed in the private rehab facility where the Russos had her transferred once all the surgeries were completed. Cate began to make trips back and forth to a cosmetic dentist and she lost track of how many procedures and thousands of dollars the family had now spent. Such generosity they were showing her!

Then one day, her memory began to return.

It happened while she was futilely trying to brush her teeth with her jaw still wired shut. After rinsing off her mouth with water cupped in her hands, she straightened to look in the mirror. Instead of seeing her swollen eyes and cheeks, a brief image of Joseph's darkly savage face stared back from the mirror. Her knees buckled, and she found herself sitting on the bathroom floor.

Over the next hour, she remembered pieces of their conversation in the restaurant and her speedy exit. Soon, she was reliving the argument that had started on the sidewalk and led to the slap and that first punch in that alley. An electric shock ran down her spine as she began to recall, to understand, what he had done to her. She walked over to the phone next to her bed and lifted it, poised to call 911. Then she looked around her, slowly replacing the receiver, and folding her arms.

Joseph Russo had planned it out very well.

For the past four weeks, she had been languishing in a posh plastic surgery aftercare center, the kind catering to rich matrons getting facelifts. The medical staff, including Dr. Littleton, had gone to great lengths to restore and heal her face. Of course, no one would believe her story of the attack now. Much of the bruising had subsided, and although she still ached from the shoulders up, she realized how well she fit the profile of a cosmetic surgery patient that had gone through all this hell for the sake of vanity. *Oh, sure, your ex worked you over. A common response to all that medication—delusional!*

Uri the driver had been the only witness. "No way to trit woman," he'd said more than once. Since she'd moved to the recovery center, a different driver brought Will every time he came to visit. When she'd asked, Will just shrugged and said Uri had gone home. If home was in the Ukraine, then there really was no one to tell the real story. The realization had felt like another blow to her face. She felt a twinge of pain in her jaw and popped an extra pill to help her drift back to numbness.

Cate's roommate Heather came to see her finally. "So glad to see you're so much better," she said flatly, eyeing the upscale furnishings of the hotel-like room. "I, um, needed to put your stuff in storage, 'cause I needed to get a new roommate in there."

Cate stared at her. *Really, Heather, so much need?*

"Sorry. Just needed to get back to some kind of financial schedule I could depend on. I actually had to call that creep and tell him about your share of the rent being due. The check came, no prob, but *ugh*."

By "creep" did she mean Joseph? Since when did he pay her rent? *Since you haven't worked in nearly two months, chum,* answered the voice in her head. Where would she and Will go when she got out of there? She had no way of even starting to look for a new place. No phone—the bill hadn't been paid. No money for that or even for transportation around the city. She was almost twenty-five, with an eight-year-old child and less money than when she'd arrived in the city as a runaway teen.

Then Cate remembered what she had been planning right before the attack. She would contact Margaret and apologize. *Sorry for stealing the money and running away. So very sorry. Can I come home and study accounting now?*

Margaret would send airfare so she and Will could fly home to Arizona. Then she would happily work as Margaret's slave on the family ranch in exchange for putting this whole disaster behind her.

Her head spun with ideas, but her body felt lethargic from the round-the-clock painkillers. Oxycontin—oxy—was something Cate had never taken recreationally, not even when the cool kids were into it. Now it was a lifeline, numbing the dull throb of her neck pain, headaches, and broken jaw. But she felt so loopy most of the time that she couldn't concentrate. She would try to cut down on the dosage when she got out of there.

Right now, she needed to reach out to Margaret. Yeah, her big sister would save the day, she just knew it. Cate would call her right now if … she could remember the ranch's landline number. She leaned back against her bed pillows to concentrate and promptly fell asleep.

Chapter 39

The new home of Cooper Union Art School loomed above her, all jagged angles and bulging lines. It looked frightening to Cate, on so many levels. Like a metal box, frozen in the act of exploding into a dozen sharp-edged chunks. This was where she would be getting her fine arts degree and living, if she accepted Joseph Russo's offer.

"If," she repeated, standing on the busy sidewalk. *If* meant swallowing her anger and pride. Ignoring her fear of the man who had nearly killed her. Ignoring her need for justice. Ignoring her need for Will ... at least for the time being.

Of course, the Russos had filed for legal custody of Will the moment Cate had begun asking for his return. Joseph was so confident she'd go for a financial settlement—especially now that recovering from her "accident" hadn't allowed her to work the sixty-hour weeks like she had before. Once she'd refused the first offer of a settlement, the family court summonses had arrived regularly at Dexter's apartment where she was staying.

Cate had laughed scornfully at the Russo lawyers in their expensive suits and professional smiles. Her pro-bono lawyer had convinced her to file a countersuit against Joseph as a means of regaining custody of Will, not to mention going after him criminally and civilly for the attack.

"That monster Russo ought to be doing time," the lawyer had said at their first meeting, shaking his head and sighing as he read her testimony. But within days and without much explanation, the lawyer had begun urging her to step away from the lawsuit and settle. There was no doubt in Cate's mind Joseph Russo's "handlers" had gotten to him.

Not a problem, Cate had thought. Hers was such a good case she probably didn't need a lawyer to explain it to a judge. She would tell her story in court and then Will would be released back to her. She hadn't been allowed to be alone with her son since his visits to her in the hospital, but she would soon remedy that.

The morning of the court hearing, Cate had sat on a wooden bench, waiting to go into family court. One of Russo's suited flunkies sat down next to her with a manila envelope and casually pulled out several eight-by-ten glossy shots of her buying oxy from a guy in Washington Square. Then he pulled out a sleek silver iPad, which showed a video of her jamming pills into her mouth as she stumbled away from the dealer. She felt strangely detached, marveling at how well she played the part of a strung-out drug addict—the disheveled hair, the shuffling step. An award-winning performance, really.

"We have so much more, Cate. The dumpster diving, the panhandling," the man had said with such patrician disgust that it made her want to take a kitchen knife and stab him, and then herself. Instead, she'd stood and stared down at him icily.

"Yeah? I'll take my chances in there." That had been a colossal mistake.

Standing in front of the restroom mirror and washing her hands, she couldn't stop seeing herself as a strung-out vagrant. Choppy hair still growing out from the surgery, her pale face with its dark circles, and the wrinkled boho dress under a stained hoodie.

She had a vision of the judge ordering her arrest on drug

charges, then smiling at Joseph Russo as he awarded him full custody of Will. Justice served today. Next! She'd shaken off the images, dried her hands, and gone to claim what was rightfully hers.

Cate hadn't been prepared for so many Russos to be seated in the courtroom. The children missing, but Leona, Dina, and various Russo relatives Cate recognized from the Long Island parties had packed half the courtroom pews.

When the judge asked Cate where her counsel was, she'd told him she was representing herself.

"Your honor, I just want my son back. He belongs with me. I … I don't want him to be raised by Joseph Russo, or any of the Russo family, for that matter."

"From what I understand, Miss Finley, you relinquished custody to the Russos last May due to injuries sustained in an automobile accident, correct? And there is evidence you've developed a drug dependency since then—"

Anger began to seethe in Cate's chest. She hadn't relinquished her son. They had stolen him from her and then waged a campaign to make her look like an unfit mother.

"What? No, sir—your honor—that wasn't an accident. He—" She'd turned and pointed at Joseph, who had snuck into the seat next to his lawyer at the plaintiff table. "He attacked me, knocked me to the ground, and beat me with his fists—over and over." She felt her voice rising to a high wail. "He tried to kill me!"

The Russo lawyer was up and walking toward the bench.

"Your honor, this woman is clearly under the influence of drugs and is delusional. The child's grandmother and custodian, Leona Russo, filed a court document saying Miss Finley poses a threat to her grandson. She requests that any contact with the child be denied until Miss Finley has entered a drug treatment program—"

The rest of her life Cate would remember the moment when a tiger got loose and roamed the courtroom. She raged forward at Joseph, almost reaching him before the court bailiffs caught up to her. They each grasped an arm and dragged her back, but not for long. She bit one and kneed the other in the crotch. Suddenly free, she ran to the one person who had shown her compassion and empathy—Leona Russo. Crouching down, Cate stretched her arms out to the woman, who shrank back against her daughter-in-law like a character in a B-rated horror film.

"Leona, please don't let them do this. I never did anything to you *or* your family." Cate was trying to make eye contact, but Leona kept her gaze on the floor. "If I'd known you were planning to steal him—for money, Leona, really?—I would never have come to your house that day. Will is my baby, *my* child, not yours. Not any of yours!"

By then, the bailiffs had caught up with Cate and shoved her face down while they handcuffed her and perp-marched her out of the courtroom. She'd sat in lockup for twenty-four hours before a court-appointed lawyer got her transferred to Bellevue on a seventy-two-hour psychiatric hold. By then, she'd been well on her way to withdrawing cold turkey from the oxy. After she was released, she'd practically crawled back to her friend Dexter's apartment and slept under a blanket on his living room couch for an entire day.

When she awoke and could keep food down, she sat at the kitchen table and looked over the packet of documents that had been dropped off the previous day.

The official offer letter contained bulleted items for her to consider before making her decision:

1. You have no residence.

It was true, she had been camping on the couch at Dexter's,

which also served as a meeting place for the art collective. With the courts involved, it would never pass as suitable lodging for Will.

2. You have no full-time job.

Sort of true. While she didn't have a full-time income, her window display work with the art collective amounted to nearly forty hours weekly, if you counted the extra cleaning she did around the apartment for couch-sleeping privileges.

3. You lack any family support, locally or otherwise.

That one hit home. Reaching out to Margaret via the old ranch number hadn't gotten any response. Clearly, she had burned her bridges when it came to her Arizona ties.

4. You have an on-going addiction to painkillers that has expanded to street drugs.

Well, no argument there. The oxy had her, and when she couldn't get that, she bought whatever she could get—Percocet, codeine, once even methadone. Some mornings, she could barely recognize herself in the mirror.

On the final page came Joseph's offer. In exchange for giving up all pursuit of custodial rights to her son and signing a nondisclosure agreement, the Russo family would prepay her art school tuition and board, plus give her a monthly living stipend of five hundred dollars while she attended. So, this was the dangling carrot—the chance to revive her art school dream. All it would cost her was her son, Will. It was a deal with the devil.

Cate read and reread the offer until her head ached and her eyesight had begun to blur. The truth was, she hadn't been able to tolerate much text reading since "the accident," and so she skimmed the document, reading only what was in bold or capitals. Then she had walked the streets for an hour, ending up at the library where she scrawled a letter to Will on some paper she'd pulled from the copy machine.

Seated at a table next to the stacks, she looked down at her writing. *Someday, I hope I can make it up to you, that I can become in your eyes the mom you deserve. I love you so much, Will. I ache at this choice in front of me. But you should not suffer from this hard life I've created, these mistakes I've made. Just know that you have NEVER been one of those mistakes. I love you, Willis Daniel Finley. I love you to the moon. xoxo Mom.*

She'd wondered how she could get it to him out on Long Island, where she'd even get an envelope to mail it. She envisioned Leona eyeing the letter suspiciously and feeding it to her shredder unopened. In the end, worn out and dope-sick, Cate tossed the letter in a trash bin as she stumbled back to Dexter's. With depression rolling in like a fog, she took her last two pills and fell asleep on the couch at ten-thirty in the morning. The next afternoon, panic lodged in her ribcage and withdrawal already wrapping its fingers around her throat, Cate walked across town to her first Narcotics Anonymous meeting.

Chapter 40

June 10, 2014, New York City

She sat cross-legged in front of the blank seven-foot canvas, her back to the light streaming through the window. It was ethereal light today, sifting through the clouds of a spring storm and reflecting off the jagged metallic surfaces of 41 Cooper Square. The building that had frightened her with its audaciousness four years ago was now a haven, if not a home.

Faced with the final project of her last semester at art school, Cate spent between eighteen and twenty hours a day either in class or working in the studio. Now she stared at her towering blank canvas with not an ounce of inspiration in her. All she could think about was a boy named Will, who was celebrating his thirteenth birthday that day. Her son had become a teenager.

Well, why don't you take the train out there and wish him happy birthday? the tiger purred in her ear.

"I ... I'm not going to do that."

Why not, girl? Just saying, it's a free country.

This was how she talked to herself these days, a bold inner voice talking with her broken, cautious self. No one at that first Narcotics Anonymous meeting had believed she could kick oxy without medical intervention or at least therapeutic support, but they didn't know her grit, and they surely hadn't met her tiger. The same force that had lashed out in the courtroom on that horrid day four years ago had morphed into her spirit animal, guiding her through the emotional jungle of recovery.

"Talk-it-out therapy" was how she termed it. It went hand in hand with her favorite technique of making lists.

Faithfully attend Narcotics Anonymous meetings—*check*

Get off the pills and stay off—*check*

Accept Joseph Russo's tuition offer—*(grr) sigh, okay, check*

Enroll in art school—*check*

Get a waitressing job again, weekends only—*check*

Focus on her future with her son—*check*

Take the train to Long Island and crash her son's thirteenth birthday party to show him and the Russo family how great she was doing?—*Wrong. Bad idea. Don't do it.*

Okay, so the technique wasn't flawless.

#

Two hours later, Cate was on the Long Island Rail en route to Sea Cove Country Club. She knew about the party because she lurked online as someone named Brigit Bernini. It had been easy to build a profile page and get her friend request accepted by Dina Russo, Joseph's long-suffering wife. Cate had searched online for a profile photo, finding one that could have been Dina's twin, only slightly less pretty. Then she listed all of Dina's likes and dislikes, including books (pitifully few) and films (shockingly violent for the mother of daughters).

Gazing out the train window as the urban landscape morphed into suburban shrubbery, Cate clasped the framed and wrapped portrait she'd painted from a photo that had been on Dina's Instapix page. It showed Will in his baseball uniform, his face lit by the midday sun, reaching high into the air to catch a fly ball.

You are simply going to say happy birthday to Will and be prepared to walk away before you cause a scene, she told herself sternly. The tiger merely rolled her eyes.

The ease of finding the Sea Cove Country Club came as another surprise. Just off the Oyster Bay branch at Sea Cove station, Cate took a short walk to the entrance. A vast carpet of bright green lawn lay beyond the entrance, guarded by a skinny young man in an ill-fitting uniform, who nervously peeked at her from the guard house.

For once, Cate had spent some time on herself, blow-drying her hair and slipping on a Palm Beach floral shift and conservative flats, both of which she'd found for under twenty dollars at a resale shop. Artful makeup and a sunny smile completed her look. Her hair had grown out past her shoulders and she'd left it her natural dark chestnut. No matter what else happened today, Will would see with his own eyes that his mother was thriving, despite the lies she imagined the Russos had been telling him about her.

The guard stepped toward her uncertainly, apparently not used to foot traffic. She reached into her bag and pulled out an invitation to Will's party. Trust Dina to post a photo of the garish document on her Facebook page this morning with the comment, "Happy 13th birthday William. We love you so much." So easy for Cate to make a reasonable facsimile in the art school's computer lab.

"And it's Willis, not William, you twit," she had mumbled as she'd pulled the finished copy out of the printer.

Cate strolled along the road to the clubhouse feeling confident and emboldened. This was no time to be a shrinking violet. Find Will. Find Will before the Russos—or more likely their handlers—found her.

"Yes, hello," said a balding man in an impeccable black

suit as he stepped forward to greet her. "May I direct you toward an event?"

She pulled out the invitation again and he smiled, pointing to a grouping of tables and chairs far out on the greens. Cate's heart sank. They would see her coming—a woman walking across the vast lawn on her own would draw attention. She needed cover.

And then they appeared right next to her—a family of four, complete with a toddler in her mother's arms and a gawky boy of about Will's age. She let them pass and fell in step behind, all the while searching for her son.

Just as they got to the gathering, Cate spied Dina walking forward to greet the family. She peeled off and joined a group in front of the portable bar. She didn't drink—ever. Bad things happened when you drank, especially in unfamiliar circumstances. But she grabbed an empty plastic cup and held it in front of her as she moved through the crowd.

Some boys were chasing a soccer ball about fifty yards from the festivities. One of them yelled, "Hey Will, over here!" and a lean, dark-haired boy stepped in to kick the ball down the green. She let out her breath and watched as her son, flanked by the boys, ran past her to chase the ball. *I made that human*, she thought. *I created him, and now he's a teenager.*

Uh oh. Two muscular men were walking toward Cate. She looked past them at Dina in the distance, her arms folded and face grim. Cate turned and hurried toward Will, calling his name.

"Will! Hey, Willis Finley!" He turned and looked in her direction. She broke into a trot, closing the gap between them. The club's security police were starting to walk down the hill toward the party now, no doubt summoned by Dina Russo.

Cate reached Will and saw she'd have only a minute before

the Russo men caught up. She smiled at her son and took off her sunglasses. "Hey stranger, remember me?"

The look of terror on his face was unmistakable. *Oh my God, he's afraid. What have they told him?* Her hands shaking, she offered him the wrapped present.

"Happy birthday, Will. I ... I wish you well." He took it from her thrusting hand, then backed away as the two men approached. The distress on his face told her all she needed to know. She was a monster to him. The stuff of nightmares. She turned away to shield her tears from him, then straightened and headed back toward the road. The suited men fell in step beside her.

"Um, Mrs. Russo thought maybe you could use a lift back to the city," said the closest suit, firmly and meaningfully, but not unkindly. "We've got a car parked right by the guard station."

When they got to the guard gate, Cate kept walking toward the train station. There was no way she was getting in a car with them. But just as she attempted to walk out the gate, the two men grabbed her shoulders and pushed her into the back seat of a parked black SUV. In the seat next to her sat Joseph Russo.

"I must say, you're looking very pretty these days, Cate."

She didn't reply for fear the tiger might take charge. It probably wouldn't help to give him a black eye with his men looking on. An awkward silence built as she looked out the window, clenching her fists.

"Yes, very pretty indeed."

Cate turned and studied Russo. He'd gotten pudgy in the last decade. Thick around the middle and no height to offset it. Will would probably tower over him soon. As if he'd heard her thoughts, Joseph's voice turned cold.

"Cate, I'm not going to spend much time on this, or you.

Here is what I want you to consider."

Out came another iPad with a video already playing. It was of her in a hotel room. No doubt the room she'd awoken that morning, feeling soiled and injured, nearly fourteen years ago. There were two people in the video, but only one whose face wasn't blurred. In the video, Cate writhed and moaned, seeming to be in pleasure. The male, manipulated her body in various positions as he raped her. The camera work was on an expert level, showing close-ups at times and then panning out full length to show her bucking body. Cate pushed it away and shrank against the car door.

"What the hell is wrong with you?" she said, unable to look at him or keep the shock from her voice.

"Cate, listen carefully. Stop fucking with us. Sign that non-disclosure we gave you. And if you *ever* show up at another family function like you did today, I will make sure that this video finds its way onto Will's laptop." His voice dripped with sarcasm as he added, "I suspect you're too conscientious a mom to want to see your son, er, *influenced* like that."

Cate was hunched over weeping into her hands by then, so Joseph slipped an envelope into her purse and opened the car door.

"I hate to see a woman cry like this when it's so unnecessary, Cate. Please, try to behave along the guidelines we've set up for you. And sign the goddamn NDA." The door slammed and she was alone.

By the time the car dropped her off at 41 Cooper Square, Cate felt gutted. Seeing the video had made her relive all the trauma of that day. *What kind of monster would do that to a woman, let alone show it to his own child?* She felt nauseated and deeply shamed.

The art school building was as quiet as a library as she made her way to her studio. Before her loomed the canvas, still awaiting her creative brilliance.

She needed to cleanse herself, cleanse her brain of those images. Cate stood in a hot shower for twenty minutes and then put on her paint-stained cutoffs and a torn gray Gold's Gym t-shirt. Sitting cross-legged in the middle of the floor, she focused on sweeping away the stress and horror of the last few hours. For a full hour, she just stared at the blank canvas. Then she went to mix her paints.

When her studio mate Patrice came in to do some painting later that evening, she murmured, "Hey," up at Cate, who was balanced high on a ladder and dabbing meticulously at the Day-Glo colors on her palette. Neon yellow to orange to red to purple to blue to green. The blend on each hue was painstaking. A distinct image was taking shape in the center through the absence of color. It was a white silhouette of a small figure in a baseball cap, reaching straight up as if to pluck something out of the sky. A printed photo of Will catching the baseball lay where she'd dropped it at the foot of the canvas.

Her instructors gave her low marks for an unfinished senior project, but she knew it was finished. By the time she graduated, just eight weeks shy of her thirtieth birthday, Cate had gotten her first commission to paint another six-foot mural—the hyperreal face of a tech company CEO on a neon graffiti background. Three more commissions followed. Her floor-to-ceiling canvases, tagged with "Catify," were trending on social media fine art sites like Paintsy and Cre-art.

At the end of that year, with accumulated mural money, Cate bought a vintage camper truck, which she named "Max." She kept it parked at a fellow student's parents' house in White Plains, after telling them she planned to take it camping in the Adirondacks when she got some time.

Chapter 41

July 15, 2016, New York City

Who would have thought that sneaking out against her parents' wishes to climb the granite monolith looming over her family's ranch in rural Arizona would pay off so nicely for Cate's art career?

"Do not climb it, not with Drew, not with the college kids—not at all! Hear me?" Her father would chant this like a mantra every time he caught her gazing in the rock's direction.

"I'd prefer you didn't, love," Fiona admonished gently, aware how much her daughter loved to push back on any hard rules. So, Cate had climbed because Doc forbade it, but not too often because her mother had called her "love" in her melodic Irish lilt.

Now she was actually getting paid to climb, along with a slew of other street taggers. Featured in a music video, they hung by harnesses and brandished paintbrushes on a building-high mural of colorful neon images. All while some trending hip-hop artist made his moves for the videographers below. Okay, there wasn't much pay involved, but huge bragging rights.

After the director wrapped the shoot, Cate nimbly rappelled down forty feet and landed on the ground to gentle applause from the onlookers. She couldn't help smiling. This was fun, not work. Tomorrow she'd be back up there, without the crowd and cameras, putting finishing touches on her commissioned painting so she could collect her wages—a meager stipend, but at least it paid some bills.

As she unhooked her harness from the lines, she felt a man sidle up and stand next to her. She snuck a sideways glance at him. Probably late twenties, well-tailored Armani suit, clean-shaven face, dark complexion. A restless brute beneath a smooth exterior. Instantly, she knew what he was and who had sent him.

"Hello, I'm Tyson." He held out his hand to shake hers, and she stared at it. His voice was light and ever so friendly as he continued. "I have a message to deliver from a friend of yours." Suddenly her heart was thumping in her chest. She focused on slowly and deliberately stuffing the climbing harness into its pack.

"Define *friend*," she answered, not meeting his eye.

"Someone who's made it happen for you and who now needs your support and cooperation."

"Support, huh? You mean he wants me to campaign for him? To get out the vote?" She snorted at her own joke and headed down the sidewalk, knowing the man would tag along. They always did.

"Your, um, benefactor has noticed all the attention your artwork is getting these days—that it might put you into the media spotlight and tempt you to, well, reveal a certain shared history. So, he's, um, he's—look, if you could just stop a second." Cate halted and turned to stare at him icily. "He'd like you to sign this nondisclosure. It was, um, apparently returned to us unsigned."

Judging by his earnest expression, they hadn't let him in on the prank. Oh, she'd sent back a signed NDA the day after her son's birthday party—the one where Joseph had shown her just how far he was willing to go to keep her in line.

The night she finished her senior project, she hadn't been able to sleep. Instead, she'd locked herself in the computer lab, working well into the next dawn's light. Studying the copy of the NDA, she'd captured just the right font, ink color, and letterhead in a new document. Then she'd added all the legal language, minus the paragraphs restricting her right to speak freely on her exact relationship and history with Joseph Russo. Instead, she'd inserted:

The undersigned parties agree to no binding or restraining measures of any kind that would prohibit Caitlyn Finley from reporting the history and particulars of her relationship and interactions with Joseph M. Russo, either in the present or at a future date.

As she'd hoped, no one at his office had taken a second glance at the document once they'd checked it for her signature and initials. But apparently, now that Joseph's campaign had grown legs and Cate's artwork had begun to attract attention, someone had pulled it out for a closer look. After all, Joseph Russo was expecting to win a seat in the State House of Representatives that fall.

Now Cate pursed her lips and returned young Tyson's hard stare.

"By 'shared history' do you mean the time he drugged and raped me? Or maybe the time he hauled me into an alley and put me in a coma with his fists? That shared history?"

The change in the man's face was almost comical, like he'd had a whiff of something hideous, some ghastly mess. He looked around to see if anyone had overheard her, then stepped in with an air of exasperation.

"Okay, look, I'm not going to … get into this with you. I'm just relaying the message for my boss. Don't really know why he picked me for this. I do real estate and environmental law."

"Bully for you." She shoved the last of her harness into its bag.

"I came east on a summer internship to work for my cousin Joseph, and he liked the way I handled things, I guess. Wants me to help him get elected state senator and then governor in four years. Me? I just want to get back to the West Coast. Not my jam here." His distress was making him chatty, severely compromising the Russo code of silence.

"California?" For a moment, he didn't seem to understand her question.

"Oh, uh, yeah. Based in San Bruno, but I just got a job offer from a big environmental law firm in San Francisco." Tyson realized she'd gotten him off-track and straightened his shoulders. Back to work. "Anyway, I'm not going to, you know, twist your arm about the NDA. But my message is that it needs to get signed, and you need to steer clear of giving any interviews, especially with his opponent, who will be looking for stories like yours."

Well, that was candid of him. "Thanks. Tyson, right? Tyson... Russo?"

He smiled and handed her a card and an eight-by-ten envelope. "Burroughs. My mom is Joe Russo's half-sister. When Mom decided to leave the family compound twenty-five years ago, she took me and got all the way out. That was enough to cut her off from any inheritance."

That, and being female, Cate mused. Cate nodded and gave him a sympathetic smile as he handed her a card. She knew a little about escaping family ties, too. She pocketed the card, then waited until his car drove off and tore up the nondisclosure. It brought instant gratification, followed by the usual anxiety.

\#

Joseph won the nomination in his district and began a rigorous battle with his opponent. Cate continued to accept high-profile mural commissions, while watching for the next NDA-bearing emissary. Strangely, they stopped coming. One October night, she returned to her studio apartment to find a clump of feathers fluttering in her mail slot. She gingerly pulled out the dead pigeon. A string tied around its neck held a card reading, "A dead bird tells no tales." Her inner tiger sneered at the corniness, even as Cate began pulling out her suitcases. Instinct told her it was time to run.

Two hours later, when the Uber driver let her off at the teal and white camper truck in White Plains, she breathed a sigh of relief. Her untraceable route began with the debit card used for the trip, tied to an online payment account under her artist name Catify. She was done with New York but Joseph Russo didn't need to know that ... yet.

Heading for the interstate that would eventually take her west, Cate felt a strange serenity come over her. She was controlling her destiny, and even though that path was taking her away from the one person she cared about, her son Will, she knew it would lead her back to him. She had an uncanny sense that a certain environmental lawyer now back in northern California would be crucial to her West Coast plans.

But just a day later, Max broke down in Omaha. When Cate heard it would cost her just shy of a thousand dollars to fix the truck, Cate realized for the second time in nearly two decades, she would have to ask Margaret for help. Leaning against the driver's door of her truck, she dialed the ranch number from memory, using the burner phone she'd bought across the street at the superstore.

Chapter 42

She never gave out her cell number. Not socially, not for work, never. Internet messaging was the way to reach her, even though it had forced her to finally get a smartphone with a prepaid data plan.

One day, a message came in through her Paintsy page, the one with only the name Catify attached. The online fine arts marketplace had assured her their customer information was deeply encrypted and non-hackable. Yeah, right.

She sat in her camper truck, parked beside yet another sun-drenched crowded park in the San Fernando Valley, and stared down at the message on her phone.

Hello Catify, I'm sending this because I'm searching for someone who looks a lot like that one photo you have on your page. Her name is Cate Finley, and she's my mom. I need to reach her pretty quick. If you could pass along my cell number—

Heart suddenly racing and feeling breathless, she had deleted the message before reading any more. Pretty sloppy of Joseph. Did he think she'd been brain-damaged during the assault eight years back?

An hour later, another message came through Paintsy again.

Hello again, could you possibly get a message to my mom? I'm going out of the country for school and wanted to talk to her before I leave. I think about her. A lot. Just wanted to say hi to her is all.

Again, the flickering breathless feeling. She put the phone on the table and gazed out at the homeless people wandering through the park. It was "Indian summer" in Los Angeles, with heat nearly as bad as Phoenix. Soon would come raging Santa Ana winds and the threat of wildfires.

She slid all the windows open and flipped on the small battery-run fan. Then she read the message once more and began tapping her phone.

Cate said to ask you, what was the song she sang to you at bedtime when you were six years old?

Within two minutes the response came.

You mean in 2007 when I turned six and we moved back to Manhattan from upstate?

She stared at the response and gritted her teeth. "You're trying too hard, Joseph. To hell with your stupid mind games."

She reached to clear the screen, but before she could, another message pinged.

Bobby Shafto's gone to sea, silver buckles on his knee, he'll come back and marry me, pretty Bobby Shafto. It's Irish. My grandmother Fiona taught it to you. It's your birthday, Mom. I just wanted to talk.

Cate sat looking at the screen as minutes rolled by. Then she took a long breath and tapped on the keyboard.

Send me the number again.

A minute later, she was listening to ringing—once, twice, and he answered, "Hello?" A rich, deep voice that had already breezed past puberty and firmly arrived in adolescence. Was she really the mother of a young adult? She felt a wry smile and shook her head. It hardly seemed possible.

"Hello?" he repeated, "Is ... are you there, Mom?"

"Will? Hey, hi." Awkward silence. Her chest pounded like a bass drum. She wanted to rush on, but fear stopped her. Was Joseph standing there next to him? She didn't think she could bear it if he was now doing his father's bidding.

"Hi, Mom, it's really you? Really?" He gave an uncomfortable laugh, or was it the sound of relief? She wanted his voice to soak into her every pore. Her son, her boy. She ached to hold him again like she'd done back when they both were babies.

"It's me, Will. God, it's been..."

"My thirteenth birthday, over three years ago."

"Yes." Memories came. Of Will's frightened face as she handed him his present. Of sitting in Joseph's parked SUV at the country club, seeing the horrific video images on his tablet while his velvety smooth threats violated her ears.

Another uncomfortable pause. Cate looked around the camper, suddenly seeing how small and shabby her world had become since then. If her son knew how she really lived ... Better that he believed the online myth of her glorious artist's life with its dazzling and colorful photos of completed murals. It was so easy to fabricate a grander life on social media.

"Hullo? Mom?"

"I'm still here, Will. Are they ... are you doing all right there?"

"Huh? Oh sure, it's ... it's all good. I'm fine." His voice faltered. "Gonna—going to," she heard him correct himself, "head off to boarding school for the next two years. Switzerland. How about that?"

Why? What did you do wrong? she wanted to ask him, Hadn't she learned from her own experience that boarding school was simply a convenient place to stash an unwanted family member? Maybe Joseph had collected his millions and had no further use for Will. If that was the case, why not just send him back to her? She knew that answer, too. Joseph Russo would never give up his leverage over her. Never.

"Switzerland, huh?" She tried to make her voice sound conversational. "Are you excited about that?"

A sigh on the other end. Then his voice sounded raw and emotional.

"I think it's for the best, Mom. There's too much—" A pause, then, "The house is getting pretty, um, crowded. With the new baby coming…" He trailed off and there was another heavy silence between them.

Well, well, she thought, *the Russos have spawned again.* But it was the maturity and sadness in his voice that ripped at her heart. How could she have given him up? She should have fought for him harder … and longer.

When he spoke again it was lighter and with more finality.

"But I wanted to wish you a happy birthday. I think about you all the time, Mom. You're my family, too. I think that … you're very, um, brave. Just wanted to say that to you before I, you know, jet out of here." He paused for her to say something but the sob she was suppressing wouldn't let her mouth open. She heard him clearing his throat.

"Maybe sometime … I could come for a visit."

A sudden picture of this bright and shining young man getting his first look at how she lived flashed through her mind. She saw a disheveled woman standing next to an ancient camper truck on a filth-laden street in Los Angeles and it was more than she could bear.

"Gosh, Will," she tried to clear the tightness in her throat, "This has been—such a great birthday treat. I wish you all the best over there at school, I really do. It's going to be a … a great experi-ence." The words felt so weak and impersonal as they tumbled out of her mouth. She'd been poised to tell him, *you are my greatest creation, Will*, but by then her mouth had stopped working.

"I love you, Mom."

She could only nod and weep, even as her thumb disconnected them.

A moment later, her rage filled the camper. The big cat roared and savaged inside her. She wanted to kill Joseph Russo, to sink tooth and nail into him and rip him to shreds. Until that moment, she'd never truly wished death on anything in her life.

It had to go somewhere, so after a while she let it flow into her art and worked through the night. Hours later, as the sun rose on another blazing California morning, Cate stared with satisfaction at the five finished canvases in front of her. The last was of Will, painted from memory. A color-saturated portrait of him at five years old, standing alone in the woods and grinning out from under an enormous red umbrella while the neon rain poured around him.

Chapter 43

August 13, 2019, Copperton

Entering Jimmy Lee Baker's law offices had triggered a memory from nearly a lifetime ago, of Cate holding her father's hand and proudly toddling up her first stairs. Back then, the law practice had belonged to Jimmy's father, Harold "Buck" Baker, who had supplied all the legal help Daniel "Doc" Finley needed for his cattle ranch and veterinary business. The offices spanned most of the third floor of a century-old building on the corner of Copperton's two busiest streets and across from its quaintly historic Courthouse Square.

Cate and Jimmy sat opposite each other in his mahogany-paneled corner office. She had just finished telling him a vastly condensed history of her life on the East Coast, and he seemed eager to move on to the paperwork on his desk.

"To be honest, Cate, I don't know who Margaret used for the ranch's legal work these past two decades. For certain, it wasn't us. According to our files, this will," he picked up the papers she had brought in the ancient folder, "is the last piece of business Dad had with Doc and Fiona. Mailed to them the same week they headed off on that trip to Baja."

He set the papers down on his left, then picked up a newer document.

"This is a copy of the current recorded deed, listing Margaret as sole owner. Looks like it's been in place for four years. Strangely, until this deed was recorded, neither Margaret's nor your name showed up anywhere on the property title after the estate's final settlement. That's a decade and a half where someone savvy enough could have snuck their name onto the deed and mortgaged the hell out of the property. At this point, there are no liens against the property, but this," he picked up another document, "is a petition to modify the deed to list Margaret Jean Finley and Estelle Brown Parker as joint tenants with right of survivorship."

He picked up the will again.

"The will that you found at the cabin, which matches the one I found in our archived files, lists you as co-heir of the estate, stipulating you would receive your share on your twenty-first birthday. Unless you remember signing away your share once you became an adult, this current deed, along with the petition, can be nullified through the court." A smile crept onto his face. "Good news for you, bad for Estelle."

Cate took a moment to look over the document, as she tried to control the tempest brewing in her gut.

"Jimmy, I ... can assure you I didn't sign anything away because no one *contacted* me about any inheritance when I turned twenty-one—or thirty-one for that matter."

At the age she should have inherited, she'd been a single mom with a toddler, living at poverty level and bartering for food. Getting access to some money would have changed her life.

I would have my boy with me, she thought. *I could have paid my own way through art school and we'd be living in a decent place.* Had she inherited the money back then, Cate would never have needed to meet with Joseph Russo at that restaurant on the day the lights blinked out. *I could have gone on with my life and never taken a dime from that monster.*

Jimmy was shaking his head as he looked over the deed.

"Sad to say, this stuff happens often in families. Given the, uh, strained relationship you and Margaret had, Doc and Fiona should have named a third party as executor." He slipped the will back into a folder marked "Finley Estate."

"So now what?" Cate was aware that all this time Jimmy had spent on her was costing money she didn't have. She did a mental review of possessions she could sell for some quick payment funds.

"Let's assume that the other side isn't going to back down quietly. We'll need to file a protest of the current deed—bring what's known as a 'cloud' to the title, and also file suit against Margaret's estate. I doubt she made a will, given the circumstances of her death, but she may have listed Estelle in other ways as her beneficiary. In that event, you and Estelle might wind up as co-owners of Finley Ranch." He caught her stricken look and hurried on. "But in the meantime, I'm going to file the paperwork and secure a court date."

Cate closed her eyes and slumped in her chair, fatigue beginning to settle in.

"Jimmy?"

"Yeah, Cate?"

"What do I owe you for all this?"

He gave a laugh and Cate opened her eyes to see him grinning at her.

"I really want you to stop worrying about that. Everything going on in your life? We can discuss it after this case is settled—in your favor, I might add. I'll just have you put a dollar down on our retainer agreement, like we did before."

He chuckled, and she could tell he was trying to lift her mood. Another thing she needed to accept—charity from old friends, not just from strangers.

#

Downstairs on the sidewalk, Cate strolled along, gazing at the current crop of stores that populated Hooch Holler, a nickname given the street during its wild-partying gold- and silver-mining days.

She had been surprised to see growth and prosperity in Copperton. The migration of rich retirees and other urban escapees had attracted a half dozen Starbucks, a couple of Walmarts, and even a Trader Joe's to the dusty southwestern town. But the historic street where she now strolled still favored cowboy bars, Indian souvenirs, and the occasional Western art gallery.

As she walked back to where Max was parked, her phone rang. An actual call coming in instead of the usual text. She checked the screen nervously and saw it was from Dexter at the Los Angeles gallery where she'd left her finished portraits.

"Hey there, you sell my paintings?"

"Cate, are you sitting down?"

"Ha, not quite. I'm window shopping on Hooch."

"You're drinking at this hour?"

"No, Hooch Holler. It's—I'm in downtown Copperton."

"Okay, get ready for some good news."

"Dex, I am so ready for it. Spill."

"Well, this morning, I was fiddling with those mini paintings you left. I thought I'd just, you know, arrange them all on one wall, edge to edge, like a giant mural. Looked great."

Cate hopped into the seat of her truck and closed the door so she could hear better. It was instantly an oven, so she rolled down the windows.

"Dex, I'm listening. All twelve, huh? Must look very colorful.

Send me a pic."

"Yes, looks smashing, but there's more, Cate. The very first customers in the store were two interior designers from Santa Barbara. Fell in love with all the faces, the color flashes, the fact that the components could be ordered differently on the wall. Light bulb exploding overhead—pow!"

"Wait, they—they bought them? All of them?"

"Now get this: Just minutes earlier, I had put a price on all twelve assembled like that. Thirty-five hundred. Sold! Not even a blink. And these clients are high volume designers. They want more panels, just how you made them."

Thirty seconds went by.

"Cate?"

She was silently laughing, tears streaming down her cheeks.

"I'm here. You ... you have no idea. I'm so ... grateful. Thank you, Dex. You made my day."

He heard her emotion and spoke carefully.

"Shoot, I didn't even ask. How is the sister search coming? Did she turn up?"

"Not good news. The sheriff's office found evidence that she's ... she's passed."

She heard uncharacteristically raw emotion in her friend's voice. "Oh no, Cate. No ... I'm so sorry, really."

"And she's left behind a mess that we're trying to make sense of." A tsunami of emotions was rising in her and Cate suddenly longed for the cabin's solitude. "So, thank you ... so much for this good news, my friend."

A new thought came to her.

"Hey, I need a piece of physical mail sent here, so don't post a payment to my online account, okay? I'm texting an address where you can mail the check. Love you ... and thank you so, so much."

She tapped out a brief text, sent it, and clicked the phone off. Putting the truck in reverse, she was about to back out of the parking spot when someone leaned all the way into the open passenger window. Startled, she glanced right and met the cool even stare of a human pit bull.

Chapter 44

Just inside the passenger side window loomed Gabe, the mystery man from Estelle's dinner party. The party where Cate had eaten drugged food and crawled up the stairs. Where she'd lain weak and helpless on the floor in her childhood room, listening to conspiring voices on the other side of the door. Had one of those voices belonged to this man?

"Hello, Cate. You look like you're feeling better today."

He was fearlessly committed; she'd give him that. She considered backing out quickly with half of him in the truck and causing some real damage. *But do you really want more run-ins with the police in this town?* sensible Cate asked. She shifted back to neutral.

"What do you want?"

"Well, a sheriff's deputy named Gomez tracked me down via my New York office. Said there was some confusion about that dinner party last week? The one where you left in the middle—"

"Oh, the one where Estelle Parker and company drugged me?"

That shut him up for a moment. Then he laughed, tilting his head slightly as he studied her.

"You're ... you aren't what I expected to find here in Arizona."

"Oh, so trite. Will you step back, please? Someone's waiting for this space."

In one smooth move, he slid back out the window, held up an index finger at the car waiting for the space, opened the truck door, and hopped in.

"Hi, Cate," he said amiably. She glared back, silently kicking herself for not keeping the windows up and the doors locked.

"Um," he said, looking around him at the stores, "maybe you can drop me off someplace I can get some lunch?" He let a moment go by as she handily maneuvered the truck out onto the street, then sped forward, freeing up the parking space.

"Maybe I could ... treat you to lunch," he said, trying again. Then, in a more confidential tone, "I might have info about the dinner party."

"Well, confirming there *was* a dinner party works in your favor."

She turned onto one of the streets that traveled east from the courthouse. They drove toward Copper Valley in silence, with Gabe glancing at her every minute or so. When they pulled into a fast-food drive-through on the edge of town, he let out a chuckle.

"Always doing the unexpected, aren't you?"

She stopped in a line of six cars. "Takes one to know one."

More chuckling. "Touché. You got me there." Then he noticed the sign. "The famous In-N-Out Burgers? I've heard stories."

"This food will make you want to move west—but don't." She smirked down at the tiger, purring in her lap.

As the truck inched along to the order window, Gabe seemed uncomfortable with the silence.

"I heard about your arrest. Sorry I couldn't have helped with that business. Defense is my specialty."

She turned to size him up and nodded. "Thought so. That's why I told Gomez to have a look at the New York State Bar website. So, what were you doing at that party, Gabe-who-didn't-give-a-last-name-when-we-met?"

"If I'd said, 'Hi, I'm Gabe Janssen,' would you have stuck around?"

The other candidate's brother. Now it all made sense. "Well, I have been dodging you people for the last six months. You can understand why, right?"

Gabe looked out the window, but she'd caught the smug grin.

"Let me help you with this," Cate said in a matter-of-fact tone. "You've heard I have some potentially damaging dirt on Joseph Russo. You're here to get me to go public so your, um, family member can beat Russo in his bid for governor."

He opened his mouth and then shut it.

They sat in silence, the truck inching forward until she gave their order at the window. "Two Animal Style with two cheese fries and two root beer floats."

"Good Lord, woman. I refuse to believe you eat like this all the time, slim as you are. My LDL is jumping for joy."

She stifled a laugh and drove forward. At the pickup window, she waited while Gabe counted out some bills. With two bags of food in tow, they drove to a lushly green neighborhood park and pulled up next to a picnic table.

Seated at the table, she watched Gabe take his first bite of burger. He chewed for nearly a minute, eyes closed and emitting a panther-like purr.

She took a bite and laid her burger down, grabbing a napkin from the stack on the table.

"Okay, here's your chance, Gabe. Talk."

Grabbing a napkin also, he patted his mouth before speaking. "We know Russo has been harassing you into keeping silent about your, um, history with him. In the current environment, that alone could be damaging to his campaign. You wouldn't even need to give details about the assault that put you in the hospital a decade ago."

It was useless to ask how he knew any of this. All such information wore price tags. But did he think she'd never fantasized about being the one who took down Joseph Russo? That she remained quiet due to low self-esteem or Stockholm syndrome?

"Gabe, I'm not going to lead you on. I won't get involved." *At least not until a certain young man turns eighteen and is safely away from the Russo family,* she thought. "It's not worth the risk right now." She studied her last bite of burger. "Also, there's a little thing called a nondisclosure agreement."

"Which you still haven't signed." This caught her off guard. "Oh, I've been doing this legal stuff a while. There are channels of communication—backroads, if I may. There's no nondisclosure, and that's why I'm here to ask if you want justice."

Cate gave a derisive snort, took a sip of her drink, and then studied the straw as she spoke.

"Joseph doesn't really need an NDA. He only needs to keep me quiet. The day I talk to news outlets, a … a certain video gets released, making me look like a … like a sex worker."

She hadn't said the real reason was the threat Joseph had made to show it to her son. Sure, he was older now, but she didn't want to live in a world where Will had seen his mother's graphic rape video.

"That's the best-case scenario," she went on. "Worst case, the fascinating mystery of my disappearance gets aired on *Dateline* a few years from now."

Dead Cate tells no tales, she thought, remembering the bloody feathers poking out of her mail slot.

"What makes you think we won't protect you, Cate?"

"It's not a matter of *won't*; it's *can't*. I don't want ... to keep on like this, constantly looking over my shoulder—"

The truth of what she'd just said stopped her short. Suddenly she was up on Cabeza Rock again clinging to a perilous ledge above the valley, gazing across at what she ached for—to feel safe, feel loved, to reunite with her son ... to set down roots. She looked back at Gabe. How could he help her? How could anyone help her?

"I thought I'd be safer here in Arizona, but it seems somebody here is also bent on my destruction." She crumpled her empty wrapper and tossed it twenty feet into the trash can. "Tell me, Gabe. How is it you were at Estelle's dinner party?"

There was a long pause while they eyed each other.

"She and I have, uh, known each other since her days as a dancer in Nevada. Helped her with ... some legal stuff."

Cate flashed on the article about Estelle's rich dead husband and how quickly she'd weaseled out of being a suspect. A good defense lawyer can make that magic happen.

"Around the time our people started hunting for you in New York, I learned you were originally from northern Arizona. Coincidentally, I'd heard Estelle was putting together a pretty big development deal in these parts and that a Finley Ranch was involved. On a hunch, I flew out here to see Estelle, but really to meet with your sister—Margaret? Apparently I arrived just after she went missing."

"You wouldn't have gotten much about me from Margaret. We'd been estranged for nearly twenty years."

"And yet, you came to help look for her."

They exchanged smiles. Pit bull versus tiger.

"So, are you a partner in her development deal, Gabe?"

"What? Oh, no. She was actually a little annoyed I was here in Copperton. Didn't want me to come down to the ranch, but

I persevered."

Cate had been peering at his face, looking for signs of treachery. If he was lying, it was professional grade.

"I was a newly-hatched lawyer, hired to rep her when the Vegas D.A. was investigating her husband's, um, suspicious demise. Such a brilliant actress, not to mention some decent eye candy back then. Exotic dancer and all. The D.A. never could get anything on her—solid alibi, and, as I said, a drama queen on the witness stand. Next time I see her, a couple years later, she's a bounty hunter wielding a nine-millimeter Glock like a child's toy."

He chuckled at his own joke, then gave Cate a sober look as he grabbed the last of his fries.

"You talk about dangerous, the Estelle I know is—"

Cate held up her hand. "Whoa, preaching to the choir. I've seen her skills firsthand. I just want to know if ... she's vulnerable. If there's any dirt that might make her back off."

Gabe was quiet for a moment, as if weighing his options.

"Doubt it. She and your sister go back a long way—school days, maybe. This is her own deal."

"Well, bringing her to justice is taking all my attention these days, Gabe. Sorry, nothing to spare." She picked up the rest of the trash, wadded it, and pitched it into the can. "But, if Estelle's real estate deal were to go south, I might be convinced." *Though not without a decent safety plan for Will and me.*

Gabe's eyes widened as he sipped on his float. It seemed unlikely he could help her, but she'd let him ponder it for a while.

#

Cate had dropped Gabe off back at the Square and was putting the last of her team penning cash into Max's gas tank when Jimmy rang her.

"Okay, we have officially brought a suit against the current deed holders, Estelle and—until there is a death certificate—Margaret. Stay tuned. And Cate? I thought of a way you could start working off the legal bill."

"Really? Need some murals painted?" She envisioned a Catify mural, its neon colors splashed against his aging brick office walls.

"Uh, no, but I need a place to stash Cochise for a while."

"Co-chise...?"

"That horse you rode in the team penning. Marisa and I are taking a … a break. I'm, um, living in the apartment at the office."

"What? Aw, no, Jimmy. I'm sorry to hear that." Tiny Marisa and Jimmy had been the "mini-me" version of her and Drew back in high school—smitten and inseparable.

"Yeah, well, it's been coming a long time. Now she tells me she's tired of cleaning up after my ponies. I'm selling the other two—don't really have time for that these days—but Cochise is coming twenty—my dad's last horse. It would be great to find him a pasture to hang out in and, um, enjoy retirement."

This was a different Jimmy, sounding so lost when he talked about his personal life. All his boisterous professional manner fell away and she realized the request wasn't about paying down her debt. He was trying to protect an animal that his ailing father had raised and cherished.

"I … I don't know, Jim." She was in the dark field again, watching her own beloved Bella writhe in pain from gunshot wounds. Had Estelle really been the monster behind the trigger?

It would be insanity to try and bring another horse into the Finley stables right now, but there was space at Bronnie's cottage—a large side yard hidden from the ranch house. She could imagine Bronnie nodding her approval at this gesture for a friend in need.

"Hey, uh, do you have any fence panels you can bring down? I could keep him in the grassy area next to the cottage until you and I get the ranch squared away."

Relief filled Jimmy's voice. "Sure, you got it, Cate. Fence panels, hay, and one horse coming your way tomorrow morning. Thanks for helping me out."

Cate climbed into her truck and turned over the engine. It was risky, but she knew why she'd said yes. She thought about that early morning not long ago, when a young girl had crossed the cow pasture, so excited to start caring for the horses she adored. Then she thought of what Rae had seen instead.

Chapter 45

Two in the morning and she wasn't sleeping. The last time she could remember getting any rest had been in the cabin, the morning she'd opened her eyes to Levi's smiling face.

Every time she curled up on Bronnie's living room couch, burrowed under a lavender-scented crocheted blanket, the questions began in her head.

What's happened to Bronnie?

Where is Margaret's body?

What connects Margaret to Estelle?

and ending with,

Where the hell is Bronnie?

Finally, she got up and wandered into the messy office.

Two days since Gomez and Friendly's visit, and the crime scene techs had yet to appear on the scene. "Office looks tossed," Friendly had said when he saw its state. And then he and Gomez had left. What was with the sheriff's department, anyway? Slackers.

Standing at the doorway, poised to do some snooping, the first dilemma presented itself. If a forensic team was on the way, whatever she touched would be compromised. Each time she handled a file, she might ruin evidence. So, what could she safely do?

Hands clasped behind her, she scanned the disheveled office, taking in the jumble of pens, staplers, paper clips, and papers strewn over the floor. She stopped in front of a free standing computer desk. A dust-free square clearly marked where something the size of a laptop had sat. Did the kidnappers take it when they took Bronnie?

"You're assuming she was taken and didn't just escape this Finley family craziness."

Using a tissue, she peaked in all the desk drawers before concluding that everything left in the little office was in plain sight on the floor. Noticeably absent from the room were files and a file cabinet. Wherever did Bronnie keep her office records, if not in her office?

On a hunch, she stepped across the small hallway and opened the bedroom door. Immaculate. A bed you could bounce a coin on, clothes neatly folded in her chest of drawers, and a partially shut closet of white or pastel hospital scrubs. When she slid the closet door open, she saw shoes in straight little pairs beneath the hanging clothes and an overflowing laundry hamper at the far end. Cate turned to go, stopped, and looked back. Amid the pristine furnishings and carefully organized belongings in the bedroom stood this overflowing, messy hamper. Hm.

She walked over and slid the closet door the other way to get a better look. Dirty underwear strewn on top, lots of it. Beneath that were smelly, mildewed towels. She really had no desire to touch the mess, because, *ugh*. But something was working at her. She burrowed her hand into the pile until she touched something hard, smooth, and flat. Clamping thumb and finger on it, Cate carefully pulled out a silver laptop.

Was this Bronnie's idea of personal security? Dirty clothes? And why didn't she take her laptop with her?

Cate envisioned Bronnie awakening to someone trying to get in the front door, burying the computer in the hamper, then dressing and slipping out the side door to her car and driving off. Had they followed her? Caught her halfway up Cold Springs Road? *Where are you, Bronnie?* She needed to phone Gomez for updates on the silver Volvo.

She stared at the laptop until she realized she had the perfect excuse to touch it. They'd been sharing it while she stayed at Bronnie's. She carried it into the office, set it on the computer desk, and hit the power button. The screen lit up, telling her there was fifty percent charge left on the battery and revealing that Bronnie had no password protection. Either she didn't have anything worth protecting or she hadn't had time to turn on the password.

"Let's take a peek, just to be sure," she murmured to the calico kitten that was playing with a pencil at her feet.

Like the bedroom, Bronnie's electronic desktop was neatly organized. It was also empty of useful or interesting clues. No bank info, but there was a file marked "Pending Retirement," and one marked "Internet Downloads." In the latter, she appeared to be collecting recipes and clever social media memes.

The Wi-Fi icon was searching for a signal, suggesting Bronnie might have used her phone as a hotspot when she was home. Per her parents, Internet access in rural Arizona had been neither easy nor cheap when Cate was growing up and probably wasn't much better now. Most likely, Bronnie made use of the free Wi-Fi at the hospital.

Cate looked out the window to see long fingers of daylight stretching across the garden fence and realized with a start that it was already six. What had she done these past four hours? More thinking than sleuthing. It was exhausting, whatever you called it, or maybe the lack of sleep was finally catching up with her. About to close the laptop, she idly clicked on the email icon. An explosion of folders appeared on the screen. After opening a few, Cate sat back with a grin. She'd just discovered Bronnie's secret filing system.

"She scans all her important documents and emails them to herself as attachments," Cate announced to the empty room with more than a little admiration. "Very tidy."

There were folders and subfolders, including one titled "Finley family"—Margaret, her parents, and herself. There were folders on the Finley Ranch, the cottage, and a variety of organizations including one called "Stop Cabeza Rock Estates!"

Cate brought the laptop with her into the kitchen. She put on some coffee and sat at the counter clicking through the emails.

A headache had begun, and her eyes were already beginning to lose focus. She dug her drug store readers out of her backpack and pressed on with her search.

The folder labeled "Cate Finley" caught her eye immediately. The files inside were mostly JPEGs. She clicked on a subfolder titled "1980–1990" and summoned a handful of candid shots, showing a newborn in her cradle, Fiona holding a cheerful toddler, a finger-painting five-year-old, and a gawky grade schooler, who looked a lot like Will at that age.

What the... Cate thought, leaning back from the monitor. *This woman was chronicling my life in photos and I never knew her. Why?*

Then she found a subfolder containing carefully scanned images of all the missing artwork from her bedroom wall.

"Thank you, Bronnie," she whispered. Her face felt hot, and tears were welling, but she resisted the urge to take a trip down memory lane. No time for that.

She opened the last subfolder simply titled "2000's." The first email in the folder had a JPEG attachment, sent from s_littleton@nyulangone.org. She clicked and the JPEG opened automatically. An electric shock ran through her, along with a high-pitched whine. Fifteen long seconds went by before she could move. Then the voice in her head spoke.

Set the coffee down carefully, Cate. Look away. Breathe in, breathe out. Don't look at it again.

The photo was enormous, nearly the full screen, taken up close. Seared into her mind were the bulging grapes for eyes, the bright red blob of skin where a nose would have been, the torn upper lip hanging and a black gap where teeth should have been. Cheeks so stretched and swollen that the entire head looked like a painted balloon. But she had recognized her hair, streaked with purple at that time.

Cate stared at the counter, shaking her head. Without looking up, she slammed the cover closed and leaned forward, face in her hands, her ears ringing.

How? How had anyone ... ever ... gotten this photo? A wave of nausea followed by panic waged war on her insides. *No place is safe*, she thought. *I'll never be safe again.*

Then she heard a vehicle pulling up to the cottage, its noisy diesel engine idling. Through the window she could see two men emerge from a truck hitched to a livestock trailer. They began unfastening some fence panels that flanked the sides of the trailer. A horse whinnied anxiously.

More panic. *I can't see anyone like this,* she thought and ran to the bathroom. In the overhead light, her own frightened but fully healed face looked back at her, just as it had a few hours ago, just as it had yesterday, last week, and for a long time now.

She took some deep breaths and closed her eyes. *Easy, girl. Steady on,* crooned the voice in her head she had come to rely on. It felt like she was quieting a frightened animal. But it worked. Still a little shaky, she pulled on jeans and slipped into her running shoes. Then she went out to greet Jimmy and a horse named Cochise.

Chapter 46

Rae came over early the next morning to help feed and clean up after the horse and Cate made breakfast for them both. Afterward, she coached the girl on brushing Cochise and cleaning out his hooves, and together they braided his mane and tail.

When Cate sent her to put away the muck rake and shovel in the gardening shed, the girl returned with five orange kittens squirming in her arms. Cate rolled her eyes in mock exasperation and set down a plate of milk on the kitchen floor.

"That brings the feline count to an even dozen," she told Levi later on the phone. "Bronnie's in serious danger of becoming the neighborhood cat lady."

"Has she turned up?"

She could hear metal pots clanging as Levi prepared to feed a dozen stateside members of his 'āiga, who were coming to see his mama, the *matai*. She imagined a house filled with happy, excited people who were all catching up on each other's lives and felt a pang of loneliness. What must it be like to have close family like that?

"Nope, no Bronnie. It was her car they pulled out of the ravine, but there were no signs of her having been anywhere near it." She sighed and tamped down her anxiety. "They're doing a ... a DNA scan on it now—finally! Things move as slow as molasses around here."

"Is there a missing person's report yet?"

"I've tried to find her family to get that going, but none

are listed in her files." Suddenly she remembered a photo she'd seen on Bronnie's laptop, scanned from a faded black-and-white snapshot circa the 1970s. A woman with a teen girl and two much younger children. It was too faded to see much detail, but she felt like she'd run across the same shot somewhere else recently. In Margaret's room?

Levi was rattling some pans in the background.

"Bae, I got to go put this back on the stove. Making my barbecue ribs tonight."

"Did you just say the *b* word?"

"Before anyone else." He was actually chortling, making a sound she'd never heard from him. Being with family was doing him good.

"Okay, I miss you." *I miss those lips and those strong arms around me*, she thought with a sweet ache. "I'll see you soon... *bae.*"

She put the phone down, still smiling, and then looked over at the computer charging on the kitchen counter. That photo would still be on the desktop when she opened it.

Cate squinted and only caught a quick glimpse before she clicked the file closed. The sender's name caught her eye this time. Dr. Stuart Littleton. How could she forget "Stuart Little"?

Staring down at the email, new questions plagued her. Other than both being in the medical field, what was the connection between Bronnie and Dr. Littleton? How had he gotten her email address—through Margaret? But why hadn't she heard from her sister during that time? And then the recurring question: If Bronnie's friendship with Margaret and Fiona went back several decades, why couldn't Cate remember her?

After a moment, Cate typed her full name into the file search window. There were twenty-two hits for Caitlyn Finley, five in the

Inbox, seven in the Sent folder, ten in the Trash.

The earliest email was dated May 4, 2009, the day after the attack. Sent from admissions@nyulangone.org to mfinley1970@yahoo.com, and then forwarded to bronwyntaylor@cmc.org. There was a photo of Cate lying in a hospital bed, hooked up to monitoring machines.

The accompanying message read:

The person in the photo is an emergency room patient at Tisch Hospital in New York and we are seeking confirmation of her identity. She carries an Arizona driver's license and student ID card, both expired, identifying her as Caitlyn Willis Finley, as well as a business card with this email address. She is thought to have been in a hit-and-run automobile accident and we are attempting to treat her injuries. Please respond back confirming her identity, your relationship to her, and consent for treatment. A large deposit has been placed on account for her treatment, but, due to the mortality risk, we need consent from a family member to proceed. Please print and sign the attached document and fax it to the number listed below.

Sincerely,

Barbara C. Trent, Intake Coordinator

NYU Langone Health/Tisch Hospital

Fax 212-264-5555

Not until that moment did it dawn on Cate that her family would have been contacted in such an event, even if that family was one estranged sibling.

Most of the other emails were between Bronnie and the hospital in the same twenty-four-hour period. Then came the email from Dr. Littleton, sent directly to Bronnie:

Greetings Ms. Taylor,

I understand you are acting as the contact for the Finley

family. I am the surgeon who will be operating on Cate's face to-morrow AM. I am looking for any photos you might have of how she looked before the accident. I try to do this as a courtesy, usually procuring photos from the patient herself. However, since Cate is not fully conscious, I'm requesting any images from her next of kin. These should be close-up frontal face shots, although if you have any close-up shots in profile that would be a plus. Attached are sample photos.

I thank you for your prompt response to this request.

Sincerely,

Stuart A. Littleton, MD

Reading the email now, Cate felt shocked that so many medical procedures had taken place without her knowledge or consent. Joseph Russo's hand was all over this, from claiming it was a car accident, to scheduling her "emergency" plastic surgery, to later moving her to a high-end recovery center where she had access to plenty of oxycontin.

Like a classic sociopath, he'd covered his tracks while appearing to be concerned and caring. By the time Cate remembered the attack, she had little proof it had even taken place. She wished she'd known about this photo back when she was fighting for custody of Will, but it might still be of value to the Janssen campaign. Not that she relished anyone seeing her in that condition.

Three more emails caught her eye, all from Margaret. One simply said:

Taking the red eye to La Guardia. Will call after I see Cate.

Cate stared at the email for a charged moment. Her sister had come all the way to New York to see her in the hospital? The second email was dated May 10, 2009.

It could have been her, or someone stole her ID. She's out

cold and swathed in bandages, so who knows? What did she do to get in this shape—shoot off her mouth again?

Someone with deep pockets shelling out for this. I'll stay over and see if she's awake tomorrow.

She couldn't remember seeing Margaret's face at the hospital but did recall a dream where she heard a low, throaty voice, saying, "Cate. Cate, wake up! What did you do this time, Cate?" So, it hadn't been a dream after all.

The last email from Margaret was dated the following day.

Showed up at the hospital today and she's been discharged! She wasn't even awake yesterday! They said a private ambulance came and got her. Her phone goes straight to voicemail, which is full. Now how do I even find her? Serves me right for giving a damn. Headed for the airport to get a standby ticket. Home tonight.

Chapter 47

August 16, Cabeza Valley

Not until Cochise called out a hungry whicker at daybreak did Cate realize she'd slept through the night for the first time all week. She put the coffee on to drip and set a platter of food on the porch for the kittens before heading over to the haystack.

As Cate stood watching the gelding tear into his hay, someone stepped up next to her at the rail. Thinking it was Rae, she turned with a smile and then flinched. Not Rae. After having been missing for a week, young D.J. Ruiz now stood beside her and scowled at the new horse.

"Don't let Estelle see him—she'll mess him up good," he said.

She glanced at his profile, then back at the house, tempted to put distance between them. But this was her chance to get some answers to what happened to the horse ... and maybe the missing women.

"Like Bella." Not a question or a challenge, but a statement.

"Look, I didn't shoot your horse," his voice cracked and suddenly he looked deflated. "Estelle came by and told me to get rid of it, just like—" He broke off and stared out at the pasture. Cate tried to slow her heart rate.

"...Just like Margaret?" It came out in a whisper.

As if to deflect the question, he shrugged a shoulder at the pink house.

"That little girl found something she shouldn't have. Best

you watch over her, too. Estelle's going to try and get rid of any ... *evidence* before the cops close in."

"If you mean Margaret's phone, it's too late. Sheriff's office has it."

He looked hard at Cate, then turned on his heel and started off across the pasture.

"D.J., wait! Where are Rosa and Diego?"

She hadn't seen the older Ruizes on the property since she'd returned from the cabin. He kept walking and spat out a laugh over his shoulder. A sharp, savage sound.

"*En México.* I drove them down there myself last week, after I saw the cops at Desi's. I'm going back, too, before they put out an APB on me. Hell with this place."

Cate's chest was thumping, and she could feel moisture under her arms. Was he getting away with aiding a murderer? She ran after him and caught up as he was climbing the pasture fence.

"Wait, don't go. Don't you ... owe me the truth?" He jumped back down and whipped around to face her, just as she stepped back out of his reach. "Look, I believe you if you say you didn't do it. But if it was Estelle then she needs to be arrested ... and punished. Please help us. If you know anything about my sister's death—"

"Your sister." A dark look crossed his face. "I know she wasn't who you *thought* she was." Suddenly, he looked spent again, a strange sadness edging his voice. "I ... I moved her body, but maybe they know that by now. Estelle said to do it or my folks would suffer. So I moved Margaret's body from there," he pointed to the grove of trees in the pasture, "to there," he finished, pointing to the Ruiz house. He looked back at Cate and said, "That night? I heard them fighting over Margaret's truck keys—Estelle wanted them, and I think that's why she ... did what she did."

They'd fought over a horse transport? Maybe it was the hundred-thousand-dollar resale value, or maybe Estelle wanted to make it disappear to fit the story she planned to tell about Margaret's whereabouts. Or maybe both.

He reached into his pocket and tossed her some keys. "Here's my set. I cleaned up the mess in the trailer, by the way. Gotta go."

He wasn't quite fitting the scenario of an accessory to murder. What was Estelle holding over him—over the whole family, apparently?

In the distance, Cate saw Diego's truck parked by the bridge.

"D.J., your parents—how can I reach them?"

The nasty look was back on his face. "You know they're not legal, right? After all this time. It was a well-kept secret until Estelle went snooping and started using it against them. She's the devil—*La Diabla*."

He gestured up at the main house again.

"Doc and Fiona could have helped them with immigration way back when but didn't. Then Margaret had years to help them but didn't. Cheaper to keep it the way it was. Anyway, they were already planning to go back to Chihuahua. So, when the little girl talked and the cops showed up, I packed them up and we scooted. *Adiós*, Finleys."

He turned to head back down the road. Cate had one more question pressing on her.

"D.J., what about Bronnie?" He shot back a look of annoyance, but she pressed on. "Do you know anything about her—or her car at least—going off the road?"

He spread his arms in mock innocence. "Hey, I was in Mexico, but plenty of tweakers in Copperton would've done that for a few hundred. Anything else?"

"Well … I'm guessing it was you who put that bogus powder in my backpack instead of the real thing. Thanks. It, uh, shortened my jail stay."

He bowed sardonically. "I leave you another parting gift—my sister Leelee. She's under the spell of *La Diabla*, because of that stupid mustang horse, so there's no talking her into leaving. Good luck with her." Then he spat and strode off.

Cate leaned over and took a few deep breaths to calm down. She pictured Leelee, who had seemed so friendly when Cate first arrived. The girl wouldn't even look at her yesterday when Cate had snuck over to the stable to borrow some grooming equipment and a water bucket for Cochise.

The voice in her head was nagging her to call Gomez. The sheriff's office would contact the border agents and nab D.J. at a crossing. But the kid's motivation had been to protect his family. That was honorable, right? Helping and protecting your parents?

She found herself thinking more about Bronnie's disappearance than her own sister's. Margaret, whose aloofness and tyranny had made it so hard to talk with her, let alone love her. Finding the adoption papers had explained plenty, but Margaret's deception over the will had widened the gap between them. Yet, her sister's note had told Cate to read all the papers in the file. Had she finally felt remorse after all these years? Then there was D.J.'s curious statement, "I know she wasn't who you thought she was." Why hadn't she asked him what he meant?

The week had been a game changer, starting with her discovery of the red file box at the cabin and including the emails on Bronnie's laptop documenting Cate's time in the hospital. This virtual stranger had gone to great lengths to help Cate. Who was Bronnie really? And a more crucial question, now becoming an hourly mantra: *Where* was she?

Chapter 48

"Good morning," Jimmy's voice boomed out of her phone's speaker. "Hope you got some rest over the weekend."

Out on the back patio, Cate yawned, set down her sketchpad, and took a sip from her coffee mug.

"I don't think I'll rest until Bronnie shows up. But I am trying to knock out some paintings for that gallery in SoCal I told you about."

"Well, the judge has moved up your court date. He wants to see us this afternoon at one," Jimmy said over the phone speaker.

"That was fast. Are we ready?"

There was a pause.

"Cate, this is for the assault charge, not the petition to challenge the will."

"Oh, the sham assault charge." She had almost forgotten that headache.

"Yep. Turns out the techs couldn't lift any usable prints off that fireplace poker, nor did the wounds on Estelle's face match the supposed weapon. And since Copperton's finest crime scene investigators couldn't find your fingerprints on anything else, beyond your backpack and the dining room table, the other side will need to explain just what you used and how a one-hundred-and-fifteen-pound woman was able to do that damage to a five-foot-eleven, two-hundred-pound woman."

Cate snorted. "Unless I have superpowers."

"Speaking of which, what kind of whammy did you put on our friend Gabe? He thinks you're a goddess."

"Hm," Cate yawned, trying to sound bored with the conversation. "So, I'll be at your office at noon and we can drive to the courthouse in your air-conditioned Beemer."

Cate clicked off her phone and picked up a partially finished study she'd been sketching—the mustang stallion Destino in profile. The charcoal drawing had captured his mystical pale eyes, her use of shading rendering them stark and ghostly. Cate remembered how he had danced and preened, arching his neck obligingly as she took shot after shot from the pasture fence. Then, like a celebrity rock star saying, "No more photos!" he had abruptly whirled and raced off across the pasture to join his herd.

Her painting of him would be a peace offering to Leelee, an attempt to bridge the gap between them these days. The final version would be on her signature acrylic gloss backdrop of subtly blended neon colors, over which she would paint the horse in photorealistic matte. A familiar sensation was coming over her body—the sweet ache of creation.

Finally, the clock told her it was time to head for Copperton. Outside the kitchen window, Rae hung on the fence talking to Cochise, as she spent much of the time doing these days. Caring for this horse was doing her good, just as Cate had hoped it would. She made a mental note to go by the used horse tack store in Copperton and get a smaller saddle. She'd promised the girl a riding lesson this week.

Cate opened the window and called out, "Hey, headed into Copperton. You can hang here with Cochise—just let Desi know where you are, okay?"

The girl flashed a broad grin and shot two thumbs up in agreement.

On the way to town, Cate stopped by Bronnie's rural route mailbox. Tucked among the letters and junk mail was what she had been looking for—an envelope with a check for the dozen paintings. It was also her first piece of mail at a physical address. She would swing by the ADOT office and apply for a driver's license before the court appearance. Slowly but surely, Cate was conquering this "adulting" thing. Levi would be so proud of her.

Chapter 49

Rae

She walked the horse down the lane, stopping to let him crop some of the brilliant green. It was cool how just watching a horse eat grass could make parts of you feel better, like you were the one having the meal.

When Cate came back from town with the saddle, she would have to help Rae with this fear she had. Learning to ride was something she wanted but also something she was crazy afraid of. It reminded her of climbing onto the freeway railing, with a voice in your head yelling, "Save yourself, get off now! Don't die!" It was shameful to think such thoughts. Cochise was her friend. He was kind and gentle. He wouldn't buck her off ... would he?

Way down the lane she saw a dark SUV turn off the main highway and start driving toward them. Rae knew what to do and led the horse over to the side of the road, turning to face the approaching vehicle, like Cate had shown her. She stood petting Cochise and murmuring quietly so he wouldn't be afraid as it got closer. But just as the car was passing it stopped. The engine turned off and a door opened on the shotgun side. Rae could see Leelee Ruiz behind the wheel, through the partially rolled up window. She waved, but Leelee just looked at her phone, ignoring her.

"Why, hello." The shotgun rider had come to stand right in front of Rae. It was the woman she'd seen in the pasture a while back, arguing with Leelee's brother. Estelle was the woman's name.

Estelle was taller than Margaret had been, with black hair and broad shoulders like a man. She had big breasts—"knockers," her brother Davy used to call them. In her black jeans and boots and wearing a red-checked shirt, she looked a little like Wonder Woman, if Wonder Woman had been in a fist fight. Rae could see dark bruises under her eyes, covered by makeup and she had a Band-Aid taped over her nose.

"Is that your new horse?"

Rae didn't answer. She was afraid to say whose horse it was. She knew Cate and this woman were not friends.

"He's a pretty boy." Estelle gave the horse some fast slaps on his neck that made Cochise lift his head in a scared way. "What's his name?"

"Um, Cochise. Like the engine."

"Well, well. Cochise like the ... *engine*? Or In-di-an?" The woman laughed, but it wasn't the kind of laugh you shared. "Well, shall I give you a leg up onto Co-chise, Rae?"

Had she told this woman her name? And now the woman had come over to where Rae stood, getting ready to put her up on Cochise—without a saddle!

"Come on, just bend your knee—go on, bend it—yes, that one, and I'll lift you up, up, uh-up and over!"

And then she was sitting on Cochise's back. He lifted his head from grazing, like he was waiting for her to tell him something.

"You've ridden him before, right?" As if she was telling Rae, not asking her.

Rae was clenching the long mane in her hands and looking down at it, willing herself to be brave, to stay on, not to start crying. The woman walked Cochise down the lane as the black SUV started and followed them.

In a little while, they passed Desi's pink house. Desi and the kids were at dentist appointments in Copper Valley. The woman, Estelle, kept leading her up the road toward Finley Ranch.

Once, Cochise stumbled and it felt like he was going to fall down. She gasped audibly and clutched at his mane. Estelle looked back at her with her eyebrows raised, as if daring her to say something. Rae just straightened again and looked at the road ahead, the tears hiding in her eyes.

Cate would wonder where Cochise was. Desi wouldn't know where she'd gone. But she didn't know how to tell this woman to stop leading her up the road. It was like they spoke different languages.

Chapter 50

August 19, Silver Springs Courthouse
Cate

"Miss Finley ... Miss Finley!" Cate looked up, startled. Inhaling deeply and unclenching her fists, she willed herself to look at the judge. Today, the courtroom was all but empty and not nearly as intimidating.

"Miss Finley, I just told you that all the charges against you have been dropped. Do you—is there something you would like to say?"

She felt irritated. Sure, there was plenty she wanted to say, but there might be consequences for saying it in court. Then Tiger Cate spoke.

"Do I get an apology?"

The judge took off his reading glasses to look at her. "Excuse me?"

Jimmy scrambled to save his client.

"What Miss Finley, uh—what we would like to know is when the restraining order related to these charges will be lifted so that she can regain access to her family's residence. I've filed a petition based on a verified and legitimate will that lists Miss Finley as co-heir, along with her deceased sister, to the Finley estate—"

"That sounds like a civil matter, Mr. Baker, and nothing I can do anything about in this session—"

"Okay, forget the apology," Cate broke in, "you know, for the wrongful arrest."

"Cate, don't—" Jimmy muttered.

"You've just said I didn't do any of the things I've been charged with. Why am I still barred from my family's home?"

Exasperated, the judge looked at her a moment and then back down at his papers.

"Mrs. Parker has produced an employment contract that gives her full access to the Finley Ranch premises."

"A contract with a now-deceased woman," Jimmy interjected.

"That is still being determined, pending verification of forensic evidence—and *also* not a part of this session."

Now the judge looked downright cranky.

"Caitlyn Finley, you've come here today to learn the status of assault charges against you stemming from an August sixth encounter at the Finley Ranch. They have been dropped due to insufficient evidence. You leave here today with a document saying as much. I *advise* you to use that document to address *any* issues you have regarding restricted access to family property, in the established procedure afforded you in such cases. I also advise you to hire," he peered meaningfully at Jimmy, "more qualified representation in the future. Case closed."

Outside, the two stood in silence for a moment before Jimmy spoke.

"He's right. This is out of my league. A case of the proverbial 'snatching defeat from the jaws of victory.'" He thought for a moment and gave his temple a hard tap.

"On the other hand ... I think I know what he was— Cate, I'm going back in to do something, and it might go quickly or might take a while. Can you wait for me in the car?"

Cate had spotted a familiar man leaving the county court

building and walking out to the parking lot.

"Sure, okay."

She turned and headed out to the parking lot, hooking her finger through Jimmy's offered car keys on the way. The man she'd spotted was just opening the door to a late-model Lexus coupe when she caught up with him.

"Hi, Hugo. Remember me from Estelle's dinner party?"

Lost in his own thoughts, Hugo jumped at the sight of her standing two feet away. *Almost screamed like a little girl, didn't you?* the tiger snickered.

He recovered nicely and smiled at her with cool British reserve.

"Oh, hello. It's ... Cate, correct?" Charming and noncommittal. Good choice.

"Say, Hugo, will you be seeing Estelle anytime soon? A clandestine meeting of the four of you—at my ranch again, perhaps? I want you to give her a message."

In response, he checked his watch, jingled his keys, and tapped a toe to some unheard music.

"Tell her I'm coming over to claim my estate. Tell her my lawyer is filing an injunction in civil court to invalidate any claim she or you or those two other monkeys might have concocted to grab the ranch. Got that? Oh, and one more thing: Tell Estelle the dudes who stole and trashed Bronnie's Volvo have named her as their client."

The last part had been pure fabrication, but she couldn't resist. She watched Hugo press his lips into a line. Then he turned and fumbled with his key fob.

Now walk away, little sister, and don't look back. She was shaking, but she set her shoulders and headed to Jimmy's BMW. Behind her, a car door slammed sharply, and a luxurious engine rumbled to life.

When Jimmy opened the driver's door a half hour later, his smile was both wide and sheepish.

"It, uh, dawned on me that the judge had been trying to get me to take the document he'd signed to the county registrar and fill out a form. Once that was done, it was simple to get the order of protection dropped, especially since," he counted on his fingers, "he'd dropped all the charges and there was absolutely no proof you'd done anything beyond climbing a trellis at your family's home. But it *annoyed* him that we didn't know this."

"So, this was a pissing contest?"

"Let's just call it legal red tape." He handed her a small packet of papers. "For your files, Sunshine."

He put the car in gear and they headed out of the parking lot. Cate smiled at her friend and flicked his shoulder with her fingers.

"So, a pissing contest?"

"Yep."

Chapter 51

Cabeza Valley
Rae

She loped the brown and white horse around the small pen like she'd been doing it her whole life. Leelee had shown her how and now it felt so easy. Her legs gripped his wide barrel and off they went, without a saddle or even a bridle. What a good horse he was. She was *riding*, and it was so much easier than she ever would have thought.

"Sit straighter," Leelee called out. Her voice was high and sharp, and she held a long whip in her hand. From the center of the pen, the tall girl guided Cochise around, tapping the ground in back of him to go faster and in front to slow, stop, or turn him. They'd started at a walk so Rae could get over being nervous. Then they trotted, which was bouncy and scary at first.

"Put your hands down flat on the sides of his shoulder and push to smooth out the bouncing," Leelee had instructed, with Rae trying to obey. It had felt strange at first, but it worked.

Next came the "lope," as Leelee called it.

"Western cow horses lope and English jumping horses canter," she'd explained.

Rae listened and nodded, trying to do it right. She felt her brain sucking up all the knowledge. She would always remember the moment she stopped being afraid and her heart soared with those red-tailed hawks overhead. In the distance, a herd of mule deer grazed next to the pastured horses with no one shooting at them and not afraid for their lives. She thought this might very well be hawk, deer, and horse heaven. It was *her* heaven for sure.

Rae had forgotten that Estelle was watching from the rail until she heard a cell phone ring.

"Hello? Yeah? What—tell me that again?" A pause. "Is that so?" Estelle's laugh sounded angry, not happy. Sharp, like a whip cracking. Then she leaned over toward Leelee, but loud enough for Rae to hear. Her voice was friendly and scary all at once.

"Why don't you and the girl come up to the house for some tea and cookies when you get done down here?" She shot Rae a grin and then headed up the hill, still talking on her phone. "Well, I don't care if she *mumble mumble* ... Great, let her come. I'll be *mumble mumble*."

Leelee had nodded, but her face had a fierce look as she watched Estelle walk away. Rae had thought they were friends, but there was nothing friendly about that look.

Leelee turned back to her and said, "Hey, Rae, when does Desi get back?"

That was a good question. "I don't know. What time is it now?"

"Four o'clock."

They would be making the long boring trip home from the dentist in Copper Valley. Shania would be whining that her mouth hurt or felt numb. Gregory would be playing games on his mother's phone. Rae was glad she was here instead.

"Probably an hour. Can I ride 'til then? I want to show them and Cate what I learned."

Leelee looked toward the ranch house and bit her lower lip.

"Maybe a half hour more. Then I have to feed."

"I can help. I know how 'cause Cate taught me."

Another angry look, this time at Cate's name. Maybe she was just in a bad mood.

"I really think you should go home instead. Desi will be looking for you."

Chapter 52

Copperton
Cate

With the criminal charges firmly in the rearview mirror and some help from Jimmy to cash her art gallery check, Cate decided a makeover was in the budget. At a walk-in salon in Copperton, she got a wash and cut for a small fortune and wondered what had happened to truly affordable haircuts.

Cate glanced in the mirror at her new look—a long layered bob brushing just past her shoulders, with a hint of the pink platinum kissing the ends. She liked her natural hair color—dark chestnut shot with natural highlights from days spent painting in the California sun. She felt more in control of her destiny than she'd ever felt in her life. Being an artist didn't mean you had to look like you lived on the street.

On her way back to the truck she passed a tattoo parlor and, on impulse, circled back to walk through the door. Vintage rock wafted softly out of an equally vintage CD player—Counting Crows singing about lions and lambs.

An attractive flame-haired woman in her forties with elaborate sleeve and neck tattoos flashed a welcoming smile at Cate ... ah, fresh canvas. After a brief chat, Cate pulled out her phone and brought up the image she'd drawn earlier in the week. The head of a tiger, eyes staring dead on at the viewer.

"Whoa, nice artwork," the woman said in an Australian accent.

"Can you outline it on my back? Low and centered?"

The woman clicked a few buttons on Cate's phone and soon the tiger image was emerging from the printer behind the counter.

"If you've got the time, I've got the ink. Let's get started."

#

Singing to the radio on the way home—a local station playing country hits from the early 2000s—she thought about the blank canvases neatly stacked in the camper and felt eager to get started on them. The music reminded her of mornings in California, awakening in the camper to scrambled eggs and conversation with an enigma named Levi. Would he like her new cut and body art? Would Bronnie?

Bronnie!

With the trip to the courthouse and her need for some personal time, Cate's brain had neatly skipped over the fact that Bronnie was now missing a week. The angst that had been her constant companion through the last seven days peeked through the rosy curtains.

She'd left a message for Gomez, but apparently he had other cases on his plate. In her mind, it just wasn't adding up that the sheriff's posse wasn't looking harder for Bronnie, let alone Margaret's remains. She'd seen enough true crime shows to know they would need much more evidence to charge Estelle with murder.

Some kind of festival was happening in downtown Cabeza Valley as she approached its outskirts. Cate passed a banner that read, "Save the Rock! BBQ and meeting tonight." It was the event Desi said Bronnie had been organizing before she disappeared. Cate turned off on a side street.

Ahead of her were cars parked haphazardly along the road-way, their owners making their way toward the Cabeza Valley Grammar School auditorium, which doubled as a community hall. A pickup truck pulled out in front of her and suddenly there was an empty parking spot. On impulse, she swerved into the space. *Why not?* She felt a thrill of adventure. This would be her first time min-gling at a community event in over two decades.

Cate hopped out and joined the horde of people walking toward the auditorium entrance. To one side three well-dressed realtor types—a man and two women—sat at a table displaying brochures and sign-up sheets on clipboards for a raffle. Glossy, professionally-printed posters announced, "Cabeza Rock Estates—Put Our Community on the Global Map!" Perched on easels were the same architectural renderings from Estelle's dinner party. Cate looked around, but neither Estelle nor her entourage were pres-ent. The crowd was mostly ignoring the Estates table in favor of the Save the Rock display.

Someone tapped her on the shoulder, startling her—Dep-uty Miguel Gomez. Dressed in his off-duty black tee and jeans, he looked considerably more relaxed than the day he and Officer Friendly had come to search Bronnie's house. Worry had creased his face that day, but today he was beaming. Cate did not return his smile.

"Did you get any of my messages?" she asked, feeling sud-denly cranky. "I've left several."

His smile was replaced by a guarded look. "Eh, I've had to be out of town ... but I did hear that D.J. hasn't shown up at any of the ports of entry. They've got an APB out for him in Phoenix. Oh, and congratulations on your assault charges being dropped in court today."

"Wow, *some* news travels fast."

"County clerk is a friend of mine from New York. You got the order of protection lifted, too, I see."

"Yep, free to go kick in the front door at *Casa* Finley and get myself shot, I guess."

He stared back with raised eyebrows.

"Oh, my God, I'm kidding."

Big grin. "I knew that. Just messing with you. You're probably a lot savvier now than you were a couple weeks back."

"I am. For instance, I'm just itching to ask you a question right now."

"Me? Okay, go ahead."

She folded her arms and scrutinized him.

"Where is she, Miguel?"

He returned her stare, then slowly his face melted into a sheepish grin. "Pardon?"

"When the crime scene techs didn't show at the cottage after your visit—didn't show all week, in fact—I thought it was weird. But seeing you right now? I know how devoted you are to your friends—how far you would go to protect them. You're too damn calm and happy for Bronnie *not* to be alive and well."

Suddenly, Miguel was grabbing her wrist and leading her toward the empty playground. Cate's heart pounded furiously. It had been a hunch, born of frustration. People hadn't been telling her all they knew about Margaret's disappearance, or about Bronnie's.

"So, where is she? Someplace safe, I hope."

Silence, but he looked like he was working up to something.

"Miguel, I'm staying at her place and caring for her animals, just a stone's throw from where my sister's probable murderer is hiding in plain sight. Please let me in on anything you know—for my *own* protection."

He held his hands up to quell her rising volume.

"Okay, okay." He looked at the ground a moment. "She's safe."

Cate opened her mouth to speak and he held up a hand.

"Last Sunday, I *was* worried and just about to put a bulletin out on her when she called my cell. Said her car had been stolen from the hospital and she'd taken a cab to a motel in Copper Valley. She was thinking about leaving town—grabbing a shuttle to Phoenix and flying east. Margaret's death and then the car theft—it really got to her. I told her I could find her a safe house in the area. That way she could, you know, say goodbye properly to everyone, if that's what she wanted to do."

Cate noticed that Miguel had started to blush and mumble a bit toward the end of his speech. So, they were definitely more than just friends. Probably had been for a while. As if reading her mind, he spoke again.

"Bronnie and I, we have history—back on the East Coast. She was a nurse in Boston and came in to help triage people when 9/11 happened. Lots of guys on the force were getting smoke injuries."

"And you were K-9 … search and rescue?"

He nodded

"We sort of bonded during all that. We were, um, even married for a while. Yeah. In the end, not the best plan for either of us, but we're good friends now."

There was an awkward moment while Cate tried to envision them as a younger couple. Mic feedback from an outside stage set-up brought her back to her question.

"So, where—?"

"At a friend's place in Paulson, about an hour north—"

"I know where Paulson is located. I grew up here, remember?" she snapped before she could stop herself. All this subterfuge was irritating.

"Okay, well, there's a weapons training retreat out there, very low profile."

"Don't tell me it belongs to another buddy of yours." He nodded and hurried on. "Bronnie's got a story you need to hear. I don't know all of it, but I've heard enough to agree she shouldn't have kept you in the dark this long."

It was starting to sink in that Bronnie was indeed safe. Alive and in hiding, but at least not another victim of the psycho Amazon. She felt her anger subsiding.

"So, what about the car over the cliff?"

"That was a message to her, apparently. Cate, Bronnie's in hiding because she's pretty sure she's next on Estelle's list."

A tingle in her backbone. "You sure she isn't after *me* next? Show of hands—who's been in both the ER *and* county lockup thanks to that woman?"

Miguel's steady gaze gave her the feeling she'd said something incredibly stupid.

"Cate, when Estelle had a gun on you at the house, she could have shot you as an intruder. Happens all the time. Do you know why she didn't?" Cate had no answer. "Bronnie can tell you."

"Great, Miguel. What fun. I can't wait."

A moment went by as they stared each other down. Then Cate gave him a faltering smile. "I'm ... I'm glad she's okay. Let her know the house and animals are doing well. Oh, and more kittens showed up."

Cate thought about all the emails she'd read in the past day. Missing details about her hospitalization and recovery in New York.

"TellherIlookforwardto...togettingsomequestionsanswered."

She turned, feeling the tears coming, and headed back toward Max. As she passed the tables, she saw a small crowd had gathered in front of an empty podium with a mic setup. It looked like the Estates agents were preparing to speak to the crowd.

The sight fanned the hot anger she'd been trying to suppress all afternoon. Those people—Cabeza Valley Estates AKA Estelle Parker—were not going to win. Before she was aware, she had sprinted up to the podium and stood looking out at the crowd. Then she leaned into the mic and began to speak.

"Hello, Cabeza Valley, I'm ... I'm Cate Finley."

Some cheering erupted and she spied Desi's husband, Pastor Jake, standing to one side with a small group of people who were all smiling and waving at her.

"I just want to say that Finley Ranch is definitely not for sale and won't be part of this development deal or any other deal. Not while I'm still breathing."

Louder cheering greeted her as she waved, stepped down, and ran toward her truck. As she passed Miguel, he grabbed her arm and pulled her back around, his expression tense again.

"Listen. We're closing in on an arrest warrant for Estelle. Do not go up to the house and try to confront her. This is rapidly coming to an end, but, in the meantime, be smart and don't give her a reason to hurt you, Cate."

"You men," she said, thinking of Levi's comment before he left. "No worries, I won't do anything stupid. Just ... don't dawdle." She brushed past him. "Have Bronnie text me about a meeting."

Her phone read five-thirty when she turned onto Loose Cow Lane. At the cottage, Cochise was munching contentedly in his immaculate pen. Cate saw Rae's small form racing across the pasture to the pink house, where Desi stood waiting with Samson.

A rare peacefulness enveloped Cate as she greeted Bronnie's multitude of meowing kittens on the porch with open arms and poured cat food into their dishes. Was this the new normal? She'd gladly take it, for now.

Then a text from Bronnie appeared on her phone.

Cate, I am so sorry. Come to Tonto Ridge Tactical Training 340 Rd. 5N in Paulson 2morrow at Noon. Will explain everything.

Chapter 53

August 20, TRTT, Paulson, Arizona

After a restless night, Cate dragged herself through the morning feeding and cleaning up after animals, checking her art supplies inventory, and straightening the house. Now she was headed north to the little town that sat just south of Interstate 40, wishing she hadn't skipped breakfast.

An hour later, arrowed signs bearing TRTT in block letters began appearing at intersections. Following the arrows, Cate finally spied a long fort-like building the color of mud and perched on a low hill in the distance. A low profile at first, it grew more substantial as she approached. This had to be Tonto Range Tactical Training.

Then she saw Bronnie, standing in the sparsely filled parking lot, dressed in a heather gray t-shirt with the black TRTT logo, khakis, and some chukka boots that looked new. The woman approached the truck and as Cate emerged she threw her arms around her, whispering "I'm sorry" incessantly in her ear. Finally, she led Cate around to the back of the building, which looked to be part hotel, part institution. Everything was contained inside the walls with no attempt at landscaping the exterior.

They ducked through partially opened gates, past a guard who nodded at them, and finally came to an RV parked against the back wall, well out of sight of the main road. Bronnie opened the door, and they both climbed in. A breakfast nook to their right held water bottles and sandwiches. Bronnie gestured to sit and Cate did, folding her hands in her lap. Bronnie sat opposite, looking uncertain.

"Cate ... again... I'm so sorry—"

"Yes, I got that." Then, somewhat softer, "All this cloak-and-dagger stuff is nerve-wracking, Bronnie. Miguel said if I came today you would fill in some details."

"Details, yes... Details."

For the first time since they'd met, only two weeks ago, Bronnie looked haggard. Whatever secrets she'd been holding in were visibly tearing her apart. Cate was almost afraid to find out what had caused this change in Bronnie.

They sat looking at each other for several minutes. Finally, the older woman roused herself and began to talk.

PART IV – The Truth

The pure and simple truth is rarely pure and never simple.—Oscar Wilde
And the truth shall make you free. —John 8:32

Chapter 54

March 12, 1980 Albuquerque, New Mexico
Bronnie

The old Woodie station wagon sat with its motor running in the No Parking zone outside the Christian Children's Home in northwest Albuquerque. Inside, two young girls stood with their mother, Ruby Taylor Brown, in the cramped little office. Their older sister, Bronnie, had positioned herself at the window to keep an eye on the man who sat waiting in the family station wagon.

All the talking was done. Ruby had wept openly as she'd signed a sheaf of papers releasing custody of her two younger daughters, Margaret and Stella. Bronnie had wanted to dry her mother's eyes and murmur encouragement the way she was used to doing at home these days. It would be over soon, and Ruby knew it was for the best. The girls couldn't stay in the house with that man, the one waiting in the car. Not since they'd told Bronnie and Ruby everything that had been going on.

The man only had one functioning eye now, the other swathed in a bandage. Two days earlier, the younger girl, Stella, had seen to that. She babbled on proudly about it every chance she got. It was an eye for an eye, she said. He was lucky he wasn't dead, blah blah.

The girl had lunged at him with a kitchen knife, and the tip had caught him in the eye socket. Sliced the eyeball in two while slashing the lower lid and upper cheek. Hard to put a thing like that back together.

Bronnie had held a towel over the bleeding mess until the paramedics arrived. Having graduated high school mid-term to start her certified nurse's assistant training, she was secretly thrilled to be putting it to use already. Another part of her was thrilled that her stepfather—the bastard—had gotten it in the eye. She would have aimed much lower.

Despite her husband's serious injury, Ruby couldn't be talked into going with him to the hospital. She was still reeling from what the middle girl, Margaret, had told her—that he had been molesting and sexually assaulting them. Touching them, making them touch him, and so much more. A ten-year-old and an eight-year-old ... and it had been going on for years.

"At first, he did it alone with just me," Margaret had said in a strangely calm voice. "Then he wanted Stella to do it, too. He made me go get her. Then he made us both ... kiss it." She spent the next ten minutes saying everything else he'd made them do.

"They cannot stay here," Bronnie had told her mother with newfound authority. "I'll be moving into the dorms at the college soon, and those two need to be in a safe place until you figure out how to get rid of that monster. If you don't want me to go to the police, you better come up with a plan, Mother."

Ruby had looked at her meekly, a cavernous sorrow etched into her once-beautiful face. Over the last few years, their relationship had gradually shifted. Now the daughter was the voice of strength and reason for a mother overwhelmed by life.

"I miss Dad," Bronnie had said as she rinsed off the breakfast dishes that morning. There was no doubt that the specter of Chet Taylor—an Army officer who had lost his life in the final years of the Vietnam War—loomed in their minds at that moment.

Ruby sat at the kitchen table, weeping again, her face in her hands. At only thirty-six, her mother seemed frail and broken from the loss of her one true love and the cost of some terrible choices in romantic partners since then. A string of hard-luck boyfriends had come and gone, lured by her military widow's pension, and, ultimately, put off by her neediness. Then came Bob Brown—a one-night stand whom she'd married on a lark. Supposedly, he had fathered Stella, but what parent could do to his own child what he had done? By rights, he should be in prison.

Ruby had taken a martyr's breath and shaken out her shoulders. "I've decided that if he tells the police anything, I will say I pulled the knife. Those two have been through enough."

"Something tells me he won't be talking to the police about this," Bronnie had replied dryly. "Here's the number for the children's foster home. Call now, so we can take them there before he gets back."

But before they'd finished packing the car, Bob Brown had arrived home in a cab. In a rare fit of remorse, he had insisted on driving them, perhaps afraid they were all trying to flee. Bronnie had sat in the back seat with her sisters, feeling protective and fierce. She kept her eye on Stella, who was laughing maniacally at her father and kicking the back of his seat. Just her funny ways, their mother would often say, just her funny ways.

When the admission work was completed, their mother stood fussing with the girls' outfits like they were about to take a Christmas picture.

"I am coming back here in a month to fetch you," Ruby murmured as she gave each an impassioned kiss on the head. "Three months, tops."

Ten months later, she still hadn't returned.

But Bronnie had gone weekly to see her siblings. Stella, a born extrovert, settled into group foster care nicely and held court with a half-dozen little girls her age. Margaret, who had always been a loner, seemed perpetually buried in a book during Bronnie's visits.

"What are you reading?"

"Black Beauty."

"Again?"

"I like it. It's a good story," the girl would reply stonily.

Over that first year, Margaret had checked out from the library and read a stack of the most famous horse stories written. The Black Stallion, My Friend Flicka, Misty of Chincoteague, King of the Wind, and National Velvet, among others. No doubt it kept her mind off her current situation and fed what Bronnie imagined was an ongoing fantasy of being adopted by a horse trainer from the Ruidoso Downs racetrack.

Bronnie had chuckled and ruffled her sister's hair, ignoring the sullen glance she got in exchange. While Stella was adapting well and showing no obvious signs of damage from her past ordeal, Margaret was escaping further into a fantasy life of books. But she was doing what she needed in order to survive in the orphanage. They were all tightening their emotional belts.

Not until the first week of 1981 did Bronnie realize the extent of her mother's fragility. Two days after the child-molesting, pension-stealing, wife-abusing Bob Brown moved out—leaving her bank account empty and the rent in arrears—Ruby took the remainder of her sleeping pills, downed a half-quart of vodka, and eased herself into a steaming bubble bath. Bronnie found her submerged body the next morning. Such a serene look on her face, as if to say, "Sure, I've been a screw-up, but I got this one right."

Chapter 55

February 25, 1982

Bronnie parked her rental across the street, grabbed the colorfully wrapped package, and darted through traffic to the curb in front of the austere youth facility. Had Albuquerque always been this busy? Having recently returned from the Indonesian island where the Peace Corps had stationed her for the past year, the crowds, frigid weather, and traffic sounds of her southwestern hometown seemed unfamiliar and jarring.

A lot had happened to her sisters in the year she'd been in the Corps. Stella had gone into an adoptive home and why not? She was a gregarious, outgoing girl who had her father's talent for singing and merriment, not to mention his con-artist charm.

Her adoptive family had two other children—an older boy named Fred, and Tina, a girl Stella's age. They'd been trying for a third child for years but had lost hope. So, they settled for adding the adorable little orphan girl they'd met at the children's home, thinking she would be a grateful and happy addition to make their family complete. Never thinking she might have darkness that followed her everywhere she went.

Six months ago, Stella had clubbed her adoptive sister Tina over the head with Fred's baseball bat, apparently as a joke. Apparently thinking the girl would get right up, shake it off, and chase Stella around, after which they'd all have a great laugh. Only after emergency surgery to relieve pressure on her brain and a tense week of waiting did Tina regain consciousness. Her parents claimed she still wasn't right.

Given the circumstances, the adoption was reversed. Stella was sent to a psychiatric hospital for "evaluation," then to a different children's facility, one with locked doors. She would be there until she was eighteen.

Bronnie had avoided visiting her until now, but today would be her last chance on this year's leave. She had planned to arrive late morning, knowing lunch would be at noon and she could beat it out of there while Stella was distracted by food. She needn't have worried. This wasn't the kind of institution that encouraged close or extended contact between inmates and their visitors, for everyone's sake.

A suddenly preadolescent Stella was waiting for her in the visiting room. She looked thin and bad-tempered, her legs crammed under a table that seemed built for toddlers. Still, the girl smiled at Bronnie and exclaimed in surprise at the belated Christmas/early birthday present. The gift had been costly, but Bronnie was grappling with her guilt over the plans she'd made. After her Peace Corps stint ended next year, she was planning to finish her nursing studies at a subsidized college on the East Coast, where some friends from the Corps lived. She wasn't planning on returning to the Southwest for a long while.

"Oh, how precious—what is it?" Bronnie noticed how quickly Stella could shift from stormy to that charming smile, the one that worked magic on adults.

"It's a portable cassette player you can carry with you and listen to with headphones. I checked and they'll let you have it at least in the lunchroom." She glanced around the room at the handful of guards leaning against walls, ready to step in if a family visit got ugly.

"I love this—thanks, sis!" She blew a kiss over the table, then smiled at the burly guard who had shifted his position to get a better view of their conversation. At almost eleven, Stella was all long limbs and lean torso. Bronnie was a little shocked to see her breasts budding already. Her sly, roaming eyes were now framed by prescription glasses. A brainy Lolita on stilts.

"You are welcome, my darling," Bronnie answered gaily, mimicking how their mother used to croon to the baby of the family. Had all that fawning and pampering led to Stella's dangerous state of mind? No, it had been the sexual abuse plus a certain gene pool, all courtesy of Bob Brown. The court-appointed lawyer had told Bronnie there was hope among the doctors that her sister would grow out of her antisocial behavior. She had murmured agreement, all the while thinking, *Uh huh, when pigs grow wings.*

"Um, Stella, I want to ask you something."

"Yeah?" Stella responded. She was fiddling with the Walkman, trying to figure out where the accompanying batteries went. She looked at that moment like any normal preteen, and Bronnie dreaded asking her question.

"Why?"

Stella looked up and straightened her black-framed glasses.

"Why what?" As if she had no idea what Bronnie might be curious about.

"Did you do that to the little girl?"

An amused smile crept onto her face. *Oh, that why.* No doubt she'd been asked more than a few times.

"First of all, not a *little* girl. My age, right? And fat. Just rolls of it."

That could not have been why she attacked the girl with a baseball bat, it just couldn't. Bronnie stared back, waiting. Stella lifted her glasses and rubbed the bridge of her nose where the heavy frame had left a dent. Without the glasses, Stella's gunmetal eyes were calm and undisturbed, just shy of amused.

"Well, she was going to tell, wasn't she? What me and Fred were up to. He'd told me no one was home, and so we were doing it, you know, and she just walks in without knocking."

"Doing what exactly?" But her fingers were tingling. *That could not have happened. No.*

"We were just having fun, you know? Feeling each other up. Course, our clothes were piled on the bed. That probably set her off."

Bronnie opened her mouth to say something, then shut it again.

"Oh, wipe that look off your face. It wasn't—" Stella mimicked the loud voice of a street hustler, "it wa'nt no big deal, man. Shee-it!" A guard came to attention and stepped in toward her, and she dropped back to her own voice. "I *told* her I would make her sorry. I warned her what would happen."

"Stella, you nearly killed her," Bronnie whispered, aware of the guard still hovering.

"So I hear," the girl said, puffing out her cheeks and shrugging her shoulders. "I tried to talk to her, but she ran. Kinda ticked me off, her running away like that."

An image of a lion bringing down a gazelle flashed before Bronnie's eyes and she shuddered. As she passed back through the security check at the front entrance, Bronnie wondered whether society might not be safer with Stella permanently housed in such a place.

The half-hour drive to Christian Children's Home was hardly enough time to recover. Another jolt awaited as her usually shy sister Margaret swung wide the front door. On the cusp of adolescence, the girl had already bloomed into a young woman. Now taller than Bronnie, Margaret was more rounded, her chestnut hair falling well past her shoulders. The girl glowed with good humor and something else Bronnie couldn't quite define. She looked *nurtured*.

Bronnie found herself hugged and dragged through the front door, all while Margaret filled her in on the last year. Before she knew it, they were stepping into a large room set up for Sunday brunch. Margaret led Bronnie by the arm to a couple who had been looking out the window, plastic cups of punch in their hands. The man was older, well into his fifties, with the tanned face of someone who'd spent his life outdoors. Next to him was a striking if not beautiful woman in her forties, with alabaster skin, bright auburn hair, and aquamarine eyes.

"Bronnie, this is Doc and Fiona Finley. They ... they've taught me so much about horses and riding and horse care, and—" Margaret was choking up, and Bronnie stared at her in amazement. Her stoic little sister was undone.

"We've learned a lot from her, too," Fiona murmured in a slight Irish lilt. "She is a delight."

"Hi. Daniel Finley," the man said in a deep baritone, reaching out to shake her hand. His steel gray eyes twinkled with amusement. "I've been mentoring the 4-H group in this area for years," Doc said. "When Margaret showed up, she was remarkably good with the horses. She said she'd had no previous riding or horse experience. True?"

Bronnie nodded. "Only in her dreams." They all laughed, and then they filled Bronnie in on her sister's meteoric rise in the horse show scene, from novice to champion in her age group.

Later, Margaret showed Bronnie the trophies in her tiny

room, which lined most of her designated shelves.

"Next show season, I go into the older age category—fourteen to seventeen. I'm trying to prepare now." She closed the door to the hallway and turned to Bronnie in a conspiratorial whisper. "Hey, I need to tell you something."

Bronnie felt her stomach lurch as Margaret self-consciously leaned against the wall in the cramped space. She had a hunch what she would hear and had been trying to prepare herself.

"Doc and Fiona, they're moving to Arizona later this year. They've asked me if I want to go with them. We would live on a ranch that's been in Doc's family for almost a hundred years." Margaret turned her faded denim eyes on Bronnie as tears spilled onto her cheeks. "I guess they want to adopt me, I mean legally. Is that, I mean, would that be okay?"

Suddenly, Bronnie was tired of being the older, knowing sister. Stella's adoption had been a disaster, so who knew? She smiled back half-heartedly and answered, "You tell me, Margaret. Will it be okay?" Then she reached out to embrace her younger sister, regretting having introduced any doubt into such joyous news.

"You deserve to have a happy life, Margie," Bronnie whispered into her hair. "On a ranch with horses to ride? Oh, Lord, yes—the jackpot! Mommy and Daddy would be so happy for you."

She held her damaged little sister for what seemed like a long time. For years afterward, she'd regret not having held her longer that day.

Chapter 56

April 13, 1984 Phoenix

Margaret's voice had sounded small and fearful on the phone. It wasn't a voice she'd heard her sister use before, not even when their abusing stepfather had lived with them. Margaret the stoic, she'd been. Margaret the steady one. Hearing that hysteria in her voice had made Bronnie agree to fly out West. She couldn't spare any time away from her nursing studies in Boston right now, not with finals looming. Yet here she was, all the way across the country, on Daniel Finley's dime.

She'd departed a blustery New England seven hours earlier, dreading her arrival back in the Southwest. But Phoenix's sleek, sunny airport with its ultra-modern architecture had stretched its arms out to welcome her like a fashion-savvy girlfriend. So much for her notion of old cowpokes shuffling down dusty Arizona streets.

Bronnie stood at the counter, gazing at the schedule of buses that ran between Phoenix and Flagstaff to the north, Las Vegas to the northwest, and Tucson to the south.

"Where to?" asked the smiling man at the shuttle counter.

"I need to get to a place called ... Cabeza Valley." As she spoke the name, someone gently tapped her shoulder. The woman standing there looked familiar—the red hair, pinned up now, pale skin and blue-green eyes. It was Fiona Finley, Margaret's adoptive mom.

"So glad I caught you in time," she crooned, her Gaelic lilt barely masking the stress in her voice. "Doc thought we should wait in the car outside baggage claim, but Margaret spotted you in line." She pointed through the baggage claim exit doors where a brown and beige Suburban was taking up a substantial amount of curb space.

Bronnie felt relief mixed with sudden foreboding. She still didn't know why she was here, what couldn't have been hashed out over the phone. As if she'd heard the thought, Fiona leaned in and spoke quietly.

"We've had a time of it with her. She actually ran away for a short while, up to a cabin in the mountains. Scared us witless. We only know because the horse she rode up there got loose and began making a racket when he was halfway back to the ranch."

"Did you find out why she ran?" Might just be teenage angst, but that didn't sound like calm and stolid "Mag the Drag," as Stella loved to call her.

"Still a mystery. She's suddenly quite standoffish. Won't let me hug her and wants to stay in her room. She's refused to attend school and we thought she was having issues there, so I've made arrangements to homeschool her. But she won't talk with me about her trouble. Said she would only tell you, Bronnie."

They reached the car, where Doc stood. He gave Bronnie a brief but heartfelt hug and opened the backseat door for her. Margaret was huddled against the far door. Bronnie slid in, reached over, and rubbed her shoulder.

"Hey."

"I'm so sorry," was all Margaret could whisper. "I'm just … so sorry."

The drive up into the mountains would have been a scenic trip under other circumstances, but Bronnie spent it sneaking looks at her sister's face and speculating about the nature of the "crime" she'd committed. The girl looked done in.

Two hours later, when they were piling out of the Suburban, Bronnie barely had time to register the spectacular vista of cottonwood trees, green pastures, and craggy peaks before Margaret grabbed her hand and led her down to the stables. The two sisters sat on the haystack, the younger cramming herself into a gap between two bales, as if for security.

Bronnie studied her closely. "Okay, let's hear it."

"I'm—"

"Pregnant," Bronnie finished for her. Not a question, no condemnation, just a fact.

"How—?"

"What else could get you acting like this? Unlike some in our family, you don't hurt people. Maybe remorse over an animal, but don't you think *those people* would totally understand and share your grief? Do you know how far along you are?"

Margaret pushed her palms into her eyes.

"Christmas vacation," she said without moving her hands. "This guy Alejandro—everybody called him Pony Boy—a cousin of Diego, the ranch hand. He was here from Mexico for a few weeks and I got to hang out with him and learn about starting colts. He's really a great trainer..."

But Bronnie was too busy recovering. She had been bracing herself to hear about a seemingly benign adoptive father turned sexual predator. She blinked away tears of shame. That sweet veterinarian and his wife were her sister's saviors. He didn't deserve such suspicions, but they were bound to come.

"The day before he was going to leave for Mexico, we went into the stable apartment and were, um, kissing. I didn't know how to stop it..."

As Margaret spoke about the incident, Bronnie saw her sister turn back into the helpless victim she had been with their stepfather. Bronnie pulled the girl into her arms and rocked her. They talked and cried for almost an hour. There would be a long evening of explaining and planning ahead of them.

It was Margaret who recovered first and stood up decisively.

"Okay, let's go." She said, dusting the hay off her jeans with a new resolve. "We've got to find a clinic that will do it."

Bronnie put her hand up.

"Wait, what?"

"We have to get rid of it. I can't have a baby, I'm only fourteen!"

"And you're four months pregnant. That's almost halfway, Margaret. Whatever you did to get rid of it at this point would be medically dangerous, especially if you did it on the sly."

A needle poked at Bronnie's temples, and she rubbed it. This had been a ploy all along. The girl had needed an adult to carry out her plan, and her twenty-two-year-old sister was the obvious choice. She shook her head slowly and sadly.

"I'm not taking you anywhere, Margaret." Margaret looked truly shocked as Bronnie continued.

"First of all, we'd need Doc and Fiona's car. Second, I'm pretty sure they'd need to sign a release. I saw something in one of the newsletters at school. A few states have tightened their laws on underage terminations, and I think Arizona and Texas were two of them. Lastly, don't you think the people who've come to love and care for you need to hear about this?" Margaret was still staring and shaking her head slightly.

"I'm going to kill myself."

"No, you aren't, and here's why. Those two people up there believe in you. You've given them a chance, and they've given you one. I saw the joy you three shared at the children's home, and it made me so happy. For a while, I forgot about all that's happened to us—Dad, Mama, Stella's trouble. You … you gave me hope, Margaret, you really did."

Margaret was bent over, weeping noisily into her hands.

"Now, let's go up the hill," she felt the quaver in her own voice, "and give those worried people a break. Tell them the truth."

Bronnie did most of the talking, while Margaret sat staring at her lap. Fiona looked shocked, indeed, while Doc seemed less so. No doubt his medical eye had seen the physical changes in Margaret over the past fifteen weeks. After the talking was finished, there was silence. Then Fiona came to sit on the couch on the other side of Margaret, who was still looking down. The woman patted her hair, and then suddenly the girl turned and grasped her around the shoulders, laying a head on her chest.

"I'm … so … sorry I failed you." A flurry of more sobs from Margaret.

As Fiona patted her, Bronnie watched the woman's face and saw only wonderment. She looked far from devastated or disdainful. Certainly not happy, but comprehending the potential gift placed before her. For years, she and Doc had been childless. Now they would have two.

Chapter 57

As she drove the Suburban back from Phoenix, Bronnie glanced at Margaret, half-turned in the passenger seat and scowling at the contents of the back seat. A bassinet, various bags of infant clothes, towels, and blankets, and a contraption for expressing milk that the girl had declared looked "utterly barbaric" took up most of the back seat.

"What a waste of time and money," her younger sister muttered.

"Well, we had a good lunch in Scottsdale, and it's not like you were going to spend the day astride a horse or anything."

"Nope, but soon, I hope."

Bronnie snuck a look at her sister. Despite her sour mood, Margaret was carrying her pregnancy well. She looked stout but fit, with the extra bulk covered by oversized t-shirts. The whole family had refrained from any social interactions all summer. The girl still did her daily chores around the stable, sweeping stalls and raking up manure piles, along with grooming horses. Doc had vetoed any heavy lifting, but the fresh air and activity were certainly helping her mental state. That and the knowledge she'd soon be riding again.

Fiona had been bundling her midsection, adding more stuffing by the week, starting at five months. She was currently pulling off the full-term pregnant look, stuffing two fiber-filled pillows into a leotard each morning and draping herself in oversized shirts and tunics. Now, two weeks before the due date, Doc and Fiona had snuck off to Tucson so they could celebrate their anniversary and have a brief respite from the pretense.

After Fiona had loaded up her Toyota and come to kiss the two sisters farewell, Margaret whined for the umpteenth time:

"I don't know why we even need this ... this—"

"Charade?" Fiona offered. "Simple. It's a small town, where people have little to do but snoop and gossip. Why not save you from that flak and bring this baby into life with a clean slate? It's not his or her fault, but people will still chatter."

As she'd watched the couple drive off, Bronnie had a private moment of wonder at Fiona's bravery and, well, commitment. In a scant year, she'd gone from no children to becoming the mother of a teen and a soon-to-be newborn. Bronnie hoped it would work out, especially for the new arrival.

Margaret was eyeing her skeptically now that they were alone. "Are you—do you feel, you know ... ready to, um, deliver a baby?"

Bronnie laughed, but it was a good question. She'd been asking herself that for a month, ever since returning from her summer internship with a midwife practice in Massachusetts. Her nursing schoolmates had thought it a curious postgraduate choice, but Bronnie had assured them her specialty in neonatal care could only be enriched by a midwifery experience.

Now she smiled as the mountain road began to lift them out of the baking Sonoran desert.

"Margaret, you are aware that many pioneer women delivered their own babies, right?"

"Gross." Margaret made another revolted face. She straightened in her seat and announced, "I am never in my entire life talking to another boy ever again."

Bronnie smiled and looked over at her. "It wasn't the talking that got you this way."

That night, at the dinner table, Margaret's water broke. Despite all her preparation, Bronnie's stomach lurched with anxiety when she saw liquid dripping from the chair onto the floor. After she helped Margaret change into a new nightgown and cleaned up the mess, she phoned the hotel where Doc and Fiona were staying in Tucson.

"Water broke and she's having her first contraction. Come home, now!" As if to underline this, Margaret let out a cry.

"Ow, ow, *owww*, that hurts!"

"We'll be there in three hours and change," said Doc. "You've got your protocol to follow, right?"

"Yes, sir," Bronnie said, "but please hurry." Before she stepped back into the dining room, she relaxed her shoulders and put on a calm expression. "Let's go get you comfortable."

Doc and Fiona had set up the delivery room in a downstairs guest room. Fiona had covered the single bed in plastic sheeting before making it up with sterilized linens. Bronnie had purchased a stopwatch, antimicrobial soap, sterile gloves, sterile receiving blanket, shoelaces for tying off the umbilical cord, and surgical scissors.

"Ow, ow, ow-woo!" Margaret called out. Another contraction. Fifteen minutes apart now. At ten minutes, she would officially enter labor. Bronnie threw a sterilized sheet over a small mountain of pillows on the floor and helped her sister lie back on them. Over the next hour, Margaret got up, walked, squatted, and leaned back on the pillows again.

Bronnie scrubbed in, waited, and silently prayed for a normal presentation. Over the three months she›d interned, she had attended at least one birth a day. Apparently, summer in the Boston area meant non-stop babies. She›d seen a variety of births, from relatively swift and textbook to disastrous. One in particular—a breach—left Bronnie in awe of how the midwife had saved the situation. It was a complicated procedure, not for newbie midwives, and she prayed this baby was pointed in the right direction.

When the contractions were three and a half minutes apart, Bronnie insisted Margaret climb onto the bed, even if she wanted to sit upright. She stuffed pillows behind the girl. Doc and Fiona were still an hour out. This delivery would be on her.

She mentally checked off all the steps that would lead to holding a live, crying baby in her arms. A half hour later, she saw the crown of a little head and thanked her maker for a normal presentation.

"Margaret, tuck your chin, curl your body forward, and push," she crooned.

Whimpering and drenched in sweat, the girl tucked her head.

When the couple burst through the front door twenty-five minutes later, Bronnie was clearing fluids from the baby's mouth and nose with a suction bulb.

"Girl," she called out, just as the baby emitted her first bleating sounds. "Placenta arrived. Looks intact and normal." She and Doc exchanged professional nods.

The couple quickly changed into scrubs and did the fifteen minutes of sanitizing protocol Bronnie had provided. Meanwhile, Bronnie lay the baby across Margaret's chest.

"Hey, what're you doing?" she said, trying to squirm away.

Bronnie spoke gently to her exhausted sister. "It ... it would help your body heal if you could breastfeed for a little bit."

Margaret shook her head no until Fiona sat down beside her and murmured in her ear. Margaret was crying but let them attach the baby.

Doc was on the phone with Caren Mintz, a pediatrician who'd become Fiona's close friend and confidant. She was the only other person they'd brought in on their secret. She agreed to meet them at her offices in a half hour.

"We'll let you sleep, love. Bronnie will stay with you. We just need to get the wee darling checked out." Fiona kissed the groggy girl on her forehead, and they left with the swaddled infant.

"Well, that's done," Margaret said, her voice tired and shaky. Then she turned her back on her sister and fell asleep.

Chapter 58

August 20, 2019, Paulson, Arizona
Cate

It was well past three before either of them wanted to move from the table in the RV. Cate had wept and dried her eyes three separate times. She had tried to form a few questions and then gone mute again. She felt dull and overwhelmed. A wave of anger had passed over her, then more tears and something that felt like despair.

"Cate, no one could be sorrier than I am about keeping you in the dark this long. Frankly, it was Margaret's wish that you never find out, but then the note you found ... she must have had second thoughts." Bronnie pushed the box of tissues closer. "You know Fiona and Doc couldn't have loved you more. Fiona confided later that, after years of trying to conceive, your arrival had been an answered prayer."

Cate sat for a long time, trying to voice the turmoil she felt, the deep-rooted loneliness. Who was she, really? Where did she belong? When she did speak, her voice felt raw and tender.

"Yes, they did love me. They ... are my parents, no matter what. Without them, I might have ended life in a surgical basin or ... a dumpster." She took a long breath and drank some water. "So, Margaret was my bio mom and some guy named Alejandro was her sperm donor."

She got up to leave and wobbled a little, feeling drained. "Okay, well, thanks for the, um, info. I guess I'll be going now ... Auntie."

"I'm sorry, Cate."

"What?" She turned to look absently at the woman.

"Introducing you to your family history this way. It's a harsh reality."

"I was just remembering all those years ago when I found a letter addressed to *Starr Parker* on the back steps. That was big sister Margaret sending some bucks to Stella, right? The little sister who eventually killed her. How ... how does someone do that to their own ... flesh and blood?"

Bronnie took a sip of water and a deep breath.

"There are a number of answers I could plug in here, but the only one that makes sense is that Stella isn't wired like you and me—from an early age, I might add. That combined with, well, the sexual abuse. It created a ... a very dangerous personality."

"Yeah, nature versus nurture." After a moment Cate added with a reassuring smile, "You seem to have turned out alright."

Her phone rang for the first time all day and she pulled it from her pocket. Desi.

"Hi there."

"Rae's not—she's not with you by any chance?" Her voice sounded stressed.

"No, check over by Cochise's pen."

"He's ... not there, either. Shania thought she saw her riding across the pasture, headed towards Cabeza Rock with two other people... I was hoping one of them was you."

"*Riding*? Riding Cochise?"

"Didn't she tell you? Leelee gave her a riding lesson on him, up at the ranch stables yesterday."

Prickling began in her hands and arms as she imagined Estelle watching the two girls from the house and plotting her next move.

"Uh, no, she didn't tell me. Could she be out riding with Leelee, then?" And Estelle. With D.J. gone, Estelle would be the other rider, Cate was certain of it. "Look, I'm headed home from Paulson. I'll be there in an hour. Text me if she turns up."

Cate looked at Bronnie.

"You have Miguel Gomez's number, right?"

Bronnie fished her phone out of her purse. "I'll call him for you."

"I don't trust anyone else at that station, and they need to send deputies to the ranch immediately." A flash of D.J. standing by the horse pen and warning Cate. "Rae could be ... in danger."

Cate headed for the RV door.

"Maybe you should stay, Cate. You don't want to escalate things."

"If there's a squad car already in the area, it might get there before me. But, if not, I want to let Estelle know they're coming. Something tells me the only thing that will stop a sociopath like her is fear of getting caught and going to jail."

Cate climbed out of the RV, but then leaned back in. "Tell Miguel they may be headed up to the cabin."

Feeling energized, Cate sprinted to her truck. Why hadn't she taken that red file box with her when she came back down? She mentally went over the contents that were left in it—a couple of folders and a small key.

"Please turn over, Max. Please, please, please!"

The truck responded by quickly roaring to life. There were five miles of rutty dirt road before she picked up the state route.

She thought about D.J.'s comment at the horse pen: *That little girl saw something she shouldn't have. Best you watch over her, too.*

The trip home was a nerve-shattering process of watching for patrol cars in her rearview mirror and weaving the truck around slow-driving retirees on the highway that looped around Copperton.

Desi had said the riders were headed for Cabeza Rock National Monument. The sensible choice was to drive straight to the Monument parking area and wait for the deputies. But Cate was pretty sure the three would be turning up toward the cabin and the tiger was telling her not to bother waiting for the cops. Everything she needed was at Bronnie's.

She was warming up Bronnie's quad when a text hit her phone. It was Levi.

Headed back to AZ. Anything been happening?

Cate put her face in her hands and began to laugh. Her hands felt wet and she realized she was weeping instead. **So much is happening, Levi. So much.**

She put the quad in gear and stepped on the gas, then immediately screeched to a halt and went back inside to get the Walther. Checking that the magazine was fully loaded and that the safety was on, she placed it in the side compartment of the quad.

A voice—definitely not the tiger's—whispered in her ear that it was one thing to protect yourself from a home invasion and quite another to go gunning for someone, but she brushed it away. She needed to get Rae to safety. Hopefully Leelee and Cochise, too. But Rae was her priority.

Cate spotted fresh hoof prints on the muddy trail. They headed toward Cabeza Rock, then made a sharp right at the trailhead that led to the cabin. She sent a quick text to Bronnie.

They r def headed to the cabin.

Just below the crest of the trail, the ancient quad sputtered and drew its last breath. She hadn't checked the gas gauge before leaving. Rolling it off to one side of the trail, she shoved the gun in the back of her jeans waistband and continued on foot.

Another forty feet and the trail would level off. Cate would be able to see anywhere in the high valley pasture from that vantage point. The challenge was not to let them see her first.

Chapter 59

Finley Cabin

Rae

Estelle rode first up the steep mountain trail, riding the white geld-ing named Pete. Then it was Rae on Cochise, followed by Leelee on the blue-eyed mustang named Destino. He was called a *cream-mel-low* and Pete was called a *gray*. But they both just looked white to Rae.

They climbed way up the mountain, above the valley. Rae was trying not to hang onto the horn so much, but it made her a little dizzy to look down on all of it—the flat green meadows they'd left behind and the tree-lined creek that cut through fields like a shiny snake before crossing the cottonwood lane. Then she saw a spot of pink—the two-story house where Desi was probably getting dinner ready.

A twinge of guilt stabbed her. "Always tell Desi where you are," Cate had told her. But there had been no time between Estelle bringing out the beautiful saddle for her to ride in and the three of them taking off on the horses. A "trail ride" was what they'd called it. *More like a dream ride,* she thought. It was everything she had wanted a horseback ride to be.

They'd been climbing forever when, finally, Estelle and Pete climbed over a rock pile and disappeared. When she and Cochise got to that spot, Rae saw it leveled onto a flat field.

Estelle urged her horse to go faster, stabbing him with the

spurs on her boot heels. Pete trotted forward and then began to lope. Definitely a cow pony lope. Cochise did the same, and it felt easy to stay on, now that she had the saddle. Behind her, she heard Leelee fighting to hold back Destino, who wanted to be in front, she guessed.

They came up to a little house that reminded Rae of the ones in old western movies—all wood with no paint anywhere. A front porch with a string hammock on one end and a water pump with a trough in the front yard. Estelle slowly dragged her leg over her horse's back and stepped onto the ground like her back was hurting.

"You stay with the horses," she told Leelee, tossing her reins behind her. Leelee jumped off fast to grab them and then gave Estelle a dirty look as the woman went inside the cabin and slammed the door.

No one had said whether to stay on or get off, so Rae slowly slid down Cochise's side as he began to munch on grass. Through the window, she saw Estelle throw things out of a wood bin, then pick up a red box and turn it upside down so the insides, mostly papers, fluttered out.

"It never occurred to me she would put this where the little bitch could find it," the woman was shouting. "Damn you to hell, Mags!" Rae hadn't seen anyone get this mad and it made her feel scared.

Then came noises of heavy things being moved. Estelle was red-faced and had cursed a lot by the time she opened the door again.

"Rae, sweetie, come in here. I need your young eyes."

There didn't seem to be a way to refuse, so Rae gave her reins to Leelee, who still looked angry, and slowly climbed the stairs.

The inside of the cabin was a wreck—a table and chairs and a small bed were on their sides and pushed against the walls. A chest that looked like a bench had been pushed over, and its insides were scattered across the floor.

Estelle's voice was sharp, but she spoke slowly, her eyes pinned to the floor. "I. Am. Looking. For. A. Tiny. Silver. Key." She held up her thumb and index finger to show how tiny. "It *used* to live in this lovely red box in lovely Margaret's bedroom. Very important key, Rae. Ve-ry…"

Rae scanned the floor looking for a small piece of silver metal. Her eyes weren't all that great—Desi had been talking about taking her for an eye test—but she thought this probably wasn't the time to say that.

She did a circle of the room, looking hard at the floorboards. Then she looked in the empty bench chest by the window. The sun had sunk behind the mountain and the light in the cabin wasn't good. She was hungry and getting nervous about being up in the mountains past dark.

Please help me find this key, Lord Jesus, she prayed. Just then, her toe hit something sticking up from the floorboards. As she tapped it, it went further between the boards. She leaned down to feel for it, but it was wedged in tight. Estelle saw what she was doing and aimed her phone light on that patch of floor.

"Ha! I think that's it, my girl. Let me see if I can dig it out with my knife."

She pulled a large folding blade from her jeans pocket, flipped it open, and began digging between the boards. A silver tip emerged, and she tweezed it out with her fingernails. She held it up to the light triumphantly.

"The magic key!"

It looked like a regular door key, except three sizes smaller.

Estelle carefully tucked it into her front jeans pocket and stood up.

There were voices outside the cabin and Rae stood to see Cate holding Cochise's reins and having some hushed words with Leelee. Rae's stomach lurched, not so much in hunger this time, but because she'd screwed up. She'd ridden someone else's horse without even asking permission.

"Raelene," she heard Cate calling. "Rae, come out here, please."

Rae headed to the door, preparing to tell Cate she was sorry, but she felt Estelle grab her wrist. She looked up and the woman was grinning and looking at Cate out the window.

"She's a little busy," Estelle called out the door. "How about you come in here instead, Caitlyn?"

Chapter 60

Cate

Cate climbed the cabin steps and nudged the door open. There was Rae, unharmed but looking terrified in the grip of the angry Amazon. The cabin had been thoroughly tossed—a tangle of papers, file folders, and furniture.

"Well, hello, Caitlyn-with-a-*c*-and-a-*y*." Indicating Cate's hair, she said, "Hey, nice 'do.' You almost look like a grown-up. Come on in." Estelle grabbed a chair and set it upright without letting go of Rae's wrist. "I have a proposal I'd, uh, like you to consider."

Cate was mesmerized by the woman's manic attitude—like she'd had ten shots of espresso. She sensed heightened danger, too, and tried to squelch the prickling on her skin. Showing fear would only make the woman bolder.

"Another PowerPoint presentation, Estelle?"

"Nope, just little ol' me talking to little ol' you. Excuse me a moment, though." She reached into the black leather saddlebag she'd brought inside and pulled out some handcuffs and her Glock.

Salty sweat was making Cate's new tattoo itch uncomfortably under the waistband where the Walther hid. She discreetly reached behind to adjust the weapon, but Estelle seemed to guess what was hiding there. She aimed her weapon straight at Cate.

"How 'bout you slowly take out whatever you've got back there and lay it on the floor for me?"

So, here it was—the stupid thing Levi had been so worried

about. What had she been thinking, taking along a weapon? She was an artist, not a freaking FBI agent.

She pulled the weapon out and laid it down. Estelle kicked it out of reach without even looking down. Then she turned to Rae and held out the handcuffs.

"Put this one on your wrist, would you, darling girl?" she said to Rae, her voice needle-sharp with controlled rage.

"You know, Estelle, the cops are on their way with an arrest warrant. Your best hope right now would be a speedy getaway."

"Yes, you're right. But judging by the speed at which the cops around here do anything, I think we can wrap up some unfinished business."

Estelle grabbed the cuffs away from Rae, deftly snapping one end on the girl's wrist and dragging her to the woodstove where she closed the other end around one of its legs, all the while holding the Glock on Cate. Rae slumped on the floor next to the stove like a tethered dog.

"Truly sorry about all the subterfuge, but I needed to get you away from your impressive support system, Caitlyn." She stared at Cate for a long minute. "You're not the pushover I thought you were, are you? Not nearly as manageable as Margaret was, poor dear."

Cate tried to summon her inner hostage negotiator.

"Estelle, isn't this just between you and me? Why don't you let the girl go?"

The woman chuckled as if Cate had told her a joke. Then she pulled out her phone and glanced at it. "Ah, we *do* have cell service here. Sit, please."

Cate perched on the edge of the chair. On the run up the mountain, she had come to terms with her priorities. Last time she was faced with a hard choice, she'd walked away from a child that was rightfully hers, leaving him with dangerous people. Not this time. Whatever it took to get Rae free, she would do it.

Estelle turned on her thousand-watt smile and laid the Glock on the table in front of her.

She delicately picked through her saddlebag. Out came a file folder from which she selected a multi-page document.

"Since your midget lawyer seems determined to claim your Finley Ranch birthright in court, here's my offer." She held up a silver key. "This is for a safe deposit box that belonged to your, um, fake Finley parents." She leaned toward Cate conspiratorially. "I say it that way because, if you've been spending time with Bronnie, you probably know the real story of your birth, heh-heh. By the way, welcome to the family."

"Estelle, just get on with your little presentation before it's so dark I can't read those papers."

"Ah, good point. To speed things along, I'll tell you what it says, shall I? It's a legal bill of sale listing your interest in the ranch in exchange for, well, what's behind door number one. Ta-da! Here's what might be in that deposit box. Long ago, when your sister-mom and I were chummier—before she started getting paranoid and trying to hide shit from me—she showed me the contents: cash, US savings bonds, and even a coin collection—all of it valued at over a million. It may be worth a couple million by now, who knows?"

Cate felt a wave of *déjà vu*. Once again, someone was trying to steal something that was hers to begin with. This was a deal worthy of the Mexican cartel. In essence, *I'm forcing you to give me something of yours and, in exchange, I'll give you something that already belongs to you.*

Now she wished she had come in the door with her Walther

blazing. Next best option was to draw out the conversation until help arrived.

"Come on, Estelle, I have no idea whether there's even anything in that safety deposit box. I mean, forget the fact that you're trying to bargain with what doesn't belong to you in the first place."

The woman made a chagrined face, nodded, and set down the key.

"Again, I've overestimated your gullibility. Bad on me. Time to ramp up the stakes."

She stood up wearily and ambled over to where Rae sat and rested the muzzle of her weapon on the top of Rae's head. Rae moaned while Cate racked her mind for a new angle.

"Really, Estelle? You'd do that with two other witnesses present?"

"You're right. Luckily, I have a full magazine." An impish grin came over her face. "But do you really want her to witness your demise first? That's just cruel."

Through the doorway, Cate caught sight of Leelee Ruiz seated on a horse and watching the door. It had been a mistake to tell her to wait for Rae to come out. She should have told Leelee to ride like hell away and call the state troopers or the FBI. Instead, she'd expected a safe and simple outcome to a hellish reality.

Because the only way this paperwork would hold up in court was if Cate wasn't alive to oppose it. The plan would be to kill her and the girl, and either frame Leelee or maybe just kill her, too.

As this chilling realization settled in, Cate threw out some bait.

"Wow, Estelle. So way back when we first met, all that texting you did on your phone was, what, to a dead woman? Award-winning performance."

Estelle grinned at her, shrugging her shoulders and tilting her head whimsically. Then, still holding the Glock on Rae, she shook loose some papers from her saddlebag and slapped them down on the table.

"I think it would be better for everyone's health if we stuck to the business at hand."

In the corner, Rae had begun to whimper like a puppy.

"Okay, I'll sign. Got a pen?"

Estelle tossed her one and Cate hovered over the document, showing she was poised to sign.

"Wait, this transfers the property to a Cabeza Rock Estates LLC?"

"I'm a partner. We're just cutting out an unnecessary step."

"So, you and the realtor twins..."

Cate felt her pulse racing again and shot a glance out the window. Where was the sheriff? It had been over two hours since Desi's phone call.

"Won't someone need to, um, notarize my signature?"

Estelle chuckled.

"Ah, Catie... Becoming a notary public is practically standard in real estate these days. Just put your John Hancock on that piece of paper and I'll do all the rest."

Cate stared at her until the woman aimed her Glock at Rae again. Cate scribbled her name on the paper. Estelle nodded and grabbed the document away from her to check her signature.

"Don't you ... need my ID to notarize something?" Her new Arizona driver's license she'd been so proud of just days ago. "I left it in my truck."

"Oops on you! No worries. I made a copy of your old license when you left your backpack at the house." She pulled it out of the document envelope and held it up. "Did some artwork of my own to update it—are you impressed?"

Cate watched as the woman signed and stamped the papers neatly and tucked them into her saddlebag.

"Well, I need to take off now. Places to go and people to see." She stepped into Cate with a sudden menace. "Where's your phone?"

Cate stared her down and then finally pulled out the burner phone she used as a camera. Estelle grabbed it, dropped it on the floor, and stomped on it with her boot heel. Then, with a flourish, she set the safety deposit key on the table. "With my compliments."

Suddenly, a hard look came over Estelle's face. "What's that you say? 'Oh, Auntie Stella, I'm not really interested in the contents of the deposit box'?"

Estelle scooped up the key and jammed it in her jeans pocket.

"You're probably right about it being empty. After all, Margaret was clueless at business. Well, off I go. Hope to never see you again." She stopped at the door and then slowly turned back. Her gaze went from where Rae crouched to the table where Cate sat.

"You know, you have been far too compliant, Caitlyn. Something's ... just not right here. I'm wondering what's up your dainty little sleeve."

She sighed as she pulled her weapon from its holster. "So, maybe this is for the best after all. A little extra insurance in case you feel like talking to the cops."

She walked over to the girl, leaned down to unlock her cuff, and then used it to drag her along toward the door.

A wave of anxiety strummed Cate's ribcage as she racked her brain for words that might distract Estelle.

"So, you killed your own sister to get your hands on this property? Pretty cold-blooded, Estelle." It sounded lame to Cate's own ears but did the trick of getting the Amazon's attention. Estelle turned and looked straight at her, her eyes suddenly gleaming with moisture.

"Imagine you are four years old and asleep. You are shaken awake and it's your big sister Maggie, pulling you out of bed. She leads you down a dark hall to another room where the monster waits for you. He ... uses you to ... get off—so many ways to do that—while your sister stands by. When it's over and the monster is asleep, she leads you back to your room and gives you candy." Estelle leaned over to gently pet Rae's hair, her face suddenly reddened. "I was only four and she fed me to him. She sacrificed me!" Then she threw Cate a mocking grin. "Just imagine how much fun it would have been for some man if Mag had decided to raise you herself."

Cate flashed back to Margaret's letter she'd found in the red box. *I'm no good for anyone.* She'd carried her guilt for decades and it had made her an easy target for Estelle.

"But wasn't Margaret six or something? That's pretty young to know what you're doing—"

"—Shut up! *You* don't know what you're..." Her eyes drifted past Cate and she noticed the Walther on the floor. As the woman's attention shifted to picking up the gun, Cate grabbed her chance. She tumbled off the chair and rolled behind the stove. A loud bang assaulted her ears as a bullet ricocheted off the iron stove. A second shot rang out and Cate felt a sharp sting in her left bicep. She lay still, hoping Estelle wouldn't check on her. Her ears were ringing loudly and in the background she could faintly hear Rae's piercing screams.

Leelee yelled from outside amid sounds of the horses pawing and snorting.

"Estelle! You need to get out here! I hear engines coming this way—Estelle!"

"Okie dokie. Put the little girl back up on the Paint, please." A scuffle of lighter footsteps at the door and the sound of Rae weeping.

Yes, get her on Cochise and do the plan. Go, go, go, Leelee!

The floorboards creaked and Cate heard the jingle of the woman's spurs coming closer. She braced for another shot. Instead, Cate felt her good arm grabbed and something snapped around it. The handcuff now tethered her to the stove.

There was the unmistakable strike of a match before the jingling boots ambled toward the door. Cate opened her eyes and an old cardboard box of fire starters next to the wood pile was in flames. Smoke was already beginning to waft through the tiny shack.

Outside, she heard Estelle say, "Why'd you put her on your horse?"

"Um, just easier to manage that way," Leelee answered meekly.

Cate lifted her head and glanced through the open door as saw Estelle hanging the strap of her bag over the saddle horn of the other horse. Next to her stood Cochise, head down and docilely cropping grass.

Gasping as smoke began to fill the room, Cate reached under the stove to remove the hatchet she'd remembered from her stay at the cabin. She hoped it would do the job. Cate positioned the cuff that was attached to the stove leg, then picked up the hatchet awkwardly with her injured arm. Breathing shallowly, Cate focused on the hinge of the cuff and broke it on the third blow. She scrambled to the door as her lungs sought air to breathe.

Outside, Estelle had dragged herself into the saddle while Leelee stood holding the horse's bridle.

Time was running out to do something or Estelle would continue her mission to destroy the people and animals close to Cate.

Not this little girl, she thought. *No one, ever again.*

With the pain and numbness in her arm increasing, she dragged onto the porch railing and flung herself over the back of the spotted horse, grabbing the horn and hoping he wouldn't buck or bolt in response. Miraculously, Cochise took one step forward and stopped, clearly experienced with jackpot ropers jumping on him from all different directions.

But the horse Leelee had given Estelle, the one the woman had mounted in a hurry, seemed to lack that same gentleness. The surprise of a body hurtling onto Cochise's back caused Estelle's horse to whirl and bolt toward home. Halfway across the field, he became airborne, pitching and bucking as his rider struggled to stay in the saddle.

Once again, her father's sage advice came to Cate:

Always look a horse in the eye before throwing your leg over the saddle.

Had Estelle done that she might have noticed the white horse whose saddle she was climbing onto wasn't Pete the ranch gelding but Destino—Leelee's blue-eyed half-wild mustang. And Destino didn't like spurs. Hadn't Leelee said so a few weeks back at the round pen? As soon as he felt the sharp stab in his sides, the burly horse had dipped his head, hunched his shoulders, and executed a string of bucks worthy of a first-rate rodeo bronc. And, like so many bronc riders before her, Estelle did not stay on the full eight seconds.

Cate and Leelee stared at the motionless mound that was Estelle, looking for any sign of movement. Papers from the woman's saddle bag were blowing in all directions, some even chasing the mustang, who had stopped to graze after getting rid of his irksome rider.

Cate slid off the horse and reached down to pick up the Walther from where Estelle had dropped it. Making sure the safety was on, she slipped the weapon back in her belt and headed across the field to the prone figure.

Estelle lay motionless on her back as Cate approached. She was breathing shallowly, a hoarse rasping sound coming from her throat. As she knelt down, the woman startled her by speaking in a halting whisper.

"She ... wouldn't ... give ... me ... the ... truck ... She ... ran away ... got ... what ... she ... de-served."

Had the woman just confessed to Margaret's murder?

Cate felt her arm oozing blood. The wound beginning to scream at her, but there was one more thing she needed to do. She slipped her fingers into Estelle's jeans pocket and retrieved the key to her parents' safe deposit box. Then she walked back to where Leelee bent over Rae, who crouched on the ground hugging herself.

Trembling and breathless from sobbing—the girl was in full meltdown again. Cate knew she should stay for the police, but to hell with that. She had just enough strength to get Rae back to Desi's, but not if she delayed.

As she reached out for Cochise's reins, she struggled to catch her breath.

"I'm going to ... take her back ... down the hill on Cochise. Can you call 911? Have them send an EMS unit. Just tell them what it was ... a riding accident. I don't know ... what's happened to the sheriff." She felt suddenly weak and was beginning to shiver. "I can't wait for them up here."

Leelee gave her a grim nod and Cate took hold of Rae's arm and helped her off the ground, getting a bear hug in response.

"I have an idea," Cate murmured into the girl's hair. "How about we both ride this big old boy out of here? Leelee will help you get on first, then I'll climb in the front. You just hold on to me like they do on the backs of motorcycles, okay?"

She felt the girl move her head up and down.

Minutes later, with Leelee staying behind to greet the EMS helicopter and the cabin fully engulfed in fire in the background, Cate started to ride across the darkened field toward the trailhead.

"Rae, I know it's dark, but I wonder if you'd rest your forehead against my back and keep your eyes closed until we get to where the trail goes down."

She felt Rae do so, and they silently rode past Estelle Parker's prone body. No need to add that sight to the girl's collection of nightmares. Once past, she focused her waning strength on getting the three of them safely down the mountain trail.

Chapter 61

Cate awakened groggy and with a sense of *déjà vu.* White on white hospital room, the same kind-eyed nurse with short gray curls bending over her arm, fiddling with something. Bronnie. Deputy Miguel Gomez stood just behind her.

"Time is it? How did I…" The last thing she could remember was the view down a dimly lit mountain trail and Rae's hands gripping her around the waist.

"It's just past midnight," Bronnie said with a check at her watch.

"Rae? The horse?"

"They're fine. The horse is in the big cow pasture and Desi put Rae to bed with some medication. Jake was going to run you up to the hospital when this guy rolled in and took over."

She stepped aside for Levi, looking worried and haggard, who moved in to lightly touch Cate's face.

She smiled at him weakly. "Hi. I've been bad. When will I learn?"

He leaned forward to give her a light kiss on the lips, and she whispered, "You have the gun, right?" He nodded, scowling, and shot a quick glance at the deputy.

Bronnie was continuing with her explanation. "…Said you sort of slumped forward on the ride home, probably blood loss and delayed shock. She said she had to steer the horse and hold you in the saddle." *That little girl,* Cate thought, feeling her eyes water. *Just who is taking care of who around here?*

Gomez turned to the other two, his hands in a herding gesture.

"I really need to do some, um, police business here. Do you mind waiting outside?"

They filed out and Gomez pulled up a chair, an odd mixture of embarrassment and irritation on his face.

"I'll cut to the chase—we got her for your sister's murder. Not that she's likely to go to trial any time soon, bad off as she is. They flew her to Good Samaritan in Phoenix and, if she doesn't croak there, she'll wind up in the prison ward of the state hospital."

"State hospital... You mean for crazies?"

His look turned to pure disgust. "Yes, that's right. She lawyered up before her little joyride up the mountain and was already mounting an insanity plea."

Cate was beginning to remember pieces of the day, coming to her like parts of a dream. She'd heard her birth story ... she'd signed a paper ... been shot ... heard words mumbled from a woman lying in a field. *She ... got ... what ... she ... de-served.* Could that be deemed insanity or vengeance?

Something else was on Cate's mind: Leelee's brother, D.J.

"Did you locate the Ruiz's kid, D.J.?"

Gomez had his scowl back.

"Well, we had an APB on him at the border crossings, not to mention through DPS. Nothing. The kid certainly knows how to hide, but we'll find him eventually."

"Is Leelee ... is she a part of any of this?" She hated asking, but the girl had been close to Estelle all this time.

"We questioned her, and for now it looks like she thought she was on a ride with her student and the ranch manager. I told her not to leave the area for now, that more questions would be coming." Gomez gave a Cate a quizzical smile. "So interesting how a riding accident brought Estelle to justice."

For a long silent moment, he and Cate shared a meaningful look.

"So, you want to tell me just how you got shot?"

Chapter 62

September 4, Cabeza Valley

Cate's shoulder was finally beginning to heal, Bronnie having cautioned her not to overdo it. For the past week, she'd busied herself "moving into" the ranch house and relying on Levi for all the lifting. The guy worked magic with a broom and vacuum, too. Other magic was happening in the master bedroom, which they'd begun sharing since Cate's release from the hospital.

The first time they'd pulled off their clothing, bathing in a sea of sexual longing, she'd gasped at the extent of his tattoos. Beautiful, stark, patterns across his back and down his thighs and calves. She knew they were sacred to his Samoan roots, so she tried not to make a big deal of it. After all, a dreamcatcher owl peered out from her breast and the line drawing of a tiger glared from her lower back. The body decoration was a common tie, but their bond ran deeper than just ink. She felt committed for life, though a part of her wondered what that would mean.

Ambling to the stables this morning, she caught Leelee lugging a fifty-pound bag of feed from the bed of the ranch truck to the feed room.

"Hey, there," Cate said, walking to open the feed room door for her. It still felt awkward between them. There had been no talk of what happened up at the cabin, although each of them had given a statement at the sheriff's office.

"I never thanked you for what you did up there. You saved

the day. I mean, she probably wouldn't have gotten away with any of it, but you never know."

Leelee cracked a smile. "It was your freaking brilliant idea to switch the two horses, Cate. I knew she never paid attention when she got on Pete." Then her face darkened again, and she suddenly looked very much like her brother. "I hate her. What she did to Margaret, to my family? It was just deserts."

Cate nodded in understanding.

"Just deserts, all right. I think you're the bravest person I know." Tears began to stream down the lanky girl's face and Cate resisted an impulse to embrace her. Leelee had a proud streak and Cate wasn't Rosa. Certain boundaries needed keeping.

"So, are you going to stay on here? I understand if you want to leave, but please don't. This could be Diego and Rosa's retirement home if they want it. I'll help them get an immigration lawyer. I—we owe your family so much."

Now they were both crying and Leelee was shaking her head.

"They keep thinking D.J. will turn up down there and they can talk some sense into him. He's a fugitive and *Papá* thinks the cartels will exploit that."

Cate nodded, remembering the pain of having to choose between her own child and a way forward.

"But *you'll* stay, right? For Destino's sake."

Leelee brightened at the sound of his name.

"So, you won't be selling him, then?"

"Sell the hero of the day? What kind of monster would do that? No, you own that horse now. I'll make up a bill of sale that says so. One dollar, please."

Then they laughed and Leelee reached into her pocket.

Chapter 63

She set a pretty good pace; he loved that about her. Each morning since they'd moved into the master bedroom at the main house, she'd risen at dawn, put on running shorts and a tank—plus a sweatshirt now that the temperature had dropped—and headed for a run down the road toward the big rock. She was quiet enough getting ready, but it didn't matter. He missed the feel of her next to him under the sheets. Once her body left the bed, sleep was over for him.

It had been her idea to sleep together, and how could he refuse? He'd ached for her for so long. Now he harbored the hope of making it permanent, of marrying the woman. It was something he would need to break gently to his mama. But it wouldn't be the first time someone from his äiga married an outsider. He and Cate would make it work.

The greater hurdle was coming clean about his deception. Their meeting in the park that day hadn't been random. His old army buddy Tyson Burroughs had asked him for a favor.

"Hey, man. How are you doing in 'ol El Lay?" Tyson had asked him eighteen months earlier. "Meet anybody famous yet?"

It had felt good talking to Ty—a guy he'd first teamed up with in boot camp and then spent three years alongside, doing active duty in Iraq. Tyson had switched to reserve after his mandatory three. After passing the bar, he'd moved on to practicing environmental law in northern California.

Levi had soldiered on, putting in for more active duty and the higher pay grade that came with it. That ended the day the IED exploded next to his platoon's tactical vehicle outside Kabul.

Six months after the incident, Levi was still on medical furlough and dealing with crushing migraines. He'd picked up some civilian work babysitting an IT setup at a hospital in the San Fernando Valley. That was when Tyson caught up with him.

"How am I doing, Ty? I'm dying 'a boredom here," he'd complained on the phone call.

"Hm, so, you're working in the Valley?" Tyson had asked.

"Yep, ground zero for the homeless masses."

"Feel up to doing some surveillance for me?"

"What, you want eyes on some polluters?" Levi watched a woman push a shopping cart overflowing with rubbish past the hospital entrance. "I'm looking at a sidewalk full of them right now."

"What? No, that's not ... not what we do. Anyway, this is for, um, a family member back in New York. Sort of a welfare case. I need you to keep tabs on a woman for me."

"Okay, that sounds more promising."

Then Tyson had filled him in on the job. It didn't pay that well, but he would only need to send a biweekly report and bill for a maximum of twenty hours per week. Levi got a description of Cate and her vintage camper along with a list of her frequent haunts around the valley. Just by coincidence, one of them was at the park next to his IT job. What were the chances Cate would park there the very next night? He hadn't even planned to start surveillance until the weekend.

She pulled up in her distinctive camper truck, right next

to the bench where he'd sat down for a momentary catnap before starting his hospital IT shift. A meet-cute convo had started up, leading to a friendly alliance with the target. At least, that was how he related it to Tyson. His friend had chuckled and given him full rein to have daily "convos" with Cate, as long as she thought he was nothing more than a homeless vet.

Cate was scary-beautiful in that earthy way some women have who live close to the bone, their emotions tucked deep inside. It all poured out of her eyes—sometimes fierce, sometimes sultry, sometimes wells of sorrow when she didn't think anyone was looking. The pale green irises contrasted her olive complexion like a human version of the Bengal cat an auntie of his kept back in Samoa.

The woman had been raised right. Her tiny camper stayed clean and ordered, with her art supplies neatly stacked and her personal items tucked away and labeled in drawers and bins. He also saw how guarded she was—wary of revealing too much, even after they'd gotten to know each other, and she'd invited him to bunk there during his off-hours.

He was conflicted about sleeping in the camper under false pretenses, but Tyson had thought it was a swell idea. It was handier than the daily commute back to his crowded house in Baldwin Hills.

Then came the day she vanished. Of course, it would be during one of his migraines. After a brief phone call with her, she went silent. When he texted Tyson that Cate was off his radar, his friend's reply had surprised him.

Let her go. Abandoning the project. Thanks for all your help was all it said.

But, by then, he couldn't let her go. So, he'd asked another army buddy, who did electronic investigation for law enforcement, to ping her phone. That gave him a direction to go.

The going had been slow. First, get the truck out of impound. His buddy in law enforcement had pulled some strings. Once the paperwork was updated and the truck had a new battery, he'd given notice at the IT job. Then he'd driven across a blazing desert in August and wound up in the mountain town of Copperton, Arizona.

On the day he arrived, the local newspaper had run a front-page story about a Cate Finley being jailed in a local assault case. Getting intel on the case had required a half-dozen phone calls and flashing some military credentials.

Jimmy Lee Baker had been stoked to have him as a character witness. Getting his sister Talia to overnight his uniform had been a chore, but seeing the look on Cate's face that day in court? Feeling her arms around him again? Priceless.

Now he tracked her on the jeep trail like a bloodhound on a scent. He'd dropped about twenty pounds doing these early morning runs. Almost back to his boot camp weight of two ten. From experience, he knew that at some point she was going to stop running and find a rock to climb. He cut through a few granite outcroppings and then stopped short.

She sat cross-legged on a small patch of dry grass, staring hard at him. Then she smiled.

"Knew that was you behind me."

"Yeah, couldn't, um, sleep any longer." He walked up and sat next to her. Their arms instinctively found each other, and she leaned into him.

After a while, she pulled back and looked into his eyes with that familiar tiger intensity.

"You're not here to watch me climb. You ... have something to tell me." A statement. Like she knew his soul.

"Kind of, yes. I have." She turned away and stared out at the vista. He followed her gaze. Across the valley, the sun was breaking over the mountains.

"Will it make me cry?"

"What? No, I don't … I don't want it to, Cate."

A soft sigh from her as she kept her eyes on the distant mountains.

"Okay, spill."

And so, he did.

Epilogue

December, Cabeza Valley

Perched high on a ladder, Cate added the final trimming to the oversized Christmas tree while two ginger tabbies—rescues from Bronnie's feral litter—batted a plastic ornament around the main hall of the ranch house. It felt surreal to be here celebrating Christmas again after two decades.

Levi had bought the tallest tree he could find in Copperton, and she'd found the old box of ornaments in the work shed. All the original pieces were there, even the tiny cowgirl on a miniature golden horse that they'd used instead of a star. Desi and her kids were bringing over popcorn strands later, and Levi had driven back to Copperton after suddenly realizing he hadn't picked up any twinkle lights for the finishing touch.

In September, after discovering her father's office safe was empty, Cate hadn't been too hopeful about the safe deposit box. Although the bond certificates were missing, the extensive coin collection remained. It had been her father's prized possession, the result of forty-five years of collecting.

She had brought the collection home, set it on a shelf in the office, and gazed on it daily for a week while she held a mental conversation with her dad. Then, eyeing the ever-growing stack of ranch bills, she'd called a coin broker in Scottsdale.

Selling only part of the collection had allowed her to get into a used Subaru Forester and service the ranch's debt, plus pay

Leelee back wages, hire a new ranch hand, and stock up on feed for the animals while she and Levi decided the future of the ranch. They had already decided their future would be together.

Bronnie was missing in action these days, having rented her place out and moved to Copperton. She said she needed to get some distance, physically and emotionally, from the place Margaret had drawn her last breath. This had stemmed from a visit to her baby sister Estelle, now a quadriplegic committed to the state hospital in Phoenix. Bronnie had worn a wire the day Estelle finally revealed that she'd thrown Margaret's body off the bridge over Cabeza Valley Creek, watching while the monsoon flood waters carried her away. The forensic investigators were still looking for Margaret's remains in the now dry creek bed that ran from Cabeza Valley down to Wickenburg.

But what had truly sealed Estelle's fate was D.J. Ruiz turning himself into the Yavapai County Sheriff's office and asking for a plea deal. Although he was currently spending time in county jail on unrelated warrants, he had been promised no further prosecution in the murder case in exchange for his testimony against Estelle. Leelee and Cate had shared the news with Diego and Rosa over the speakerphone, and they'd all wept with relief.

In October, Cate had sat at her father's desk again, this time to fill out the victim's personal statement form the Janssen people had emailed her. Apparently, others had come forward to describe Joseph Russo's criminal behavior toward women over the past two decades. Cate had taken a deep breath and written out her experiences with Joseph Russo, starting with their second date on September 6, 2000, and ending with the dead pigeon stuffed in her mail slot with a note reading, "A dead bird tells no tales."

For a long while, two folded documents had lain on the office desk, ready to be included in the mailing. The first was a copy of her birth certificate, which she'd rescued along with her parents' will from the red file box, just days before the cabin had burned to the ground. The document proved she was just sixteen when Russo drugged and assaulted her in a hotel room. The second paper was another birth certificate copy—her son, Will's—filed by the midwife in upstate New York. With all Joseph's fairly public effort to gain custody of Will so he could make bank on his uncle's fortune, he would have to explain to the voters how a sixteen-year-old girl had given birth to the child.

Even with the birth documents, her statement probably wouldn't lead to criminal charges, given the statute of limitations. But it would hopefully keep Russo out of office … and plenty pissed at her. She'd mulled it over for a week, wondering if she was about to do one more stupid thing. Then early one morning, the tiger had sealed the documents in Jansson's pre-addressed envelope and sent it on its way.

Tonight, Cate could hear pans banging and voices singing along to a local pop station as Leelee and Rae baked batches of Christmas cookies in the kitchen. Cate had been working on connecting Diego and Rosa with an immigration lawyer. Even so, getting their daughter to commit to staying on at the ranch had been surprisingly tricky.

When they'd talked about it earlier in the week, while sorting saddles for the annual Copperton Rodeo tack sale, Leelee had finally come clean.

"You and Levi are starting a new life here. I feel like, well, a third wheel."

"What? Leelee, let me tell you a story I learned recently." Cate drew a breath. She was still adjusting to her real birth story and hadn't shared it with many people. "Margaret wasn't my sister. She was my mother." She paused; no reaction. Just Leelee blinking back and smiling.

"Oh, my God, you knew?" It had probably been common knowledge in the Ruiz family for decades. "Well, if you knew that, then you must know that your second cousin Alejandro—Pony Boy?—is my real father."

"Wait, what? Pony Boy?" Her eyes widened—this was the news.

Cate had simply nodded. No need to go into the circumstances around the pregnancy with all that Leelee was dealing with in her family right now.

"So, forget this third wheel crap. We're family," she'd said, pulling Leelee over to the wall mirror that hung in the office and holding her face next to the girl's in the reflection. "I mean, how else do you explain our matching green eyes?"

Remembering that day, Cate smiled as she balanced on the ladder to hang another ornament. She'd spent twenty years feeling like an outsider, so this new sense of belonging—of being part of a family again—was priceless ... a priceless gift.

She heard a car coming up the drive and guessed it was Desi and family bringing the popcorn strings for the tree and roast beef sandwiches for supper. A knock on the front door reminded her she'd latched it out of habit.

"They're here. I'll get it," she called toward the kitchen and climbed off the ladder.

Cate flicked on the foyer lights, noticing it had gotten completely dark outside. Unlocking the oversized door, she swung it wide.

He stood in dim light on the flagstone, facing away. When

he turned around, Cate sucked in her breath and stepped back, her stomach clenching and hands lifting to her face protectively. The dark hair, the heavy Neapolitan brows and swarthy complexion. Expensively tailored black jacket over a white shirt, open at the neck. He came toward her in the darkness, and for a moment it was a decade ago in a deserted alley, when savage fists had nearly ended her. Then he stepped into the foyer light and she saw she'd been mistaken.

He was taller and leaner than Joseph, his smile shyer. Damn spitting image, otherwise. He dropped the carry-on bag he'd been holding and held out his hand to her uncertainly, like a child learning to greet strangers.

"Hi, Mom," he said. "It's ... it's been a while."

And then she was pulling him into her arms, feeling a warm human—her baby boy—through the wool jacket and wondering, *Is this really happening? How is this not a dream?*

Cheek pressed against his shoulder, through blurry tears she saw the big Samoan walking toward the two of them, grinning and carrying luggage.

The End